EVERY
WORD

Ellie Marney

EVERY WORD

Tundra Books

Published in Canada and the United States of America by Tundra Books, a division of
Random House of Canada Limited, a Penguin Random House Company

Library of Congress Control Number: 2014951817

Library and Archives Canada Cataloguing in Publication

Marney, Ellie, author
     Every word / Ellie Marney.

Reprint.
Issued in print and electronic formats.
ISBN 978-1-77049-775-7 (bound).—ISBN 978-1-77049-777-1 (epub)

     I. Title.

PZ7.M366Eve 2015   j823'.92   C2014-906432-2
                                            C2014-906433-0

Cover designed by Five Seventeen
Cover images: (young woman) © Jen Grantham / Stocksy.com; (background)
© jackjayDigital / iStockPhoto.com
The text was set in Minion

www.penguinrandomhouse.ca

Printed and bound in the United States of America

1 2 3 4 5 6   20 19 18 17 16 15

 Penguin
Random
House

FOR MY AMAZING SONS –
BEN, ALEX, WILL AND NED

Lady, you bereft me of all words,
Only my blood speaks to you in my veins

– SHAKESPEARE

PROLOGUE

I'm standing on the verandah of our old house, barefoot in my summer nightie. Nighties get daggy by the time you're nine or ten, I guess. In this dream, though, I'm still a kid, and the cotton tickles my skinny knees.

It's just after dawn. All the birds chorus to the morning – currawongs, kookaburras, our tired old rooster. The sky around the house is a dark-bleeding blue, a bowl of water dripped with food coloring.

Dad's there too, his boots not yet coated in dust, his hat still in his hands. Together we take in the crinkling underexposed world that will soon become the day. We wait for the sky to change color, the blue to harden and flare, to spread from one horizon point to the other.

'Bushfire weather,' Dad says. 'Something's coming. Can you feel it?'

Yeah, I can feel it. It's the fear of every rural, every cockie and farmer on the land. In a few hours, we'll all be on edge. The sun will be searing, and Mum will belt Mike for playing with matches.

Sparks will fly.

The wind will pick up and the whole yard will smell of prickling anticipation. Open your mouth, and you'll taste dust and heat. In this weather, you can sense the uncertainty. The control you think you have – over the property, over your fate – is just an illusion.

James Mycroft's eyes are the same blue as that early morning sky. His energy is the same, his deep brown curls shifting in the warm breeze that makes my skin tingle.

'Can you feel it?' he says.

And when he takes my hand, we are both seventeen. The nightie that swirled around my knees as a child now barely kisses mid-thigh.

He tugs me closer. Radiant heat brings the red to my cheeks. I put my hand on his chest and there's something smoldering under his skin. Something inside him that licks and burns, something crackling, a sense of forces barely contained.

Bushfire weather – my father's fear, the dangerous day, the hot dry wind that scurries through the yard and tosses your hair.

When the hot wind races, a change will come. A man could die, a crime could be committed, a history of secrets could bubble to the surface like lava. I could flare up and be reborn in the fire of Mycroft's eyes. Because you don't know what will happen, in this weather. Anything could happen.

Anything at all.

CHAPTER ONE

'Okay . . . here's the strategy. I punch Patty in the face, you get past her.'

Mai Ng's helmet is askew and bits of black fringe flop into her brown eyes. It's very disconcerting, being able to see her eyes. Normally she'd have her black-framed glasses on, but you can't wear glasses on the track.

She's panting hard, but we're all panting, blowing like horses, hands on hips.

I'm covered in sweat and bruises, legs shaking above my skates. 'Does the term "foul out" mean nothing to you?'

'Doesn't matter.' Stacey swills from the water bottle between gasps. 'She's gonna foul anyway.'

'That's true.' Bernie tucks her hair back, tightens her wrist guards.

Mai grabs the water. 'And Patty's been fouling without proper penalty all night. Let me do it. It's the final. If we win, they can disqualify me all the way into next season.'

I squeeze my waist, try to control my breathing. 'You might break her teeth.'

'Twenty seconds,' Chris says, adjusting her bra strap. She's watching the jam timer.

Stacey shrugs. 'Patty's got a mouthguard.'

Mai grins, shark-like. Bernie sighs. 'You know what I've got to say, people. It's wrong. Very wrong. And you're all extremely bad girls for even suggesting it.'

I pull up my drooping footy socks. 'Why don't you back-burn her instead? Then Chris can pass the star to me and I can take off.'

'Ten seconds,' Chris says. 'Happy to pass.'

Mai doesn't look convinced.

Bernie makes an executive decision. 'Go the backburn. If that doesn't work, then belt her. But, y'know, in a restrained manner.'

'Time,' Chris says, then raises her voice. 'Furies, form up!'

The five of us skate into position. I roll on my stops at the pivot line, the speakers start pumping out 'Rocksteady' by the Bloody Beetroots, and the noise of cheering is unbelievable.

This is it. We've got two minutes of full-contact chaos in this last jam to make the Fitzroy Furies the undisputed champions of North City Roller Derby. I intend to make those two minutes count.

We're all wearing matching black tank tops with the Fitzroy Furies logo, a silhouetted Kenworth Truck Babe wearing roller-skates. There's plenty of variation in the rest of our boutfits though. Chris wears gold-spangled hot pants, Stacey's red tennis skirt has bold slits up each thigh, Bernie's got her fishnets. Mai, true to form, has added another picture to the front of her tank – I get an eyeful of Trogdor the Burninator growling his majesty across her boobs.

My flannie shirt (snipped out at the back so I can flash my number) is unbuttoned over my tank and cut-off jeans. The rest of the team likes my 'hayseed' look, but the cut-offs are so snug I can practically see my own bum crack. I've also got a red-painted slash from temple to temple, so it's not totally farm-girl porn. With my red mouthguard, black-striped helmet, wrist guards, elbow and knee pads, I look ready for battle.

I tie my trailing shirt-ends up under my bust and glance at the crowd. Mai's boyfriend, Gus Deng, exposes incredibly white teeth as he smiles straight at her. My mum and dad stand near Gus. Dad's dressed in his taxi driver's outfit. He's taken three hours off work to come and see me bollocks around the circuit, and I'm suddenly regretting these outrageously revealing shorts.

My brother, Mike, clutches the barrier with both hands and Alicia Azzopardi stands between him and my parents. Mike's grinning like a loon, bursting with energy. It might have something to do with Alicia, who's smiling at Mike as much as at me. I'm glad she made it – she seems to spend all her spare time packing lately.

And on Mike's other side, towering over most of the people around him and probably pissing off a lot of shorter spectators, is Mycroft.

He's wearing jeans and his black T-shirt, he's stripped off his red hoodie and tied it around his waist, and his hair is like a riot in a rubber band factory. His jaw works furiously as he chews on a tab of nicotine gum – he hasn't had a cigarette in eight weeks, so it must help somehow – but he's grinning at me.

My whole body shivers like a wave about to break. My hands fold into fists.

Mycroft leans on the barrier and yells 'High Voltage!' – my derby name – through the throng. A sizzle of electric current passes from my eyes to his.

Mai jostles me on the left, eyes urgent above black Comanche stripes. 'Focus, girl.'

'I am focusing!'

'On the *jam*, you noob.'

The whistle sounds. I stumble into a slow start, then sensation comes back into my toes and I'm off.

There's nothing like skating around a slippery roller-derby track at a hundred miles an hour to get your heart pumping – although my heart was pumping already, from the look Mycroft gave me, so it's academic.

I lean into the curves, feel the tape on my ankles as the muscles in my calves strain. I tense my arms, ready for the first collision, cranked and racing and completely *alive* . . .

Someone wallops into my back with what feels like both elbows. 'Comin' through. Outta the way!'

I stagger on my skates as Patty 'Mama Said Knock You Out' Oustterman heaves past in her Crushers shorts and schoolgirl tie.

'Steady! Stick to the pack.' Bernie grabs my arm, hands me off to Mai's tender care. 'Watch her, and get ready!'

Mai glares at Patty's pink-striped shirt. 'I'm gonna mess that bitch up, so help me.'

I match Mai's speed. 'It's not about Patty, it's about the win. Focus, you *noob*!'

We've done a full circuit in a whirr of skates and sweat. The jam timer blows the double-tap whistle that signals the start. Now it's on for young and old.

I get jostled, scratched, bashed into – not all by members of the other team. We're skating strategically now, so Chris can lap the bunch. Every time a gold sparkle zips past us we get a cheer, feel a rush of energy. I concentrate on blocking the Crushers and staying on my feet.

I don't look for Mycroft, can't afford to. I'm too easily distracted these days. A look, a word, a scent – I'm like a tuning fork that resonates to one deep-thrumming pitch. The sound of Mycroft's voice is enough to send wings through my insides, make my skin go nuclear. And a touch, even a gentle one . . .

Somebody slams into me. I slam back with my arse before I realize it's Chris.

'Shit, sorry!'

'Dickhead!' She's puffed out and sweaty, fumbling with her helmet. 'Stace and Bernie have got Patty boxed up. I'm passing the pantie, you dill, take it!'

She passes her starred helmet cover to me – I am now the jammer, the team point-scorer. This was our strategy all along, because I'm not exactly the world's best blocker, but going at speed I'm hell on wheels.

I am the Fitzroy Furies' secret weapon.

'Got it! Go!' I shout.

Chris backs away to wall off anyone approaching. The Crushers' jammer is coming up, and Patty Oustterman glares at me from behind Bernie and Stacey, who are fighting hard to keep her contained.

Patty looks ready to murder someone. But I've had experience with that.

I bend my knees and *fly*. My hair streams back behind me and a breeze cools the perspiration under my helmet: my arms are pumping, elbows back, body streamlined. The sound of ten skaters barrelling together on the track, with a hundred spectators yelling encouragement and the bashing music from the speakers, is like a roll of thunder in my bones.

I lap the bunch once before Patty gets loose. She lets out a roar, like an unchained lion. I know from experience that it's not quite the same as a *real* lion, but it's not a bad effort. In two seconds her hot breath will be right at my ear.

I pour it on. My thighs are really killing me now. I dodge my way past two Crushers, crouching to duck the flailing arms of one, and I'm about to get in a second lap—

Patty grabs my collar. 'Get behind, you stupid bumpkin!'

I'm choking, and the whistle's blowing a penalty, but Patty just holds on.

Then Mai's on my other side. 'Block this, you Collingwood slag!'

She elbows Patty in the face. There's cacophony as the Pack Ref goes ballistic with the whistle, Patty screeches, the crowd explodes with catcalls. Patty's hand comes loose and I can skate.

I bunch up and burn off.

I'm coming up on the last Crusher and I have no idea how close the time is, but I'm not gonna make it.

Then Bernie's there with her arm stuck out. 'Into orbit, Rachel!'

I grab her hand and she swings me around herself like a hammer-throw. We let go at the same instant – I whip into the final curve with booster rockets on my skates. I pass the last blocker as the Head Ref blasts the whistle. The crowd goes completely nuts.

Mai's screaming, I'm screaming, the other Furies are pumping their fists into the air. Someone lets off a mass of confetti, poppers go off in streams of foil and tangled paper tails. The noise is deafening.

We spit out our mouthguards and toss our helmets. Chris and Stacey cling to each other, jumping up and down on their skates. Nobody is looking at the Crushers yet – we're all just delirious with the feeling of *winning*.

Bernie takes my fingers in one massive fist and shakes my arm half out of its socket. 'Awesome! Oh my god!'

Mai hugs me. 'That was fantastic!'

'I can't believe we won!' I squeal into her ear. We hold each other's arms and lean back and scream like insane people into the air. Nobody cares, because you can't hear a bloody thing.

Eight weeks ago, I wasn't a Fitzroy Fury. Eight weeks ago, a harmless old man was murdered, and I saw the aftermath. I ended up being groped by a scalpel-wielding homicidal maniac, and nearly getting eaten by lions. Eight weeks ago, I was contemplating leaving Melbourne for good, and James Mycroft was just my eccentric mate from two doors down.

That was eight weeks ago.

A lot can change in a very short time.

CHAPTER TWO

Six the next morning, the hullabaloo starts.

Mike pinballs between his room, the bathroom and the kitchen. It's a mystery why my brother feels compelled to make such a racket when he's getting ready for work. My Saturday hours at Tognetti's mini-mart have been switched to after lunch, so by all laws of natural justice I should get to sleep in. But that is clearly not going to happen.

Mum and Dad have already left for work – or in Dad's case, haven't yet returned from night shift – so there's no one to disturb except me. Mike's just being Mike; this morning he doesn't give a toss about who else is around while he sings in the shower, clatters the kettle, and bangs his wardrobe doors.

I roll over, try to get back to sleep. But then I realize what six a.m. means in the larger scheme of things, and I jump out of bed.

'You're very chipper this morning.' I lean against the kitchen bench and slurp scalding black coffee.

'Yes, thank you, I am.' Mike's trying to get his hair into some kind of order while simultaneously making toast.

'Don't butter your head. Alicia won't like it.'

'Cheers.' He licks jam off his thumb. 'Shit, I've gotta go. You're still gonna help with the casserole, yeah? Dinner tonight, remember?'

'Yes, and yes. You've only reminded everyone about twenty million times this week. It's not like we're gonna forget.'

'This family, anything's possible.'

Once Mike's gone, I dive for the shower. The blast of hot water wakes me up. I wash my hair, which smells of liniment.

The final traces of my warpaint from last night go down the drain in a soapy swirl. I've sloughed off my alter-ego: 'High Voltage', souped-up speedster and roller-derby whiz, she of the sexy shorts and the flying golden-brown hair. I'm back to being me: Rachel Watts, seventeen-year-old displaced rural, who still thinks trams are fun, and misses the sound of currawongs every day.

I towel off and pull on my clothes and boots fast.

Outside, the late May morning snap-freezes my damp hair. I have Mike's brown woolen jumper on permanent loan. In Five Mile, I would have woken up to frost – in Melbourne, it just gets pretty damn cold. It makes the current arrangement between me and Mycroft particularly awkward: we've been seeing each other for eight weeks through his front window, me on the verandah and him in his room.

Basically, I'm under house arrest. Because of the whole scalpel-wielding maniac thing, and the lion thing, and because of my general bad behavior surrounding all that, I was officially barred from spending quality time with Mycroft unsupervised.

Mycroft pops over for study sessions at my place in the afternoons, and dinner in the evenings some nights – something of a major achievement in itself. We see each other five days a week at school, and since the hot water service at his place broke down a fortnight ago, he even comes by for the occasional shower. But we rarely get any time alone. He's been in my room once, just once, and Dad made me keep the door propped open with a chair.

The lack of privacy has had the complete opposite effect to what my parents intended. Now I think about Mycroft *all the time*. It's starting to addle my brain. It's getting to Mycroft too. Every time I look at him lately it's as though he's got something boiling inside, barely contained . . .

The whole situation is getting ridiculous, and sitting outside on Mycroft's verandah is becoming more and more uncomfortable. Hopefully my parents will come to their senses before winter sets in.

But right now all my family members are occupied, which gives me a unique opportunity to go AWOL. It's the only major benefit to getting up this early on a Saturday – if I get to his house in time, Mycroft will let me in while he dresses for work.

The job thing's been happening two afternoons a week after school and every Saturday morning for eight weeks now, with no sign that Mycroft's losing interest. Once I would have said it was as likely as Mycroft giving up smoking, but that only makes me wrong on two counts.

I cut through his yard, bound up the steps of the verandah. The wooden park bench under Mycroft's window is dotted with dew spots, where condensation from the eaves has spattered down from above. The window is closed, the dark blue curtain drawn, but there's a glow of light within. I rap with a knuckle, chafe my hands together as I wait.

Limping steps echo inside, then the curtain is pulled aside and Mycroft's standing there, toast shoved in his mouth. He balances a mug of tea in one hand, with the toast plate on top, as he uses his other hand to push up the window.

I perch my bum on the ledge, my feet on the bench, basking in the wash of hot air from the room. Then I take the toast out so I can kiss my boyfriend good morning.

I can say that now: *my boyfriend*. It took me a while to get used to the words. I'm still getting used to the way my body reacts when Mycroft and I touch: this hot flush goes right through me. My mind goes on vacation, and my breathing catches, so I'm gasping every time he does simple things – putting his arm around my shoulders, or touching his lips gently to mine, like now.

Mycroft tastes like butter and condensed milk, and I laugh. 'You warm enough in there?'

He settles his toast plate on the desk. 'I was before you made me open the window. Bloody hell, that air is freezing.'

'Is Angela asleep?'

'For her sake, I certainly hope so. She copped a late shift.' He takes a slurp of tea and brushes crumbs off his front.

Mycroft's got a speckle of red on his neck, where he shaved too fast, and his hair is a dark-chocolate tangle. He's wearing hiking socks and black jeans and the white T-shirt Mai helped me buy for him after he got out of hospital. The typescript on the front of it reads *If you're not part of the solution, you're part of the precipitate.*

There've been a few changes inside Mycroft's bedroom, the pithily named 'Stranger's Room'. The desk is now squashed into

13

the corner, near the window, to accommodate our new arrangement. Mycroft's laptop, with snarled supplementary wiring, still takes center stage, but the massed paperwork beneath the Anglepoise has a more orderly air.

The model of the guy with no skin – christened 'Skeletor' by Gus last month – is now wearing a black tulle tutu, courtesy of Mai. On her last visit, Mai got a lot of mileage out of the fact that *she* could enter the inner sanctum of Mycroft's room, while I was stuck outside on the park bench.

Mycroft's rearranged his chemistry-setup-slash-dresser over to the far side. His old crutches still lean nearby – he hasn't needed them for a while, although he still can't put too much weight on his left foot because of the reconstructive surgery after his brush with the lion. His futon on pallets has shifted back along the right-hand wall, to make room for a small bookshelf. A retro orange lamp (salvaged off someone's hard rubbish pile) is gaffer-taped on top of the bookshelf, so he can read in bed. The Christmas lights are still twinkling sweetly around the walls, now complemented by an electric four-bar heater at ground level that glows at all hours of the day and night. His aunt's electricity bills must be killing her.

The heater turns the room into Mycroft's private tropical oasis. I still can't get my head around the idea that a guy who spent his childhood in the land of snow-shovels and icy moors can be so sensitive to the cold.

But the way I'm looking at him now should be warming him up.

I waggle my eyebrows. 'D'you think you could manage to let me in?'

'Seriously?'

'Mum and Dad and Mike are all at work.'

Mycroft gets my full meaning, and I don't have to ask twice. He almost drops his tea in the rush to pull the curtain further back. I slide into his room, so warm and familiar. So warm, in fact, that I have to strip off my jumper.

'Help you with that.' Mycroft tosses the jumper onto his bed and gathers me up.

We kiss at full pelt, teeth clacking together and noses bumping. I taste blood.

'Mm – ow.'

'Shit. Sorry.'

We try again. My hair gets in the way, and Mycroft's hands are trying to move everywhere at once – my cheeks, my hair, my waist.

I grab for his shoulders. 'Stop. Just . . . one second.'

Mycroft rubs his nose where we bumped. A breeze chills the back of my neck – I glance behind me. The window's still wide open with the curtain pulled aside, letting in refrigerator air and the curious stares of any passers-by.

Mycroft grabs the wooden sash. 'I'm on it.'

He finishes struggling with the window. I pull the curtains together with a snap. 'Right. Sorted.'

'Shall we try this again?' Mycroft slides his hands around my waist as I turn.

'Yes.' I grin. 'Without the crashing this time.'

'Right. No bump and grind. Slow dancing.' Mycroft pushes gently until my back hits the wall. His eyes flare as he leans in. 'Got a bit carried away before, sorry. You're *here*.'

'I'm here.' I nod and smile.

'Inside my room.' His lips turn up delightfully.

'Uh-huh.'

'Mm.' He flattens one hand against the wall, lets his other hand roam as he lowers his head. His fingers trickle over my arm, down to my hip, to settle and stroke there. 'Special occasion, then.'

'Celebratory, yes.' I put my hand on his chest. I'm having trouble thinking up replies. My brain is dissolving as his lips nibble softly across my jaw to my ear, like a darting school of fish.

'Should've worn my tux. But what happened to your roller derby shorts?'

'You liked those, did you?'

'Definitely. They should probably be illegal.' The corner of his mouth is quirked, but his voice is low, hungry. His English accent has thickened. 'You should wear them more often. School, even.'

'You reckon? Principal Conroy would have a heart attack.'

'I'm nearly having a heart attack right now.'

He is, too. His heart is thumpa-thumping there, right under my palm. But he keeps himself a critical centimeter or two away – that tiny space between us is pulsing. I close my eyes. My head starts to feel very light.

Mycroft sways against me, breathes onto my temple. 'God, you smell fantastic.'

My being here is well outside the statute of limitations. My parents have laid down the law. And I had thoughts about that – honestly, there were *Thoughts*. I just can't seem to remember what they were right now.

I grin with my eyes shut. 'James, I—'

That's all I get out, and it's enough. He captures my mouth with his own, and my legs go wobbly as my body liquefies.

My hands fill up with the feel of Mycroft, the softness of his curls. I catch his taste on my tongue, inhale his scent. The room is vibrating with the heater's buzzing breath and the murmur of our wanting sounds, until it's just one complete sound.

Our bodies strain together. I draw on his bottom lip, slide my hands down his back, then up under his T-shirt. My fingers skate across the ridges of his old scars, find smoother parts of him as well, and there's nothing like this feeling of silky warm skin.

We break apart, panting.

Mycroft scoops back my hair. 'Rachel—'

And I say '*Shh*', because we don't need to talk. Not now, when all my blood feels hot.

I kiss him again, gasping deep. I hear this rush in my ears, my heart pounding like temple drums. I'm consumed by a wild memory of the very first kiss in the study hall at school, and the thought I carried around for hours afterwards: *What would it be like with his shirt off, the two of us pressed up against the wall near his bed . . . What if it was deeper, stronger . . .*

In that instant, I want to *know* what it would be like.

Deeper. Stronger.

I push him back, yank my T-shirt up and over my head.

Mycroft's blue eyes light with a high, serious burn. He arches and strips off his own T-shirt. I squeak when he puts both hands under my bum, lifts me up and presses me harder against the wall. Then my arms go around his neck, my legs around his waist, and I squeeze him tight – now our bare chests are together, with only my sports bra in between.

We look at each other, kiss again. Mycroft's lips trail down my neck, his curls tickle my ear. My head bumps the wall, but I keep my hands moving because Mycroft feels so soft and so incredibly good.

My cheeks are on fire – I don't need a mirror to see the flush in my face. I don't want a mirror to see the things we're doing: picking up speed, rubbing against each other, fretting with hands and arms and mouths.

We've had so little privacy for so long, and this is the explosion that results. I kiss his throat and he gasps, bites on my shoulder. I turn his head to get back to his mouth, and these kisses are so deep that he is a part of me, he is mine and I am his.

We're locked together, so completely absorbed in one another's bodies that we don't hear the tacky Casio-organ intro. It's only when Mycroft's phone starts vibrating against my calf that I figure out the noise I'm hearing. It's the daggy Racey classic 'Lay Your Love on Me'.

I groan – not in a good way and not because my boyfriend seems to be obsessed with late-seventies British pop songs.

'Oh shit.' I let out a shaky breath and push at him. 'Mycroft. That's your alarm.'

'What?' Mycroft stops sucking on my earlobe and goes still.

'Mycroft—' I detach his lips with an effort. 'Your *alarm*. You've got to go to work.'

'Shit.'

He releases me slowly, and I slide down the wall in a graceless way until my boots hit the carpet.

Mycroft staggers back, breathing hard, tugs out his phone and thumbs off the music. He pulls at his hair and steps forward again, like this is some bizarre do-si-do.

'Bloody hell.'

I don't have a comeback for that. This is the way it always goes – we never get any time alone, and then it's like a chemical reaction. Or a thermonuclear explosion.

Mycroft rests his forehead on mine and sighs. 'You should have come earlier.'

'Mike left, then I had a shower. Didn't think you'd enjoy me smelling of Deep Heat.'

'Deep Heat,' he murmurs into my ear, 'is good. Deep Heat I can handle. Not being able to look at you sideways when your folks are around – *that* I can't handle. Your mum hates me.'

'Mycroft, if she hated you she wouldn't feed you three square dinners every week. Not to mention giving you free access to our bathroom and fridge.'

'Maybe I can trade off the fridge for some other things I'd like free access to.' The growl in his voice makes my insides turn to toffee. But then he leans away and breathes out his nose. 'I've got to say, Watts, your house-arrest thing is getting extremely old.'

'Tell me.'

'Your house-arrest thing is getting extremely—'

'No, I mean *I know.*'

'I know you know. I'm just reiterating. Ah, bloody hell, come here.' He reels me into a hug.

I hug back until I have to push him away again. 'Oh god . . . Stop. You should change. You'll be late for your tram.'

We separate so I can fish around for my long-sleeved tee, and Mycroft can drag on a tank top and the white shirt hanging off the knob of his dresser. Apparently Professor Walsh is happy to have Mycroft in the lab, provided he's stringently punctual and dresses a little more appropriately. Jeans are okay, but T-shirts with chemistry in-jokes scrawled across them don't qualify.

I flump down into Mycroft's office chair and watch him fumbling with the purple laces of his new Cons as he sits on the sloppily made bed. My breathing is still jagged.

'So what's Professor Walsh got you working on this week?' I sip Mycroft's tea, lukewarm now.

'Dunno. Last week was the slides prep. Boring as hell.' He pulls on the laces; one comes up shorter by about five centimeters. He frowns and tries again. 'My no-complaints policy seems to be paying off, though. Getting to help with those autopsies was a fairly massive leap forward. And the Professor had a look at that upcoming *Diogenes* article on MVA physics, even made a few suggestions.'

Motor vehicle accidents are a very touchy subject – that article was hard for Mycroft to write, and harder for him to share. That Walsh agreed to look at it makes me appreciate him even more than I do already.

'He likes you, you know,' I point out.

'Well, I'm assuming so, or he wouldn't have offered me a job.'

'He offered you a job because he knows you're smarter than half his Forensic Pathology lab assistants mashed together and rolled into a ball. But that's not why he likes you.'

'Really?' Mycroft glances up as he knots the still-uneven laces. 'So why, then?'

I pick up the abandoned toast, consider it, drop it back on the plate. 'I think you remind Walsh of himself when he was younger. Not your wacky part, I mean. The thirst for knowledge part.'

'Maybe the tall part, as well.' Mycroft stands up, illustrating.

'Maybe.' I grin. 'So are you still the only baby in the labs?'

'Yeah, but come on. The youngest pathologist is twenty-five. They just treat me like part of the crew now.' He starts buttoning, then haphazardly stuffing his shirt into the back of his jeans. 'Check the newsfeeds for me while I'm in the gents? See if there's anything more about that Shakespeare thing.'

He walks out, using the wall to help with his limp. The physiotherapist said the problems with Mycroft's foot should clear up within a few weeks. He still feels it most in the mornings.

I swivel to the laptop and bring up the newsfeeds, Mycroft's bird's-eye view on the world.

Mycroft keeps track of anything related to forensics, of course. Also any scientific curiosities, and whatever else happens to catch his fancy. Some of what he follows makes it into the articles he puts up on the blog I built for him, *Diogenes*. Under that genderless, anonymous pseudonym he can expound his latest theories (backed up by online research and a fair bit of crazy experimenting) about whether fingerprinting cold-case evidence using the gold vacuum deposition method is really viable, or which ingestible biotoxins would show up in routine autopsy testing.

Other stuff he just checks out for fun, like the thread I'm pulling up now about the theft of a priceless book from an English library. Maybe he's taken an interest because it's about the UK – I honestly don't know. He's got all the reports backdated though, so I can read on from where he left off.

'What's the story?' Mycroft asks as he limps back.

'Nothing much new from last week.' I scroll down, scan the first few lines. 'It hasn't popped up at a London antique shop or anything.'

'No, they won't be stupid, these guys.' He pulls on his red hoodie. 'They must already have a buyer. Trying to fence a Shakespeare First Folio – you may as well be trying to flog the Crown Jewels.'

'I still think it was the conservator,' I say. 'He had access, he would have known the place—'

'For god's sake, Watts, it's not Cluedo.' Mycroft rolls his eyes, fiddling with his jacket zip.

'No, come on, it makes sense. Professor Plum, in the library . . .'
I grin and keep reading. 'Anyway, looks like everyone at the Bodleian has been questioned by police, and now they're . . . Hang on.'

'What?'

I read the feed from late last night. Read the lines again. My mouth opens, but nothing comes out.

Mycroft grins at me. 'Watts, what is it? Come on, I'll miss the tram.'

He leans across the back of the chair and looks past me to the laptop. For one demented second, I want to cover up the screen with both hands. But Mycroft's already spotted the headline, in hideous black and white, and it's way too late.

Mycroft's grin droops, melts. His breath escapes as if he's been winded. When he reaches for the mouse, his fingers are shaking.

I want to keep looking at him, as if somehow that will keep him together, keep him whole. But my eyes arrow back to the laptop, because I have to read the words again to make sure they're real.

And the words say *Shakespeare Librarian Dies in Freak Carjacking Smash*.

'Mycroft.' I put my hand on his, on the mouse.

He flicks my hand away, scrolls down the short paragraph of text. All the animation has bled from his face.

'*Mycroft*.' Airy panic rises in me.

'I've got to go to work.' Mycroft's voice is thick and weird, like it's oozing out of quicksand.

He straightens, blinking and looking around as though he's not really seeing anything. He grabs for his backpack, which is slumped against the side of the desk, then thrusts my jumper at me and bustles us both through the bedroom window.

He's kicking me out. This isn't how I imagined my visit ending at all, when I first tantalised myself with the idea of sneaking into Mycroft's room without my family around.

Out on the verandah, I grab his hand and squeeze. 'Hey. One carjacking isn't the same as another, it doesn't mean—'

'I *know*.' He scuffs at his face with his other hand, struggles back to normalcy. 'I know. I'll . . . I'll ask Walsh, he has connections in London.'

'Okay.' I knead his fingers. 'That's good.'

'I should . . .' He shakes his head and his hair shivers. 'Look, I've gotta go. I'll see you this afternoon.'

'See you *tonight*.' I put my hand on his cheek, bring his face around. 'Mike's bringing Alicia over for dinner, remember? You promised you'd come.'

'I . . .' He closes his eyes, nods. 'Right.'

'Tonight. We can talk about this. Are you okay?'

'I'm . . .' His expression vagues out. 'Fine. I've got to go.'

He kisses me in his front yard, just a quick, soft-lipped peck. The look on his face, as he walks off down Summoner Street to catch his tram, is awful. Shadowed and serious and absent, as if he's in shock.

I stand there for a long moment, my hands and cheeks numb. This is not good. Mycroft hasn't looked like this for ages. Not since December last year.

Mycroft never mentions the carjacking accident he was involved in, the one that killed his parents. It's like his scars – obvious, but too sensitive to touch. I only know what I've read in his Anniversary Book, the photo album where he keeps a ghastly montage of clips and articles related to the incident that changed his life forever.

Maybe the last few awesome months have lulled me into complacency, but the anniversary of Mycroft's parents' deaths isn't a date I can forget. It's the same date as my birthday.

I'm not surprised he's affected by this latest news about the London carjacking. Any reference to his old life in England, or car accidents, or family, has a tendency to ruffle his feathers. But I'm still shocked to see him react this badly.

The most frustrating thing is not knowing what to do. I don't understand the situation properly, because Mycroft never talks about it. I'm powerless, useless without more information.

My hands ball into fists. Ammunition – I need something to fight this with.

I jog back to my house, my tiny room, which is freezing compared to Mycroft's. My clunky laptop gives a wheeze of protest when I kick it to life. One of the things I've considered buying with the police reward money is a new laptop. I need one, but I haven't been able to take the step of spending the cash. It feels like ill-gotten gains. Mycroft and I got to split a five-thousand-dollar bonus for finding Homeless Dave's killer, but what did Dave get? A horrible death and a cheap coffin.

What I read about the carjacking case in the newsfeeds doesn't exactly put my mind at ease. The main headline is from the London tabloid *Metro*, and details are sparse:

London (A.M.) – Police have identified the body of a man follow-ing a fatal car accident early this morning, near High Wycombe. Daniel Maurice Gardener, 44, an Australian national, was a Rare Books conservator with the Bodleian Library in Oxford. Police are still investigating the recent scandalous theft of a copy of Shake-speare's First Folio, the prize of the Bodleian collection, valued at over 6 million pounds.

Sources within New Scotland Yard claim that police are questioning an Oxford alumnus, Farrell Al-Said, regarding the Bodleian theft. While Gardener had been exonerated of responsibility in the case, he recently contacted police to assist with their enquiries into the theft. The accident occurred three miles from the deceased man's residence. Metro *sources claim he was en route to New Scotland Yard at the time of the accident.*

Full details have not yet been released, but it appears that Gardener was the victim of a carjacking attempt. Police have detained a woman in response to an anonymous tip-off, but will not confirm if the woman is a suspect. Detectives have said that although the accident appears unrelated to the Oxford crime, they will be instigating a full investigation.

The Bodleian Library website is even less illuminating. I trawl through other sites. A broader search turns up an article from seven years ago, covering the deaths of one Edward Mycroft and his Australian wife, Katherine – I've seen it before, in Mycroft's album.

I read back and forth between the old article and this new one, about Daniel Gardener. Words like *Carjacking* and *Freak Smash* and *Accident* and *Fatal* recur so constantly they become a blur.

The two cases *can't* be related. Mycroft's hyper-sensitive to this sort of thing, so of course it set him off. He can't seriously be thinking there's a connection between two freak carjackings, seven years apart . . . Is there something I'm missing?

I frown at the screen, trying to figure out where these dots connect, when Dad wanders past the open doorway of my room. He must have come home after work, and I didn't even hear him.

'Up early, pumpkin.' He walks over, a mug in one hand, his taxi driver's shirt smelling of sweat. He plants a kiss on the crown of my head. 'You still hyped from last night's win?'

'No.' My eyes are still fixed to the screen. 'I mean, yes. But not right now, no.'

'Righto, then.'

'Mm.' I tear my eyes free. 'Sorry, Dad, hi. I'm just researching something.'

'School stuff, is it? Your exams are coming up fast.'

'Not for months, Dad, come on. But this isn't for school. It's, um, this case in the UK . . . This big book of Shakespeare's plays got stolen.'

'Shakespeare, eh? *To be or not to be . . .*' He slurps his tea, squints at the laptop. 'Valuable, is it?'

'It's worth about six million pounds.' I collapse useless tabs absently.

'My word. Seems a bit crazy, for a book. If my house was on fire and I could only go back for one thing, a book or a person, I know which I'd choose.'

Dad squeezes my shoulder and wanders out. I'd smile at his good mood, but his throwaway comment makes me shudder.

Mycroft wants to know, more than anything in the world, what happened to his family. Why they were attacked on a London expressway, how he ended up lying in blood, watching his parents die. If his house was on fire, and the answer to those questions lay inside, there's no doubt in my mind Mycroft would throw himself back into the conflagration. He'd risk a burning building, risk anything, to find out the truth.

A picture of Mycroft – his face blackened, his lanky body licked by flame – comes into my head, and sticks there.

I can't get rid of it.

CHAPTER THREE

'Mash?'

'Please.'

'Bread and butter?'

'No thanks, I'm good.'

'Rachel?'

'Just a little piece—'

'There's a big piece for you. Mycroft?'

'Mm? No, I'm fine.'

'Mike, put that up on the bench, would you, love, thanks—'

It's as tight as a fist around the yellow laminex kitchen table. Dad, Mycroft, me – wishing for more elbow room – Mum, Mike and Alicia, not put out by the squeeze.

This table wasn't really made for six. We've had to drag in the extra chair from my room, and Dad's sitting on the stool that usually lives under the eaves out the back.

'How's the casserole?' Mike asks, pouring the wine into four tumblers. Mycroft and I miss out.

'It's not bad, actually,' Mum says. 'It's a great relief, knowing you've managed to pick up some domestic skills.'

I open my mouth, but Mike bangs his knee against mine under the table. Alicia catches my eye and grins. I grin back, and she *knows*, I'm quite sure of it. We can't help giggling at each other.

Mike starts smiling. 'What? I'm getting better with the cooking, aren't I?'

Alicia and I erupt into laughter. I liked her even before I discovered Mike fancied her. It's crazy he took so long to work up the guts to ask her out.

'You must be looking forward to Europe,' Mum says.

'Oh yes.' Alicia's eyes are still sparkling. 'I'm meeting up with mates in Paris. We'll be traveling to Spain, and then I'm going to Malta to see Dad's family.'

'Sounds like an adventure,' Dad says.

'Yeah. I've been planning it for months, but it seems to have come up incredibly fast. Packing is giving me nightmares.'

Mike pokes at his plate with a slice of bread, mopping up gravy.

'Don't forget about us while you're away, eh?' he says gruffly.

Then Dad asks Alicia what motivated her to go into psych nursing as a line of work.

'My younger brother has schizophrenia,' she says. 'I planned to do nursing, but I guess growing up with Martin has encouraged me to go into psych.'

'I suppose you get asked that question a lot,' I say, after she replies so quickly and easily.

'Yeah, a bit.' Her face goes radiant. 'But I really love my brother, so I don't mind telling people.'

I remind myself to tell Mike he can date Alicia forever.

It's another debt of gratitude I owe Homeless Dave. If it weren't for Dave, I wouldn't have met Alicia at Royal Park hospital. I wouldn't have discovered Mycroft's history as a former patient there, or encouraged Mike to go for a job. The way all these disparate events flowed together is still a kind of miracle to me.

If Mycroft was his usual bouncy self I'd be even happier, but he's picking at his casserole and mash, grimly distracted. He's often distracted by something he's working on – a paper, an experiment – but this is different.

Mycroft's phone brays. He checks the screen and scrapes back his chair.

'Sorry, I've got to take this.' He walks out through the back door to the garden.

Mike squints at me across the table. 'Something up with him, or what?'

I wriggle my mouth and shoulders, reach for another piece of bread and butter I don't really want to eat.

Mycroft helps with the dishes afterwards, his usual contribution to the household. He's still acting a bit like an automaton, though. It's unnerving.

I keep a careful eye on him while I'm drying, as his hands move through the motions of scrub, wash, rinse, repeat. 'So did Walsh have more information?'

'What?'

I stop, the plate in my hand still dripping. 'The London case. The carjacking. You said you were going to ask the Professor—'

'Oh. No.' Mycroft frowns at the taps over the sink. 'I mean, yeah. But they still have to do the post-mortem and stuff, and I won't get access to that info anyway. Walsh might . . .'

'What? Walsh might what?'

'Nothing,' he says. He bites his lip.

29

Mum and Dad are seeing Alicia and Mike off – they're going to a movie. Cutlery clashes, the plates I'm drying clatter together in their stack. It all sounds loud next to Mycroft's silence.

I swat him gently with the tea-towel. 'Hey. You're doing it again.'

'What's that?'

I frown. He should know this. 'If you're feeling shit, just say so.'

It's a line he's used with me before. But he's blinking at the rainbow skin of grease on the dishwater.

'That's the thing,' he says. 'I don't know how I feel.'

His face and voice are expressionless. A chill slides into me. I put a hand out, splay my fingers across his back and feel the fabric of his shirt, the movement of his ribs as he breathes. I'm not sure whether the gesture is meant to steady him or me.

'The carjacking thing—'

'It's okay,' he says, but his eyes are distant. 'I'm just . . . thinking.'

Pretending again. The thought comes unbidden into my mind, rocks me. Mycroft's habit of pretending he's okay might have faded, but it's still there. I just didn't think he needed to do it with me anymore.

'Mycroft—' I start, then Dad comes back into the kitchen, belly-laughing towards Mum in the living room, and the moment is gone.

Mycroft pulls the sink plug and turns. 'All right if I have a shower, Mr Watts?'

Dad collects his windbreaker for work. 'Go for your life. Hey, Mycroft, when's your aunty gonna get your hot water service fixed, eh? She want me to come and have a look at it?'

'Oh god, don't let him,' Mum calls out from the living room with a giggling groan. 'If I had a dollar for every bloody time Terry said he'd fix some essential service around our old place—'

'Get off!' Dad yells.

I turn back to Mycroft, but he's already moved away to the bathroom.

The rest of the dinner clean-up is my job; I dry pots and wipe down benches with a frown on my face. Then there's nothing left for me to do except wait for Mycroft, so I can walk him home. Dad pecks my cheek on his way out to his taxi shift, and Mum's watching telly, so I head off to tidy my room, which is a slob-fest. Maybe when Mycroft emerges he'll come in and we can talk. Even with the door propped open, it'd be better than nothing.

I pass the bathroom at exactly the same moment Mycroft steps out of it in a towel.

Steam geysers out from the open doorway behind him. Drops of water sheen his neck, and his clothes are bundled in one fist. His hair is softly damp, ricocheting everywhere. His feet are bare, his chest is bare – actually, pretty much everything about him is bare, because apart from the ratty towel around his waist, he is naked.

Everything inside me suddenly *gets* that.

I stare at him. This is outside the statute of limitations but oh my god, I can't *stop*. His body is lean-muscled and strong. His wide shoulders and chest make that classic upside-down triangle, pointing towards his waist. There's that gentle curve, the silken spot between his abdominals and his hip bone. His scars are white zippers on his stomach, across his ribs. Delicate dark hair arrows down from just above his navel, disappearing under the towel.

Mycroft's lips part, his eyes flicker. He's registered the TV noise in the living room, the absence of parental figures in our immediate vicinity. Before I can speak a word, he takes three limping steps – near, nearer, nearest.

He edges me backwards through the door of my room, drops his clothes bundle, pushes the door silently closed. His eyes are intent. I feel that intention throughout my whole body.

Our faces are together – we're not kissing, but we're breathing each other. We're breathing so hard the air around us is heating up. Mycroft smells like lathered soap and something else, that dark, rich guy scent. His lips move gently over my face, different spots all around: my eyelids, my cheekbones, my forehead, my jaw. I am shaking.

My hands lift, like butterfly wings opening, and I touch him. His skin is soft as a new leaf. I trace his collarbone, the muscles of his chest. My fingertips slide across his ribs, his scars, down to his stomach, his hips. We do not make a sound.

I run my fingers through the fine hair around his navel, dip the tip of my thumb into the hollow there. Mycroft shudders, deep as a sob. He holds my eyes and all I can see is blue, blue, blue . . . I am dissolving into color. My body is blurring, spreading out, thinning at the edges.

I reach up to take a handful of his curls, pull his face closer, because if I can only taste his mouth now I will flip into oblivion. But if we kiss, if we start, I don't know what would make us stop.

Mycroft holds himself away. He lowers his head against the force of my hand, leans slowly and kisses the side of my throat. It's like a brand, and I gasp. He stares into my eyes, before kissing my lips so lightly it feels like the soft press of a bubble, the stroke of a feather, the touch of a baby's cheek.

I'm trembling so hard, panting, my legs like jelly. I have to hold on to him to stay upright.

He swallows thickly. When he speaks, his voice is just a husk. 'Let me get dressed.'

I nearly cry with the disappointment of it. Instead, I make this weird involuntary nodding movement, take two shaky steps to the door. Closing it behind me I glimpse Mycroft leaning, one hand on my desk and one hand squeezing his nape, his head hanging down.

In the hallway, nothing seems solid. I have to hold on to the wall to walk towards the kitchen. Even then I don't get far. I end up just standing in place, trying to breathe again, my eyes blinking, open-close-open.

What *was* that?

I mean, I know what it was. Since Mycroft and I became a couple we've done plenty of kissing, made a few explorations, always kind of grinning at each other. A mix of grinning and gasping, both of us alive to the *potential* of what might happen, of where we might be headed.

This was not that. I don't know what it was. It had a quality about it . . . A finality.

It's rattled me to the core. I stand there, staring at the cracks in the hallway paintwork, completely shell-shocked.

When Mum calls my name from the living room, it takes me a couple of tries to get my throat working. 'Yeah, Mum. I'm . . . I'm gonna make a cuppa.'

The space of the living room seems so open. There's no wall for me to hang on to anymore. Mum's relaxed, her feet up on a cushion – maybe it was the wine she and Dad had at dinner.

'You feeling all right, love?' She gazes up at me, her dark eyes crinkling with care. 'You look a bit white.'

'I'm okay.' My voice sounds odd and I walk on slow feet into the kitchen.

When I make it back to my bedroom, there's no one there. Mycroft's scent washes through the room, washes over me. He's already left by the front door.

———

I go to bed.

I'm not tired, but I'm exhausted. The combination of the early morning, and the hours I spent at work, and the frizzle of tension over dinner – Mike and Alicia's excited hum, Mycroft's rigid shoulders beside me – it's all got me wrung out. Then the moment in my room, with Mycroft standing half-naked in front of me, my hands skimming lightly over his body . . .

I can't lie here, feeling all this. I can't do it.

I drag myself up, slip into my uggies and pull Mike's jumper over my pyjama top. Sneaking out of the house seems so natural, and now I'm out on Summoner Street, close to midnight, the lines of neighboring roofs picked out in silver.

A stiff breeze lifts my hair off my neck, makes me shiver. I tuck my hands into my armpits and sprint down to Mycroft's house. Pass the gate, the path, tiptoe over the verandah boards.

Cold air makes a foggy border of condensation around the window and the curtain is drawn halfway. From my shadowed spot on the verandah I reach out to rap on the glass . . .

Something makes me stay my hand. Then I look, really look, at the tableau inside.

Mycroft is sitting at the desk in his office chair, lit from the front by the Anglepoise. The rest of the room is dark. The Christmas lights have been turned off, even the heater's glow is absent. He's got his puffy headphones on, shutting out all noises except the ones in his head: if I'd knocked, he may not have heard me.

I can see over his shoulder, and the sight chills me inside as well as out.

One of Mycroft's knees is up, and the Anniversary Book is propped on it. As I watch, he exhales a stream of smoke from the cigarette between his fingers – it billows outwards, like light from a dying star – and turns a page. It's the first time I've seen him smoking since he got out of hospital, and I get a sick feeling there's a few things I might have been missing.

Mycroft's hands – touching the album, lifting the ciga- rette to his lips – shimmer with suppressed tremors. The faces of his parents blink out from under the plastic: young, loving, frozen.

Dead.

My breath catches in my throat. I can't knock. I can't break this spell. This boy who makes my heart lose rhythm, whose hands have touched my skin, whose mind is bright as diamond. This boy who cannot let go, whose past is buried in the ground, in another country . . .

I've nursed sick animals before, and sometimes they just give up. Their eyes fill with this helpless lethargy, and there's not a lot you can do after that. Now I'm filled with the same awful feeling – that whatever's broken inside Mycroft might be well beyond my ability to fix.

I stumble off the verandah, stagger back down the street and let myself into my house. My fingers and toes are glacial. I climb into bed, leaking tears, with my jumper and ugg boots still on.

The sensation that there's nothing but chaos inside and out takes a long time to fade.

———

'Eaerrhhhh . . .'

Bears are growling in my sleep. Through my dreams. I try to fight them off, but I can hear their deep-throated calls, smell their acrid breath . . .

'Eaerrhhh . . . Rache, get up.'

Now one of them is batting me with his enormous paws.

'Come on, Rache, wake up!' More growling. 'Waaake uuup. Rachel, I've got to tell you something—'

I pull the quilt up over my face. My bear brother tugs it down.

'Rachel.' There's a bit of a struggle with the quilt. 'Rachel, wake up and tell me I'm not losing it. Just be honest.'

'You're losing it,' I mumble. 'Whatever it is, you lost it ages ago.'

I don't want light and cold on my face. I want to stay inside my warm cocoon. But Mike is insistent.

'Rache, I think I'm in love.' There's a pause. 'I mean it. You can't be in love after one night out, can you? Rache—'

Now he's got my full attention. My attention is bleary-eyed and suspicious, but it's present.

I push the quilt off. 'In love.'

'Yeah.'

Mike's face has this glow. I mean, he looks horrible this early on a Sunday morning – his dark hair is sticking up everywhere, he's thrown on clothes willy-nilly, and he hasn't had a shave. But his face is all . . . open. Happy. He's grinning, amazed.

'You're in love with Alicia,' I say.

'Yeah.' He licks his lips, makes a snorting smile. 'Yeah. Bloody hell.'

'Bloody hell,' I echo. I'm smiling, though.

'She's . . . God.' His voice has a wobbly uncertainty. 'I can't do that, can I? One night, be in love . . .'

I raise an eyebrow.

'I mean, I don't wanna . . .' He wriggles, looks away. 'She's . . .'

I prop myself up on my elbows. 'My brother. Speechless. Now I've seen everything.'

He snorts and smiles again, ducking his head. Then the words are jumbling out of him.

'We went to this pub down Sydney Road, right? And then she said she'd rather just hang out instead of going to a movie and sitting in the dark for two hours not talking to each other. So we went for a walk down Royal Parade, near the park, and we were talking for about *three hours*, Rache, until it was nearly midnight. And then it started to get freezing so she drove us to this cafe near the Westgarth Cinema, with, like, old couches and stuff up the back, so we could—'

'Snog.'

'Yeah, but *Jesus*!' Mike tugs at his hair while I watch, eyebrows raised. 'It was like . . . I *dunno* . . . by the time we got home it was nearly three, and she just . . . She told me she really likes me, like *really*, right there on her front step. But she's *leaving* tonight, so this whole thing is crazy. And I dunno if I'm going a bit mental, but I haven't felt like this before, and I think I . . . I mean . . . Maybe . . .'

I sit up and throw my arms around his neck. 'Oh, Mike.'

He hugs me back, squeezes hard.

It's *perfect* that Alicia and Mike have fallen for each other. I want to cheer. And Mike's all-out confession . . . I love my brother for it. It's more straightforward than anything Mycroft and I have ever had.

My eyes are burning. They're already swollen from last night, but I tell myself this heat is different. It's because I'm so happy for Mike.

'I feel weird,' he says, disentangling.

I grin. 'You look a bit weird.'

'Nah, seriously, I feel a bit . . . floaty or something. My hands are all shaky, see?'

He holds them up to show me. I don't point out it's probably partly from exhaustion.

'Anyway, I couldn't sleep, so about an hour ago I went over to Mycroft's to look at the hot water service. I was trying to be real quiet so I wouldn't wake Angela up. Mycroft's already headed off, so at least I didn't have to worry about—'

'Pardon?' My grin was high and bright, and now it's . . . not.

'Pardon what?'

'The bit about Mycroft heading off.'

'Well, he's gone.'

'What do you mean?'

'Off. Gone on hols? Absent.'

My face goes flat. 'Bull.'

'You didn't know?' Mike looks confused. 'His stuff is all packed up.'

'*No*, I didn't *know*.' I'm out of the quilt now, staggering upright, searching for clothes.

'Oh. Right.' My brother's expression is *not* right. He's watching me as I lurch around the room. 'Look, I didn't mean to—'

'Get out. I've got to get dressed.' I spill out of my uggies, grab for my jeans.

'Rachel, don't have a turn. It's probably nothing—'

'Get *out*.'

'Okay, Jesus . . .'

Mike retreats, and I zoom around like I'm on the track, my hair bouncing and flying.

I'm out the front door in under ten seconds, sprinting down to Mycroft's house, vaulting the fence.

The window of the Stranger's Room is closed, the curtain still pulled halfway, but I don't stop to check. I streak around the side of the house, bang open the back door and stride down the hall as though I'm possessed. I must *look* possessed – hair all over my face, boots untied, Mike's jumper rumpled over my pyjama shirt. Heaving my shoulder against the door to Mycroft's room is a totally unnecessary use of force because the door isn't locked, and then—

The Stranger's Room is neater than I've ever seen it. The desk has been tidied, laundry has disappeared, shelves groan with teetering piles of paperwork. The chemistry set on the dresser has been packed up and put away. The bed has been stripped.

The laptop on the desk is gone.

I check the dresser. Mycroft's wardrobe is incredibly limited, and half of it is missing. His backpack is gone from its spot beside the desk. My guitar still leans against the wall, like a lonely girl at a country dance.

There's no note.

I'm standing in the middle of Mycroft's room, shaking my head, when I get the feeling someone is watching.

'He left early,' a throaty voice says. 'About four.'

I spin around.

Angela Hudgson's dirty-blonde hair is tufted from her pillow. She's pulled a nylon dressing gown sharply around her front, as if she's trying to mummify herself. Her eyes glide quickly around the room she almost never gets to see. Although she and Mycroft have been less twitchy with each other lately, Mycroft's space has always been a no-go zone for her.

Before I can say a word, Angela turns and heads back down the hall. After another three-sixty around Mycroft's room, I trail after her.

Angela's standing in the kitchen, near the rumbling kettle. This room used to be a musty underused dungeon. A few weeks back, Mycroft and Mike and I got together to give the walls and cupboards a coat of creamy paint. Dad fixed the dripping taps and installed a second-hand patio setting. The change is dramatic – the old fridge still clunks in the corner and the windows are cloudy, but it looks like a room you could actually eat in now. I know Mycroft and Angela have shared a cuppa or two here, testing the waters.

Angela looks tired – she always looks tired – and I realize she's doing me a favor. Normally she never gets up before ten, but she's awake now, ready to answer my questions.

I'm so bushwhacked, though, I blurt the first thing I can think of. 'He didn't tell me.'

Angela coughs, an involuntary hacking into the heel of her hand that makes me think of smoker's lungs in photos on cigarette packets. 'He didn't have much notice, from what I gather. His boss called him about midnight, and he packed up and left.'

'His boss?' I gape. 'Professor Walsh?'

Angela nods. It comes to me that I haven't asked the most important question.

'Where did he go?'

Angela looks at me as though I should know the answer. And before she even opens her mouth, I realize I *do* know.

'London,' she says. 'He's gone to London.'

CHAPTER FOUR

The light on Summoner Street is starting to sharpen with that rosy, welcome-to-the-polluted-city glow as I let myself out of the house. Streetlamps wink off. Trams and cars shamble down Sydney Road towards another gray Melbourne day.

Last night – I'm thinking of last night. Of the phone call Mycroft took at dinner. The way he stood with me in my room, with the door closed and our breath intermingling, the way he shuddered when I touched him, the way he barely touched me in return, just left those light, papery kisses . . .

My steps gain momentum, until I've barrelled into my house, rushed to my room. My phone's on the desk, and when I check my texts, there it is.

Going to UK with Walsh. Don't be mad. Will stay in touch. M

Five-twenty this morning. And he had the audacity to include a smiley.

I'm going to kill him. But there's someone else I need to kill first.

———

Detective Senior Sergeant Vincent Pickup, of St Kilda Road Police Headquarters, Homicide Division, looks like a ginger tomcat that was dumped in a hessian sack and thrown in the river, before clawing its way out and drying on the bank.

He's wearing what appears to be the exact same suit he had on the last three times I saw him, possibly with the same shirt. His nose and cheeks are a knobbled, pockmarked mass and his ranga hair has been flattened with the palm of his hand.

Pickup's eyes, though, are steady, like pale blue chips off an Arctic glacier. Right now, he's got them squarely focused on me.

'Sunday,' he says. 'You know the days of the week, I'm assuming. Saturday and Sunday are supposed to be rest days. Days of rest, that means.'

I stand in front of his desk in my camo pants and long-sleeved black T-shirt, my satchel strap slung across my chest. Looking reasonable and polite is almost beyond me. I'm so angry I can hardly change expression without hurting my face.

'That's rich, coming from you. *Days of rest* – since when have you ever had a weekend off?'

Pickup sighs. 'Okay. Fine. Out with it.'

'You knew Mycroft was going, didn't you?'

'Miss Watts.' Pickup knows my first name, and has used it on occasion. So he's either giving me the official line or he's trying to browbeat me. 'Scotland Yard agreed to a direct request from Daniel Gardener's family for an Australian forensic expert. Professor Walsh was contacted early yesterday by the embassy, after being recommended by a pathologist colleague in England. Walsh explained to me that Mycroft was researching something that had relevance to this case in London, and that he'd gain valuable experience by participating. That doesn't mean—'

'It means everything! And he's not a detective!'

'I'm aware of that.'

'Excuse me, but that's *crap*. You would have known Mycroft was—'

'Mycroft petitioned Walsh yesterday for the opportunity to go. He's been—'

'He's not a bloody field agent! He's in high school!'

'Mycroft has a very particular set of skills, something the Professor felt would—'

'Oh, for god's sake!'

I throw up my hands, but Pickup is giving me his best line in glares.

'Look. This was as much of a surprise to me as it is to you. Mycroft helped out with the Perth case, but that was online. This London business . . .' Pickup sits forward, jerks his chin at a collection of forms in front of him. 'Walsh put the paperwork in yesterday, but your boyfriend wasn't part of the equation until late last night. Mycroft offered to pay for the ticket himself, assuming the department can reimburse him at some later stage. Walsh has vouched for his expertise, and he'll be paid as an outsourced assistant – note the word "assistant" – while he's in the UK, so it's not like we're ripping him off. He won't be in any situations that involve a personal risk. It seemed like a reasonable—'

'You don't get it, do you?' I stare at Pickup, willing him to understand. 'This isn't about whether Mycroft's getting paid, or whether he has the expertise for the job. I mean, don't you lot do background checks, and psych profiling, and all that shit? Don't you have any idea what this case means? I can't believe you'd just—'

'Enlighten me,' Pickup says.

He looks tired. It *is* a Sunday. He's in here, working some other case on his weekend, and now he's got a mad seventeen-year-old girl wringing her hands in front of him.

I pull my satchel strap over my head and plonk down on one of the deliberately uncomfortable metal chairs. 'Detective, Mycroft's originally from London. You know that, right?'

Pickup gives me a dose of eyebrow. 'The accent sort of gives it away, yes.'

'And you know his parents are dead.' I take a breath before the big reveal. It's Mycroft's personal stuff. I'm not sharing it lightly, but it still feels like a betrayal. 'They were killed in a car accident seven years ago. The police called it a carjacking attempt.'

'A carjacking.' Pickup's expression doesn't change, but it gets an immediate stillness.

'Yeah. But it wasn't. The police found bullet casings at the scene. Somebody shot into their car on the A1.' It feels thin, like I'm drawing lines of connection that don't exist. But they exist for Mycroft. 'Look, they never figured out who did it, or why. His dad was an academic, some kind of analyst, but there was no—'

'And Mycroft's tried to follow this up, has he?' Pickup's sitting up a bit straighter.

'Like a bloodhound. You know how he is. The file he's got is just . . . scary. Huge.'

'This bloke from Oxford who got killed . . . That's another carjacking.'

'Yes.' Thank god Pickup isn't as dim as he looks. 'As soon as Mycroft saw the words "carjacking" and "London" in the same sentence, he was on it like a shot.'

'And you think Mycroft'll go nosing around in London, trying to make two and two equal twenty-two.'

'Yes.' This massive weight has been lifted, just by saying it out loud to someone who believes me.

Pickup sucks his front teeth, his eyebrows gathering together like a pair of red ferrets.

'Okay. This is what we do. I call Walsh, word him up. Tell him to keep an eye on Mr Busybody, make sure he doesn't go bugger-ising around in things that don't have anything to do with the case they're supposed to be on.'

My shoulders slump. 'Detective, d'you honestly think Mycroft's going to do as he's told? He might be bright, but when it comes to issues of personal judgment he can be sort of a dickhead.'

Social moron. I get a gut-wrenching flash of Mycroft's hot lips on my cheek, my forehead, my eyelids . . . I swallow and refocus.

Pickup is sucking on his teeth again. 'All I can do is tell Walsh. We'll just have to rely on him to keep Mycroft on a short leash.' He grimaces. 'Mycroft respects Emmett, and he wants to keep his job. Let's pray that's sufficient.'

He's giving me this sympathetic look, but it's a pragmatic look too – *our hands are tied.*

My own hands itch to throw something. I twist my satchel strap, fray my worry into the canvas-weave. 'It won't be enough.'

Pickup's face softens momentarily. 'Rachel, you don't know that.'

'I know,' I say, but I'm looking away, remembering Mycroft's face when he saw the newsfeed: the way his grin dissolved, went watery, the way his hands shook.

Mycroft is on a plane, on his way to confronting his bloody past, with no one but his slightly eccentric boss to back him up.

A dreadful sense of foreboding sprints around inside me, and I can't ignore it – the last time I ignored it, Mycroft and I ended up in the lion pen at the zoo.

Pickup sees my expression change from anxious to fearful. 'I'll contact Walsh, okay? As soon as they touch down.'

'Thank you.' He's doing his best, which makes me feel worse.

Pickup stands and frowns at me, scratches under his ear. 'Rachel, will you take some advice from an old man? Your lad . . . He has to learn how to sort out his own messes. He's nearly eighteen. You can't be wiping his nose for him. You have to just trust he's gonna act like a grown up. He'll muddle through, he'll be all right.'

Pickup's right – I know he's right. But there's a glass knife cutting a thin groove into my gut.

'Detective, Mycroft was a passenger in his parents' car. He saw them die.' I feel my face turn bleak. 'Mycroft's good at acting like a grown up – he's always good at acting . . .'

I can't say anything more or I'll cry. The tears are right behind my eyeballs. I escape Pickup's office, wishing I had wings to take me out of this place, to another country.

————

That's it, then. There's nothing I can do except fret all the way back home on the tram. At least I've got roller-derby training in the afternoon.

I catch Mai in the change rooms as we're slamming lockers shut. She swings around, boggle-eyed. 'London. Like England, and the Queen, and—'

'Yes. That London.' I concentrate on pulling on my skates.

Mai tears off her black hoodie – the one with the graphic of Darth Vader constructing a macramé Death Star – and thumps down onto the bench seat beside me.

I show her the text and she blanches.

'Bastard. *Don't be mad.* Yeah, right. And what does *Will stay in touch* mean? Has he been?'

'No. But he's probably still flying . . .'

Mai shakes her head. 'I can't believe he left without telling you.'

'I know. And I reckon he knew he was leaving. He went outside to take a call at dinner last night, and when he came back he was . . .' I yank up my knee pads, trying to keep my face angry, not pathetically soft and wet. '. . . different. And he kissed me in this funny way.'

'A funny way? Like, what, he stuck his tongue up your nose or—'

'No. It was . . . weird. Intense.'

Mai kinks her eyebrows. 'Because intensity and Mycroft are always mutually exclusive.'

'No, I know, it just . . . It felt different.'

Mai gives me the same look she did when I said I occasionally listen to country music. 'Rachel, if you're telling me you think Mycroft was kissing you goodbye, like he was breaking up with you or something, it will just totally shatter my world view.'

I keep my face down. 'I don't know what it meant.'

'Oh, hey.' Mai squeezes my shoulder. 'It's okay. Maybe he was worried about being gone for a while, so far away, and he didn't want to . . . I don't know. That sounds like bullshit, doesn't it?'

'Yes.' It's as though I'm swallowing tar.

'Or maybe it's just that it's London. I mean, Mycroft doesn't talk about England. He doesn't talk about his life before at all. It's pathological. Whatever his baggage is, it's serious.'

'Yeah.' I can't bring myself to explain how serious. Not right now.

'Rachel, if he's talked to you about England, then he must trust you.' She tugs on the laces of her skates, removes her bangles, one by one.

I shrug. Most of the details about Mycroft's life 'before' I've gleaned by accident, or from leafing through his Album on the sly.

'Which means he must care about you,' Mai continues. 'So he can't be breaking up with you. There you have it – quod erat demonstrandum, et cetera.'

She grins, as if this sophisticated logic is enough to soothe my fears. But I'm dwelling on the idea now. I've always known there's a tangled mess beneath Mycroft's cool-geek veneer – but if he cares about me, trusts me, then why doesn't he tell me more about his past?

'So what *do* you know about him?' I ask.

'I know he's living with Angela because his parents passed away. He doesn't have any siblings. He's English. He's a pain in the arse. That's it.' Mai shrugs, chews her lip. 'So he's over there with his boss?'

'Yeah.'

'Will he be okay?'

I stop in the act of pulling my hair into a ponytail. 'What?'

'Will he be okay? I mean, the only time Mycroft's mentioned England was his birthday, July last year, and he went manic. Got incredibly blotto and let off these homemade fireworks in Fawkner cemetery, nearly set his hands alight before Gus and I dragged him home . . .' She glances over in time to see the horrified expression on my face. 'Sorry, this probably isn't helping, is it?'

'Not really, no.' I've gone stock still.

She hurries on. 'Look, Mycroft will be fine. Either way, there's not much you can do. I mean, it's not like you can just jet off to London, can you?'

'No,' I say, and it kills me to say it. I can't talk about this, I can't think about this anymore. Thank god there's training.

The track is solid, the track is good. I get to bash into Bernie a few times, and I'm strangely focused. When I'm skating, the surface of the world is liquid and I'm sailing over it. The drum of rolling contact travels through my feet and up my legs into my torso, into my head.

I can forget about Mycroft, forget his cryptic text message. Everything recedes but older memories: the sounds of traffic outside the hall are muted by the rattle of quad wheels, and I can almost smell gum leaves, sense the miles of open space . . .

I'm feeling better by the time I walk in the door of the house, examining the rink rash on my forearm. It's after six-thirty, so Mike should have made dinner – yep, there's the greasy smell of sausages in the air. I think he's burnt something again.

Everything is oddly quiet. Dad must've already left for work, Mum is out. The door to Mike's room is closed, music seeping through softly – he must be in there, mourning Alicia's imminent departure.

I dump my skate bag and head straight for the shower. When I step out, I swipe a hand over the fog on the mirror and take a good hard look at myself.

My hair flops over my shoulders in limp strands. It's clinging to the blonde streaky thing, and getting ridiculously long. I've got nice skin, and biggish brown eyes. My face is a bit paler than it used to be and a few pensive wrinkles have collected between my eyebrows – I relax my face, and they disappear.

I don't know what it is about me exactly that Mycroft finds so appealing. I'm not remarkable-looking in any way. Just as ordinary as dirt.

The fog starts to dissipate from the edges of the mirror. I take another look at my face. There's something else in my expression.

Stubborn eyes.

I've always taken it for granted. But maybe Mycroft saw the obstinate look in me right from the start. Maybe he knew, as soon as he glanced my way, that I was a hanger-onner. That I would stick around long enough to break through his shell and see him, the real him, the James I know, in spite of all the obstacles . . .

An idea forms in my brain.

No.

It's stupid. It's a stupid idea.

I drag on fresh underwear, struggle to pull my jeans up my damp legs.

It's not like you can just jet off to London, can you?

No, you can't. No way. Not unless you're Alicia – planning the trip months in advance, scheduling time away, saving money . . .

I tunnel into my long-sleeved T-shirt and yank a flannie over the top. Socks over wet feet, boots. I scrub my hair with the towel, rake it into a knot at my nape.

Back in my room, I check my texts. Nothing new, just the same message as before.

Going to UK with Walsh.

I don't know how long a flight to the UK takes. Maybe they had a stopover somewhere. Maybe he can't get reception on his phone. Don't they make you turn off your phone on the plane?

I spin a slow circle inside my tiny mushroom-colored room. There's the cranberry-and-tan quilt on my bed. My desk. The bars on the closed window. When Mycroft came over that night it was raining, and he reached through the bars to touch my cheek . . .

It's crazy, this longing I feel for him when he's not even around to appreciate it.

And underneath, I sense this thought process moving. Assessing.

Sports bag – I'd need that. It'd be big enough. Laptop – probably not. Phone – will it work? Underwear.

I escape from my room, because this is too big. I can't think about this. I need a second to re-stabilise, or . . . I need a sounding board. Someone I can bounce things off, to give me some perspective.

I stumble across to Mike's door, twist the handle and walk in. 'Mike, tell me I'm not losing it—'

Mike is lying on his bed. Or rather, not lying, more propping himself on one elbow, with his other hand kind of tangled between Alicia's legs. She has her skirt rucked and her shirt unbuttoned, lying beneath him, one knee up and one arm raised, her fingers in his hair. And Mike has no shirt on, and they are kissing so deeply that I feel an empathetic stab of *whoah*, because this is raw unadulterated passion, and I—

'Oh god, sorry!'

I whip around and trip over the edge of the rug in my hurry to get out. My back flattens against the wall in the hallway, then my brain kicks me and I lean across and pull the door closed.

My face is red-hot.

I stand in the hall, my hands pressed to my cheeks. There should be something on the market – *Brain Wipe 3000*, or something like that. Extra strength. The way you can get beer in Light, Full, or Heavy. Something Heavy, so I can get rid of the image of my brother *feeling up his girlfriend on his bed*. Because there's a limit, you know, to what little sisters are supposed to see, although at least it's stopped me from thinking about Mycroft and the whole—

Mike comes out into the hallway, pulling on a T-shirt. He closes the door to his room behind him.

He's giving me the blank look, but his cheeks are flushed. '*Knocking*, it's called. That thing where you knock on the door.'

'Sorry.' I glance at him. 'Your fly's undone.'

'Right.' He zips himself, completely unabashed. 'What were you after?'

And there's got to be something I interrupted his X-rated romantic goodbye for, so I blurt it out. 'Mycroft's gone.'

Mike chases back his hair. 'We established that this morning.'

'To London.'

'London. Shit. That's a fair way.' He clears his throat. 'So was there—'

'I'm worried about him.'

Mike sighs a little. 'Well, he can be worrisome. That's true.'

'His parents died in London.'

'I didn't know that.' Mike's words are slow.

'Didn't know what?' Alicia pokes her head out into the hall and then emerges properly, tucking her now-buttoned shirt back into the waistband of her suede skirt.

Mike turns and sighs again, more deeply. 'It's okay, Leesh. Mycroft's gone to London, and Rachel's worried about him.'

Alicia twists back her long espresso-colored hair and looks at me. 'Yeah, okay. I can see it.'

'What can you see?' I say, immediately more anxious.

'Nothing.' Mike glances at me sternly. 'He'll be okay, Rache.'

But suddenly, it's clearer than it ever was before. Mycroft has gone to London, where he believes his parents were murdered. Not killed in an accident. *Murdered.* And Mycroft watched them bleed out. Watched them die.

He's going back to all that.

And I'm standing here, worried that I might be *interfering.*

I am a *moron.*

'He'll be fine, Rache,' Mike says, but I've already walked off.

I head into the kitchen, past the living-room couch with Alicia's multi-strapped, chock-full backpack sitting there ostentatiously – why didn't I notice that before? I prop my bum against the table and stare at the stove. It's spattered with brown grease, from when Mike fried the sausages. I stare at the frying pan, full of congealing fat, and the dirty tongs, as though they were beamed down from Mars.

Mike has trailed me in. He looks at me and starts talking fast. 'Oh no no no. Rache . . . *Rachel.* It's not happening, okay? So you shouldn't even be thinking it. D'you get that?'

I keep staring at the frying pan.

'Shit. Ah geez . . . Rache, you *can't.* Ask Alicia, there's heaps of organizing, and you can't just—'

'I know that.' My voice seems to be coming from a long distance away.

'So you *can't go.* Rachel, think for a second.'

'I am thinking.'

'What's she thinking about?' Alicia says. 'Where does she want to go?'

'London.' Mike's eyes must be deadly, from the tone of his voice.

'I love London,' Alicia says brightly. 'That's why I made it my first stop before Paris. I lived there for a while, three months on exchange. It's fantastic.'

'We're not *advising* her to go,' Mike grinds out. His gaze cuts right through me. 'We're advising her to exercise her brain. Let Mycroft work his own shit out.'

'If it was *you*,' I say to him, 'if *you* had lit off to London, with the intention of walking back into some unspeakably awful personal-history fuck-up, I'd go to help you out. No question.'

'How is it unspeakably awful?' Mike stares. 'You didn't say anything about unspeakably awful.'

'I'd go,' Alicia says. She shrugs. 'I mean, people ask you to go to their wedding in, like, Bali. But they don't ask you to come to support them when they're having a breakdown, or in pain. It's dumb. It's some Australian stoicism thing, I don't understand it.'

'We don't *know* that he's having a breakdown,' Mike says. 'And it's not Bali, it's the *UK*. It's two days on the plane or something.'

'Twenty-three hours,' Alicia says, grinning. 'It's still a long way.' She looks at me, and her expression gets this sunflower openness. 'Rachel, I don't know what you had in mind, but my flight leaves in four hours . . .'

'No *way*,' Mike says.

'Seriously?' I can't breathe for a second.

'Well, if you're that worried about Mycroft . . . Are you sure?'

I nod slowly. 'Yeah, I think I am.'

'You should check online, see if there are any seats still available.'

'Stop *helping* her!' Mike yells, but it's too late. I've pushed past him and back through the living area, down the hall to my room. My knee jigs compulsively as I wait for my laptop to load.

'*Please*, Rachel.' Mike shifts from foot to foot at the door to my room. 'Mum and Dad are gonna go fucking *mental*.'

I look straight at him and play my final card. 'You owe me. Your track record, remember?'

He smooshes his hands over his face and talks through his fingers. 'Jesus Christ. Why did you have to turn seventeen? Why couldn't you have just stayed twelve? You were *cute* when you were twelve.'

Alicia pushes past him and stands behind me, leaning so she can see the screen. 'There. That's my flight – and there are three seats left, excellent. You've got a passport?'

'Yeah.' I'm surprised I remember. 'From when we were going to my uncle's funeral in New Zealand. But then he ended up being buried in Mildura . . .'

'And you don't need a visa, because you're traveling within the Commonwealth.'

'Oh. Good.' Visas. Crap. I've no idea what I'm doing.

'Bloody hell.' Mike bangs his head quietly against the doorjamb, looks away down the hall. 'Bloody fucking hell.'

'Have you got money?' Alicia asks.

'I've got two and a half thousand dollars,' I say. 'From the police reward.'

The idea still seems bizarre to me.

'Great, you'll need it.' Alicia nods at the screen. 'See, the flight is about sixteen hundred dollars return, but if you want to get there without stopping in Dubai for two days on the way home, you'll need to spend a bit more. And London's not a cheap place to visit. We'll need about a hundred bucks a day each, for accommodation and expenses.'

'Okay.' I'm doubly glad now I haven't spent any of the money.

'I was planning to stay with old friends in Camden, but I know a few YHA hostels that should have rooms . . . Will you need to be in central London?'

'I have no idea,' I say. I gulp at the enormity of what I'm about to do. 'I . . . I could find out from Detective Pickup where Walsh and Mycroft are staying.'

'Okay, good. And if we're together I can show you around . . .' She turns to grin at Mike. 'I think it's a great idea. I can stay with her in London, and it'll keep everyone happy.'

Mike's arms lift and he puts his hands on his forehead, as if he's trying to hold his head together.

'People say that. People say *Mike, I've got a great idea*, and I always get the chills.' He sighs. 'But who cares what I think?'

CHAPTER FIVE

'Have you got that jumper?'

'I'm wearing it.'

'Right. Phone, passport, ticket . . .'

'Yes. Yes. Yes.'

'Money?'

'I just withdrew it from the ATM. Mike, you saw me, you were standing right next to me . . .'

'Okay. Have you got somewhere to put it?'

'Just . . . I don't know. In my purse?'

Mike gives me this desperate, frazzled look, his mouth open as if he's about to speak, but then he changes his mind and licks his lips and nods. 'Okay. Okay.'

'Mike, it'll be all right,' I say. Half of me wants to tell him to snap out of it, and doesn't he think this is stressful for me too? The other half wants to hug him.

Alicia grabs Mike's hand and we walk towards the check-in desk. I can't believe I am doing this. I have never been on a plane.

Ever. This is my first trip to Tullamarine, although six and a half months ago on the way down from Five Mile we stopped near Bulla and watched the planes coming and going. They were big, bigger than I expected. This is all a bit bigger than I expected.

The check-in area is enormous, noisy and neon-loaded, and I'm not sure which glossy aisle I'm supposed to be walking towards.

'. . . so if you tell your folks I'm with her, that should set their minds at rest,' Alicia says to Mike, while grabbing my arm and pulling me in the right direction. 'Tell them it was my fault for suggesting it.'

'God, they'll think you're a bad influence.' Mike's expression is panicked, but he's looked like that for hours now.

'Well, maybe I am. Don't tell them anything, then.' Alicia grins and tugs her backpack strap. 'Look, don't worry about your mum and dad. I mean, they'll have to see that it's better if Rachel comes with me rather than jaunting off on her own.'

'I can't believe you're doing this,' Mike says, echoing the thoughts in my head, only I'm not sure if he's talking to me or Alicia. But she's the one who puts her cheek against his, and when they kiss I have to look away.

It's nine o'clock, and the plane leaves in an hour. I didn't know it was possible to do this, just make a decision and act on it so fast – book and print a ticket, pack in a whirlwind, then bust out the front door for the furious drive to the airport.

Now I'm standing in International Departures, near a group of Chinese students going back to Guangzhou. They're all wearing crazy shoes – runners with thick velvet straps, pink laces on hi-cut trainers, brown Converse with graffiti. A girl with red fluffy moccasins looks as though she's standing on top of two small dogs.

I don't know if I've packed enough: my little sports bag, emptied of its skates and safety pads and towels, is now stuffed with jeans and underwear and long-sleeved T-shirts. Everyone else is carrying massive backpacks with ten million straps, or Samsonite suitcases.

The man at the check-in counter looks almost disappointed. 'It's under ten kilos,' he says, as if he's expecting me to pull a heavier bag out from behind somewhere.

Alicia tells me I'll have to ditch my bottle of water and take out all the crap from my satchel – my lip balm, my toothpaste, of all things – and put it into plastic ziplocked bags for Customs inspection. We don't have time for a coffee, just a quick visit to the loo, then Mike's standing in front of me with this hard expression on his face.

'Rachel, listen to me for a second. You've gotta remember something. A guy thing.' He glares at me, willing me to pay attention. 'He won't want you there. Even if he's hurting—'

'I know,' I say.

'Do you? Because it's not gonna be all hugs and flowers when you see him.' Mike pushes a hand through his hair, and all the dark strands go haywire. 'Remember Dad, when Uncle Owen died?'

'I remember,' I say.

'Rache—'

'Nobody should have to grieve alone, Mike,' I say softly.

Mike drops his head and sighs. 'You know, this is officially the most fucked-up crazy thing you've ever done.' He scrapes his stubble with one hand. 'There was the lion thing, but . . .'

'I know,' I say. I'm really standing here, really doing this. Saying I can't believe it doesn't make one bit of difference.

'You're totally dropping me in it with Mum and Dad. You know that, right?'

'Yes.' I take his hand in both of mine. 'And I'm sorry. But I've got to go. I . . . I don't even really know why.'

'Just a bad feeling, is it?'

'Yes,' I whisper.

And it's insane, because for a bad feeling you call, or text. You send an anxious email or even travel a little way and drop in. You don't *fly halfway around the globe.* But this bad feeling powers over me, overwhelming. My breathing is smothered. I feel as if I'm drowning. It's all I can do not to cry.

'All right.' Mike stares at me for another second, then he's pulling me forward into a bear hug, solid and warm. His smell reminds me of dirt, and sheep's wool, for some reason. I hug back until my arms hurt. Mike puts his hands on my shoulders. 'I get it. Maybe I wouldn't have before I met Leesh, but I do now.'

'I know,' I say, and I'm actually crying now.

'Stay with Alicia.' He squeezes my shoulders hard. 'And don't put up with any bullshit from Mycroft. Personal dramas aside, there's no excuse for being an arsehole. If he thinks it's okay to just piss off without saying goodbye, then tell him . . . Tell him he better not come back to Summoner Street unless he wants a word with me.'

A booming, disembodied voice rolls around the cavernous roof-space of the International Departures area.

'That was our boarding call,' Alicia says.

'Make sure Mum and Dad know this was my idea.' I squeeze and squeeze. 'Tell them it wasn't your fault.'

'They won't believe me.' Mike laughs. 'Jesus, I can't believe you're taking off with my girlfriend. And my jumper.'

'I'm a cow.' I hoist my satchel over my shoulder. 'I'm sorry. Thanks for the jumper. I'll be back by Friday.'

'You'd better be.' Mike grabs Alicia and kisses her hard, looks her straight in the face. 'You know, I think I might be in love with you.'

Alicia just stares at him. 'Oh my god, you have to tell me now! Mike—'

'They're calling for passengers,' I say.

'Go.' Mike squeezes my arm and releases.

'Mike,' Alicia says, and she leans in towards him. She whispers something in his ear, and I see his expression become intent, and then shocked, and then amazed . . .

But there's no time to dwell on it, because Alicia has taken my hand.

My last glance back shows Mike, his palm up, fingers straight, in that classic country wave. He has this anxious longing on his face, and maybe it's for Alicia, or maybe it's for me, to just forget this insanity and stay. Or maybe he's wishing he was coming with us. I don't know, and it's too late to ask, because the doors have swooshed closed and I am on my way to London.

———

They do make you turn off your phone on the plane. And god, I wish it hadn't happened – that I'd been cool and collected – but I threw up on takeoff.

When the seatbelt sign gets turned off, I spend a few minutes in the toilet cubicle, which is no wider than my body, staring at myself in the mirror. *What have I done?* I've gotten on a plane without telling my parents where I'm going, leaving my brother to sort out the mess. I've effectively wagged school for a week, I haven't told Mai what's happening – oh shit, I haven't called Mai!

And Mycroft isn't even going to be pleased to see me, when I rock up to his doorstep in London.

I stand in front of the mirror, hyperventilating, until I figure out that's a sure way to make myself throw up again. I close my eyes, force my breathing to slow, splash some tepid water on my face. I keep my eyes off the mirror as I tidy myself up, before stumbling back to my seat.

'Feeling better?' Alicia gives me a gentle smile.

My seatbelt joins together with a Zippo-lighter snap. 'A bit.'

The cabin lights have come back on in a subdued way. Alicia says it's so people can start adjusting to the time-zone changes if they want to.

'Really, it's best not to sleep yet. I mean, I know it's nearly eleven Australia time, but that makes it about lunchtime in the UK.' She yawns and stretches. 'God, we're going to be horribly jet-lagged. But let's catch some rest after Abu Dhabi.'

'Thank you.' I look at her. 'Really. This is . . .'

'Rachel, it's okay – I invited you, remember?' She looks at the seat in front of her, shaking her head in astonishment. 'But oh my god – Mike! I can't believe he said that, just as I was leaving . . .'

'He told me,' I say. 'He woke me up and told me this morning. I think he was busting to tell someone. I'm glad he actually managed to tell *you*, before you got on the plane.'

Alicia just grins at the seat back, then looks at me and snorts, then grins some more.

We fly into the eye of night. Flying is weird. The moon is huge out my window – I thought it was reflecting off the sea, but I realize it's reflecting off the plane's wing. It swims in a halo of golden light, like an egg yolk floating in a pale sway of foam.

Alicia chats to me about her Europe plans for a while, then turns on her e-reader. People in the seats around us are going to sleep. Stress keeps me awake. There are so many reasons why going to London is a dumb idea.

What if Pickup's right? Mycroft's a big boy, maybe he can take care of himself. Maybe he doesn't need a hand-delivered care package. Maybe I'm jumping the gun on this, maybe I'm on the road to major embarrassment . . .

Maybe, maybe, maybe.

Alicia starts to fade as the hours slip away. 'I worked all day yesterday, and I've been awake all night. I'm buggered.'

'You said not to sleep before Abu Dhabi.'

'I know!' She pushes back a smooth fall of dark hair and blinks hard. 'Talk to me a bit. Tell me something.'

'Like what?'

'Tell me again about this thing Mycroft's gone to London for.'

'Oh, the case. It's a carjacking . . .' I flip open my satchel and pull out the articles I printed before I left, all held together with a bulldog clip. I peel through the stack of photos and information until I find the picture I want. 'This guy. His name is Daniel Gardener. He was a conservator at a library called the Bodleian, at Oxford University.'

'I've been there.' Alicia smothers a yawn with one hand. 'What's a conservator? Is that like a librarian?'

'A special type, who repairs and maintains the books.'

'Okay, so this Gardener fellow was killed, is that it?'

'Yes. But before that, the Bodleian Library had something very valuable stolen.' I show her a shot of one of the most famous books in history. 'Shakespeare's First Folio is the first known collection of his plays in one volume. There are only a few hundred First

Folios left in the world, and they're each worth millions. The police questioned Gardener about the theft.'

'They thought it was an inside job?' Alicia says.

'Well, they questioned everybody, and Gardener was cleared. And they've arrested someone for the theft – an ex-Oxford academic named Al-Said.'

'So they've caught the guy.'

'Apparently. But a few days ago, Gardener contacted the police, saying he had more information about the Folio. And then yesterday, Gardener was killed in a carjacking. The police have picked up a woman who they think is responsible, but the Folio is still missing . . .'

Alicia yawns again, shakes her head against it. 'So how does Mycroft fit in?'

'Mycroft's boss at the forensic pathology unit, Professor Walsh, is an ex-colleague of the English pathologist on the case. Gardener is Australian, and his family has asked for an Australian presence, so Walsh is going over to contribute. Mycroft managed to wangle his way into going too.'

'That doesn't sound too bad. It sounds like a good opportunity.'

'Yeah, it sounds great.' I grimace. 'Except Mycroft has a kind of personal connection to the carjacking business.'

Alicia's eyebrows go up. 'What, he used to jack cars?'

'No. His parents died in a carjacking. It was seven years ago, but I don't think he's really . . . recovered properly yet.'

'God, that's terrible.' Alicia frowns. 'Well, that makes things a bit more complicated.'

'Yeah.' Complicated by a factor of a hundred. A thousand.

'And that's the unspeakably awful personal-history fuck-up? You think Mycroft might have flashbacks or something in London?'

'I think Mycroft sees . . . similarities between this carjacking and the one that killed his parents. I think he might be planning on doing some investigating of his own. And I don't know if he's really . . .'

I hesitate on the right word.

'Stable enough to hold it together?' Alicia suggests.

I wince. 'I don't know. But he's been obsessed with his parents' deaths for a long time.'

Alicia pats my hand on the armrest. 'Then I think you're right to be worried.'

We hang on to alertness for a bit longer, but the fug of body heat in economy class soon starts working on us. My eyes are drifting closed when the cabin lights come back on. Soon after, I discover that Abu Dhabi airport is huge, with this bizarre statue in the middle that I think is supposed to be a palm tree, but to my foggy brain looks a lot like a kaleidoscopic volcano spewing glass. It's beautiful, but it's a bit too *Alice in Wonderland* for me at whatever-it-is in the morning.

Alicia suggests we get coffee near the departure lounge, which looks more sane. The glass walls overlook a crop of airplanes – they're dotted around everywhere like mushrooms . . .

'I really need to sit down,' I say.

My eyes drift around. Signs with a mix of English and Arabic, guys in white robes with flowing headgear, enormous hoardings advertising products I've never heard of . . . I've just gotten used to leaving Five Mile and living in a new city. How can I possibly be sitting in the airport terminal of another *country*?

Alicia breaks into my state of shock. 'So this is your first international rescue mission?'

'This is my first international anything. I've never even flown on a *plane* before.' I feel odd. Calm, but in an out-of-body kind of way. 'Seriously, this is all totally outside my range of experience.'

Alicia grins. She has a good grin, wide-mouthed and crinkly-eyed.

'But I want to be there for Mycroft.' I think for a bit. 'To make sure he doesn't do anything crazy.'

'Okay. But is there another reason?'

I look at my coffee. I dredge up my reply from deep inside, and it comes out more baldly than I was expecting. 'He just . . . left. Without saying goodbye. I don't know why, or what's going on, or what he feels, so . . .'

'You want to set the record straight,' Alicia says.

I nod. She's expressed it much more succinctly than I could.

She sits back in her chair. 'Then, Rachel, I guess you have to ask yourself whether you can handle a worst-case scenario. If Mycroft breaks up with you, will it be a wasted trip or will you still support him?'

God, what a question. I think about it for a long moment. I'm trying to be dispassionate, but it's very hard: a great ripping feeling washes through me when I consider what breaking up with Mycroft would mean.

'It would hurt,' I say.

'Yes.' Alicia nods. 'Break-ups always hurt.'

'But . . .' I swallow firmly. 'I would still want to be there for him. If he needed me. Because he's my friend. We were friends before we got together. If he needed my support . . . it wouldn't be a wasted trip.'

'I'm glad you came along, then.' Alicia smiles at me, and I can see the spark of her, beneath all the jet-lag weariness. 'C'mon, let's see if we can have a shower. They'll have showers around here somewhere. You packed your towel in your carry-on, like I told you?'

We abandon our coffee, and I'm hoping that a blast of hot water will wake me up, give me some strength for what's coming. I'm putting a lot of faith in hot water, but right now I have to believe in something.

CHAPTER SIX

'Rachel.' Someone is shaking my arm. 'Wake up. We're coming into Heathrow, you should see this.'

I don't care if we're coming into Moonbase Alpha. I want to sleep. I *have* to sleep. My whole body groans in protest when Alicia shakes my arm again.

'C'mon, we're in London. Rachel, it's amazing!'

I open my eyes. We spent ages flying over cresting waves of cloud. Now I push up the window shade and see misted pasture-land below. But this is not the ocher expanses of dust I'm familiar with. It's a quilt of tiny plots, worn-tracked and hedgerowed, and *green*, my god, so green. Clusters of buildings are sprinkled on the landscape, like hundreds-and-thousands on fairy bread.

I blink out the window and notice something else. 'There's a river. A very dirty river.'

'It's the Thames.' Alicia sounds faintly appalled.

I rub at my face. Far below, the Thames looks like a wide olive-drab ribbon, with tiny boats cruising up and down its length.

I press my cheek to the glass. 'There's a . . . shearing shed. A shearing shed with lots of tank-water pipes running off it. Is that really . . .?'

'Yup.' When I glance at Alicia, she's grinning. 'Heathrow Airport. It's really real. We're really about to land, and we're really in England.'

I start to share in the excitement after that, although my reactions are still a bit sluggish. In the first few hours after Abu Dhabi I tried to read through the Gardener file, but I couldn't concentrate. Then I started to get dizzy, and realized that I'd been awake for nearly thirty hours, and actually your body needs sleep like your lungs need air, just to function. I crashed out against the closed window shade. Now I have an imprint of the shade handle pressed into my cheek, where the stupid in-flight pillow slid down.

Getting off the plane takes longer than getting on, because there are five hundred million people all queuing for entry into the UK.

After a tedious wait, a bottle-blonde matron stamps my passport, then disarms me by smiling and saying 'Welcome to England!' just as I'm about to move away from the desk.

'Thank you,' I say. I must look completely lost: even total strangers are giving me encouraging smiles.

We change Australian dollars into British pounds – an extremely terrifying experience, handing over my wad of bank notes only to be given back another wad half as large – and then slog onwards.

'Luggage,' Alicia reminds me.

At the carousels, I collect my sad little sports bag and Alicia hefts her backpack. Then we're disgorged onto the main Arrivals concourse. The first waft of air from the massive sliding glass doors cools my face.

London air. I'm in London.

'Right.' Alicia disentangles her hair from her backpack straps and straightens her crumpled shirt. 'We're here. Now do you want to find out where Mycroft is staying?'

'Um. God.' I have a moment of panic, until I remember. 'Let me check . . .'

I scratch in my jeans pocket for my phone. The screen says it's eleven in the morning, London time, which is actually eight in the evening, Australia time. My brain needs a re-set, because that one reminder gets me yawning.

Amid a flurry of ALL CAPS texts from my parents, that I have no intention of reading right now, is the message we need. I shake my head awake.

'Okay. Detective Pickup has sent me a phone number for Professor Walsh.' I squint at the number. 'Do you think I should call?'

Alicia squeezes her nape wearily. 'Why not?'

I note down the number, buy a local SIM card for my phone from a machine, and stand with Alicia in the Arrivals hall while the swarm of people moves around us. Someone behind me says *An then ah said, well ahm not payin fifteen pahnd for that . . .* and these are English voices, English people. It might have been *Alice in Wonderland* in Abu Dhabi, but I'm truly down the rabbit hole now.

I call, looking out at the buses and black taxis puttering through the underground tunnel of Terminal Four.

The ringtone chirrups, then there's a firm warm voice I'm familiar with. 'Hello, yes. Walsh here.'

I'm incredibly relieved the call didn't go to voicemail. 'Professor Walsh, this is Rachel Watts—'

'Who?'

'Rachel *Watts*. I'm calling from—'

'Are you in England?'

I stare at Alicia, who looks expectantly back. 'How did you know that?'

'No international prefix. You *are* in London, then?'

'Yes.' I can hear traffic noise; it sounds as if he's driving. 'But—'

'Thank god,' Walsh says.

'Pardon?'

'I said, *thank god*. Your boyfriend seems to be seesawing fairly wildly between genius and insanity at the moment, and I'd very much like—'

My shoulders slump. 'Is he there?'

'What? No. Look, right now, I need you to help me with damage control.'

'Damage control?' I grimace. Alicia's eyebrows go up.

'Yes,' Walsh says. 'Where are you?'

'I'm at Heathrow—'

'Right. Take the Express – do you see it?'

The Express? I mouth to Alicia. She nods. 'Uh, yeah,' I say.

'Wonderful. Take the Express to Paddington and then change to Victoria Station. Come out on Buckingham Palace Road and I'll meet you there.'

'Okay,' I say. 'But is Mycroft—'

He disconnects. The phone beeps in my ear.

'He hung up,' I say, rather unnecessarily.

Alicia pulls her backpack up with a little grunt. 'Where do you need to be?'

'Victoria Station.'

'Okay,' she says. 'Victoria Station – I know where that is.'

The mere thought of catching a train, after flying halfway across the world, exhausts me. But Alicia leads the way, whipping through to a blue exit signed *Heathrow Express.*

I chew my thumbnail as she buys tickets. 'He said *damage control.* That sounds bad, doesn't it?'

Alicia's actually *smiling.* 'Reasonably bad. But hey, that's what you're here for, right?'

'Right.' I chew some more. 'Right.'

Alicia squeezes my arm. 'Rachel. Relax. There's no point making yourself sick about it. And you'll be no good to Mycroft if you're a bundle of nerves.'

I nod, blow out a jittery breath.

On the train, Alicia's face shines as she looks out the window. 'Oh god, it's so lovely to be back in England!'

It is kind of thrilling, and I'd like to be more enthusiastic for Alicia's sake – this is her big trip, after all. But my skin is electric with tension.

People are literally *everywhere* at Paddington Station, weaving and cross-weaving in a dizzying tapestry. The escalator to the Underground is unbelievably steep, as if you're riding towards the bowels of the earth. The metal steps vibrate, and I grip the rubber handrail.

Alicia buys us both blue Oyster cards and shows me how to make mine work. I'm fumbling around with the newness of it all.

But I'm tougher than this. I can do this.

I've pulled all-nighters at shearing time, I've waited for foxes in the dark with Dad's rifle, I've climbed out of a *lion pen,* goddamnit. Yanking my satchel strap higher on my shoulder, I tie my hair back in a knot.

Victoria Station is an aircraft hangar, and lit up like Christmas.

Shops line the concourse, so I could buy books and aspirin and lingerie here if I wanted. I could walk across to a shop called Marks & Spencer and buy juice and croissants for three pounds to pep me up.

The only problem is, I can't walk anymore. I don't think I can stand up much longer, actually. But that's okay, because as soon as we exit the station I spot a miniscule brown Honda tooting its horn near the bus loop. A long hand waves from the driver's-side window.

'Rachel.' Walsh leans across the passenger seat. 'Good to see you, hop on in.'

He's double-parked in the bus lane, revving the engine. Alicia and I heave our bags onto the back seat; Alicia tumbles in after them while I get in the front. The Honda is actually too small for Walsh. I have no idea how he and Mycroft both fit their gangly selves inside at the same time – even *I* feel too large in this car. My satchel gets caught around my knees and elbows.

'Hi.' I smile tiredly at Walsh while pulling my satchel strap out of the door. 'Um, Professor, this is Alicia Azzopardi, whose trip I've piggybacked on.' I wave my spare hand to the rear.

'Hi,' Alicia says. She looks relieved to be sitting down.

Walsh smiles back. 'Pleasure.'

He's rangy as ever in tweedy trousers and a khaki shirt. He looks different from when I last saw him – it takes me a second to figure out that I've never seen Walsh not wearing a lab coat.

The rest of him is comfortably familiar. His glasses are on a string, and his hair is still receding on top like a monk's tonsure with a thin fringe of gray around the edges.

He's looking at me and Alicia in his usual calm way. 'Well, here we are. Nice flight?'

'Long,' I say. I can't think of another word.

'They usually are, from Melbourne.' Walsh hunches over the steering wheel and noses aggressively into the traffic. I'm shocked to discover he drives like a maniac. He's worse than my brother. 'All right, we're going to High Wycombe. I said I'd pick up Mycroft on the way.'

'How bad is he?' I grip the sissy bar above the passenger-side window. 'I mean, just . . . you know. Give me the outline.'

Walsh nods cheerfully, swerves around a traffic island. 'He was rather terrible on the flight over, from what I gather. Unfortunately I didn't realize the full extent until we landed, which was when I left business class.'

I think for a moment. Sigh. 'He was legless.'

'Ha! Yes. Legless, armless, you name it.' Walsh seems almost entertained by the idea. London scenery flashes by at breakneck speed. 'I'm not sure he was aware of how badly alcohol can affect you mid-flight. He threw up in a bin at the Arrival lounge.'

'Oh shit. How did he manage to get that much booze? He's underage.'

'Ah. I think he might have been taking advantage of the fact that being six foot two can lend you an air of gravitas.' Walsh snorts, shakes his head. 'Anyway, he was very rough during the briefings at Scotland Yard this morning. And then I got your message via Pickup.'

'Yes.'

'Rather wish I'd known about it all before I agreed to let him come along, if you don't mind me saying. But that's not your fault.'

We career through the traffic, which seems to be going much more slowly than us. The buildings around us are squat, double-storeyed, with the occasional gothic tower or church steeple spiking skyward. Pigeons race each other for the rooftops. I see flagstone pavements, and shop awnings, and signs for places called *WHSmith* and *Pret A Manger*, but nothing I recognize. I don't really have any idea where in London we are.

Walsh doesn't seem angry, but I'm sure he's worried about how Mycroft's behavior might impact on the case they're supposed to be working on.

'Where's Mycroft now?' I ask.

'Back at his hostel, the Empire Star. We have an appointment to view the scene of the accident in High Wycombe, and I'm hoping he's sobered up enough to cope.' He gives me a sideways glance: a slight navigational lurch ensues. 'Throwing up in a bin is one thing, but throwing up on a crime scene is generally considered bad form.'

I rub the back of my neck. 'I can imagine.'

'I'm sorry, my dear, you must be very tired.'

'A bit.' That's the understatement of the year, but I've got other things on my mind. 'Professor, I don't know if Mycroft's going to be particularly thrilled to see me.'

Walsh smiles. 'Quite immaterial at this stage, I'm afraid.'

'Just so you know.'

'Consider me mentally prepared.' He grins again, and down-shifts with a dramatic crunch of gears as we screech to a stop against a curb I didn't even see coming. 'Right, here we are.'

A maroon door graces the edge of a white corner terrace. The perspex sign, with red letters reading *EMPIRE STAR HOTEL Bed and Breakfast*, juts out from the facade. Lichen-spots of peeling paintwork decorate the building. A hanging planter trails green fronds over a spidery black ironwork fence.

I push out of the car. Alicia's leaning back, looking up. The Empire Star appears to be a slightly grotty Victorian tenement.

Further down the dead-end court on the left are more brown-gray terrace houses, with white window frames and black exterior pipes. Under the overcast sky, it all looks very English.

There's a piece of cardboard reading *Vacancy* stuck on the hostel's maroon door. Alicia's eyes perk up.

'I think it would be better if we stick together. Why don't I go to ask about rooms.' She drags her backpack onto her shoulders, takes my sports bag.

'Okay.' I sigh.

'Rachel.' Alicia plucks at my sleeve. 'Remember what Mike said. And . . . in my experience, people sometimes have to crash and burn a bit before they realize they need support.'

Crash and burn. It's uncomfortably like my mental image of Mycroft stumbling into a burning house. I nod and pull away to find Walsh, who's already heading for the entrance.

By the time I reach him, he's being received at the door by a broad-faced guy wearing a turban, a wide-collared pink shirt and burgundy trousers.

'Ah, hello,' Walsh says. 'We've come to see—'

'Yes, yes,' the guy says. 'Your friend on second floor. You will tell him there is no smoking in rooms, please. This is a no-smoking hotel, yes?'

'Certainly,' Walsh says, with a faint grimace, and the guy lets us through.

There's a gold-framed mirror in the narrow foyer. Seriously, I don't think I could squeeze through this hall if I was much fatter. Red velvety carpet deadens the sound of my boots and travels with us up the tight, steep stairs.

We go up another flight, sucking in our breath on the turn. At the top of the landing, the carpet pattern changes into some

76

sort of terrifying paisley explosion. This gives way to yet another pattern – a dark shadowed floral – on the next flight up. Clearly the Empire Star isn't going to win any awards for interior design.

The squeezed-in-sideways door on our left is white wood, with a number '3' hanging loosely on a nail. Walsh's rap is loud. He pushes me forward and I wipe my palms on my jeans.

I hear faint music, hear it switched off. Smell the noxious tang of stale cigarette smoke.

'*Sec*,' someone calls from inside the room, only it's not someone. It's—

The door opens and he's looking down, pulling up the collar of his red hoodie. Unlit cigarette balanced on bottom lip. Hair in chaos. Pale, with the brown circles around his—

Mycroft's eyes meet mine.

CHAPTER SEVEN

Mycroft's cigarette drops onto the hideous carpet as air puffs out of him. Not an actual word, more like he's been punched in the chest.

'A visitor,' Walsh says, over my shoulder.

'*Rachel?*' Mycroft says, and then, 'The *fuck*?'

It's pretty much exactly like I imagined. That doesn't mean it doesn't *hurt*. It hurts so much I want to fold my arms across my chest just to keep myself together, but I can't do that. Not now, not yet.

Walsh checks his watch, clears his throat. 'The coroner's office said two-thirty. I've got about one-fifty-five.'

'No,' Mycroft says. He smells boozy and, god, he looks truly awful. 'No no no. No *way*.'

But now that I've seen him, all my built-up apprehension melts into something else. My vision goes red. Did he really think that it would be *okay* to kiss me as though he was saying 'au revoir' then nick off overseas without a word?

'Nice to see you too,' I say.

Mycroft looks like a deer in the headlights. A really pissed-off deer. 'How the fuck did you get here?'

'I dunno. Backstroke?' I roll my eyes and turn to Walsh. 'Can we go to the scene now?'

'Certainly,' Walsh says.

'No *way*,' Mycroft repeats. His face is all dark crevices as he stares at Walsh. 'Look, I'm sober, okay? I don't need anyone holding my hand at a crime scene.'

'Who said I wanted to hold your hand?' I snap.

'I don't encourage hand-holding,' Walsh says, in a conciliatory tone, 'but an extra pair of eyes might come in useful. Let's be off, shall we? The car's just outside.'

'This is *bullshit*,' Mycroft says.

But Walsh has started moving and so have I. Mycroft has no option but to tug the door closed, snag his smoke off the floor and follow.

Walsh has already bundled down the stairs. I keep my eyes on the blood-red carpet underfoot and grip the white banister so I don't trip down the incline. I hear Mycroft limping behind me.

We squish past Alicia and the proprietor in the hall. Alicia's dangling a key and grinning.

'Hi, Mycroft! Rachel, we're room seven!'

'You came with Alicia?' Mycroft glares at me when I glance at him over my shoulder.

'Yes.' I give Alicia the thumbs-up. 'Great! Get them to hold my key!'

'Wonderful.' Mycroft's wearing a bitter grimace. We follow Walsh out to the car. 'What about Angela? Did you bring her too?'

'Of course not.'

'Well, thank god for small mercies.'

I jump into the back. Mycroft takes shotgun, throwing himself into the passenger seat with repressed violence.

Walsh folds himself behind the wheel and revs the engine. Mycroft glares at me again around the passenger headrest.

'Do your parents even know you're—' He looks at my face. 'Shit.'

'Yeah,' I say. 'Shit.'

Walsh is casting me looks through the rear-view, which I ignore.

'Perfect. Just perfect.' As Walsh tears out into the traffic, Mycroft grips the sissy bar too, which gives me a vindictive little stab of pleasure.

Walsh concentrates on the road, and Mycroft concentrates on glaring out the window. I have a strong urge to cry but I suck it back, keep my eyes trained on the street. It's my first real look at the city and I wonder if I'll always remember London this way, with a sense of melancholy.

We backtrack past Victoria Station. The London sky is a pearly gray, not my idea of early summer. Red double-decker buses career past, and the occasional ancient tree is decked in lacy green buds. The buildings here are all a bit staggering: gracious and serious and *old*, like proper old. What's most amazing is the scale of the buildings – I feel totally dwarfed. We go past a park with a massive monument I recognize, but I've only ever seen Marble Arch in pictures.

Walsh glances over at Mycroft. 'How's the head?'

'Fine.' Mycroft stares out to the left.

'That's good,' Walsh says evenly. 'If you check in my bag you'll find the notes from this morning's briefing. Thought you might like a refresher.'

Mycroft reads notes, Walsh keeps his eyes forward, and I gaze out the window. We drive in silence for nearly half an hour. It starts raining, a glowering drizzle that reflects my mood. This moment, this break from action and argument, is almost enough to do me in – my eyelids start getting heavy and I have to bite the inside of my cheek.

We've been on a motorway, and the view has changed from tenements and chimneypots to verdant pasture edged with wild-flowers. We drive off the motorway into a little town of brick cottages. Pubs and shopfronts have names like 'Shammy's Fry' and 'Tom's Jellied Eels' and 'George and Dragon'. Traveling up the side of a hill, the view outside changes again as we enter a wooded strip.

Walsh has put on his wipers, smearing the windscreen. He squints through the smear. 'The lead detective, Detective Constable Inspector Gupta, has questioned a woman called Irina Addington about Daniel Gardener's death.'

'Right.' I lean forward. 'The paper said they'd detained a woman.'

'It was Ms Addington herself who contacted police. Apparently she and Daniel Gardener were romantically involved, and the accident was the result of her misguided attempt to scare him, after a quarrel.'

'A quarrel about what?' I stifle a yawn.

'He wanted to end the relationship. Found her too intense, she said.'

'Shooting at your ex from the roadside qualifies as intense, yes.' Mycroft's murmur seems to be directed at the window.

Walsh makes a snort. 'Anyway, after the accident she felt compelled to come forward. Gupta seems confident that her remorse is genuine. He's going to provide us with . . .'

He trails off as we see red and blue lights flashing up ahead. Walsh pulls into a turn that looks like the start of someone's long, genteel driveway. On the other side of the road lies a gorgeous stretch of hedgerowed paddock that would make my dad drool.

'Right, here we are,' Walsh says.

'Where's here, exactly?' I scrub my flannie sleeve over the foggy window beside me.

'Near Lane's End, just out of High Wycombe,' Walsh says, which means nothing to me at all.

'We're west of London. About halfway to Oxford.' Mycroft's voice is quiet. He's watching the revolving lights on two police cars parked on the road shoulder. He twists himself around to stare behind me, out the rear window of the car, and his voice changes. 'Is that . . . Gardener's car is still here?'

'Yes.' Walsh pulls a light rain jacket from the foot-well near me. 'The location is fairly isolated, so Gupta said they wouldn't put it in impound until after we've viewed the scene. Highly unusual procedure. SOCOs have already been through, of course.'

I'm not really processing what Walsh's said. But when I follow Mycroft's gaze and peer over my shoulder, I see a car mashed into the road edge behind us. It's a write-off – smashed glass and buckled roof, half-buried in a tall stand of hawthorn bushes. The car's gray paint has a sheen of drizzle as it sits patiently in the boggy grass on the road shoulder.

'This is where the girlfriend shot at Gardener's car?' I ask.

'Yes.' Walsh opens the driver's door. 'Well, from in front of us. But this is where the car ended up. Hold on a moment.'

And I suddenly realize that a man died here. In the car I'm looking at. His own girlfriend shot at him. In his panic he swerved, and his car reeled, tilted, rolled . . .

Walsh has gone over to consult with the two figures in front. One is a police officer in a uniform and a rain slicker. The other is a slim, short man wearing a dark-green gabardine coat, the shoulders dampened by rain. I can't see his face, only a shock of black hair, but his bearing and brisk hand gestures scream authority – DCI Gupta.

I watch the men talk. The Honda's engine ticks as it cools.

Mycroft's sitting sideways, staring out the rapidly fogging driver's-side window. His face is pallid, wrung out. He's got his unsmoked cigarette in one hand, tapping the end on his knee, flipping it in his fingers, tapping the other end . . .

'So you just got off the plane?'

I startle, take a breath. 'Um, yeah. About . . . three hours ago.'

Three hours ago I was on a plane. Now I'm viewing a crime scene outside London, with my furious, hung-over, maybe-ex-boyfriend and his forensic pathologist boss.

'You must be knackered.' Mycroft's voice is colorless and his eyes are fixed forward. Brown shadows under his cheekbones hollow out his face.

'Yeah,' I admit. 'A bit.'

We don't say any more. Two days ago we were kissing each other senseless. Now we can barely have a civil conversation.

Walsh returns and taps on Mycroft's window. Mycroft cranks the window down, letting in a gust of damp air.

'Here's something for you.' Walsh hands him a small metallic lozenge. 'That's Irina Addington's interview footage from this morning. My tablet is there, in the bag – you can have a bit of a look before you start.'

'We want to see if the details she's providing and the details of the scene match up, yeah?' Mycroft fumbles at his feet for Walsh's bag.

'Indeed,' Walsh says. 'One moment – I need to speak to Gupta before he leaves.'

He darts off again. Mycroft winds up the window and settles the tablet on his knee, jabbing the USB Walsh gave him into the port. A video starts playing on the screen.

I lean closer. 'Can I see?'

'What?'

'Turn it so I can see.'

With exaggerated bad grace, Mycroft turns the tablet. I watch the woman on the screen as she blinks, pushes her blonde hair back with shaky fingers. A smooth edge of desk is visible in the foreground. Irina Addington is wearing a scarlet coat. Her eyes are smudged from crying, and her lipstick has almost worn off.

That's right, she says. The sound on the recording has a nasty echo. She's answering a question I didn't hear. *I-I mean, I wasn't aiming at* him, *just, just at the windscreen. The passenger side. I didn't mean to—*

'She sounds scared,' I say.

'Shh.' Mycroft frowns.

. . . course *I didn't mean to kill him!* Irina swipes at her nose with the back of her hand. The paint on her nails is chipped; one nail is torn right off. *Look, I panicked, okay? After the row I just* lost it, *I wasn't really thinking of consequences, but then when I saw Daniel's car* . . .

We listen as the testimony plays out. Irina Addington describes the scene of the accident, her shock at what happened. Her voice quivers, falters; her eyes dart around.

Mycroft's still frowning when the video concludes. He thumbs the screen dark, rolls the cigarette still in his fingers, presses his lips together. I think he's about to turn and say

84

something to me, when Walsh suddenly raps on the car window. I jump.

Mycroft opens the door. 'That was . . . interesting.'

'And useful, I hope.' Walsh gestures to the smashed car outside, which I'd almost forgotten about. 'Shall we?'

'Where do you want to start?' Mycroft tucks his cigarette behind his ear and his voice has changed again. Brusque, professional, with a tense edge to it.

'Over in the impact zone, there.' Walsh points. 'We're just going to have an initial look, then you can help me backtrack. Sound all right?'

'Fine.' Mycroft clambers out of the car.

Walsh peers through the open door at me. 'Are you coming?'

'I think I'll stay.' Mycroft gives me a curious look. I stare back at him. 'I said I wasn't here to hold hands.'

Mycroft shrugs, turns away. 'I'm going over to have a look.'

'I'll get the camera,' Walsh says.

I help him retrieve a small blue bag. He pulls it over his shoulder and rests a hand on the car door.

'Are you sure you want to stay here?'

'Yes,' I say firmly.

Walsh looks at Mycroft's retreating figure. 'How does he seem to you?'

A compulsion to just lie down and go to sleep wells up all of a sudden. But this isn't about me. I keep my eyes on Mycroft.

'Angry,' I say. 'Nervous.'

'Yes, I thought I detected a bit of that.'

'Overall, I think he'll do better if he's angry.'

'Let's hope so.' Walsh's smile is considerate. 'Trot over if you see a need.'

I nod, and Walsh closes the door. I wriggle around so I've got twin views, through the back window and my own window. Traffic on the road flashes past in a blur. Gupta's car is gone: he must have driven off while we were watching Irina's testimony. Two rain-jacketed figures – Walsh and the police officer – separate, and Walsh starts taking photos of the car.

Now it's just me and the sound of my own breathing. It'd almost be enough to put me to sleep right here, if I wasn't concentrating on the tall figure I can see through the back window.

Mycroft stalks around the site of the crash, hands jammed in his jacket pockets. He'll be getting very damp out there. His hair is settling into soft dark curlicues and his head is low, forward, focused. He doesn't touch anything, just strides purposefully, pretending his limp doesn't exist.

He checks the plowed-up ground around the wrecked car. Examines the black rubber marks on the road, examines the road shoulder. Backtracks along the road with Walsh, careful of the traffic, hands out now and fingers pointing here, there. He makes angles of incidence and reflection with his arms extended.

He looks completely professional. He's not a forensic engineer, but he understands a lot about this stuff – he's spent the last seven years researching velocity, trajectory, impact. It's why Walsh agreed to let him come. I realize this is the first time I've seen Mycroft in his element: this is what he must be like at work in the Forensic Investigations unit, all scientific focus and polished edges.

Suddenly I don't know what I'm doing here. Walsh was wrong. *I* was wrong. Mycroft is handling this. Sure, he had a booze-up on the plane, but I don't know many seventeen-year-old guys who would let an opportunity like that slip. Mycroft's fine, and I'm superfluous.

This wash of relief, and a strange kind of happiness, floods through me. I've blown seventeen hundred bucks on a plane ticket because my visit here was unnecessary, but that's a *good* thing.

I'm still half-smiling with this idea when I see Mycroft in profile.

He's standing by Gardener's crashed car, near the front passenger side. Walsh is photographing the front bumper, and his eyes are not on Mycroft. But mine are, and something about the way Mycroft gnaws on his bottom lip unsettles my good mood.

As I watch, he reaches a hand out towards the crumpled car roof. His fingers are tentative, uncertain, and the moment he makes contact . . .

His hand jerks back as if he's been burnt.

All my senses jump, seeing that. I don't know why. But it's brought me to full alertness. I flash hard on the conversation with Mike before I got on the plane, which seems like forever ago – *just a bad feeling, is it?*

A bad feeling.

Keeping my eyes fixed on the scene through the back window, I open the car door, ease myself out. The spitting rain and fresh breeze make me hunch. I slip my hands into my armpits and take a few steps towards Gardener's car so I can hear what's going on.

'There's very little frontal impact.' Walsh has pulled his rain-hood down. He calls from his spot, half-hidden in the hawthorn. 'Are you seeing anything else?'

Mycroft doesn't reply. He's staring through the shattered passenger window into the car.

Walsh tries again. 'Mycroft?'

'Yep.'

'What else are you seeing from that side?'

There's a long pause.

'There's . . .' Mycroft clears his throat. 'Interior staining. It's extensive.'

'Yes, we discussed that, remember? The five places where a victim can lose blood torrentially are into the chest cavity, into the abdomen, the retroperitoneum, the muscle compartments, and—'

'– externally, into the environment,' Mycroft says. 'I remember.'

But his voice sounds off, wrong. The way he says it, *I remember* . . . I wrap my arms more firmly around myself, step away from Walsh's car.

'So a hemorrhage from a compound fracture or some other wound would account for the staining,' Walsh says. 'Now, it looks like the airbag deployed, but there's some evidence to indicate that he didn't get the full benefit of it. Irina Addington claims she fired towards Gardener's car from the road-edge, in an attempt to scare him. But the passenger-side window appears to have broken in the crash. And he seems to have swerved *towards* the road-edge, not away from it. Maybe Addington's confused? Because it looks more like Gardener was shot at on the *driver's* side. Then he would have either fallen or ducked to his left . . .'

Walsh's voice keeps going, but I'm not listening. I don't think Mycroft is either. His hands hang limply by his sides.

Suddenly he reaches out and grabs the car's doorhandle, pulls hard. Glass tinkles, the door gives with a metallic creak of protest, and swings wide until it hits the turf. Mycroft looks a bit horrified at what he's done, as though he might have opened Pandora's box. He swallows hard, takes a step.

He eases himself onto the passenger seat.

I hold my breath. Walsh seems to have figured out there's something going on, because he's stopped monologuing.

'Are you right there?' He frowns at his assistant, sitting motionless in a dead man's car. 'The vehicle's not completely stable, you know.'

Mycroft doesn't answer. I take an involuntary stride forward. Rain dusts down on me, sprinkling like icing sugar. Walsh glances in my direction.

Mycroft starts speaking. 'They would have come up on the right, to get his attention. A motorcycle, probably, that's what they . . . They seem to like motorcycles. Motorcycles are perfect . . .'

His voice is muted from inside the car, I can barely make it out. But he's not talking to anyone but himself, that's abundantly clear. I wonder if he's even aware that he's speaking. The singsong tone, the rambling words . . . Mycroft is working something out, yanking it out of his own mind. Both his theory and his manner make my blood slosh coldly in my veins.

'And then they dropped back, and the bike passenger would have shot near the driver's window. Maybe birdshot. We should check for . . .' He raises a long-fingered hand, lets it fall back onto the seat. 'Birdshot would be good, because they just want something to scare the shit out of him. They don't want him to die of gunshot wounds, they've made a mistake like that before . . .'

He pauses, takes a big shuddering breath before continuing.

'So Gardener swerved and rolled the car, but he would have been going fast. He's gunning say eighty kay an hour, and rolling at that speed is probably going to do the trick. So even if he's not already dead from blunt trauma, or internal shear forces, or a high spinal injury from when his head hits the roof here . . .'

He taps above himself at something I can't see: a dent in the interior roof.

'. . . even if that's not instantaneous, then it's okay. Because it's a lonely road, and at seven a.m. there's not much traffic passing, no one to stop and help. It's okay to just leave him, he'll bleed out, probably from a massive haemothorax, after the impact from the steering wheel, or maybe just hypovolaemic shock after the pelvic fracture, or something else. Something like that, something . . .'

Mycroft trails off. His head turns slightly, right and then left, as though he's only just realized he's sitting in a pool of dried blood on the passenger seat of a crime-scene death car. With a deliberate set of movements, he gets out. His face is completely expressionless when he closes the door with both hands. He stands there as if he's holding the car in place.

The attack, when it comes, is sudden. It takes me off guard.

Mycroft kicks the car door, hard and sharp. Kicks again, then again. He kicks at the door over and over, until he's rocking the car with the force of it. The tendons in his hands are stiff as cords as he grips the roof edge. His face is white, distorted with rage.

I flinch every time his foot makes contact. I don't approach, I can't – his expression says he's beyond calming negotiation, beyond reason. It scares me. As far as damage control goes, I don't even know where to start.

Mycroft gives the door one last vicious whack before spinning around and limping quickly away. He limps past me, past Walsh's car and the police car, twenty meters away to a road sign for the High Wycombe bus. He props himself against the signpost with one hand, his head down and his back to us. I see his shoulders heaving.

I remember to breathe. Walsh glances from me to Mycroft. Breeze blows his graying strands of hair all over his head. He's looking at Mycroft as if he's some sort of combustible substance, ready to blow.

Walsh steps to the car and ducks down, examining the driver's-side window frame. I walk closer, so close I can smell the stench of old fuel from Gardener's car, see the scrambled insides of the boot from where the lid's popped open.

'What are you doing?' My voice comes out rusty, quiet.

Walsh keeps his eyes on his task. 'I'm looking for birdshot.'

Mycroft's leaning with two hands against the post now, his body very still. Something about the way he's standing tells me he's trying not to throw up.

I don't go to him. I stand behind the listing gray car, blinking and dizzy, with the spitting wind driving into my face. My diagnosis was pre-emptive. I'm still needed here after all. Whether I'm *wanted* is something else again.

Walsh picks and prods at the driver's-side door. 'I think I've got something here. Irina Addington's testimony may not be as reliable as we thought.'

I swallow over the rough edges in my throat. 'I'm glad it was worth it, then, putting Mycroft through that.'

Walsh shoots me a serious glance. 'Rachel, you're going to have to give me a few more details, I think, if we're going to make this arrangement work.'

'Details about Mycroft's personal experience?'

'Yes.' He uses a sharp tool on the door. It scrapes and skitters. 'I know he was in a carjacking.'

'Yeah.' I push back my hair where it's blown in my face and rub my nape wearily. 'It wasn't. A carjacking, I mean. It was something like what he thinks happened here. A motor-bike came up beside the family car, and the pillion passenger shot inside. The car was on the A1, it was going fast. They crashed. Mycroft survived, but his parents only lasted until the ambulance arrived.'

'God almighty.' Walsh frowns. 'All right, so now I understand his interest in this case. He's researched the scenario quite a lot, I gather?'

'Exhaustively.'

'Then we have a problem with him being emotionally compromised, but it's not really a conflict of interest because he's only assisting. In fact, his knowledge might be very useful, if we can only get him past the personal baggage. Do you see what I'm saying?'

'Yes.' It still doesn't stop me from feeling like I want to punch Walsh in the face. Instead I blink into the boot interior, and get distracted by something. 'Professor Walsh, did you say SOCO had been through this car?'

'Yes. Why's that?'

'So did they toss around the contents of the boot?'

'No, of course not. They were asked to preserve the original positioning of items for our arrival. They wouldn't toss around the contents of anything.'

'Then I don't get it . . . That spare tire shouldn't be like that.'

'Come again?'

'The spare. It's out of its bracket. And the cargo liner is pulled right off.'

Walsh leaves his task and walks over to see what I'm looking at. 'Yes. Well, when a car rolls, the objects inside the—'

'No. Spare tires don't spin around when the car rolls. They're designed to stay in place.' I point. 'See that bolt? That's a tie-down bolt. Mum had one in her car back in Five Mile, and there was one in the paddock bomb. It has to be fully wound out from the center pole before you can release the spare.'

'Then the pole must have snapped. Metal fatigue can act in funny ways during a crash.'

'No, look. That pole isn't snapped and it's not deformed, but the bolt is off.' I glance at Walsh. 'Professor, if this boot has been left completely as it was by SOCO, then someone has opened the boot and released the spare before they arrived.'

'You're saying that someone searched the boot of this car?'

'Yes. *After* the crash.' I frown. 'Could it have been Addington? But why would she do that? And why didn't she mention it in her testimony?'

'Well, she may have been in shock . . . But I'll mention it to Inspector Gupta.' Walsh notices me shivering. 'Goodness, you should get back in the Honda, you'll catch your death.'

'Okay,' I say, but I don't move.

I look over my shoulder at Mycroft, still standing by the bus stop. Should I go to him, hug him? That's what I feel like doing, but I'm scared of how he'll react. Which is crazy. How did it come to the point where I can't even trust my gut instincts on how to behave around Mycroft, how to feel?

I swallow hard, put my hands in my pockets.

A few minutes later, Walsh finishes talking to the long-suffering police officer with the rain slicker. The officer goes to use his car radio. Walsh walks over with a ziplocked evidence bag in one hand and the camera bag in the other.

'Time to go,' he says softly.

The inside of Walsh's car feels sultry after standing in the chill High Wycombe air. Walsh shucks out of his jacket and gets in the driver's side. He reverses off the verge, turns the wheel, and runs the car up to where Mycroft stands by the post.

Walsh lowers his window.

'Hop in the car, Mycroft,' he says. 'It's getting cold.'

CHAPTER EIGHT

We drive in silence again, all the way back to London.

Afternoon sun on the main arterial glances across my aching eyes. Off the A40 and onto another crazy road, still going with the traffic flow, our car slows for buses and black London cabs. On this street there's delivery vans, light commercial trucks, general traffic, the works. Hoardings above shops feature Arabic script.

Mycroft rouses himself from his stupor.

'Could you stop the car, please?' His voice is low and hoarse.

Walsh must think Mycroft's going to be sick, because he pulls over so sharply I knock my nose against the back of the seat.

Mycroft gets out. Before Walsh or I can react, he limps off. He's lost in the throng within about three seconds.

'Ah,' Walsh says.

I sit back, rubbing the bridge of my nose. I should be more worried, I know, but I just feel helpless. And so, so tired. The thought of chasing after Mycroft is exhausting. God, what am I doing here?

'Do you think he'll be all right?' Walsh asks.

'I don't know,' I admit. 'But there's not much we can do about it right now. Professor, would you be able to drive me back to the hostel, if it's not too much trouble?'

'Certainly. Goodness, you must be horribly jet-lagged.'

'I'm okay.' This is an outrageous lie. My phone says it's only quarter to four. I'm going to need a hot shower and something highly caffeinated to get me through the rest of the afternoon.

Walsh veers the little brown car out into the street. Names I'm familiar with – Oxford, Mayfair, Marylebone – flash by on street signs. London is like a giant Monopoly set come to life.

We're actually driving along Park Lane now. It's lined with grand hotels – all the ritzy vehicles parked out front make them look like high-end car dealerships.

'I really appreciate this, Professor Walsh.'

Walsh waves a hand. 'Oh, it's no problem. I've done this trip often enough now that I know how to avoid jet lag, but I still remember my first time in London. Staggering around half asleep for the first week, and I was supposed to be on exchange rounds. Menace to patients. Terrible.'

The first *week*? The concept of this bone-weariness lasting my whole trip makes my shoulders sag. 'You studied medicine in London?'

'Yes. I lived here for a few years, got dreadfully homesick. Learned a lot, though. Figured out I was better suited to forensic pathology than treating patients in a hospital.'

'Professor, have the police really got anything concrete about the Gardener case?'

'Well, we still need to confirm it's a homicide.' Walsh studies the scenery as much as the traffic as we drive along. 'Ms Addington's testimony seems perfectly authentic, but the disparities we noticed at the scene could muddy the waters. I'm not here to speculate about the suspects, though, merely present the facts, and you just saw how informative the crash site was. Having Mycroft there to read the traces and walk me through was invaluable. That last article he wrote for his blog allowed me to understand the breadth of his insight. He has extensive knowledge of skid patterns and so on. The physics of it.'

I'm sure he has, I nearly say.

'This trip could provide wonderful experience for him,' Walsh continues, grinding gears, 'but what I need to ensure is that he stays on track. I'm sorry if that sounds a bit mercenary. I don't mean it like that. I'm concerned for him, as a friend, but I'm also thinking about his future. He's already exhibiting an extra-ordinary amount of potential.'

I choose my words carefully as we drive closer to Victoria Station. 'I think, for a long time, Mycroft wasn't sure if he even had a future.'

Walsh nods. 'I understand. I'm aware that Mycroft has a few personal demons. Right now, we want to prevent them from eating him up, do you see what I'm saying?'

'Yes.'

Walsh has taken a corner and there's the Empire Star in front of us. He pulls up to the curb and fixes me with his eyes. 'So I don't want to seem impolite, but I do need to know if you're here to support him or to take issue with him.'

I should have seen this coming, but I didn't. I'm thrown for a second, until my brain kicks in.

'Professor, I'm not in London to make a scene.' My voice shakes a little. I hope Walsh will put it down to exhaustion. 'I know

Mycroft wasn't happy to see me, but I came to help. As a friend. If you think having me around will be a distraction, or a . . . a problem, then I can just—'

'No, no, that's fine.' Walsh's eyes have softened. Just for a moment there I got a glimpse of what he must be like when his attention is laser-pointed: intense, uncompromising. It reminds me of Mycroft a hell of a lot. 'From what I understand, I think you're rather a good influence on him. But my priorities here are assisting the detectives with this case and keeping Mycroft focused, so I'm sorry if I'm coming across as a bit heartless—'

'Then our priorities are the same,' I say.

And I realize that when Walsh says he might seem heartless, he means heartless towards *me*. Which is probably only fair: I'm not his protégée, I'm not his employee. I'm just 'the girlfriend'. My feelings don't carry weight in his equation at all. It makes me feel quite lost, and alone. Until I remember Alicia.

I press my lips together as I remember what Alicia said to me just a few hours ago. 'Professor, like I said, I'll do my best to help. That's why I came. But Mycroft may not want my help. He may not want anyone's help. He might need to just . . . crash and burn a bit before he's ready to accept support.'

Walsh sighs deeply and nods. He pulls up his glasses and starts polishing them with a handkerchief. 'Fair enough. Let's just hope Mycroft's in a receptive mood, then, eh?'

————

'So then Mycroft jumped ship right in the middle of Paddington?'

'Yeah. I mean, if you think it was Paddington.'

'Do you know where he's gone?'

'Not exactly. I have a few ideas, though.' I rub my hair with a towel. 'He had that "pub" look in his eye.'

'What is it about guys, that they think beer is the answer to any problem?' Alicia chews on a handful of nuts from a split-open packet on the nightstand. 'I guess it's the anaesthetic effect. But then you just feel twice as awful the next day.'

I don't have enough energy to reply. At least I'm feeling a bit more human, now that I've had a shower and I'm wearing clothes I haven't traveled seventeen thousand kilometers in.

This is the first chance I've had to rest in my new home away from home. Our room is smaller at one end than the other. Maybe all the rooms in the Empire Star are funny shapes, like living in a mouse-maze of odd compartments.

The space here is no larger than my bedroom in Melbourne, but it contains two single beds separated by a doll-sized night-stand. The door opens right onto the end of my bed. At the end of Alicia's bed is the radiator, and a large window with green curtains hanging on tinny hooks. The shower rose in the cupboard-like bathroom is enormous – you'd never get away with it at home, the water-restrictions police would be onto you in a shot.

But it's clean, and cheap, and above all *I don't care*. I'm way too tired to care.

I flop down on my bed. The duvet is ghastly pink nylon, but it's warm. My hands and toes still tingle from standing in the drizzle on a lonely road west of London. My eyes feel bugged-out, exhausted, but Alicia tells me that if I sleep now, it'll take days to get used to the time zone. I just have to tough it out until evening. But resting on the duvet, all my muscles relax. It's a short leap from there to my eyelids drifting closed.

'Will you go look for Mycroft, then?'

I startle. 'Huh? Oh. Well, he should come back here eventually. But yeah, I think so. I might give it a few hours, though. Let him get it all out of his system.'

'You mean you're going to wait until he's completely tanked and therefore more malleable.'

Alicia's lounging on her bed with her back against the wall, half her belongings unpacked around her. I see spare socks and tampons and hair products. Is this what bunking with an older sister is like?

'Actually, the booze won't help,' I say. 'But he needs to be alone for a while to settle down.'

Alicia smiles. 'You know what you need?'

'About twenty-four hours of uninterrupted sleep?'

'Apart from that.' Alicia bounces up and puts on a velvet jacket over her jeans and T-shirt, scooping her long ponytail out of the collar. The blue of the jacket makes her gray eyes glow. 'You really need a curry. And luckily for you, we're in a country where you can get curry twenty-four-seven. Come on, I'm shouting you dinner. I'll even spot you a pint.'

I feel a little groan building. 'Does that mean I have to get up off the bed?'

'Yes.' Alicia throws Mike's jumper at my head. It's warm, having dried on the radiator for half an hour.

'I need to do stuff.' I push the jumper off and rub my eyeballs through their lids. 'I need to contact my parents, and email Mai, and . . .'

'First, you need food. You'll feel better after that. Hop to it.'

'Where do you get all this energy?'

'I've been shoring up all my unresolved sexual tension since I left your brother at the airport. It's very energising.'

'Oh god, stop.'

'*London*, Rachel! We're in London! Come on!'

Alicia drags me towards the end of our street, which is populated by a number of little Empire-Star-like hostels. The drizzle has shot through, leaving behind a dark polish on the road and a faint sewage-y smell.

Sunlight blues up the sky, but you could fit the heat it gives off into a matchbox. All the English people are wearing T-shirts and jeans or skirts, no jackets. I pulled my jumper on as soon as we left the hostel's warm foyer.

'I'd love to take you to Brick Lane,' Alicia says, 'but it's really only pumping on Sundays. I guess we'll have to settle for Spicy World and a bit of a browse around Tachbrook Street market.'

'I have no idea what you're talking about.'

She winks at me. 'Come on. It's close. Everything's close in Pimlico. Actually everything's close in London generally, but Pimlico has a nice friendly closeness.'

I've noticed one difference between London and Melbourne already: the lack of green. Melbourne is full of elms and grassy corridors. This city is a lot more densely populated, so the greenery is more like a decorative footnote. But London *is* beautiful: the bunched-together houses and Victorian details everywhere are like something out of Dickens, or maybe *Peter Pan*.

We cross the street so Alicia can stop in Boots, which turns out to be a pharmacy and has nothing to do with actual boots, then we get distracted by a chalkboard sign in front of a pub. There seem to be pubs everywhere in London. This one has diamond-paned windows and an elaborate ironwork sign that reads *The Prince of Wales*.

Alicia ticks off options on her fingers. 'Fish and chips. Steak and ale pie. Pigs in blankets.'

'What the hell is that?'

'Pork sausages wrapped in bacon.' Alicia's still searching the chalkboard. 'Lamb curry. Oh god, I'm starving. Did you even eat lunch?'

She pushes me through the pub's black door and suddenly I'm assaulted by the smell of food, real food, not airplane muck. The Prince of Wales serves giant bowls of thick red curry with rice and globs of yogurt. The woman from behind the ornate bar plonks down a lunch pail with cutlery in it, plus a large number of condiments I don't recognize: Sarson's Malt Vinegar, HP Sauce, Colman's Mustard. There's tomato sauce, I recognize that.

It's all served with a pint, because apparently I can drink with a meal here if I'm accompanied. After we've clinked glasses, I point out something Alicia has apparently failed to notice.

'This beer is flat.'

'It's not flat.' Alicia slurps out of her own glass to demonstrate the beer's palatability. 'It's ale. It's not fizzy like Australian booze. And it's meant to be tap-warm.'

'Well, that's just weird.' I lift my pint glass with two hands. 'These beers are enormous. I won't be able to drink all of this.'

'Good. Because I want to look at the stalls before they finish. You can get some bargains near closing time.'

Tachbrook Street is a collection of blue-and-white striped awnings, tables with amazing cheese displays, stalls piled with fresh vegetables, and rack upon rack of second-hand clothes. I feel a bit stonkered – on top of the jet lag, the beer is making me weave. Alicia shops like a bower bird, exclaiming over fabrics and jewelry, oblivious to the looks the stallholders are giving her as they pull their awnings down.

'Here,' she says, thrusting something at me.

It's a bronze-colored puffer vest, zippered up the front, pre-loved. I like it – it's got internal pockets for valuables and when I try it on and it fits, and feels warm.

'An improvement on the jumper.'

'Hey, I like that jumper.'

'Sure. But this is better.' Alicia whips the vest out of my hand and gives the stallholder the eye. 'She still likes the jumper.'

The stallholder is a young black guy with a weak chin. 'She can keep wearing the jumper, if she likes it so much. Not my problem.'

'Do you want to sell this stuff or not?'

Alicia, it turns out, haggles like a fishmonger's wife. The stallholder hands me my newly acquired vest in a recycled plastic bag. By seven-thirty we've managed to get Alicia a pair of black fingerless gloves and a vintage skirt, and the stalls are well and truly over.

We buy some doughnut holes with icing sugar on them and scarf them down as we meander back towards Warwick Way. I stop to use the toilet in the pub where we ate – there's a curious lack of public toilets in London – and when I come back Alicia's waving me in a new direction.

'Come on, this way. I've found a cafe with internet, so you can contact your family.'

When I open my email I see a banked queue of subject lines such as RACHEL READ THIS IMMEDIATELY and MUM HERE, and I recoil. I just don't want to read them. If I open these emails I'll have to deal with my parents' anger, and I'm not ready for that. I made a decision, and I've acted on it – Mum and Dad will just have to deal with it. They can shout at me later, when I get home.

I'd love to chat to Mai on IM, but it's so early in the morning in Melbourne, she'll probably still be asleep. I'll text her later. I do need to email Mike, though. I scrabble out a message about how I've been sticking with Alicia and I've made contact with Professor Walsh and Mycroft, then I send it off. I immediately feel bad that I didn't put in any apology or sentiment, so I type up another short email with those things in it and send that too.

Alicia sends an email to her parents, then takes longer on a message to her friends in Paris. 'I've checked the train timetables – I've said I'll need a couple of extra days before I get there. That should do it.'

'Oh god, don't delay your whole trip because of me—'

'I'm not delaying my trip, Rachel. This is my *holiday*, remember? No one's expecting me before Wednesday, and I'm quite happy to have a few more days in London.'

'You're doing a lot for me,' I say, 'and you hardly know me.'

'Actually, I feel like I know all about you.' Alicia smiles. 'Mike talks about you a lot. It was one of the things I first noticed about him, that he really cared about you and his family. That, plus the fact he's sexy as hell.'

I blush at the idea that Mike could be viewed as sexy, and that he talks about me at work.

'He's younger than you,' I say, although I don't know why that counts for anything.

'Only by a year.' Alicia looks out the window. 'But he seems more mature somehow. So many guys you meet in the city are cynical or selfish, or closed-off. Mike's not like that. Melbourne is so new to him. He still has a . . . sense of wonder, I guess.'

I grin. 'Yeah, Mike can be like a big puppy sometimes.'

'That's it! But he's not a dill, and he's forthright, and genuine and . . .' Her cheeks get this rosy glow. 'Look, I could go on about your brother for ages, but you might not want to hear it.'

'Well, I'm Mike's biggest fan, but I don't want to hear about him being a good kisser—'

'He's a *great* kisser.'

'Bloody hell.' I look away.

'Awe-inspiring. *Incredible.*'

'Stop!'

'Come on.' Alicia grabs her shopping bag and stands, smiling from ear to ear. 'If I keep on like this, I'll just miss him more than I do already. Let's go to Paddington and get *your* love life sorted out.'

Evening darkness is beginning to wrap the city in its arms. We walk past Sainsbury's supermarket and jewel-lit shop windows until we reach Victoria Station's solemn stone arches.

Red double-deckers snort restlessly outside the station. The pavement rumbles under my feet, from the trains rushing below the concrete.

'Bus or tube?' Alicia asks.

'Um, I dunno.'

'Bus, I reckon. And there's . . . Oh, here we go. Run!'

We make it onto the bus. I sit near the window and watch the evening lights of London mystically appear as the bus trundles up Grosvenor Place.

'Oh, okay. I remember some of this from before.' I tap on the glass. 'That park we just went past.'

'Green Park. Buckingham Palace is just over there.'

'So that's where the Queen—'

'Yup.' Alicia buttons her jacket and fishes in the bag for her new gloves. 'This isn't the part of town I lived in. I was staying with a family friend in Camden, but I did spend a fair bit of time checking out the various neighborhoods.'

The bus gallops onwards. This time I'm not feeling miserable, so I keep spotting things – Hyde Park, the London Eye, signs for Oxford Street. They're landmarks I never expected to see in real life.

When I lived in Five Mile, the idea of traveling out of Australia never really occurred to me. I loved being there, I had everything I wanted. Moving to Melbourne has changed me, made me see a larger world. And now this, traveling overseas, is a whole new revelation. This is England. I'm in *England*. And there are heaps of other countries, exotic places like Ethiopia, Italy, Mexico. Every one of them is unique, with different people, languages, ideas . . .

The concept is intoxicating, and slightly staggering. I get a strange longing for the familiar, combined with a buzz of excitement over the new. It's a very unsettling mixture of feelings.

We pass the blue-and-white neon of the Odeon Cinema, and I press the buzzer for the next stop. This is close to where Mycroft jumped out of Walsh's car, somewhere between the M40 turn-off and the Odeon. But when we get off, I don't recognize this part of Edgware Road.

Gray spots from old chewing gum polka-dot the pavement flagstones under the streetlights. There are so many people, mostly African or Middle-Eastern. Women in hijab or full burqa carry groceries home for dinner, children trailing behind them. For a dizzying second, it's as though I'm back on Sydney Road on a Friday night.

Alicia frowns. 'Mycroft could be anywhere.'

'Just bear with me for a sec.' I spin on the spot, getting my bearings.

Then I see one of the London black cabs go trundling by, and I have a brainwave.

———

The pub is on a commission flats estate halfway down Porchester Place. It's called The Kingfisher, and it reminds me a lot of the crappy local in Five Mile. There's the same dark wood bar, the fluoro lighting above the mirrored spirits shelf, the assortment of grizzled men nursing beers. But this place is all warm inside, with giant pint glasses and English people.

I've given Alicia my new vest to take back to the hostel and gone back to wearing Mike's old jumper, so I don't seem completely out of place. A few dissolute-looking blokes stand in the corner, watching me. In Five Mile, guys wear jeans and Blundstones and their dusty blue Chesty Bonds undershirts to the pub – these guys all have more street-dirt in their look.

The proprietor has put the soccer on the telly in the background. A quick glance around the public bar disappoints, but there's a battered wooden sign reading *Tables* near a door on the left. I wander through and down a creaky step into the poolroom.

Two lawn-green tables are lit by overhanging lamps. The shadowed room is otherwise empty, except for one person. The table at the far end has balls scattered on top, and Mycroft is standing at it with his back to me.

I'm struck, in this moment, by the sheer Englishness of him. I mean, I knew he was English, but now it hits me – his height, his wild hair, the leanness of his body, the black jeans and scuffed shoes, his red-and-white striped jacket . . .

In Melbourne, Mycroft comes off as a slightly alt-punk guy, but here, in this setting, I realize for the first time that it's not a look. It's how he is. My picture of Melbourne, of Australia, has Mycroft in it, but Melbourne isn't really where he belongs. He's lived more than half his life in this country, in England, and now he's returned here, hurting more deeply than ever.

His cue hangs loosely in one hand and he's knocking back the dregs of a pint. Three empty glasses sit idly on the tabletop nearby. I don't want to think about how smashed he might be already.

I jam my hands into my jeans pockets and take a steadying breath. 'Getting a few in early, for the autopsy tomorrow?'

Mycroft's back straightens. He turns, puts down his glass with deliberate care. Meets my eyes.

'There's about ten pubs in any given two-block radius in this part of town. How'd you find me?'

'I asked the cab driver which was the grungiest one,' I admit.

He snorts, retrieves his cigarette off the table edge. 'Fair enough.'

I scratch in my pocket with fumbling fingers. 'I just . . . came to see how you were. And to give you this.' I pull out the piece of paper Alicia scribbled our respective phone numbers onto and place it on the wooden edge of the table. 'That's my new number, so . . .'

I trail off into the awkward silence. Mycroft leans over to line up his shot. In spite (or maybe because) of the sign that says *No Smoking at the Tables*, his cigarette hangs in the corner of his mouth, ready to spill hot ash onto the pocked felt.

He shoots. The balls knock together. It doesn't look as if he's trying to pocket anything.

I wait.

He lines up his next shot. 'Look, I'm not trying to piss you off, but you shouldn't be here. I mean, stay a few days, see the sights, but then . . .'

Again, I register how Mycroft's accent doesn't sound odd here, in this setting. But I also feel a smarting ache in my chest. 'You think I should just go home.'

'Yes.' Mycroft stands to his full height, broad-shouldered and glowering. 'Rachel, your mother already hates my guts. Now your parents are gonna blame me for you nicking off overseas.'

The comment about my parents is bait. I can't help but take it. 'It's none of their business!'

'You *are* their business.' He walks back to the grotty table to dib out his smoke, and chalk his cue with sharp, vicious swipes. 'At least until you move out of home.'

I get a grip on myself. 'Mycroft, this isn't about my parents.'

'Really? So what's it about?' His thick eyebrows draw together. 'Me, being such a bloody . . . I don't know what. Not being able to *keep my shit together.*'

He flings the chalk aside and stalks around to the other side of the table.

'You shouldn't have to do this on your own,' I say softly.

'Well, you can't do it for me.' Acid bitterness lines his face as he leans down, curls a finger on the cue. 'Some things I just have to sort out for myself.'

'Hey, I know that.' It's hard, smothering the urge to return fire. 'But this is too big. Mycroft, you can't control all these feelings that—'

'I CAN.' Mycroft abandons his shot to stand straight. He levels the cue at my head. 'I *can*, and I bloody *will*.'

The blue tip of the wooden cue is shaking. His lips tremble, and his eyes are hot enough to cauterise. Suddenly he lobs the cue onto the table; all the colored balls bounce with the force of it.

Something inside me breaks loose. I step forward and grip the table's edge. My words come out snake-like, striking.

'*Bullshit.*' My face crackles as I squeeze the varnished wood. 'You've been trying it that way for seven years, and where has it got you? Mycroft, if you want to deal with your shit, then fucking grow up enough to accept support when you need it! Let me in! I don't want to do it *for* you. I just want to *help.*'

He stares at me, his lips white. Just as I think he's about to start yelling, he strides towards me and grabs my hand.

CHAPTER NINE

Mycroft yanks me out of the poolroom, out of the pub – I barely have time to snatch up the paper with my phone number. We half-jog down the street; Mycroft's limping, but I'm having trouble keeping up. His grip on my hand is strong as a vise. My fingers start aching, but I refuse to say anything.

He drags me halfway down this street, across the road to turn into another. There's another turn, more walking, more pulling. Right as I'm about to crack, to complain that I can't feel my fingers anymore, that his grip is too tight, that I don't know what we're doing walking around the streets of London this late at night . . . Right as I'm about to blurt these things out, he comes to a standstill and my momentum carries me into his shoulder.

He's brought me to a ruin.

It's a narrow, deep lot. The ironwork fence in front is swathed in green safety mesh and warning signs, tagged with graffiti. Terrace houses lean on either side of the hole. The remnants of basement steps lead down to nowhere.

'They tore it down.' Mycroft lets go of me to grab onto the iron fence. 'I knew Angela had sold it. There was no way she could deal with the upkeep. But I came looking for it, after I got out of the car. This is all I found. I think it's been abandoned for years.'

Among the dirt and sandbags lies a grave-like mound of broken masonry. Whatever once stood here has long since disappeared. Somebody's left a small collection of spray cans near the fence. Scraps of other people's junk mail, limp from the rain, disintegrate against the safety mesh.

I rub my bruised fingers, stare at the demolished site. 'What was it before?'

'The executors sent me the *door key*, in a letter. Can you believe that? A key to a nonexistent door, as if that would make up for the . . .' Mycroft's short, sobbing laugh dies in his throat. He gazes at the pile of rubble. 'We had a fireplace, and a mantelpiece with cabbage roses. Upstairs was my room, and Mum and Dad's room, and if I had a nightmare, I'd go and crawl in with them. There was this pattern of shadows on the ceiling of their room, it was . . .'

Mycroft's old home. His *family's* home. I remember what it felt like to leave Five Mile, how much worse it would be if I knew it was gone forever . . .

I watch Mycroft's face. It's got this shocked emptiness about it, but I know he's not feeling empty inside.

'How could they do that?' he whispers. 'Just tear it down, without any warning?'

I swallow. 'I don't know, Mycroft.'

He turns flaming eyes on me, and, god, his voice . . .

'It's like we never existed. Sometimes I even wonder if *I* exist.' He turns back to the empty lot. An evening breeze ruffles his dark curls. 'There's nothing to hold on to, nothing real. Just a few photos in an album. Nobody remembers them. Nobody remembers we were even a family.'

I take a careful step towards him. 'You remember. You keep their memories alive.'

'Yeah.' His throat works as he searches for the words. 'And it's killing me. It's like I'm the bloody *funeral urn* for it all. My whole past is dead. I'm the only one left. And now I don't even have a place to come back to. Even the place is gone.'

I'm tight as fence wire, too taut to even shift my feet. I try to keep my voice calm. 'But Mycroft, do you think your parents would want you to keep hurting like this? And will finding out who killed them make a difference?'

'It will make a difference to me.'

'Mycroft—'

He spins around, glaring. 'Don't try to give me advice about this, Rachel, because you don't fucking *know*. Okay? You don't know what it's like.'

I breathe out deeply through my nose, unclench my fists.

'No. I *don't* know. Because you never tell me anything about it. This . . .' I wave a hand at the dirty bricks, '. . . this is the most you've ever told me. Except to acknowledge that it happened, you never tell *anyone*.'

I take a step towards him, but Mycroft makes more distance between us. His eyes arc blue in the light from the streetlamp. His cheekbones are marble-white daggers.

'What do you want me to *tell* you?' His words hammer off the brickwork of the adjacent houses. 'That I had my father's brain matter in my hair when they pulled me out?'

I blink at him, shocked. 'Mycroft—'

113

'Or should I tell you that when they were trying to saw the car apart, and it was just me and Mum left, she kept trying to say my name? But her jaw was smashed and all she could do was make this grinding noise, and finally she—'

His voice breaks and he looks away blindly. My lips are pressed together. I've got tears in my eyes. But when Mycroft turns back to me his eyes are bone dry, red-rimmed and merciless.

'Is this the stuff you want me to tell you?' His voice is husky with despair. 'Because you don't *want* this stuff, Rachel. *Nobody* wants this stuff. I don't hate anybody enough that I'd force them to listen to it, and you sure as hell don't qualify.'

I have to bear down hard then. I take a tentative step forward. 'But I do. I do want it. Because it's a part of you, and it's—'

'It's not a *part* of me!' Mycroft yells. He slams a fist against his chest. 'It's *all I am*! This is all you get, Rachel – a pile of fucking *debris*. The rest of me is just . . . smoke.'

His expression is so anguished I'm scared he's about to fall to pieces right in front of me. Then he subsides, shuddering, leaning against the iron fence. He looks annihilated. I hardly know what to say, what to feel. My chest is full and my throat is almost too constricted to speak.

'Is that why you kissed me like that, the other night?' I whisper. 'Because you were saying goodbye?'

'I finally figured it out.' He's listless now, his face bleak. 'You deserve better than me, Rachel. You're a whole person, and I'm not.'

Everything turns to winter. I force my voice not to shake. 'Mycroft, I don't believe that. And you don't get to decide what I deserve, or what I want.'

'Yeah, I do. In this case, I do.'

'No. That's not true.' I swallow. 'Are you saying you're going to go around your whole life not connecting with *anybody*? That's bull. Mycroft, the family in your past might be dead, but you're not. *You're not.*'

I step towards him and my hands lift involuntarily. I want to touch him more than anything. I don't know if I want to shake sense into him or hug him, but I want him to feel as if he's not alone.

'Mycroft, *talk* to me. Tell me . . . whatever you want to tell me. At least if you share it with me, there'll be another person who remembers them.'

'I can't.' He shakes his head, eyes turned down to the pavement. His voice is splintering, awful. 'I can't. It's not fair on you.'

'James . . .'

I put a hand on his cheek, lift his face. His cheek is wet. For a second he closes his eyes and rests against my palm.

'No.' He fumbles me away. 'Go back, Rachel. Just go back to where you belong.'

All of a sudden, my courage deserts me. I blink at Mycroft, then it's as if every single ounce of exhaustion I've been carrying spirals up inside my body. I just want to lie down – if there was a bed on the street corner, I'd curl up on it right now.

My voice is very small. 'But I flew all the way over here to bring you home.'

Mycroft wets his lips and stares right through me.

'You're too late.' His eyes are black and dull, like blunt iron. 'I don't have a home.'

It's like a fist in the stomach, winding me.

Mycroft's hand shoots up. I wonder what the hell he's doing now until I realize he's flagging down a cab.

'You should go,' he says. When the cab pulls up, he thrusts some notes at the driver through the window. 'Warwick Way, Pimlico. You know the hostel strip?'

The cab driver nods. I'm being drummed out.

Mycroft meets my eyes once, before I get in the cab, but he doesn't say anything. I suddenly realize I'm still clutching the limp note with my phone number. With numb fingers, I push the paper into his hand. 'Mycroft . . . The autopsy is tomorrow. Just . . . call me. If you think you need an anchor. We don't have to talk. I can just be there.'

He examines the paper with dead eyes, holds it out. 'I'll be fine. I don't need this.'

I grimace. 'God, you're a stubborn bastard! Take it, before I shove it down your throat.'

Mycroft looks at me, his expression vacant. I get a sudden attack of the panics. I should stay, stay with him, plead with him . . .

But I don't. I slide into the cab. I have to bite my lip and squeeze my fists tight to stop myself from jumping out again.

The cabbie looks at me in the rear-view mirror. 'You all set, luv?'

I don't trust myself to speak. I just nod.

Then the cab is pulling away. Mycroft stands there, watching me go. *What if I've screwed this up?*

The feeling I had at the crash site this afternoon pummels me again – I don't know Mycroft at all. I've traveled so far, and he's here in the wrong context, or I'm in the wrong context, or *something* – I am lost in this city, more lost than I ever was in Melbourne. The stars here are wrong, the shape of the rooftops under the London sky . . . I don't know my way, and I want to go home. I want us both to go back, so I can reframe this picture in an environment I understand. But I don't know if that's possible anymore.

I don't cry in the cab. A tendril of Mycroft's grief has seeped into my soul, and all I can feel is hollow.

———

There's a bleating sound.

The armchairs in study hall are soft. I've been having a nap, but now the fire alarm is going off. It bleats annoyingly down the long school halls.

I'm faceplanted into my pillow. I want the stupid sound to stop so I can go back to just floating around in this dark, warm space . . .

This is not study hall. And it's not a fire alarm. It's my phone.

A headache starts clambering behind my eyelids. I groan.

I unravel an arm, grab the phone. 'Mmerm.'

Nothing.

'Who is this?' I clear the gorse out of my throat. 'Look—'

'It's me.'

'Mycroft?' A jolt goes through me. My eyelids spring apart. I'm in a darkened room, in a strange bed with a laundry-bleach smell.

'I'm outside your door.' Mycroft sounds cross.

'Oh.' The headache keeps humming. I rub a crust out of one eye and kick my legs to dislodge the blankets. 'Hang on.'

The floor is a shock after being in bed – carpeted, but freezing. I shove my hands in my armpits and try to stop my heart bolting out of my chest.

He's called me. It might mean anything. I shouldn't get excited, but my brain isn't working well enough to do as it's told.

When I crack the door open, Mycroft is leaning there. He looks as if he's just rolled out of bed. For all I know, he may not have gone to bed at all. He seems to be wearing the same clothes as yesterday – a crumpled white T-shirt, black jeans and his red hoodie – and his eyes are sunk in dark grottoes.

'God, you look like shit.' The words tumble out of my mouth before I can stop them.

'The autopsy is in twenty-five minutes,' he says.

I stand with one foot on top of the other, hugging my arms around myself. 'Um . . . okay?'

He sighs. 'Do you want to come or not?'

I'm processing too slowly. 'You . . . want me to come?'

Mycroft hesitates. His eyes dart around, take in the dark room behind me. 'I don't want to go off again, like yesterday at the crash site. I don't want the Professor to think I'm a complete hopeless case. Yes, I want you to come.'

I take a second to respond, mostly so I can wrangle my voice into casualness. 'Okay. I'll come.'

Mycroft bites his lip. He seems to be avoiding looking at me in my T-shirt and undies. 'Get dressed and come downstairs. Walsh will pick us up in fifteen.'

He walks off.

I close the door. I let myself grin. I let myself jump up and down. Then I check my phone.

It's nine a.m. I've been asleep for over ten hours. My bladder is so full it hurts.

Alicia is curled towards the wall in the other bed. I try to creep to the bathroom nook, but when I come out she's awake, waiting her turn. By the time I've scrambled into my jeans, T-shirt, blue flannie and new vest, Alicia has burrowed back into bed.

'Do you need me?' she asks, cowled by blankets.

'Not for this.' The bathroom pipes gurgle as I pull on socks and boots. 'I'm going to an autopsy.'

'I'm glad you don't need me, then.' Her eyes are already closing.

'Be back later. I'll let you know how it goes.' I grab my phone and satchel.

It's bracing outside, with the brightness of a sun that got up earlier than I did. My clothing is still disarrayed, but I don't even have time to zip my vest against the cold – there's the little Honda idling at the curb, its exhaust pipe making dragon puffs around its rear end. I slide into the back to discover that Professor Walsh has got the heater going full blast, and Mycroft is sitting beside me. I blink at him as he shifts over to give me more room.

'Lovely morning.' Walsh gives a cheerful wave. As he pulls out he checks his watch on the hand he should be using on the steering wheel. 'Coroner said nine-thirty, and I've got nine-twenty-one.'

'Morning.' I look over at Mycroft. 'Hey.'

Now I've woken up properly, I can see that he really *is* wearing yesterday's clothes. He's added a pair of large mirrored sunglasses – I'm familiar with those from last December – and his face looks ashen beneath them.

I cock an eyebrow. 'Hung-over?'

Mycroft raises his sunnies: his eyes look worse in the morning light, bloodshot and bleary. He doesn't seem angry, though, so that's a plus.

'Stayed out a bit late.' He drops the glasses back into place. 'Nice vest. Very lumberjack.'

'Thanks.' I scrutinise him. 'At least you didn't get arrested, like the last time you got shit-faced and ended up in Fawkner.'

'That was all a misunderstanding.' Mycroft pulls a cigarette out of a pack as terrace houses disappear behind us. 'Bloody hell. Merry England.'

I squint at him. 'Is it weird, being back here?'

Mycroft taps the filter end on his bottom lip. 'Makes me want to listen to The Clash, for some reason.'

'Please don't smoke that in my car,' Walsh says firmly. Actual proof that he sometimes checks the rear-view mirror.

'It's a rental,' Mycroft complains.

'I'm not renting these lungs. They're mine.'

I tap my own chest between the zipper teeth. 'And these are mine.'

'The boobs?' Mycroft gives my chest an appraising look. 'Well, they're certainly not fake.'

'Mycroft, stop talking,' Walsh says. I see his eye-roll in the rear-view.

'I put it down to nerves.' I'm talking to the Professor, but looking pointedly at the back of Mycroft's head.

'How so?' Walsh asks.

'He always runs off at the mouth when he's nervous.'

Mycroft sighs. 'And he's still actually present, right now, sitting in the car with you . . .'

'We've arrived,' Walsh says.

This time I don't need to ask where, because there's a large red sign saying *Coroner's Court* plonked in the front garden of the building.

Thanks to the case with Dave, I've lost my preconceived notions about morgues. The place where we saw his body was contemporary. This building looks more like something you'd see in a horror movie, with russet brick and white marble eaves and a gothic turret above the front door. Even now, in the warm sunlight, it conforms more to the expected idea of a house of the dead: stone and stately and old.

There's a black-gabled pub on the other side of the road.

Someone has yarn-bombed the entire exterior, so all the wooden bench tables have striped cuffs on their legs. Rainbow-knitted curlicues dance around golden letters, the pub's name: *The Barley Mow.*

Walsh parks crookedly on a side street. We scramble out onto the pavement. Instead of walking around to the Coroner's Court entrance, with the grand turret, Walsh heads straight for a large hardwood gate by a banked row of taxis. He bundles his briefcase and coat under his right arm so he can press the metal intercom set into the gate.

Before his thumb makes contact, he turns to me and nods. 'Right, this is where we leave you, I'm afraid. Have you brought a book to read? Because this could take a while.'

I gape, look back and forth between Walsh and Mycroft.

'I recommend waiting in The Mow,' Walsh goes on. 'They do excellent English breakfasts—'

'Ah,' Mycroft says. 'I told Rachel she could come along.'

'Pardon?'

'I told her she could come.' Mycroft jigs a bit. 'I'd like her to come.'

He looks at me. This is a bizarre peace offering, but I take it in both hands.

'Let me come.' I turn to Walsh, straighten my shoulders. 'I won't get in your way.'

Walsh looks gobsmacked. 'You can't be serious.'

'I'm perfectly serious.'

'I'd like her to come,' Mycroft repeats.

'Look, I'm glad Rachel's here as support, but this is an official Met investigation.' Walsh frowns. 'They won't let me bring a—'

'Give me a lab coat. I'll stand in the viewing area.' I stare him down. I only have a millisecond window of opportunity here. 'In the corner. In the foyer.'

'Miss Watts—'

'I can help.' I glance at Mycroft, standing there with his hands jammed in his pockets, then back to Walsh. 'Priorities, remember?'

Walsh's face is uncertain, but not enraged. If he were Detective Pickup I'd have to work harder.

The alarm on Walsh's phone goes off, and I know I've got him.

'Oh, for pity's sake.' He shakes his head at Mycroft, thumbs the intercom. 'Yes, hello. Professor Emmett Walsh and, er, party.'

The intercom makes a buzz-saw grind. The gate slides slowly across to reveal a very ordinary parking area with a series of bays painted onto the bitumen. A modern, brown brick cottage with an attached garage sits at the end of the short drive. Walsh marches towards the cottage.

Mycroft hauls me through as the gate begins to close. He grabs my satchel off my shoulder, drops it at my feet, and starts pulling at the collar of my flannelette shirt, straightening me up.

'Thanks.' His mouth twitches. 'I didn't think he'd go for it.'

'No worries.' I narrow my eyes at him. 'But any more boob jokes and I walk.'

'Sure. No, you're right. Sorry.' He looks repentant, and a bit jittery.

I glance towards the brick cottage and decide I can get away with rubbing it in a little. 'Other boys invite girls to parties, you know.'

'You don't like autopsies better?'

He pushes his sunglasses up into his corkscrewing hair, and

again I see how awful his eyes look. His whole face is colorless. I unknot my own hair, drag my fingers through and smooth it down with my palm.

'How much sleep have you had?' I ask, with a hair elastic between my teeth.

'Enough.'

'You're off your nut.' I tie my hair back into a sleek ponytail.

'Here.' Before I have a chance to startle, he's stuffing my shirt ends in at the waist. 'Are you sure you're ready for this?'

My body is doing all sorts of crazy things as Mycroft's fingers tuck and prod. I lose concentration. 'What do you mean?'

'This. A full autopsy. I've witnessed a couple already, but you've only seen the aftermath.'

'I'll be fine. I've got a strong stomach.' I zip my vest. 'And it won't be easy for you either.'

'I can keep it together.' He says it as though he's promising himself. He gives me a once-over, and doesn't look completely pleased with the result. 'Come on, before we lose Walsh.'

He hands me my satchel and we jog to catch up.

———

The mortuary building is like an old hospital that hasn't been renovated since the fifties, everything slightly dilapidated. The fluoro-lit corridors are short and cramped, and the office doors seem to be squashed together in an unbroken line.

A woman in navy scrubs smiles as she squeezes past us to the staffroom. I see fake-pine linoleum, and coffee mugs, and someone's baby photos printed up and taped to the kitchen-cabinet doors. There are no police detectives in sight.

'So is this . . .'

'This isn't connected to Scotland Yard.' Mycroft has a visitor's ID on a lanyard which he throws over his neck. 'Were you looking for bobbies? The mortuary is run by the city council. It's attached to the Coroner's Court – that's the old building around the front – but there aren't any police.'

'Hey, I just got here. I don't even know what part of town we're in.'

'Still in Westminster. The Yard is that way.' He points away to my left. 'The police have been and gone, and the forensic pathologists are mostly private contractors appointed by the Coroner. The body came here from High Wycombe hospital on Saturday. Hold up.'

Walsh is talking to a suited man along the corridor. The man looks over as Mycroft and I come level.

'. . . for when you're ready to proceed. Ah, and this is your assistant, is that right?'

'Yes,' Walsh says. 'James Mycroft. And, er, Rachel Watts.'

'We weren't informed you had another student,' the man says, but he's shaking Mycroft's hand anyway.

'That's right.' Mycroft pumps the man's hand, smiling broadly. He seriously should go into theater. 'Pre-med. Rachel's a loaner, we're lucky to have her – medical data transmission? You haven't got that yet? Ah. Soon, perhaps.'

The man looks confused, but he nods his head. Maybe he doesn't want to appear to be behind the times. 'Er, yes, I imagine so.'

I force my features into a pleasant expression. Surely my jeans and buttoned flannie and lumberjack vest can't be fooling anybody?

Walsh gives a tight smile. 'Right. Very good of you to hold off. Shall we?'

'By all means,' the man says, disguising his fluster by ushering us politely back down the corridor.

We have to leave our bags – my satchel, Walsh's briefcase – in the staffroom and sign a ledger near the front door. Above the ledger, a pinboard is strewn with notices about Fire Assembly Points and Undertakers' Hours. There's one that starts 'In the event of a Home Office classified disaster . . .' but I don't get to read the rest of it, because Walsh waves us through a nearby brown door.

We enter what appears to be an undercover warehouse – the garage I saw from outside the building. But this is not a regular garage. A normal corrugated door is rolled down, but a series of square freezer doors are recessed into one wall.

I suddenly realize there are dead people – persons – bodies – right here. Right *here*. This is the holding pen for bodies received overnight, outside of mortuary hours.

Walsh hangs up his coat on a peg; he has a folded bundle of teal-colored cloth under his arm. There's a yellow line on the floor, and everyone puts disposable blue booties over their shoes. I try to copy them without looking clumsy.

We leave the cold garage and enter an even colder receiving room with a blue resin floor and a whiteboard with 'STOCK: To Order' written on it in black marker. The walls are strangely patterned with a streaky brown fleck, which makes them look scuffed or – more unfortunately – dripping. Boxes are attached to one wall, with blue latex or thin green plastic peeking out of them. Another wall attachment, like a piece of modern art, has gumboots hanging from it.

'Right, I'll leave you here, then.' The man in the suit seems to feel he's done his duty. 'The APT will direct you once you're in the Forensic suite.'

More hand-shaking, then he departs. I shiver. Even my flannie and vest can't stave off the morgue's chill.

Mycroft and Walsh are passing each other plastic packages. Walsh disappears into a cubicle and emerges wearing the teal-green cloth – his scrubs. He and Mycroft sit to one side on a concrete ledge, divesting themselves of their shoes.

Walsh does up a disposable blue operating gown awkwardly at the back. He shakes his head and stares at Mycroft.

'Pickup was right. Your balls . . .' He struggles with a pair of gumboots, '. . . must be the size of grapefruits. That was the Deputy Coroner for the borough of Westminster.'

'English people are so easy to con.' Mycroft grins. It's good seeing him grin. 'They're too worried about seeming impolite.'

He unfolds a blue biosuit around himself, yanks up the white plastic zipper in front.

'We're meeting Richard Gordon, the APT, inside the Forensic suite. He's prepped the body.' Walsh has achieved a victory over his boots. 'Richard's an old colleague from St Bart's. He's sharp as a tack. And he's Scottish.'

'I never try the same maneuver twice in a row,' Mycroft says. 'And never with a Scot.'

'What's an APT?' I squeeze my biceps and shift from foot to foot while they get changed.

Walsh grabs two paper face masks from the box-dispenser on the wall. 'An APT is an Anatomical and Pathology Technician. They do quite a lot of the grunt work for the pathologists here.'

'Don't I need a lab coat or something?'

'No, you'll be fine,' Mycroft says. He turns to Walsh. 'Should we put her in a Tyvek?'

Walsh shakes his head.

'I don't think that's necessary. She can stand in the Evidence Room, that's only a transitional zone.' He examines me critically. 'Do you have a notepad or something?'

Walsh seems to be taking a difficult situation and running with it. I don't want to discourage him. Eyes darting, I snatch a clipboard off the wall. There's even a pen under the clip.

'This do?'

'Fine. Have you had breakfast?'

'No.'

'Might be for the best. If you feel ill, sit down or go to the staffroom and get a drink. Absolutely do not, under any circumstances, faint in the Evidence Room. Then we really will be in trouble. Do you understand?'

Walsh walks me to a nearby doorway. He glances back at Mycroft getting his boots on, lowers his voice. 'I think this is a terrible idea, but it's the first time I've seen him crack a smile in days. All right, then?'

I nod. I'm helping. This is what I came here to do. I'm quite light-headed as I twist the doorknob, and then realize I've forgotten to give Mycroft a final encouragement before he goes into the autopsy.

The Evidence Room is tiny, concrete-floored, with benchtops along three sides. Clear ziplock bags are piled in the corner of one bench. A wide window is covered with a thin sage-green curtain. It suggests a play or a performance, but the association seems too macabre and I have to push it out of my mind.

There are no chairs, no room for them. I lean against the benchtop, before the curtained window. It gives me a chance to breathe, get my bearings. I got off the plane just yesterday. Now I'm about to watch the autopsy of a man who died in similar circumstances to Mycroft's parents. I've never seen an autopsy before, only in crime shows on TV. This will be real. No gloss, no fake innards.

I close my eyes for a second, open them, and yank the curtain sharply aside.

CHAPTER TEN

A stocky man of about fifty-five in a full biosuit, including a plastic face mask like a welder's, nods at me through the window. I firm my expression and nod back. He taps on the glass, points a finger. There's an intercom on the wall nearby. I lean across, hit the button.

'Just hold it in for a moment and it'll stay on,' Richard Gordon says. The intercom makes his accented voice garbled and hollow. 'One way only, I'm afraid. If you want to speak to your colleagues during the procedure, hold down the green button and speak into the mic.'

I press the green button to test. 'Um, thanks.'

'No problem.' He nods again, moves away from the window.

I almost forget, then, what I have to do with the buttons, because there's a steel table in the room about two meters from the glass. A man is lying on it, naked, and I know that he is dead.

It's not just the circumstances; it's not that he's lying in an autopsy suite on a steel table. And it isn't the appalling injuries on his face and body. It's something else. I saw it with Dave Washburn, and I'm reminded again now: the spark has gone, the essential vitality, the . . . the soul of him has fled. I don't know how, but it's unmistakeable, even behind glass, even this far away.

Daniel Gardener wasn't bad-looking for a guy in his forties – I've seen the photos. The figure on the table is hard to reconcile with that man. The blond hair is matted with a dark glue, the eyes are closed, the lips slack. There's no drape over the body – Gardener no longer needs his modesty preserved. I still feel embarrassed for him, lying there with his genitals exposed.

I remind myself to take a breath.

I'm distracted by movement in the Forensic suite – it takes me a second to recognize the two gangly blue-suited figures talking to the shorter blue-suited figure as Mycroft and Walsh and Gordon. All three men lower their face masks, Gordon takes off his welder's plate. Their voices echo around the large steel-and-concrete room.

'. . . weren't keen to move him direct to Westminster, but the Yard was insistent. Coroner was on your side, so you got lucky. I've done first measurements, and I took urine and vitreous when he first came in, I've already noted it on the chart. They took BAC at the scene – nothing there.'

'At least there's no biohazard to worry about,' Walsh says. 'Those hairnets always make my scalp itch.'

'Do you want me to assist?' Gordon hesitates over his gloves.

'Only if you want to, Richard.' Walsh collects two bunches of latex from a box on a nearby bench. 'Mycroft is capable, and you've done a great deal already.'

'Then I won't stay. Got another three PMs in the main room before lunch.' Gordon peels off his gloves and tucks them into a yellow biohazard bin. 'Good luck with it, then. Nice to meet you,

James. Come out to the Royal Oak on Wednesday night, I'll show you how I can still drink Emmett under the table.'

Gordon grins and leaves.

Walsh smiles, says something to Mycroft about drinking. But now Gordon has gone, Mycroft doesn't have to pretend he's listening. His expression is sombre. The blue material of the biosuit contrasts with his bloodshot eyes, and you could rule a line from his eyes to the body.

All the hairs on my arms lift, looking at the intensity on his face. I want to break that connection, I want him to know where I am. I slap my hand against the glass.

'Here. Right here,' I say loudly.

I haven't hit the green button, so Mycroft can't hear me. But they've heard the slap – Walsh glances over and nods, relieved that I've found my way into the right spot. Mycroft tears his eyes away from Gardener to blink at me.

There's all-out war on his face. I see it, the way he's struggling to rip himself out of the past and into the now, to bind himself into this moment. He looks at me, back to Gardener, back to me again.

I slide my hand on the glass, hear the squeal.

Walsh steps forward and catches Mycroft's eye, hands him a pair of latex gloves. 'I'm going to need complete shots. The bag is on the bench.'

Mycroft nods automatically. 'Right. Sure.'

A red padded bag perches on the stainless steel bench at the far side of the room. Like an obedient servant, Mycroft fetches the bag and slings the camera out. It's large, with a protuberant flash.

I'm surprised to discover Mycroft seems to know what he's doing with it. He puts the strap around his neck and begins walking around the body on the table. His shots begin tentatively, gain confidence as he works his way from the head to the toes of the dead man.

'Don't forget the soles of the feet,' Walsh says.

Walsh organizes instruments on trays, switches on a large electronic scale, preps a whiteboard on the wall with premarked words like *Brain* and *Liver* and *Heart*.

I swallow, look at Gardener's body. I never got squeamish on the farm, with the occasional slaughter or euthanasia job with the sheep. Blood, animal or human, doesn't usually get me in a flap. But this could be different. This could be more . . . whole. More comprehensive.

The most frightening thing is that I don't know what to expect.

The flash from Mycroft's camera bounces off the white tiles, strobes into my eyes. I have to look away. It wasn't that long ago I saw Mycroft use his phone to take photos of Dave Washburn's body – I guess we haven't really moved on that much.

Suddenly Walsh seems to have had enough of photos and preparations. He asks Mycroft to put the camera aside and come closer to the table.

'Tell me what you see,' Walsh says.

Mycroft presses his lips together, releases them. 'We're looking for trace?'

'Yes, but I want to hear your observations. This is a critical part, before we begin the gross examination.' Walsh lowers his head. 'I know you've researched these types of injuries before. Now forgive me, but I want you to use that knowledge to better inform this investigation.'

I suck in a breath at Walsh saying that.

'Tell me what you see,' Walsh repeats.

Mycroft stands beside the body, so close that he could reach out a hand and touch Gardener on the shoulder. He doesn't do that. His lips open slightly, his face losing its tone and getting that shocky look.

When he speaks, his voice is barely above a murmur. 'There's . . . there's the marks on the forehead. Abrasions. From hitting the windscreen.'

'Not the driver's-side window?'

'No. There's no dicing pattern from tempered glass.'

'That's right,' Walsh says softly. 'Go on.'

'He's broken his nose . . .'

'Comminuted fracture of the nasal septum, yes.'

'. . . against the windscreen.'

'How can you tell it was the windscreen and not the steering wheel?'

'Abrasions go right across the bridge of his nose. And the eyebrows. They're incised wounds, with glass fragments.'

'Yes.'

'Looks like birdshot trace near his right ear.'

'Where?'

Mycroft points. Walsh leans over, nodding. 'Very interesting. That's good. We'll see if we get a match with what I collected from the car.'

'Also a depression fracture of the right eyebrow.'

'Yes. That's the supraorbital margin . . .'

They catalog from the top of Gardener's head down the face and throat and further on, describing the horrible things that can happen to a human being during a car accident.

Mycroft speaks softly, detailing the injuries – fractures, contusions, lacerations, hemorrhage. Walsh gives him the medical terms for each part, something to focus on. It's not until they get to Gardener's torso that they hit a problem.

'Now this,' Walsh says.

Mycroft swallows hard. 'Okay. He's got a haemothorax.'

'How do you know?'

'Because his fucking ribs are poking out through the right side of his chest.' Mycroft looks away desperately. His voice has risen; he puts his gloved hands on his waist. He takes a deep breath and looks again. The next time he speaks he sounds more normal. 'If he's got a penetrating chest wound, then he's bound to have a haemothorax. Most likely COD.'

'I'm not saying I disagree, but we shouldn't presume cause of death. He may have bled out from another source.'

Mycroft bites his lip hard enough to leave a dent. 'From the pelvis? Okay, you can see the haemostasis from how he was lying – leaning to his left. He's got lividity marks up the left side, which suggests some postural compression of the pelvic cavity. But the rib fractures on the right, from when he hit the steering wheel . . . that suggests a massive haemothorax. He's more likely to die of that, after blunt thoracic trauma.'

'Well done, yes. But it's good to qualify – he would have had a flail chest, so the cause of death could just as easily be hypoxia, from respiratory failure.' Walsh takes a rough measure with his fingers. 'We'll see in a minute, but I'd say fractures are from the fifth to the eighth. What do you think?'

Mycroft just nods. He's rubbing his side, right over his own ribs.

My hand is on the glass, clipboard forgotten at my side. I'm remembering running my fingers over Mycroft's chest, tracing the scars that bump over his rib cage . . .

He knows these injuries because he's experienced them. When he was ten, in the back seat of his parents' car, lying in a pool of his own blood, unable to breathe because the pieces of his ribs had punctured his lung, extruded out his skin—

Mycroft turns away from the autopsy table suddenly, walks up to my window. He stands in front of me, deep-sea eyes blinking open and closed. His lips are white as pearls, utterly dry.

I spread my fingers wide on the glass. Mycroft lifts his gloved hand, matches me on the other side, his shaking fingers spread against mine. We stare at each other. My head thrums as I breathe, and Mycroft says nothing at all.

I don't bother with the green button, just mouth the words. *Are you okay?*

He wets his lips. Nods.

Walsh looks up. 'Everything all right?'

Mycroft takes a big breath, closes his eyes. Then he opens them, gives me another glance, and turns around.

———

The rest of the procedure is hard to take in. For one, it happens very fast. Once Mycroft and Walsh have completed the external examination, and done things like scrape under the body's finger-nails, they take some X-rays. Then they slide on new gloves, put on their face masks and . . . get to work.

I'm watching from behind the glass, and my feet are getting sore from standing. But I can't move, I can't look away. Walsh shifts to the top of the table with a scalpel in his hand; I see him slice under the head. Before I can gasp, he's peeled the scalp forward and onto the face, like a red balaclava. I don't have time

135

to process what's happening. The buzzing saw is just a noise, and the exposed brain is a sculpture in gray-blue clay.

This was a man once. He used his brain to think, to dream, to imagine, to create. All his memories lived inside it, and now Professor Walsh is examining it for signs of damage. Now Mycroft is recording its weight and details on the whiteboard with a black marker.

Walsh moves to the side with his finger stuck out, like he's pointing at something. He draws three red lines on Gardener's body with his finger, from the point of each shoulder to the throat, and then a long line down to the groin. That's when I realize Walsh isn't pointing his finger: it's merely a guide for the scalpel beneath. These are not lines, but cuts.

Everything is in shades of black and red. I have time to wonder over it, the way there are so many delicate tones – scarlet shading into inky sadness, and back again. There are other colors too: the dusky green of an unripe olive, an ocher blue, the dull dark burgundy of the curtains in my old house in Five Mile. They're all recreated here, within the internal landscape of this dead man. I discover that slippery has its own color. And hardness too – it is the aged-ivory of bone. Black is the color of decay.

Walsh and Mycroft move smoothly, working around each other with a certain lightness – I think of kite flyers, or trapeze aerialists. Walsh performs the procedures and Mycroft holds here, helps there. Weighing, writing, exchanging gloves to use the camera, collecting samples.

At times Mycroft pauses to blink over at me, but he seems to be handling everything now with a more detached mind. This body is a puzzle, unpacked from its box, and he is quietly examining each piece. After my initial shock, I start to catch a bit of that too – oh, okay, that looks damaged, or yes, you can see where this broke, or maybe that's why there's a mark here.

But I'm not participating, I'm just an observer. I'm not so involved in the process that I can be totally clinical about it. I get a strange tumbling feeling when I see Walsh reach his hand in to excise the windpipe and the tongue – the tongue! How can he even be allowed to remove that? You talk with that, you *need* it, in an essential way. But Gardener does not need it, and everything must be studied, every soft part removed. Everything must go.

When Mycroft pushes the internal organs into a large plastic bag and places the bag into the body's cavity, I get the feeling again. Walsh takes a wadded-up paper towel to wipe out the inside of Gardener's skull, as if he's cleaning out a cereal bowl.

They sew up everything they have opened. They wash the body down, and it's like giving a baby a bath – lift this arm gently, then the other, just roll him a little now. Walsh takes a blue cloth and dabs at Gardener's face, smoothing his hair, sponging his lips.

A powerful memory slams into me then: Dad, wiping Mike's face when he had a fever, years ago. Mike had thrown up into a basin, and Dad made these firm, loving swipes with the cloth over Mike's mouth. Mike's lips had moved under the cloth with this supple, rubbery fleshiness . . .

I get this weird rolling sensation, like I'm on a boat or in an earthquake, and I know I'm about to faint.

I turn away from the glass and take deep breaths as I walk out through the door, into the corridor, into the receiving room. Smells of antiseptic strike up into my nose. I put out one hand and hold the wall. I look at my empty hands: I've dropped the clipboard, back in the Evidence Room. Black spots flick around in my vision, and the room is very long.

There's a steel washbasin a few paces away, so I walk to that. It takes a lot of effort. My throat feels dry. I'm desperate for a drink, but this is not a 'clean' area and I don't think chugging out of the tap would be a good idea. I also know, without question, that if I lean down I'll keel over.

I run the water and put my wrists under it, one at a time. This seems to help. I try to keep my eyes open, because closing them makes things worse.

I'm still gulping air when someone comes up beside me and places something very cold on the back of my neck. I jump before I realize it's Mycroft, and the cold on my neck feels good, makes things better.

'Slow your breathing down,' he says quietly. 'You're hyperventilating, that'll make it worse. Just take it easy.'

He holds my arm at the elbow. He's stripped off his blue suit to the waist and tied the sleeves around his hips. For some reason, the warmth of his body beside me makes me want to cry. He's still holding the cold thing at my nape. I shiver, and he moves it so I can see.

He waggles a wet washcloth. 'Cold is the best thing for it.'

I still can't speak. I just nod and hold on to the washbasin. It hums under my hands.

'You did amazingly well,' Mycroft says. 'Walsh thought you'd be sick, but I told him you were made of sterner stuff. Country girl, I said, and you're—'

I don't think about it at all. I just turn around and grab Mycroft's head and pull his face down to mine.

I have seen the aftermath of death, the incredible mechanism of the body laid bare, and I know now that each person is a kind of miracle. A spark nestles like a bird inside our chests, so deep that we can't find where it lives, but it is *everything*. It's what makes us dream and think and feel and laugh and sing. And it is a mystery, and it is mundane, and, above all, it is fragile. Any moment could be our last.

I want to feel *this* moment. I want to feel that spark kindled inside me, more than anything. I want to feel Mycroft's spark in return.

I press my lips to Mycroft's with a deep hunger. I don't care if there are people nearby who might see us. There are no considerations except that Mycroft is warm and alive. There's only an instant's shocked pause before he drops the washcloth into the steel basin and his hands settle heavily on my shoulders. His fingers squeeze, like a spasm.

I push closer. My fingers slide into his tangled hair, his curls scrunch in my hands. I open his lips with an insistent touch of my tongue – he makes a soft, helpless noise, like he can't fight anymore, and then I taste him. He tastes smoky, and his lips are my whole world, padded and pliable.

Our tongues slide together, and I'm melted honey, dripping warm. I press my body in. My hand slips to the nape of Mycroft's neck, feeling the smooth muscle under his collar . . .

'*Please*,' Professor Walsh says. 'I understand the sentiment, but we need to show a little decorum. It's a mortuary, after all.'

Mycroft and I break apart so fast there's still spit on my lip. I wipe it with the cuff of my sleeve. Mycroft's hands drop to his sides. Two hectic spots of pink have ignited his cheeks, and he's looking at me with something like awe.

I clear my throat. 'Sorry.'

'I gather you're feeling better now.' Walsh is still in his teal scrubs, minus the operating gown. 'There's still a bit of work to finish, but the police have released a parcel of effects. I thought we'd have a look.'

It's hard to get my brain working again. My body is still Flame On. Part of me is shocked I'm so aroused when we're standing only one room away from a dead man.

I nod at Walsh automatically. 'Effects. Right.'

He holds up a ziplock bag, a big one. 'Come back to the Evidence Room.'

Walsh leads, and Mycroft and I follow. Mycroft holds my arm lightly. It's like having a giant hot water bottle pressed up beside me.

He leans in close to whisper in my ear. 'I definitely like autopsies better.'

I elbow him in the side and he grins.

The smell in the Forensic Suite has permeated the Evidence Room. It's a powerful mixture of antiseptic and cold and decay. I flinch at the entrance and Mycroft squeezes my arm.

Through the wide window, Gardener's body is still visible on the steel table. A rolled-up body bag is bundled at his feet. I tear my eyes away.

Walsh has collected my clipboard off the floor and hung it on a hook. He upends the ziplock bag on a bench. 'Here we go, this is from the pockets of his pants and his jacket. See what you can make of it.'

The final effects of Daniel Gardener make a pitiful little pile. One set of keys, a paper tube filled with breath mints, some loose change – the fifty- and twenty-pence pieces are filmed with blood. A mobile phone, the display screen smashed into powder in some places, and a pair of spectacles in their brown case, miraculously preserved. His wallet is dark brown leather, new-looking – it's still stuffed with a wad of cash.

'I guess whoever searched the boot after the accident wasn't interested in money,' I note.

Mycroft gives me a quick look. 'Someone searched the boot?'

'Yes.'

'That wasn't on the report.'

Walsh prods the rest of the wallet's contents. Gardener's driver's license and credit cards are there, a plain slip of paper with handwriting scrawled on it, two postal receipts, some credit-card receipts, plus a small photo of a woman my mum's age with a teenage girl beside her. Their smiling faces are squeezed together inside the frame – the photo is from a booth.

Walsh nods. 'That will be his sister, Margaret Sutcliffe. She lives in Melbourne – that's her and the niece, Natalie, I imagine.'

'Mrs Sutcliffe was the one who raised suspicions about the case?' Mycroft asks.

'Yes. She requested an Australian presence. Her concerns seem based around the idea that Gardener hadn't told her he was involved with Addington – or with anyone, for that matter.'

'But Irina Addington knew things about Gardener that only a girlfriend would know,' I point out.

Walsh shrugs. 'Her story seems solid. Don't like to theorise.'

I'm still looking at the photo. Margaret Sutcliffe and her daughter look happy. I like Gardener for having this photo in his wallet, but it saddens me too.

'He must have cared about them very much,' I say quietly. But if Gardener cared about his family enough to keep this photo with him, why didn't he tell them about his girlfriend?

Mycroft leans closer to examine the postal receipts. 'What about these? Does the writing on that one say *Natalie's birthday*?'

'Looks like it,' Walsh says.

'This one's for petrol.' I point without touching, as I don't have gloves on. 'Is that for groceries?'

'No.' Walsh shakes his head. 'Liberty is an upmarket gift shop in Soho.'

'Here, those dates match,' Mycroft says. 'The receipt from Liberty is dated the day of the postal receipt.'

'So he's bought his niece a birthday present and then posted it the same day,' I say.

'Show me the dates again?'

Mycroft takes out a little notebook, scrawls in the details of each receipt with a stub of pencil, then slips on another pair of latex gloves. He turns over the other ephemera in Gardener's wallet.

'Driver's license is nearly out of date. What's this?'

Walsh squints at the handwritten slip. 'I'm not sure. The Inspector will tell us, I imagine.'

'I . . . I know this.' I examine the waxy scrawl. 'It's a bookie's slip.'

'Come again?'

'From the races. Haven't you been to the races? Dad used to take us to the country trots in Ouyen . . . Look, *Eat Your Words* – that's the horse's name, and he's got odds at twenty to one. He's put on fifty for the win.'

'A day at the races.' Mycroft looks thoughtful.

'Yeah, he's had a flutter. We can check the form guide to see if he got lucky.' My throat sticks as soon as I say it. Gardener isn't going to get lucky ever again.

'It's the first I've heard that Gardener was a gambler.' Mycroft waves the slip, sets it down. 'But it's hardly a major criminal endeavor, is it, one bookie's slip?'

I glance again at the photo. Daniel Gardener was a bit like a satellite. He had an important academic job, a modestly wealthy expat lifestyle, a nice-looking – if slightly unhinged – girl-friend . . . But his family lived half a world away. Now he's dead, and his life has been reduced to this small pile of flotsam.

I look back to the body on the table. My own body feels heavy, tired. When I glance at the wall clock I'm shocked to see we've been here nearly two hours.

'I think I'd like to go to that pub now,' I say.

Walsh nods, looks at Mycroft. 'I can finish here.'

'Come on.' Mycroft gently takes my arm again. 'I'll pretend I'm eighteen and buy you a pint.'

CHAPTER ELEVEN

I don't feel like a pint at eleven-thirty in the morning, but Mycroft gets one, plus a packet of something called Pork Scratchings. He settles both glasses – mine with the Coke in it, and his with the beer – on the wooden table outside as he high-steps over to sit on the bench seat with me.

He spits out the packet of nibbles from between his clenched teeth. 'Sorry, this was all they had. Didn't think you'd want a full English breakfast.'

I take a Pork Scratching, chew it for about two seconds and spack it out into a serviette. 'God, that's bloody disgusting. It tastes like deep-fried lard covered in salt.'

'Sounds about right.' Mycroft helps himself to a handful with a grin.

We're sitting in a sunny spot, although that means it's still only about twenty degrees Celsius. Beyond the knitted fringe of the pub sign, dark clouds are massing to the west.

Mycroft tosses Pork Scratchings into his mouth and fishes his laptop out of his backpack. The document he opens is a spread-sheet of numbers and events.

'Here we go. I'm trying to put together dates and times to give us a timeline on the case.' Mycroft wipes his fingers on his T-shirt before pointing things out. 'There's the Friday when Gardener worked with the Folio. Then the Head of Rare Books at the Bodleian stored the Folio in a safe over the weekend. The safe was ransacked on the Sunday night. The police questioned all staff over the next two days.'

'And they already have a suspect for the theft in custody. But was Gardener ever under suspicion?'

'He had an alibi for the night of the theft. He was in London at a colleague's anniversary dinner.'

Bubbles go up my nose as I sip from my glass – the sugar is definitely helping. 'So Sunday night, Gardener's having dinner in London when the Folio's stolen, on Monday and Tuesday he's questioned, along with everyone else, and then he's back at work on . . . Wednesday?'

'Yeah, Gardener worked a half day. Then on Thursday after-noon, he contacted the Yard saying he had more information, so Inspector Gupta arranged for him to come in first thing on Friday morning. Then – well, you know the story.'

I know *one* story. I have a feeling that in Mycroft's version of the events surrounding Gardener's death, the mileage may vary.

'Why didn't the Inspector get Gardener in straight away, as soon as he called?'

'They had their Folio guy, Al-Said. He's been involved in a minor theft of material from the Bodleian before – tearing pages out of books, I think. He was in for questioning on the same

Thursday afternoon that Gardener called. I guess that's why the Inspector didn't take Gardener more seriously.'

'And Gardener was out shopping for his niece's birthday after work on the Wednesday, so maybe it was something fairly trivial, in any case.'

'Maybe.' Mycroft shrugs, but I'm not fooled.

'So Gupta believes that Gardener's death was completely unrelated to the Folio – and you don't agree.'

Mycroft takes a slug of his beer. 'Well, doesn't it just sound too coincidental to you? That Gardener tells police he has information about the Folio investigation, and then gets killed the next day?'

'But Mycroft, Irina Addington knew about Gardener's work, his relationship with his family . . . For god's sake, she knew he preferred boxers over briefs!'

'Can't fault his taste there,' Mycroft says quietly.

My cheeks go hot. I flick a finger at one of the salty Pork Scratchings, try to stay on track. 'She said it was all over a quarrel. Don't they even have a law for stuff like this in France?'

'*Crime passionnel*, yes.' Mycroft doesn't look convinced. 'So you're saying Gardener was just unlucky enough to get mixed up with someone who's a bit out of their gourd?'

'Does Addington have a history of that?'

Mycroft taps his laptop screen. 'Be impossible to access her mental health records anyway, but that's the thing – there's not much else I can find out either. No job history, no social media.'

'Nothing?'

'Zero. Which is weird, yeah? But more than that, it's the *timing* that's weird. He contacts the police, and then – oops, his girlfriend kills him.'

146

Uneasiness stirs in my stomach. Something about this just doesn't add up. My thoughts double back to the scene of the crash, the car boot, a Folio worth millions, Irina Addington . . .

I remember the footage of her, from the tablet. 'She looked scared. Nervous. In the interview, I mean.'

Mycroft shrugs again. 'People get nervous when they've been arrested.'

I don't say *You should know*. I think about Addington's kohl-smudged eyes and bitten nails. 'Sure. But she wasn't overwrought. Not grief-stricken, like I thought she'd be.'

Mycroft grimaces, shakes his head. 'Inconclusive. What's really bugging me is that the details of Addington's confession and the scene of the crash don't quite line up.'

'She could have been in shock, got the details confused . . .' I stop when I see Mycroft's raised eyebrows. 'Okay, fine. But why would Irina Addington confess to a crime she didn't commit?'

'Hard to say without questioning her.'

'Which we'll never get to do . . .'

'Maybe she owes someone.'

'That's a hell of a speculation.'

Mycroft rakes a hand through his hair. 'This whole bloody business is speculation. Inductive reasoning, Watts – taking a number of small clues and working out the larger picture. It's very different from what the police are doing, which is *deductive* – casting a broad net and then trying to narrow down the field.'

'Right.' I try another tack. 'What about Gardener's sister? She doesn't even believe Irina was Gardener's girlfriend.'

'Exactly. Margaret Sutcliffe claims that her brother had a serious relationship, but it ended badly last year and he'd sworn off dating.' He frowns at the laptop. 'That's the only part that sticks in my throat. How would she know? She lives on the other side of the world.'

'Now you're playing devil's advocate.'

Mycroft lets his head drop back, exhales deeply, looks forward again. 'Christ, I don't know. I guess if they were that close . . . But it still seems pretty insubstantial. I mean, would *you* know if your brother was seeing somebody?'

A slice of memory sears through me: Mike's radiant face, his hair sticking up like the ruffled feathers of a bird. 'Yes. Yes, I would know.'

I sip my Coke, rub at my temple where this morning's headache lingers. This is not going the way I'd expected. I thought I'd be talking Mycroft off a theoretical ledge, but his ideas about the investigation are all sound, considered. Except for one thing – I know the force that's driving him, stewing beneath the surface of his mind. How much of his reasoning about the case is biased because of it?

'So if it wasn't an accident,' I say, 'and if it wasn't Addington who killed him – who *did* kill Gardener?'

'I'd like to know that.' Mycroft's lips are thin as he stares at the screen. 'I'd like to know that very much.'

I've hit a sore spot. Sometimes, with Mycroft, I feel as if it's the *only* spot. 'You're thinking it's the same mob, aren't you? The people who killed your parents.'

Mycroft nods. 'The MO is almost identical.'

'The circumstances . . .' I hesitate. I haven't broached this subject with him before. Now I'm talking about it here, outside a pub. I lower my voice. 'The circumstances of Gardener's death are different from what happened to you and your parents, yeah?'

'Yeah. They're a bit different.' Mycroft chews on his bottom lip.

He lets out a breath, looks away. 'The basic scenario is the same. A motorcyclist comes alongside a moving vehicle, and shoots at or into the car. One minute we were driving along the A1, and the next minute there was this . . . boom, and then . . . My dad had been shot, so he lost control of the car. We . . . we went straight into a road pylon, so my mum's injuries were . . .'

He stops. His breathing is uneven and he's blinking away into the far distance. I put my hand on his, squeeze his fingers. He squeezes back, extricates himself to fish around for a cigarette in his pocket.

'Shit, I'm still no good at talking about this.' His hand trembles as he puts the cigarette to his lips.

I keep my eyes on him. 'It's okay. Apart from last night, that's the most you've ever told me.'

'Is it?' He flicks his lighter and the flame glows on his face. 'Jesus. All right, so . . . the circumstances with Gardener were a bit different. They chose a quieter location. They didn't use a larger caliber weapon, just the birdshot.'

A mental image of Gardener's body, back in the morgue, floats to the surface of my mind. I blink to refocus. 'You're saying . . . they've refined their methods?'

'Yes, of course. They've done it this way before. My parents were never the only ones.' Mycroft takes a deep drag of his cigarette, brings up another folder. 'Here – I've chased up leads on carjacking cases in the news. There've been three, possibly four carjackings over the past seven years that stand out from all the others, because they each look more like a deliberate homicide than an attempt to snatch a car.'

He taps another file and opens a series of small windows, each with a headline and some bullet-points on the side.

'Okay, this one – Verner Plebisch, forty-one years old, run off the road in Maida Vale. Plebisch was a museum administrator. Then here, a journalist, shot in the face through her car window in Cambridge. Then there's another one, from two years ago . . .' Something – my posture, maybe, or how I've gone quiet – makes him look over. His voice turns soft. 'You think I'm crazy, don't you?'

I wet my lips. 'Mycroft, I don't think you're crazy. I think this case is really personal to you, and that might be affecting your judgment about—'

'Jesus, now you sound like a shrink.' He straightens abruptly, glances away. The lines on his forehead are tight. 'I don't know why I have to convince you of all this. You *know* the police don't always get it right.'

'Mycroft, listen to me.' I grab for his hand. 'I *believe* you, okay? I'm on your side. What you're saying makes sense – there's a lot of questions about the case that the police don't seem to have any answers for. But you're talking about changing the whole line of Gupta's investigation.'

'*Yes.*'

'Then show Gupta the evidence – the timing of the crash, the birdshot from the car, the boot search . . . Surely he'll be convinced by the difference between Addington's testimony and the actual details of the crime scene. But I don't think trying to correlate Gardener's murder with your parents' case will work. You don't know who the killers are, you need more information on motive—'

'I *know*.' Mycroft drops his head, rubbing his eyes through his closed lids. 'You're right. I know you're right. There's nothing concrete linking the two cases. I don't have any idea why my parents were killed. And Gardener has an alibi for the Folio theft, plus they've already got Al-Said in custody for that.'

There's a thinness in him; the strain of all this is showing. Mycroft's trying so hard to make a connection between Gardener's case and his parents' murder . . . I want to believe it too, that he hasn't come all the way to England – all the way back into his nightmares – for nothing.

But I have to be impartial. I came to England to support Mycroft – that doesn't mean I have to follow him blindly. The differences between the scene in High Wycombe and the witness testimony are only subtle – the minor caliber of a weapon, the barest angle of a shot, a trace of rubber on the road. Gupta may be right after all. Mycroft's ideas seem persuasive, but so does a signed confession.

Then I look at the dejected set of his shoulders, remember his face from last night, outside the ruin of his old house. *Priorities* – the case isn't the only thing that's important here.

'Hey, don't stress out.' I squeeze his arm gently. 'We'll keep digging. The signed-and-sealed testimony from Addington, the book thief with form . . . It all seems a bit easy.'

Mycroft stares at me. 'I thought you believed that sometimes the easy answers are the right ones?'

'I don't know if I hold to that anymore.'

'Do you agree with me, that Gardener was killed because of the Folio?'

'I don't know.' I see his expression. 'Hey, I'm trying to be objective here – I just don't know. But something's definitely not right about Addington. And someone searched the boot of Gardener's car – they did that for a reason. And the Folio is special. This isn't just some book we're talking about. This is *six million pounds* worth of book.'

'So are we putting together a theory?'

I sip from my glass to wet my dry throat. 'It's like that thing you said once – we don't have enough facts yet to form a theory. We just have to look harder.'

'Then I guess that's what we do.' Mycroft gives me a tired grin. 'Can I say, at this point, that I'd be lost without my Boswell?'

'Are you seriously quoting Conan Doyle at me?'

'Never.' He shakes the grin away, looking back at his laptop. 'Anyway, there's still a lot of work to do to put it all together.'

I squint at the screen, wondering what might connect all the car crashes apart from modus operandi.

'So whoever the perpetrators are, they have a history of making accidents happen. Murders that look like carjackings.' Then I notice the dates on all the files – last year, two years ago, two years before that . . . 'You've been tracking this for a while, haven't you?'

'You got me.' Mycroft smiles, barely. He takes a pull from his beer with his cigarette hand, taps the screen with the other. 'This is just the first opportunity I've had to follow it up on the ground. But stuff like this, snagged from newsfeeds and old reports, is hardly conclusive. What I'd really like to do is get every detail of this Gardener case and my parents' case and input it into HOLMES. Do a search, see if we can't find a pattern of MVAs in the last seven years that resemble each other.'

'Sorry, you've lost me.'

'HOLMES is the British online police database. If you enter all the details of a specific case, it can give you historical matches that show a similar pattern. An MVA is a motor vehicle accident, so you would enter location, circumstances of the accident, number and gender of car occupants, that sort of thing.'

'But wouldn't you just get a long list of every UK carjacking in the last seven years?'

'Not if you were very specific. Check for cars that were written off in the resulting crash, or cars that were shot at.'

'But most carjackings involve firearms, don't they?'

'MVAs in which all the occupants died, then.'

'That would rule out your parents' case,' I say. 'You survived.'

The look on his face is almost surprised. He blinks at me from somewhere deep in his mental bubble.

'Yeah,' he says. 'Yeah, I guess.'

But in that second, in his face, I see the whole world. I finally understand something crucial.

James Mycroft did die in that car crash seven years ago. Seeing what he saw, experiencing all that pain, that ten-year-old boy passed away. The person who returned was not the same. He was changed so completely, so physically and mentally transformed, it was as though a whole different individual was born. A different boy, living in a different place, with a guardian and no parents, a boy with no past and only one name . . .

All the blood rushes out of my cheeks as that name falls off my lips. 'Mycroft . . .'

'But I'd love to get my hands on that database,' he goes on. His thumbnail makes little half-moons on his bottom lip. 'If I had something more concrete about Gardener's murderers to show Gupta, I might be able to change his mind.'

'Change whose mind about what?' Professor Walsh says as he comes over to our table carrying his briefcase. His tie is askew and he smells like antiseptic handwash.

'Oh, nothing.' Mycroft glances up. 'Just an idea about Gardener's death.'

'Well, Inspector Gupta seems convinced that the case is all but wrapped up.' Walsh perches on the opposite seat, waving away

Mycroft's smoke. 'Any alternative you put forward would need to be made of gold.'

Mycroft drops his cigarette butt under his heel, squints at Walsh. 'We're checking out the house, aren't we?'

Walsh consults his watch. 'In about two hours. We'll be driving back to Lane's End with the Inspector. I've asked for a SOC officer to walk us through as well.'

'Great,' I say. 'So we might find a link, or something—'

'Yes, but there's no "we", I'm afraid,' Walsh says. 'Mycroft and I will be going, but I can't bring you with us.'

I balk. 'But I went to the autopsy. Why can't I—'

'Standing in the Evidence Room with a pretend clipboard is a bit different to attending a crime scene. Justifying your presence to Scotland Yard officers is a bit out of my jurisdiction, I'm sorry.'

'That's . . .' I'm about to say *not fair*, until I realize it actually is very fair, and Walsh has put himself out on a limb for me once already today. 'Fine. I'll just . . . have the afternoon off. Go out with Alicia or something.'

Walsh nods approvingly.

'Mycroft can contact you later if we find anything of note.' He stands up to head towards the pub doors, looks back. 'You did very well this morning, Rachel.'

'Thank you,' I say impulsively. 'For letting me come.'

'No, I'm glad you were there,' Walsh says. 'Now, a nice packet of Pork Scratchings might be in order, I think.'

He strides into the pub. Mycroft bends to retrieve his backpack and slide his laptop away.

'I'm glad you were there too.' His head angles as he zips the bag up, his hair twining at his neck. He stands, holds out a hand to help me to my feet. 'So you're feeling all right now?'

'Mm. A bit better.'

'I don't suppose you want to kiss me again?'

I give him the eyebrow. 'After you've eaten that delicious handful of fried lard? You'd want to wash your mouth out first.'

Without a pause, he lifts his pint glass to his lips. It takes about four big gulps to drain the whole, prodigious lot.

When he's done, he bangs the glass down on the table and grins at me. 'Come on. Let's go back to the hostel.'

―――――

Walsh drops us off outside the Empire Star before driving off crazily into the traffic in the direction of his own hotel. Mycroft walks me up to my floor, grabs me before I can turn the knob on room seven. My hands bunch in his jacket collar as we kiss.

I tear my lips away from his. 'Is this what it's always like, after an autopsy?'

Mycroft races his fingers up my arm, touches my hair. He smells like beer, which I don't find unappealing. 'Do you remember that night about five weeks ago? I came over to your place after work, and then you walked me home . . .'

'Yeah, I remember.'

He'd been frantic then, pushing me up against the wall of his house beside the back door. Sliding his hand up beneath my T-shirt, down the waistband of my jeans . . . I'd had to shove him away, because I was getting so turned on I couldn't see properly and I'd said five minutes max to Dad. I knew if I didn't get back home in a hurry there'd be hell to pay.

'That was the night of your first autopsy with Walsh, wasn't it?' I say. 'I thought you were just happy he'd agreed to let you assist.'

Mycroft grins, shakes his head and looks away. 'Is it fucked up that I'm so hot for you after I've seen a body cut open?'

'No.' I feel my cheeks warm. 'Before, I would have said yes. But after today, I think I get it.'

'Rachel . . .' He takes my hand. The body heat between us is intoxicating and Mycroft's voice is sinuous. 'Come back to my room. Right now. There's hours before I have to go out again . . .'

He looks at me with this dangerous intensity, his eyes indigo-dark. One of his hands trickles down my back, while his other thumb kneads my palm. My hips ache with wanting him.

'Please,' he says. 'Rachel, come. No curfews, no supervision, no . . .'

I swallow hard. 'No strings attached?'

Mycroft purses his lips. 'You know it isn't like that.'

Pulling my hand free takes so much willpower it's exhausting, but I do it. I steady my palms on his chest. 'No, Mycroft. I don't know. I don't know what you want, and I don't think you do either.'

His gaze is magnetic as he reaches out to tug on the waistband of my jeans. 'I know what I want.'

Jesus Christ, this is so difficult. I close my eyes and lean away. 'Look, I didn't come to London for a roll in the hay.'

'Then why did you come?'

It's enough of a wallop to clear my head.

'Mycroft, for someone so intelligent, you can be a bloody moron sometimes. I came because you're my friend. And I knew you were coming back to all this *shit*.' I wave a hand in the general direction of London. 'I wanted to be here, if you needed me.'

He blinks at me, his forehead wrinkled up.

'Sometimes I just need *this*,' he says, tugging my waist again.

'Sure, I get that.' God, do I get that. I put my hands on his arms, my voice gentle. 'But James, you've got all this other stuff rolling around in your head. Are you even sure how you feel? Because . . . I don't think you are. I'm not even sure myself.'

He looks so torn then I almost relent. And I can barely resist the pull of him, the way gravity seems to want us to bend together, lean against each other. I force myself to let my hands drop, step out of his circle of warmth.

'Let me know what you find out this afternoon with Walsh.' My voice is muddy with everything I can't say.

———

Alicia is lying on her bed, reading. She's wearing glasses, red-framed rectangles that make her look like a funky owl.

She pulls them off as I stumble in, drop my satchel on the floor. 'Hey. How was it?'

'Hey.' I try to keep my shit together, but I feel so awful it's impossible. I sit across from her on the edge of my bed.

'Oh, no.' Alicia sits up. 'Are you okay? Was the autopsy—'

'No, no.' My nose is already starting to clog. 'The autopsy was fine. I mean, if you can call an autopsy fine.'

'So what happened?'

'Shit.' I put my head in my hands, which is where it wants to be. 'I think I just did something really . . .'

'Rachel—'

'I just turned Mycroft down.' I gulp thickly. 'He was just . . . And I just . . . wasn't sure.'

I close my eyes. The headache that announced itself this morning is screeching for attention again.

'Oh, Rachel.' Alicia scoots to the edge of her own bed and squeezes my shoulder. 'It's okay. You knew this would be tough.'

'*Yes*, but I didn't know . . .' I clutch my forehead. 'God, this is so *hard*!'

Alicia hugs me. I put my forehead on her shoulder. Rebel tears leak out of me. It doesn't seem fair to be doing this to her when she's already helped me so much. I lift my head, wipe a wet blot-mark onto my sleeve.

'Forget it. I'll be fine. Anyway, what are you doing here?' I look at Alicia's abandoned e-reader. 'I thought you'd be out on the town.'

'Well, I did go out for brunch. And I've been in touch with the people I stayed with last time I was here. But I'm still feeling the jet lag – I came back for a nap. So you've probably caught me at a good time.'

She does look weary, red around the eyes. I can't imagine I look any better. 'What about your nap?'

'Yeah, I think if I sleep now I'll just wake up at three a.m.' She rakes back her dark hair. 'I've got a better idea. Let's go out.'

'Where do you wanna go?'

'Tell you on the way. Or are you too tired?'

'Nah. I'm a bit frazzled, but I think I'm too stressed to be tired.'

'Okay, then. Come on.'

She grabs her blue velvet jacket, and I sling on my satchel again. I wish I had another dose of that *Brain Wipe* stuff to blot out the memory of what just happened between me and Mycroft. We have to tramp down past his door to leave the hostel. I'm very aware of the fact that he's probably in his room now, having a cold shower.

But the air is fresh enough to knock some sense into me as we walk to Victoria Station and take the stairs to the Underground. Waves of people swell on the platform right around lunch hour. A disembodied female voice tells us to change at Oxford Circus, and *Please mind the gap between the train and the platform.*

Alicia stands with me in a corner of the carriage, her voice quiet. 'So have you got anything more on the case?'

I puff out air. 'Um, maybe. The police are still questioning that guy who they think stole the Folio. But Gardener was definitely murdered. Mycroft and Professor Walsh found traces of the shot that forced him off the road. There's a woman in custody at Scotland Yard who's confessed – her testimony makes it sound like manslaughter, and she's very persuasive, but something doesn't feel right. Mycroft thinks she could be a fall guy for a bigger player, someone connected to his parents' deaths.'

'What do you mean?'

'Like they were both contract killings.' I see her face. 'Look, I know how it sounds – like Mycroft's going out of his way to make a connection between his parents' case and Gardener's. I mean, his parents were *academics*, for god's sake, there's no reason to think they were mixed up in anything criminal. But I think Mycroft might be onto something and I'm starting to believe that the carjackers and the Folio thieves are linked somehow.'

'So . . . maybe the suspect for the theft is the wrong man. Maybe Gardener helped the thieves steal the Folio, then they killed him so he wouldn't dob them in to the police.'

I grimace. 'Except Gardener had an alibi for the night of the theft . . . But maybe he was involved in some other way. The police think Gardener's crash was a crime of passion thing, that he got involved with this woman who was a bit of a nutter. But so many things still don't make sense. Like Gardener's car – it looks as if someone searched it. Well, the boot, at least.'

Alicia nudges me. 'So what were they looking for?'

'I don't know.'

Lights flicker in the low-ceilinged carriage as we go through a tunnel interchange. A little way down, a group of West Indian schoolgirls in gray pleated skirts laugh and toss their braided hair.

Alicia gets an absent expression. 'Maybe the carjackers were looking for the Folio.'

I stare at her. 'The Folio was stolen from the library safe more than a week ago. Whoever stole it must have delivered it already.'

'Delivered it to who?'

'If we knew that . . .' I've been chewing my thumbnail. I force myself to stop. 'Okay, let's *assume* Gardener was involved in the theft, that he had the Folio. Why would the carjackers, thieves – let's just cut the shit and call them "the perpetrators" – why would they kill him?'

'Maybe it was an accident. Maybe they arranged the carjacking to scare him, and there was a bit of overkill. Excuse the pun.'

I shake my head. 'I don't think so. The perpetrators set up the carjacking very carefully – time of day, route, caliber of weapon. And if it's the people Mycroft thinks, then they've done this before. They're professionals. They never would've made a mistake like that. If Gardener had the Folio, he would have had some value. How would they find the Folio if he was dead?'

'I don't know.' Alicia shrugs. 'Maybe they were more scared of Gardener going to the police. Maybe they decided to cut their losses.'

'It's possible.'

'And maybe this girlfriend of Gardener's is tied up in it somehow . . .'

I rub my eyebrows. 'God, I don't know. This is complicated.'

'And a man is dead because of it. This must be one helluva book.'

160

'It is.' I've seen pictures of the Folio. I had a visceral reaction to them, like something inside me recognized the importance of this one book, by the most amazing author who's ever existed. I remember that feeling now. 'It's right up there with the Bible and the first dictionary. Without the Folio, we wouldn't have *Macbeth*, or *Midsummer Night's Dream*, or *Romeo and Juliet* . . .'

The train slows to a stop. Alicia pulls my arm and we jump off to ride the escalators up. We stand dutifully on the right – in Melbourne, it's on the left – as health-conscious pedestrians climb these steps that grind slowly towards the surface of the city. Panto stars mug at us from flickering LCD screens along the walls. A busking saxophonist's version of a Lorde song makes melancholy echoes up the tunnel.

'So what was the autopsy like?' Alicia asks.

'It was sort of . . .' My eyes make this weird widening blink as I try to condense everything I saw just a few hours ago. '. . . overwhelming. I don't know if I can describe it. I mean, it's a dead body, but there's something so human in it, in all of it. I'd try to explain, but it'd probably just sound gory.'

'Was Mycroft okay?'

'He had a rough start, but he was okay.'

Alicia presses her thumb into the black rubber of escalator handrail. 'Rachel, you know why he's so obsessed with forensics, don't you?'

'Because of his parents?'

She nods, holds my eyes. 'Because the dead can't get their own justice.'

We've exited onto the street. I squint against the sun as an *Evening Standard* newspaper van whizzes by. There's a Pizza Express place across the street, bikes parked on the corner.

A jogger flashes past us – she looks as if she's fleeing in terror, not running for pleasure.

Alicia scans the streetscape, tugs on my hand. 'Here. Just down this way.'

I glance around, trying to get my bearings. 'Um, yeah. Still don't know where we are.'

'You don't recognize the address?' Alicia grins. 'I thought it might be appropriate.'

'What might be appropriate?'

But we've reached a little tenement shop with green gables and ironwork fencing around the front. Fake gas lamps, and a guy dressed as a nineteenth-century police officer, guard the entrance to a black-painted door. Even if I failed to see the discreet *221B Baker St* above the door, I couldn't miss the big honking green-and-black sign that says *The Sherlock Holmes Museum*.

My jaw drops. 'You've *got* to be kidding me.'

'Thought it might provide some perspective,' Alicia says. She pulls my hand, biting her lip over a smile. 'Come on, Rachel. Don't pike out on me now.'

We have to go into the gift shop to buy a museum ticket. The shop's red-carpeted and homely, filled to bursting with items such as reproduction Victorian calabash pipes, and plaster busts of the great detective, and Big Ben pencil sharpeners. After the autopsy, it's all a bit disorienting. Six pounds later we're wandering out of the shop to enter the reproduction of Sherlock's house.

Once I adjust, it's amazing – a bit fruity and bizarre, but amazing. They've sourced everything perfectly, from the dark-green wallpaper and teak-painted lintels to the antique furniture and fittings. There's a violin standing on an occasional table in the cramped living room, a Persian slipper stuffed with tobacco on the mantelpiece. You can see the indentations in the cushions of the two wing-backed chairs by the fire.

Glass cases upstairs bulge with paraphernalia and Sherlock books, and the waxworks – especially Moriarty – are so lifelike and severe I get the willies. Alicia and I scurry back to Sherlock's bedroom to look for the box where he kept his cocaine.

'They were odd bods, the Victorians, weren't they?' I glance around, thinking the man himself would be appalled at how we're casually inspecting his private space. 'They were really into fussy things like turned table-legs and peacock feathers and filigree.'

'Yeah.' Alicia examines the stuff by the window near the bed. 'And it was okay back then for a guy to have lace doilies on his nightstand.'

'Did you see the book of letters sent to Holmes? From all over the world. There was one from a guy in Canada who wanted help finding his wife.' I shake my head. 'All this dedication, for a man who never really existed.'

'But he did exist. In here.' Alicia taps her head, then a spot over her heart. 'He was as much of an enigma as a real person.'

'Real people are more complicated.' Wax dribbles off the lit candle in its holder on the walnut dresser. I frown and pick at the delicate white waterfall.

Alicia looks at me through the mirror on the dresser. 'Sherlock was a complicated character. He repressed all his earthier passions in the service of intellect. And he never married.'

'He never wanted to feel.'

Alicia nods. 'Some writers have even implied it was a family tragedy in his past that made Sherlock the way he was.'

The conversation has turned back inexorably to a topic I've been trying to avoid.

'But . . . Mycroft has earthier passions. At least, he seemed to have them this morning.'

Alicia gazes at neighboring chimneypots out the window. 'Yeah, but is he really feeling them? Or is he just using them as a way to distract himself from all that grief?'

I tug at one of the brass handles on the dresser. 'Maybe it doesn't matter. Maybe it's just . . . what he needs to get by right now.'

'I don't know, Rachel. Does it matter to you?' Alicia's look, in the mirror, is hard, searching. 'Is that what you want your relationship with Mycroft to be like – where he just pushes on, trying to outrun his emotions all the time, and then when he can't take it anymore he comes to you for a bit of relief? Because I got the impression you were hoping for something more honest than that.'

I screw up my hot eyes. 'I don't know. God, I don't know . . .'

Alicia steps over until she's right beside me. She squeezes my shoulder. 'Rachel, I think you *do* know. I think that's why you turned him down.'

'So how do I get through to him?'

'You don't. You can't. You have to wait for Mycroft to let you in.'

My voice cracks a bit. 'But what if that never happens?'

'Then that will be sad,' Alicia says. 'For you, because it will hurt like crazy. But for him it will be worse, because if you can never trust anyone enough to let them in, you can never love. I wouldn't wish that on anybody.'

I have to turn away then, before I get more upset. I will *not* cry standing here, in the dust-motes around Sherlock Holmes's brass bed, of all places. 'Maybe Mycroft doesn't have the capacity for love.'

Alicia shakes her head. 'Everyone has the capacity for love, Rachel. Mycroft loved his parents. He's experienced love before. We just have to wait and see if he can open up to it again.'

She gives me a tissue, which I'm pathetic enough to need. I tidy myself up enough to leave the museum and follow Alicia back into the gift shop. She buys a keyring for her brother, shoves something else into my hands.

'Here you go. For keeping the flame alive.' She winks at me.

It's a box of London Town matches. There's a picture of Holmes with his pipe, and the slogan *Will Flame In Wind Or Rain* printed onto the front.

I slip the box into my jeans pocket and wonder if the matches will light in a deluge, considering the mess I'm in now.

I buy a slim copy of *The Memoirs of Sherlock Holmes* by Sir Arthur Conan Doyle before I leave the museum. At least now I've got something to read on the plane trip home.

'Don't forget,' Alicia says, grinning at me, 'Sherlock's closest human relationship was with Watson.'

'Yeah. Wonderful. If only I was an ex-British-army medical officer with a gimpy leg and a mustache, I'd be in with a shot.' I sigh and look around. 'So where to now?'

Alicia lifts her chin towards Baker Street Station, back the way we've come. 'Well, I've arranged to go and visit my friends in Camden. You should come, Rachel. It'll be super-casual – just a takeaway dinner and a quiet night.'

'Thanks, but I'll be okay.' I fumble for a plan. 'I'll just . . . go to the market again. Or maybe to the Tower of London or something.'

As we wander towards the station, I pull out my new book and look at the picture of Conan Doyle on the back. The black-and-white photo makes him look ordinary. He's got an extremely impressive tash, but he's a bit chubby and, above all, normal.

But Conan Doyle was a doctor with an enquiring mind. This was the man who created puzzles for the world's greatest detective, who followed all the threads through to the end . . .

'Actually, I've got a better idea.' I'm amazed this brainwave didn't come earlier. But I wasn't really thinking straight earlier. 'Mycroft and Walsh are off looking at Gardener's house. So I can just go to the next most useful place. The site of the theft.'

'That's in Oxford,' Alicia points out.

'Is that far?'

'Well, you would've driven halfway yesterday.' Her gray eyes light up. 'You could get the bus. The X90 to Oxford goes from Baker Street.'

I check my phone. 'It's one-thirty now. Will it all still be open when I get there?'

'I think so. You should be there before four. Come on, I'll show you the way.'

CHAPTER TWELVE

Relaxing in the bus is a relief. The scenery out the window has lost its urban veneer: now it fits comfortably with my inner pictures of 'England'. England is green, and yes, there are stiles, and sagging thatched farmhouses, and large spreading oaks. Apart from the occasional power line or blue A40 sign on the road shoulder, it's an old-fashioned landscape. All those childhood books of Mum's – hedgehog washerwomen, and the Famous Five banging around the countryside, dog in tow – must have rubbed off on me.

The bleat from my phone jars me back to the present.

'Hey, it's me.' Mycroft's voice sounds warm on the phone, not blunt and cutting as I'd expected.

'Hey.' I force my brain to focus. 'So did you find anything useful?'

'Yes and no. I'm still in Lane's End with Walsh and Gupta. Gardener's house has been turned over.'

I sit up straighter. 'What – someone had been searching for something?'

'Looks like it.'

Out the window, a slate-roofed cottage surrounded by a box hedge whips past.

'Mycroft, it's the same as the car. The boot search. Whoever these people are, they're looking for something.'

'The Folio? But Gupta said Gardener's alibi was solid – lots of people saw him in London on the night of the theft. And if Gardener *did* have the Folio, but people are still searching for it, then where is it now?'

'I don't know,' I say. 'I was trying to nut it out with Alicia. It doesn't make sense.'

'Well, there was one thing that made sense. Remember the bookie's slip, from Gardener's effects? We've found more. Like, a lot of them.'

'So he *was* a gambler.'

'Yep. And Gupta's found out that Gardener's bank statements had hit a recent low. We're talking serious numbers, Rachel.'

'How serious?'

'About three hundred thousand pounds.'

'Shit.' I glance around, lower my voice. 'That's a fair whack with the bookies.'

'Yeah. If Gardener was in debt to some heavy people, it might explain the carjacking. Maybe they tried to scare him into paying up, and it all went pear-shaped.'

'But it also goes to motive for the theft. He might have stolen the Folio to pay off his debts.'

'You try explaining that to Gupta. I've already given it a shot.' Mycroft's voice sounds bitter. 'Gupta's still convinced that there's no connection between Gardener's death and the Folio theft. Now he's hung up on his theory that this Addington woman might link to the gambling debt. He's saying she probably searched Gardener's house looking for the money he owed. I think he'd just like to feel that some part of the case is solvable – considering that their lead on the Folio theft has dried up.'

'What – Al-Said?'

'Farrell Al-Said is fifty-three years old, and has to carry an oxygen canister with him everywhere. It's kind of funny, because that's how he got the pages he stole out of the Library last year – he hid them in his oxygen cart. But the situation with the Folio is completely different. There's no way Al-Said could have gotten to the safe at night and then scarpered before the guard investigated the alarm. Basically, Al-Said's too infirm to have committed the theft. The police cleared him an hour ago.'

'And Gupta won't consider the idea that Gardener might have been involved in the theft?'

'Hah.' I hear the rasp as Mycroft rubs at his stubbled cheek: I can imagine his glowering expression. 'I mean, Gupta's a nice guy, but he's worse than Pickup. It's like talking to a brick wall – a really literal, single-minded, unimaginative wall. Honestly, I'm pulling my hair out here . . .'

'Mycroft, I'm sorry.' I don't know what else to say. The frustration I'm feeling about the case can't be a patch on how Mycroft feels.

Mycroft has gone quiet, and somehow the tone of his silence has changed. His breathing echoes on the line. In my mind's eye I see him chewing his lip, rolling a cigarette out from behind his ear. I should say something, but I'm too scared to start.

'Rachel,' Mycroft says softly, 'can we talk?'

An electric pulse surges through me but I squash it. Maybe it's not the good type of talk he's referring to. Maybe it's the bad kind. The *This is too complicated, and I don't think we should see each other anymore* kind. And I don't want to hear it, not right now, not in the bus, where everyone will see me if I start bawling.

'Not on the phone,' I say. 'When I get back.'

'Get back from where? Where are you going?'

'To Oxford, on the bus. To see the site of the theft.'

'God, we'll pass each other on the road.'

My lips turn up. 'Providing Professor Walsh drives in a straight line.'

'There's no guarantee of that,' Mycroft says glumly.

Out the window, newly planted paddocks whiz away to somewhere behind me. I uncurl my stiff fingers – I've been throttling the edge of my seat. 'Look, I'll see you when I get back to the Empire Star, okay? Alicia's going out to dinner, but I should be home by seven. I'll text you.'

'Okay. Great.' He pauses. 'Rachel, I'm . . .'

'Save it,' I say hurriedly. 'Just . . . wait for me. I'll see you tonight.'

I click off before I say something else, something less neutral. My seat in the bus is well-padded, but I wriggle around restlessly.

Alicia's words at the Sherlock Holmes museum come back to me: *Everybody has the capacity for love.* I know Mycroft feels emotions. He's not a robot. But it's as if all his emotional energy is focused on one thing – the deaths of his parents . . .

God, I can't think about this anymore. I wish I was home. I miss the normalcy of my family, even Mum and Dad's nagging. I miss Mike, like I'd miss a phantom limb. And the English countryside out the window is so different, so green – I miss dust, and red dirt, and kangaroo grass. Even Melbourne street-life seems appealing, at this distance.

I must nod off for a while, because the next things I see out the window are these incredible sandstone-castle structures: university buildings. The bus is pulling into a car park surrounded by more modest red-brick tenements.

I stretch in my seat, hear my stomach growling – my first priority, when I step off the bus and into Gloucester Green, is food. I scoff down orange juice and a takeaway sandwich from a Caffé Nero as I walk through the square, binning the rubbish near a sign reminding everyone that *Feeding the Pigeons Is Strictly Prohibited*. It's after three – I have no idea what time this library shuts down, but I've got to be cutting it fine by now.

I tuck my hands into my pockets as I walk. Oxford is as small and perfect as a crystal snow-globe, with cobblestones and rain-marked turrets and stained-glass windows. The whole place is a squeezed-tight medieval town, and has a distinct Diagon Alley feel to it. There are bikes absolutely everywhere, which makes sense given the cramped streets and the student population.

I follow the signs towards Radcliffe Square, thinking about university. This is a place of higher learning. I could be riding my bike around with other students like this next year. Provided I pass my exams, of course.

After rounding a spiked iron fence, festooned with bikes, I arrive at a massive door. Old wood with iron rivets, like the entrance to a dungeon or a king's castle. I'm almost expecting a moat and a fire-breathing dragon, but this is the Bodleian. A towering statue of Thomas Radcliffe stands guard at the entrance. It's a fair bit more impressive than the glass sliding doors and tatty terracotta brick of the Coburg public library.

The place looks ready to close up. A few hardy tourists mill about, bent on wringing every last drop of excitement from their visit to the world's oldest university institution.

'Hello, are you a student?' It's an older man in a tour-guide uniform. He looks tired – maybe the last group wore him out.

I don't want to go on a full tour, I just want to see the parts where Gardener worked. The only way to do that will be to lie.

I don't feel good about it, and it makes me stammer. 'Um, no. Sorry, I know it's very late . . .'

'That's all right. We're open until five, so you've still got time. How can I help you?'

'Actually, I came to . . .' It hits me suddenly, the easiest way to do this. 'I came to see where my uncle worked. He was a conservator here.'

The man blinks in confusion. 'Your uncle worked here? Do you know in which division?'

'In Rare Books. He was Australian. I mean, I've just flown from Australia, because . . .' Maybe my fumbles will make all this seem more natural. 'He died. My uncle. So I thought I'd like to come and see the place where he worked.'

My face must reflect some of my embarrassment. I always feel bad lying to people, especially sweet elderly blokes who've had a long day.

'Oh dear. Goodness.' The man gives me a concerned look. 'What was your uncle's name?'

'Daniel Gardener.' I shift my feet. 'I'm Natalie Sutcliffe.'

———

It could work. I look about the same age and build as Natalie, the girl from the photo in the dead man's wallet. She has darker hair than mine, fuller lips, olive skin.

I just hope the real Natalie has never visited her uncle, because if someone knows her from a previous visit, I'll be stuffed. If someone asks to see the name on my passport, I'll be stuffed. Basically if I'm asked to verify my identity, I'll be stuffed.

This is dumb, I realize. But it's too late, I'm committed now. A trickle of sweat rolls down my back as the man frowns.

'Well, this is the main gate for the Library, but if your uncle was in Rare Books then he would have been in the New Library building. Why don't I make a phone call and check?'

'Thank you, that would be great.'

The man moves away to use his phone. I scuff the cobblestones in the courtyard with my boots. Wonder if Mycroft appreciates the stupid things I do on his account. I don't have time to dwell on it, because the man comes back with a generous smile.

'Right, sorry. I was just checking in with the main office. Your uncle was in Special Collections in the other building. Why don't we walk through from here?'

He leads me through a flagged archway tunnel, and we emerge near another impressive building. There are so many I'm losing track.

'This place is amazing,' I say. At least that's not a lie.

'It is, isn't it?' The man looks about fondly. 'I feel very privileged to be working here. And I love books, so working in a library is a bit like a dream.'

I decide I like this man, so I feel extra guilty for fibbing. But it's working. He takes me past a large building and up some weathered stone steps into an admin area. The walls are cheese-cake-thick, white-washed. The internal staircase is dark wood and has a strong scent, some sort of lemony wood polish.

'Just up here.' The man extends a hand towards the stairs. 'The lift is rather old and slow. Hope you don't mind the walk.'

173

'No, that's fine.'

We climb up two short flights of stairs and arrive at a tiny, carpeted hallway. A woman is standing in the doorway of a room on the left, waiting for us.

'Thank you, Malcolm, much appreciated.' She nods at the tour guide – who gives me a smile and heads back the way we've come – and shakes my hand in a firm dry grip. 'Hello. Natalie, is it? Yes, your uncle spoke of you many times. I'm Collette Nichols. I'm the Head of Rare Books here.'

Collette Nichols looks to be in her early sixties. She's small but straight-backed, and working the Madame Librarian look very hard in a pearl-buttoned blouse and tweed trousers with court shoes. Her graying-blonde hair escapes in thin strands from a French roll. Black-framed reading glasses dangle from a gold chain at her chest.

She cocks her head at me. 'Yes, you do resemble Daniel. I'd say it's nice to finally meet you, except the circumstances are unhappy ones.'

Mycroft was right. English people really are easy to con. I don't resemble Daniel Gardener any more than I resemble Homer Simpson.

I just nod my head gravely. 'Thank you for seeing me, Mrs Nichols. I didn't mean to bust in on you without even telephoning.'

'No, no, that's fine. And it's not Mrs, just Ms – I've been married to my books for many years now.' She smiles at the admission. Her soft voice has that cultured plumminess I associate with English documentaries on Channel 2. Even when he's at his most aggravating, Mycroft's accent never gets this posh.

Nichols moves to one side as a guy in a blue security guard's outfit squeezes past us to enter the office.

'Sorry, you'll have to forgive all this bustle. We've had an unfortunate event here recently, so we've installed some extra security.'

'That's okay.' I give her a glance. 'I understand. The police said that something happened where Uncle Dan worked.'

Collette Nichols's lips go thin. She looks a bit flustered as yet another security man excuses himself to come back out.

'Yes, it's a terrible thing. Terrible. We had a book stolen. An irreplaceable book.' She rubs her forehead with bird-boned fingers. 'I'm sorry, I'm being rude. Would you like to come in?'

Nichols's office is cramped, like I imagine all of them are in this antiquated building. Papers and posters for old exhibitions are tacked up in tidy confusion. There are books *everywhere*, teetering piles of them, shelves groaning with them. The radiator ticks away in the corner, beside a small square patch of empty space. The carpet occupying the space is pale, discolored. A man in the corner – the blond security guard who first butted past us – is standing on a chair, screwing a small CCTV unit into the wall.

Nichols finds us both chairs near her desk. She shakes her head, still preoccupied with her loss.

'The book in question is very rare and very valuable. Consequently, the Library has gone on lockdown, which is why there are uniforms everywhere.' Her mouth forms a tight, frustrated line. 'Shutting the barn door after the horse has bolted, I believe it's called. And now this tragic business with Daniel.'

I look at Nichols, at her paper-littered desk, at her red mug with *Keep Calm and Read a Book* stamped on it. I know a bit about lying. And what I know is, in every lie you tell there has to be a grain of truth. Everything that follows from the lie

175

is seeded by that little bit of believability. Now I need to take a chance, and use what I know to be true in the service of a really big fib.

'Ms Nichols, I know about the Shakespeare Folio.' I say it like an admission of guilt. 'The police – Inspector Gupta – told me. They said my uncle had been questioned about the theft.'

Nichols inclines her head. 'Oh dear. Yes, well, that's true. But Daniel wasn't really under suspicion – we were all questioned, myself included. And I understand the police already have someone in custody. They'd established that Daniel was in London at the time of the theft.'

Clearly Nichols hasn't been updated about the release of Farrell Al-Said. But this could work to my advantage right now.

'Well the police seem to want to keep their options open,' I say. I'm making this up on the spot. 'And the Inspector said my uncle was the last person to see the Folio.'

'Yes. Daniel worked with the Folio that Friday, doing minor repairs to the cover.'

I frown. 'That was normal, was it? Bringing it out for repairs?'

Nichols smooths a hand over the tweed of her trousers. 'Well, no. It was at Daniel's request. He was gluing a number of small tears in the leather – a very nice job he did, too. I saw the work before we put the Folio away in the safe.'

I sit a bit straighter. 'So my uncle wasn't the only one to see the Folio before the theft.'

'That's right. Normally the Folio would have gone back to its secure facility by courier, but as it was a Friday, it was kept here over the weekend.' Nichols waves towards the bare patch of carpet. 'The police have the safe now, of course.'

'So how was the Folio stolen?'

'Security had an alarm on the Sunday night, and when the guard came to investigate, he found the safe open. The Folio was the only thing taken.'

I blink at her. 'Uncle Dan didn't have the combination to the safe, did he?'

'Goodness me, no.' Nichols's expression goes soft. 'Oh my dear, you're worried, I can see that. But whatever the police have said to you, I can assure you I certainly don't believe that Daniel was in any way involved.'

I swallow and look straight at the Head of Rare Books. Tell another critical lie. 'Ms Nichols, the police are still suggesting there could be a link between my uncle's death and the theft.'

'Well, I think they're drawing a rather long bow. This fellow they're questioning, Farrell Al-Said, has been involved in some nasty business with the library before.'

'I know. It's just . . .' I bite my lip. It's no effort on my part to look anxious. 'The police seem pretty eager to find a scapegoat.'

'My dear, please don't fret over it. Your uncle was a good man. A wonderful conservator, too. So talented . . .' Nichols pats my hand. 'I'm so very sorry for your loss. I remember seeing Daniel that Friday, as he left. It was just after I'd tucked the Folio away. Daniel was in his usual state of disarray – folders, and car keys, and whatnot. He had his jacket half on, and a bundle of copy paper and a sandwich in one hand . . .' She smiles fondly at the memory, shakes her head. 'I can't quite believe he's gone.'

'No. I can't . . . I can't believe it either.'

Nichols pats my hand again. 'I'm sorry, my dear. Your loss is far greater.'

'That's all right.' I look at the carpet. I wish I was Natalie, accepting all these kind condolences.

'Now, you wanted to see Daniel's office?' Nichols asks, standing up.

'Will that be okay? I don't want to inconvenience you.' I duck my head, so Nichols won't see my blush as I embroider. 'They've given me his effects, to take home to Mum. So it's just a sentimental thing . . .'

'Not at all, my dear, that's perfectly all right. Only I would please ask that you not disturb anything in the office. The police have requested we keep everything exactly as it is. But I perfectly understand your desire to visit. You've come a long way, and I'm sure if Daniel were here he wouldn't object.'

I seal my lips and smile tightly.

Nichols gestures to the blond guard, who has finished with the camera and is now putting his tools away. 'Excuse me? Please take Miss Sutcliffe here to Mr Gardener's office, on the third floor. You have your pass key?'

'Yes, ma'am.'

'Wonderful.' Nichols looks back to me, smiling sadly. 'As I said, it's nice to have finally met you. Daniel spoke of you and your mother very affectionately. This is where I'll leave you, I'm afraid. If you'd like to see the rest of the library, the guard can direct you back to Radcliffe Square.'

'Thank you,' I say. 'You've been very kind.'

I give her an impulsive kiss on the cheek. Nichols's cheek is soft, and she smells of potpourri. I tell myself the kiss is from Natalie.

This woman is so goddamn nice, and this would be so much easier if I had an official police card or something, an ID on a lanyard like Mycroft had at the mortuary. I wouldn't have to lie to all these lovely, generous people, and feel so awful about it.

Nichols looks touched. She squeezes my arm. 'I think the truth will come to light, Miss Sutcliffe. It will be a great relief, to your family and to us, when this shadow finally passes.'

We shake hands again. Nichols gives me a wave as I follow the security guard out the office and through the short corridor to the lift.

CHAPTER THIRTEEN

The tour guide was right about the lift: it has a glass-mesh window and looks as if it was built sometime during World War II. The door is barely wide enough for one person to squeeze through, and the guard and I have to cram in together.

The guard's in his early twenties, sandy-haired, fit-looking. He stands stolidly beside me as the lift's gears grind.

'Thanks for this.' This guy's supposed to be working security detail, and I'm sure he's got more important things to do than escort me around.

'Not a problem.'

The lift rises with torturous slowness. I surreptitiously watch the guard. With a little effort I might be able to find out something about the theft.

'They've got you working hard, then,' I say.

'Yep.'

Monosyllabic. Great.

He shifts his feet, glances at me. 'They got us patrolling a bit, since last week.'

'Yeah, I heard you had a bit of excitement,' I say. 'But patrolling doesn't sound too bad.'

'S'all right.' His accent is strong, like people in the English crime shows that Mum and Mike both like to watch. He shrugs. 'Now the coppers've cleared out, it's just guarding a bunch of books again, innit.'

'Were you on duty when they found out about the theft?'

'On duty?' He lifts his chin, levels his shoulders. 'Heard the alarm, didn't I? First on the scene.'

'Really?' That makes me pay attention.

'Yeah. Got asked a bunch of questions for m'trouble.'

I definitely need to grill this guy further, but the lift has finally gasped its way to the third floor. I'll have to keep my own bunch of questions for the trip back down.

The guy – his name-badge reads *Paul Knox* – looks at me again, in a quick furtive way. I wonder if he's checking me out. The idea makes me blush. He ushers me out of the lift and along a corridor identical to the last one until we reach a wooden door.

Paul uses his key. 'Here you go.'

I don't know what I was expecting, but Gardener's office is very different to Nichols's. The space is large, floored in a mustard-yellow vinyl. A number of long desks are parked on the side nearest the windows, and on the opposite side is a collection of equipment I'd find more understandable in Professor Walsh's forensics lab: fume hoods, cast-iron presses and guillotines, shelves full of glass vials.

Apart from that, it's like a normal office. Filing cabinets are mashed together, wire inboxes on top, a PC on one desk, a photocopier in the corner. A loose ream of paper sits on the table beside the photocopier, waiting to be put to use.

Of course, what draws my eyes are the books – one whole wall is stuffed with them. Books of every type, in every condition. They bulge and flow between the paper-labeled partitions on the shelves. Walnutty leatherbound books, red cloth-covered books, gold embossed books, plain books, books in boxes, books in need of repair.

Gardener worked with books every day. He must have been someone who loved books, loved words. Someone who saw beneath the weathered covers and the yellowing ink to the soul underneath.

It beggars belief that someone like that would stoop to stealing a book as precious as the Folio. But if Gardener was in hock to some 'heavy people', then the threat of getting his legs broken – or worse – could have been pretty compelling. Except there was no proof Gardener was involved in the theft, and Collette Nichols seems completely convinced that Gardener would never have betrayed the library's trust.

I walk the perimeter of the office, check every desk until I find the one with various memos to Daniel Gardener. Gardener's laptop is still there, embellished with sticky notes. A stack of scholarly journals lurches to one side. Other items are arranged in a more orderly way – paper in folders, order forms for Japanese tissue and wheat-starch paste, blank forms for requested materials.

I perch on the stool in front of the desk, let my eyes wander. This would be easier if I knew what I was looking for. Also if Paul, my friendly security guard, wasn't staring at me from the doorway.

He gives me a grave nod. 'You the niece, then. That right?'

'Yes.' I make a polite smile. Risk some embellishment. 'Mum didn't want to come. She said it was a long way, and she's waiting for my uncle to . . . come home.'

Paul nods again.

I decide now might be a good time to milk the grieving-niece persona. 'Would you mind if I took a moment . . .?'

Paul gets this light-bulb expression. 'Oh, yeah. Sure. Long as you like. But I have to station at the door, yeah?'

'Sure. Thank you.'

Once he's closed the door, I dump my satchel and start running my fingers over the desk – the laptop keyboard, the sticky notes. Breathing a quick apology to Collette Nichols, I open all the drawers and look through Gardener's things.

Each drawer holds materials he would have used in his conservation work. Card of various thicknesses. Distressed leather. String, cord, wire. There's a collection of paintbrushes, from hair-thin to fox's-tail, a number of pairs of tweezers, labeled pots of paint and glue and varnish. One drawer is full of modular foam book supports, and one has gold-leaf sheets so fine I can see the grain of the papers separating them.

A number of A4-sized shots of the Folio's cover are piled together to one side of Gardener's desk. The detail is incredible. Maybe Gardener removed the cover of the Folio and . . . No, he wouldn't have wanted to do that. He'd have devalued the book for its new 'owner'.

I'm thinking as if Gardener was involved in the theft. And even though it doesn't seem possible, it's the only thing that makes *sense*. If Gardener knew about the theft, knew something so dangerous he was killed for it . . .

I get up to study the mess of books on the nearby shelves. I even open the photocopier drawer – no Folio, just another ream of paper.

I scan through Gardener's equipment, the paper slips here and there, and an idea starts forming in my head.

Gardener was a master conservator. Nichols herself admired his work. He knew everything about the look of the Folio, especially its nearly five-hundred-year-old leather cover. Nichols said she saw the repairs Gardener had done on the Folio, before they both returned it to the safe. But did she check the rest of the book?

What if it was only the cover she saw?

I glance again at the pictures of the Folio cover, at the contents of Gardener's drawers. Everything he needed was here. Everything he might have needed to produce, in clever detail, a facsimile of the cover of one of the world's most famous books.

What if the book that was put into the safe wasn't the Folio at all – just another book with a fake cover? Nichols would've had no reason to be suspicious. Gardener could have just taken the real Folio on the very day he worked on it . . . But how did Gardener get the Folio out of the building?

There weren't any CCTV cameras in Nichols's office, because I just saw my mate, Paul, belatedly putting one in. And if Gardener was in London on the night of the theft, then who cracked the safe? Gardener must have had an accomplice. Maybe Addington was the thief. But then why would she draw attention to herself by confessing to Gardener's death? How does it all tie together?

I don't know. I'm still jet-lagged, and my theatrics for Collette Nichols have drained me. I'm running out of inspiration. The pictures of the cover are my only clues. But it's something to show Mycroft, and something's better than nothing.

I peel one of the pictures out of the pile and fold it carefully. As I slip it into my jeans pocket, Paul pushes his way into the office. I can't help but jump.

'All done?' Paul looks at me expectantly. 'It's getting close to end-of-day, is all, and I better take you off the premises.'

'Oh, right. Yeah, sure, no worries.' I smooth my sweaty palms down my flanks. Hopefully he hasn't seen me five-finger the picture.

'Come back tomorrow if you want more time, yeah? Maybe in the morning.'

'Sure. Thank you.'

We stand there staring at each other for a second. If Paul saw something, he's doing a helluva good job of not giving anything away.

'I'd like to go back down and say goodbye to Ms Nichols,' I say. 'You know, just to say thank you.'

The idea comes out of nowhere. But suddenly I want to be around other people.

Paul squints at me. 'Didn't you say thank you before?'

'Yes.' I set my jaw. 'And I'd like to say thank you again.'

'Whatever you fancy,' Paul says.

I grab my satchel up off the floor and wave a hand forward to show Paul he should lead the way. I don't want to squeeze past him to get out of the room.

Paul lets me through to the back of the lift before taking up station in front of me and hitting the button. We're stuck together in the confined space again. I tap my fingers against my satchel strap as the lift crawls slowly downwards.

'Would you mind showing me what you've got in your pocket there, please?' Paul says conversationally.

My breath stops. 'Pardon?'

Paul sighs. 'The whatever-it-is you've got in your pocket. Would you mind handing it over, please?'

He's half-turned to face me.

'Look, I saw you lift something.' His eyes are a muddy hazel color, unblinking. 'You were told not to disturb anything in the office. Now I want the thing you took. It's my job, okay?'

For two whole seconds I think about giving Paul the picture. It might be completely meaningless and it's about to get me into a spot of bother.

In the pause created by my hesitation, Paul speaks again. 'I don't have to report it, y'know. Lot of fuss for nothing, yeah? I could just take it back, and no one's the wiser. Nichols doesn't have to know. Just give me what you took.'

Suddenly I'm not sure of this. I'm not sure of any of it.

'I don't know what you're talking about.' My face is straight as I can manage.

Paul sighs again. 'Right. Fine. Have it your way.'

We continue trundling. It's not until I glimpse the light through the lift window, see it pass up and away, that I realize something.

I keep my voice even. 'We were supposed to stop at the second floor.'

'Yeah,' Paul says. 'Well, we're not gonna do that, are we? We're gonna see Stan.'

'What?'

'Stan Moody, Head of Security. You and Stan can have a little chat, maybe he can talk some sense into you before we call the bobbies in.'

Okay, I've got the wind up me now. I don't want to talk to the library's Head of Security and I don't want to involve the police. When they ask to see my ID, I'll be cactus.

I pull the folded picture out of my pocket. 'It was just

a . . . souvenir. Something of my uncle's. I've come all this way, and I just wanted something, something small.'

'Right.' Paul lifts an eyebrow as he takes the photo. 'Little memento, was it?'

'That's right.'

'Okay, then.' Paul slides the paper into his pocket and turns to face the front again.

We're still going down.

'You can let me off now,' I say. 'I mean, that's it, isn't it? I gave you the picture, so we don't need to take it further.'

'Mm.' Paul scratches his nose. 'Yeah, I still gotta take you to see Stan, I reckon.'

'*What*? But you said—'

'Yeah, we won't need to call the coppers in, so that's something.'

I feel a bit sick. I glance up at the numbers above the door. 'This is it. First floor. Just let me off here, okay?'

Paul shakes his head sadly. 'Sorry, love. Gotta cover the bases.'

The first floor appears as a square of light held in check by the mesh in the lift window. It narrows to a band and evaporates. We're still sinking. The sound of my heartbeat is loud in my ears as my mind does the Grand Prix. What the hell am I going to do now?

We sink all the way to *B* before the lift lamp flickers. There's a heavy, settling sensation, like we've landed in a space ship. The door slides open to a view of a concrete corridor and silver-foiled coils of pipe. Down further than I can see, colored cables and more piping – thin, thick, massive – are bending and joining and extending away.

Paul puts a hand on his utility belt, steps out of the lift.

'Come on.' He glances back at me. 'Let's go see Stan.'

I look at the cables and pipes, look at the corridor. Emergency lights are set into crevices in the wall. Plant machinery hisses and groans somewhere further down.

Eight weeks ago I would've been more trusting. Now I stand in the lift, immovable.

'No,' I say.

'Come again?'

'I said *no*. I'm not going to see your boss down in some random, secluded basement. If you want me to see the Head of Security, radio him to come here.'

Paul's mouth thins. He breathes through his nose. 'You're a right bossy little snob, aren't you?'

He reaches around to his left. I think he's reaching for his radio. So when he snaps his arm back and slaps me across the face, I'm taken completely by surprise.

CHAPTER FOURTEEN

Paul grabs me by the hair.

I don't have time to gasp – my eyes are watering, and my cheek and nose bloom with the force of the slap. He's hauling me out of the lift. I yell, flail with my hands, and this guy, shit, this guy is *not* a security guard.

That's the only stupid thought in my head as Paul pulls me forward. My hair is being ripped out by the roots as I pull back, away from the direction he wants me to go. I grab at the edge of the lift door, scramble with my feet, but I can't get a grip.

Paul slaps at my hands, works to get one of my wrists into his fist. 'Come here, you little—'

Suddenly I realize that trying to stay in the lift is a dead-end idea. I take my chance and twist away, ducking under his arm. He isn't expecting that – I'm free, although he's got a handful of my hair in his hand. Ripping that out bloody hurt. The sting moves me, brings me fully awake, and I run.

I run into the maze of pipes. My satchel bangs against my hip as I dodge around a stack of silver-insulated service lines, run down the other side of the concrete corridor.

Paul grunts somewhere behind me. 'Come back here, you little shit!'

Sure, Paul, I'll come back so you can grab me again, you DICKHEAD – I don't say that. I don't say anything, I'm breathing too fast, oh god. There's a bank of terminals, switches, a red emergency door.

Paul's voice echoes in the tunnel. He hasn't caught up yet. He must be having trouble squeezing between the service pipes. The red door is metal, and it's locked – I bolt for a hollow in the wall up ahead.

It's another inset door, a fire door, and it has a bar across it. I slam into the bar, feel it give, then I'm in a stairwell, taking steps up two at a time. The next door is another fire door, and I thrust myself against the bar as it opens.

Oh fuck, oh fuck. My breathing is uncontrolled, huffing and fast. Who the hell is this guy? Why is he trying to grab me? I don't know, and there's no time to work it out—

I press my hands over my mouth to muffle the sound of my bellows breath, but the air just wheezes in and out of my nose, so I drop my hands and concentrate on where I am. A book storage area. Rows of stacks, head-high, all aluminum shelves. A white grill-mesh secure area on the far side. The low ceiling is lined with fluoro strip lights.

Come on, Rachel, think! Paul, the fake security guy, will be here any second and I have to find another stairwell or I'm totally rooted.

I weave through the stacks. I hope I'm heading in the

right direction, but I can't be sure. There are no illuminated exit signs.

My legs are shaking. I'm about to turn another corner when a heavy hand drops on my shoulder and I jump.

Paul spins me around. He's grinning. 'Hello again.'

I don't think, I just react. Working with the Furies has honed my reactions a bit, plus the shock and the fear – it all combines in my brain. I haul back and punch him right in the face. It's a good punch – Mike would be proud – my knuckles don't even smart.

Paul's head snaps backward, blood showers out of his nose.

'Fuck!' He puts a hand up, his eyes glazing over.

I don't wait – I spin and grab Paul's sleeve, whip it as hard as I can. He flails and slams into a stack to my left.

But he's still got me by one arm. He grabs higher for my shoulder, crushes the fabric of my vest in his hand. This close up I can smell his breath, a minty toothpaste smell, plus the scent of fresh blood.

As he yanks me in, I pull away, fumble for the zipper of my vest. It makes a metal ripping sound, then I'm shucking the vest, turning as I slither free.

I'm halfway along the row when a massive weight slams into me. I bounce off a shelf and come down, rolling hard – the concrete floor is a killer. Paul's bent over me, his hands grab at me, finding my satchel strap, finding my waist, squeezing for purchase. I yell and wriggle out of the strap, crawl backwards on my elbows.

There's no way in hell I'm being taken like this, sprawled helpless on the ground. I've wrestled with my brother, I've boxed up sheep, I've fought for supremacy in derby bouts and won. I kick with both feet. One of my heels connects with Paul's shoulder and he *oofs* with pain.

'Shit!' He's angry now, and I don't think that's a good thing. 'Okay, you—'

I scramble up and wriggle away, but Paul lunges again. My back buckles under his weight. When my knee comes down it hits the side of the shelving, and *fuck shit fuck* – I cry out, it hurts so bad. Sparklers are suddenly firing off in my vision.

I fight against it, climb up the shelving stacks with my hands and arms. The shelving is tottery, and Paul is trying to get his arm around my waist. He wants to lift me up, feet off the floor so I won't have any leverage, but I'm not having that. I pull a book off the shelf and throw it at him. He bats it away.

Paul's fist slams into the side of my head. I cry out – my ear rings, but I've had worse in training. If he's trying to knock me out, he's doing a pretty shit job.

I whack backwards with my elbow, smash into something soft. Paul goes down behind me and swears again. It almost makes me laugh. This is the most pathetic slapping fist-fight I've ever been in.

I pull more books down, send a cascade of books onto his head. I scramble along the row, using the shelving for support, my knee crying like a son of a bitch. I'm almost to the end of the row when Paul gives a guttural cry, and then something bashes into me from behind – he's thrown himself into a full tackle.

My palms hurt when they slip down from shelf to shelf, then I clonk my head on the concrete floor. It's sudden, and the monochrome light that showers behind my eyeballs is painful, and then it's lights out.

———

When the light comes back on, everything hurts.

My body feels heavy. Oh god. I groan, with that slow treacly awareness you have after sleep. I'm lying on . . . I don't know. Jesus. I don't know.

My eyes water and my head is pounding. I wriggle my fingers. They still work, so I raise a hand to my face, massage my eyeballs through the lids.

There's a hard lump the size of a duck's egg just above my hairline on the left. Something crusty flakes off under the pads of my fingers. When I open my eyes to look, everything is dim, shadowed. But I can see black flecks speckling my fingertips. Dried blood.

I try the rest of me. My back is sore, but my hands and legs are obeying my commands, except for my—

Ow and *shit* – my right knee feels like it's been knifed. It's competing with my head for the Most Painful Part of My Body award.

I do a little inventory. Head, hands, aching lower back, knee. I'm fully clothed with my boots on. Not fully clothed – no vest. I'm lying on a mattress and there's a blanket draped over me. I push the blanket off and struggle up to one elbow, just breathing hard and taking it all in.

I'm in the dark in a bare, dank room. It's small, with wooden floorboards and walls. The roof slopes. The shell of a bath is squeezed into the corner diagonally opposite me. It lies partially underneath a large window and blocks off a door.

Slats of brightness and shadow from the window fill the bath. The light looks artificial. If it's dark, if there are lights on, it must be evening. God, what time is it?

A green bucket sits to my left, and a plastic soft-drink bottle full of . . . water? Looks like water. Further left is another door in the wall behind me. It's closed. All the doors are closed.

I blink my eyes a bit. Throwing off the rest of the blanket and sitting up seems like a big ask, but I do it anyway.

Ah god . . . My head is suddenly gigantic and made of contracting wood. Something smells like wet dog – the mattress. The room pirouettes in my vision and I lurch forward just in time to vomit into the bucket.

I choke and cough, spit up frothy bile. My hands are numb as I reach for the bottle, unscrew the cap and test it – yes, it's water. I feel absurdly grateful.

I swish some around in my mouth to rinse, then do bush hankie into the bucket to clear my nose. I wipe my fingers on my jeans and take a few cautious swallows of the water. It tastes like chlorine and something metallic, freezing cold between my teeth, but it soothes my parched throat.

Spewing has made my headache worse, but otherwise I feel better. My right leg is stuck out to the side, so I don't have to bend my knee. I'm pretty sure I'm not going to throw up again, so I push the bucket away.

I don't know where I am, how long I've been here. And my brain isn't up to the task of figuring out what the hell's going on, not yet.

Light suddenly flickers in the room. A weak globe in the ceiling has come on. I only have a moment to register this before the door over on the left opens inwards.

A man enters. 'You are awake. Yes. Good.'

He stands holding the doorknob. My eyes are still blurry. I try to focus. Somewhere in his fifties, this guy. Solidly built, with short black-peppered hair and a blunt, tough face. A stubble of graying beard, a mustache. He's not tall, but he's upright.

His clothes are odd: a black T-shirt tucked into navy track pants with a garish neon stripe down the side of each leg, matching jacket. It takes me a second to figure out what's odd about it – everything looks ironed. Who irons a tracksuit?

I blink at him. My left eyelid feels as though it's drooping.

'Who are you?' My voice is croaky.

'Yes, we will get to this.' The man's voice seems too loud, jocular. He has a very strong European accent. He gestures out the door. 'Come. You can walk, yes?'

My brain works very slowly. I lick my lips. This is kidnapping. I've been kidnapped. How weird. I should feel more scared, I guess, but I just feel really cloudy.

'I can walk,' I rasp. I'm not entirely sure that's true, but I'm stubborn. I can make it true.

'Very good,' the man says. 'Come out, please. We will chat.'

He exits. The door is still open. Who leaves the door open for a kidnapped person? I don't know. I only know I have to get up and follow him if I want answers.

I roll up onto my left knee, with my right leg out. Then I have to do a push-up maneuver to stand. I wobble, try putting some of my weight on my right leg – oh fuck, no, that's a terrible idea. I reach for the wall and hobble towards the door.

Every step sends a splinter of pain jagging through my right kneecap. My knee feels swollen inside my jeans, rubbing the denim. I almost gag again, control it.

At the doorway, I look out. I'm not in the Bodleian anymore. I'm in an old warehouse. I've been in a room that must have once been an office. Outside it the ceiling vaults up, and the rest of the space is open plan, dirty wood, disused. The area is about the size of a public swimming pool, lit by industrial hanging lamps.

A collection of dusty steel machinery lurks against the opposite wall. To my right, the warehouse extends further into cobwebbed gloom. Closer than that is a stairwell: the old-fashioned banisters roll down into darkness.

In front of me is the man I just met. He's standing with his odd upright posture, his right hand resting on a wooden table beside him. He extends his other hand out to another chair a few meters away, facing him. Under the hanging lamps, everything the man does creates sharply defined shadows and the whole thing looks like a stage set. But set for what?

I look at him, look at the empty chair. But my knee is really killing me and I need to sit down. I limp away from the door, into what appears to be my spot.

'Excellent.' The man seems pleased. He seats himself on the chair opposite mine. 'You are strong. This is good. How is your head?'

I stare at him. 'Terrible.'

'Yes. My apologies.'

His clipped accent sounds like something straight out of a bad gangster movie. I don't know the regional accents here, so I have no idea where he's from, but there's a strong whiff of the steppes about him – Russian, Polish, Ukrainian? There's a boy at school back home who talks like this. I rack my brain to remember where he's from, but my brain isn't up to much racking at the moment.

I'm about to ask what the hell's going on when someone walks closer. It's Paul, the fake security guard. He's changed into a shirt and jeans, and he's holding a mug of something that steams.

I'm pleased to note the tape over the bridge of Paul's nose, his two black eyes. He places the mug on the table next to Tracksuit Guy. He'd be bobbing his head, like a dog to his master, if he didn't have his eyes fixed firmly on me.

'There you go, sir,' he says to Tracksuit Guy, before curling his lip at me.

I smile as nastily as I can. 'Hello again.'

'Bitch,' he says.

'Sook,' I snap back. I'm not gonna let that lie.

Paul takes a step. 'You broke my fucking *nose*, you little—'

'Enough.' Tracksuit Guy holds up a hand, glares at Paul until he backs off. It's pretty obvious who's the alpha around here.

Tracksuit Guy slurps from his mug and looks at me. 'Now. We will chat, yes?'

I swallow past the stale bitterness in my mouth, ask the first useful question I can think of. 'Who are you?'

Tracksuit nods his head. It's like a little bow. 'We will not share names, please. You understand? You may call me the Colonel.'

The only other Colonel I know is Colonel Sanders. This guy doesn't look as if he's going into junk-food franchising anytime soon, so he must be a genuine military person. Or ex-military. Or a complete wanker.

'The Colonel,' I repeat.

'Yes,' Tracksuit says.

'Okay.' I swallow again, grimace. The fluoro light hurts my eyes. 'So . . . what am I doing here?'

'Yes.' Tracksuit – the Colonel – nods. His voice is very calm for someone holding court with a kidnapped person in a run-down warehouse. 'You are here because we look for something. And we think you have maybe an idea where this something could be.'

'The Folio.' My mouth is already open, so it's not like I'm gaping.

The Colonel puts his mug down and tongues his back teeth. 'Yes, the Folio.'

This is starting to come together for me now. Okay. These people . . . they're connected to the Folio theft.

And this is bad. I recognize that this is bad. But I still feel as though I'm floating above it a bit. I try to file away the fact that this is bad, for future reference. Oh boy, my brain really isn't working on all thrusters.

The Colonel continues. 'Your uncle, he did a very foolish thing. He took this thing belonging to us. And now—'

He stops then, because I've started laughing. I can't help it really. It started like a *huh* of air escaping, then it turned into a full-blown laugh. It hurts my head to laugh, but I can't stop.

The Colonel stares at me. Paul, standing at his master's shoulder, looks at me like I've gone crazy. Who knows? – I might be crazy. Maybe it's just a reaction to being scared shitless. Or maybe that knock on the head really did something to my mental synapses, because who laughs at a time like this?

'I am sorry this is funny for you.' The Colonel's eyes are dark-gray pebbles. 'But it is not funny for us. It is not funny at all.'

'No, I know . . . oh . . .' I hiccup back to normal, wipe the moisture out of my eyes with my sleeve. 'I know it's not funny. Sorry.'

'If this is funny for you, then we have big problem.' The Colonel says it like a cheesy Russian mafioso – *beeeg pr-r-roblem.*

I nod, but that makes me dizzy, so I stop. I can't stop smiling though. 'Yes. Yes, you definitely have big problem. Because I'm not Natalie Sutcliffe.'

'*Bull*shit,' Paul says, going pale.

'Excuse me?' The Colonel's face goes completely still. He could be a store mannequin, he's got about that much expression.

'I'm not Natalie Sutcliffe.' I squeeze my aching thigh, and my voice sounds tired. 'My name is Rachel Watts. I came over from Melbourne with the coronial team investigating Daniel

198

Gardener's death. I don't have police ID, but I wanted to find out more about Daniel Gardener, so I lied to the woman at the Bodleian . . .'

'But you do not lie to me now,' the Colonel says.

Paul hisses. 'She's lying through her fucking teeth—'

'I'm not.' I fix my eyes on him. 'Check my bag, it's got my . . .'

I pat around myself for my satchel before I realize that actually I haven't noticed it in a while. It's back at the Bodleian, underneath some library shelf somewhere. Damnit. I really liked that satchel. Not to mention it's got my passport, my money, and everything else in it. But that hardly helps me at the moment.

'Okay, forget that,' I say. 'But if you find my bag, you can check my ID yourself. I'm not Natalie. I'm me.'

The Colonel stares. Paul curses under his breath, glances up at the ceiling and back down.

'Rachel Watts,' the Colonel says, struggling a little with the *w*.

'Yes.'

The Colonel sighs heavily and squeezes the lined spot between his wiry eyebrows. Then he drops his hand and looks at me.

'Excuse me, please,' he says.

In one smooth movement the Colonel stands up, turns, and grabs Paul by the front of the shirt. Paul only has time to put up his hands and stammer something unintelligible before the Colonel slugs him in the face. The punch is incredibly hard and fast. I know enough about hitting things to recognize a knockout blow.

Paul's head whips to the side, blood spraying out his mouth. He's already sagging when the Colonel hits him again, in the solar plexus, with the same amount of force. Paul sinks onto his knees, makes a retching sound. The Colonel holds on to him and hits him twice more – *thonk, thonk* – in the face.

I've reared back so far in my seat it's nearly tipping over. The only reason I'm not on the other side of the room is because it all happens so fast.

Now I'm not laughing, not smiling. Now I am stone-cold awake.

I stare at the Colonel. This is not the attack of a normal person. The Colonel is not a normal person. He is a brutal, trained assault force, and now he has dropped Paul's limp body onto the dirty warehouse floor and turned back to me.

'My apologies.' He settles heavily in the chair again, breathing hard. In a few seconds his breathing settles. 'So. We have a genuine . . . how do you say? A conundrum.'

I can't take my eyes off Paul, lying on the floor. Blood is dripping from his head, but I think I see his chest move. I look back and forth between the Colonel and Paul, and my face must reflect how completely *freaked out* I am right now.

'A conundrum, yes,' the Colonel continues, like nothing happened. 'But you say you are connected to police involved with this investigation?'

I can't speak. I just nod, even though it hurts.

'Yes. So perhaps we make advantage of this.'

There's blood on the Colonel's knuckles from where he hit Paul's teeth, but he's not rubbing his hand or doing anything to acknowledge the fact that he just beat the brain cells out of one of his henchmen. His posture is still ramrod, hands on knees.

'So,' he says. 'How can we make advantage of this?'

'I don't . . .' I'm whispering. 'I'm not . . .'

'You are not police? No, of course, you are too young.'

My breath won't come back fast enough. It's making me see spots. 'I'm just . . . I'm just the girlfriend of the pathologist's assistant.'

'Ah,' the Colonel says. 'And this boy, your friend, he is with this team?'

'Yes.' My throat is the Sahara.

The Colonel is nodding away. 'And he is seeing Gardener's house? His belongings?'

'Yes.'

'Miss Watts . . .' The Colonel really hates that *w*. He grimaces, gives me a weird conciliatory smile. 'Rachel. I may call you Rachel? Thank you. This conundrum, it is not a complicated thing. We are missing information. We have some information, but not all. You see?'

I nod, more slowly this time.

'This man, Gardener . . . We make deal with him, give him opportunity to repay his debt. We arrange simple operation at his job, to make this happen. We trust him to give us this thing we have asked for, you understand? He does not give it. He hides it somewhere for himself. Very foolish.'

'Foolish. Right.' I'm beginning to see how foolish.

'Yes. We renegotiate. I visit him, and we chat, like this chat I have with you now, you see?' The Colonel waves his hand back and forth, as if he's showing me the general amity that exists between us. I don't take my eyes off him for a second. 'So we make new agreement. Gardener will give information about where Folio is hidden to my employer—'

'Wait.' I gulp and blink. My thought process is still moving too slowly. 'Your employer?'

'Yes.' The Colonel grins. 'I am a working man, yes. My own business. I work for contract.'

Contract – as in contract killing. As in arranging assassinations that look like carjackings. With a bit of kidnapping and heavying people to pay up their gambling debts on the side.

God, what did Gardener think he was *doing*, messing with people like this?

'And . . . Gardener didn't give the information to your employer?' I say. 'Is that it?'

The Colonel frowns, as though this makes him very sad. 'He calls police instead. He is seen putting package into car boot. So plans are put in motion for Gardener, yes? But afterwards, what do we find? Only package of papers for international travel. Worthless books. So it is too late for him, and for us also.'

It starts to come together in my mind, once I parse through his garbled syntax. Gardener steals the Folio to pay back his gambling debts with these people. But instead of giving up the Folio's location, Gardener tries to double-cross them. They think he's taking the Folio to the police. And the boss has Gardener killed before he has a chance to figure out the Folio's not with Gardener. Which leaves them with a dead librarian and no idea of where the Folio actually is.

Now all the remaining information about Gardener and the Folio is in the hands of the police. And I'm their only link.

So they can't kill me. I'm glad. But it still doesn't change the fact that *I* don't know where the Folio is.

I'm going to have to play this very carefully. I don't know how to do that. I'm not together enough to deal with all this. I feel nauseous. My knee aches and my eyeballs hurt.

'So . . . you need the information that the police have, to work out where Gardener hid the Folio,' I say slowly.

The Colonel smiles broadly. 'Very good! You are a smart girl. This is good.'

My head is hammering itself to pieces. 'But I'm just . . . I don't have police access. I'm—'

'You are girlfriend of boy with police access, yes?'

'Yes,' I say.

My tongue sticks to the roof of my mouth as I say it. It's the same way I felt when Mycroft rescued me off the scaffolding that time, like I'm grabbing for his hand and I'm about to pull him down with me. That moment seems like a million years ago now.

The Colonel smiles again and smacks his hands together. 'Excellent. So you will call him, and he will give information for your return.'

'I . . .' I wet my lips. 'I can't call him. I don't know his number in London. My phone . . .'

'Hm, yes.'

The Colonel pulls something out of his jacket pocket, holds it up. It's my phone, now a handful of smashed plastic.

'Hm,' the Colonel repeats. He sucks his teeth again. 'What is your boyfriend's name, please?'

'Mycroft.' I look at the wooden floor, look back up. 'James Mycroft.'

'And we cannot call police directly, that would be not good. So . . . this is another conundrum?'

I don't need a reminder of what happens when the Colonel hits a snag. There's a visual reminder right here. Paul is a limp shadow, still leaking blood onto the floor behind the Colonel's chair. He groans, soft and low. The Colonel has not looked at him once.

I hear my voice as though it's coming from outside myself. 'My boyfriend has a blog. It's a forensics site, he checks it . . . He checks it all the time. There are comments fields, you could leave him a message.'

Mycroft, forgive me. But I am scared, and maybe he can trade info with these people without ever having to meet them.

'A blog?'

'Yes. It's called *Diogenes*, you can google it . . .'

'*Diogenes.* I like this name.' The Colonel smiles again. 'You know Diogenes is name of special club. From old story of *Serlok Holms* . . . How do you say this?'

'Sherlock Holmes.' All my bones feel weak. I am piss-weak, and so tired. 'Yeah, I know. Look, please just . . . He can give you the information online. The police don't ever need to know.'

'Yes, yes.' The Colonel nods his head, and I'm wondering if he's heard a word I said after 'Diogenes'. 'Rachel, you are very helpful girl. Very helpful.'

I almost reel with relief. The relief comes tinted with self-loathing – how can I have caved so fast?

The Colonel stands up. I cringe, but he merely extends a hand towards the office door. 'And now, I think, it is time for you to go back to your room. You will rest. Please. It is late. You look tired.'

I don't take my eyes off him. I ease myself up, wincing against the pain in my knee, and feel my way back to the door, step inside. The Colonel walks closer, reaches for the doorhandle. I hop back, bracing against the wall.

Just before he pulls the door shut, the Colonel suddenly dips his spare hand into his jacket pocket. When his hand emerges, he's thumbing a small square of foil and plastic.

'Here. Almost I forget.' He holds the thing out towards me. 'Panadol. For your head.'

I gape for a moment. When I reach out to take the foil square, my hand is trembling.

'Thank you,' I say in a strangled voice.

'This is no problem,' he says. 'We are not animals, yes?'

Then he shuts the door in my face and the light bulb goes out.

CHAPTER FIFTEEN

If I were some kind of secret agent, I'd check out the room, measure distances, look for means of escape. I'd listen through the walls to get a clue about who these guys are and what they intend to do with me.

I'm not a secret agent.

I have a bit of a cry. I clear my nose into the bucket again. My throat is raspy, so I have a few drinks from the soft-drink bottle.

I take the Panadol.

Sitting on the mattress, I know I should check my knee, but I'll have to pull my jeans down to look properly, and I'm too scared and uncomfortable to do that. The air in here is freezing, so I shiver in the dark with the gray blanket wrapped around me, with a sore head and an aching knee.

The world outside the room has disappeared. Nobody knows where I am. Mum and Dad and Mike are far away. I told Mycroft I'd meet him tonight – he and Alicia must have figured out something's gone wrong, but how will they even start searching for me? One girl stuck in a random abandoned warehouse.

Oh god, I'm alone.

In my mind, I replay the scene when the Colonel whirled around and beat Paul half to death for kidnapping the wrong girl. When I'd been fighting Paul myself, trying to shake him off, I could've happily throttled him. But the Colonel's attack was so different. He was so *cold*.

I don't know if you can appeal for mercy from a man like that.

I huddle in my blanket. I'm just a girl from Five Mile. I'm just me, Rachel, and I know about sheep, and quad bikes, and tram timetables. I'm doing Year Twelve, and my exams, Jesus, my exams, and this is not real, this can't be *real* . . .

After a while I fall asleep.

I wake up really early, still on jet-lag time. There's no warmth in the room at all. Aquarium-blue light glows from the window. The streetlamp or whatever it is outside is still on. My head hurts and my jaw aches – I must've been grinding my teeth in my sleep. But I feel more clear-headed.

I keep the blanket around me as I sit up to take stock of myself. I'm more methodical this time, working my way from top to bottom. The duck's egg on my head has gone down by half, and there's still dried blood in my hair. My cheekbone and eyebrow feel sore on that side, probably bruised. My back is really stiff.

But my knee is now a real problem. It's swollen inside my jeans leg to the point where it's stretching the denim. The heat of it radiates through the fabric. Every movement of my leg is agony. If I tried to bend it, I think I'd pass out.

But I have to move, because I'm busting. It takes a lot of gasps and hisses to get myself up, and I have to hold the wall while

I unbutton my jeans. But now I can't squat over the bucket, because I can't bend one knee. I end up working out this ridiculous system where I lean against the wall and do all the bending on my left leg. It's the stupidest way to pee ever, but it gets the job done.

I limp slowly with the bucket into the far corner of the room, so I don't have the smell of urine and vomit next to the bed. While I'm up, I check the door blocked by the bath. Locked. Not that I could push the bath out of the way right now.

The window is large, and there's a security grille covering it on my side. It's screwed into the wall with those screws that need an Allen key to get them out. Damnit.

I can see outside, at least. I'm on the second floor – the window looks down onto a bitumen access road and another warehouse, a rusted-out hulk of exposed metal struts and peeled-back siding and graffiti. The streetlamp illuminating my room is an old-fashioned sodium arc lamp, wired to the building on a tall wooden pylon. A plywood-cladding fence extends from the corner of the other warehouse, away up the road. Weed-infested garbage leans against that.

There is no one around, no people, no cars. Not one bloody thing.

In other words, I'm being held captive in a disused industrial lot, a place warehouses go to die, god-the-fuck-knows-where in England, by a Russian ex-army guy who is looking for a book worth millions of pounds and has already killed one person that I know of.

This can't be happening. No fucking way is this happening. This is a nightmare.

I close my eyes and lean my forehead against the cool metal

security mesh. My knee throbs from standing too long. The pain brings me back to life.

I force my head up. This is not a nightmare, this is real. I need to get it together. I can't just stand here waiting for the cavalry to arrive.

I look out the window again, search beyond the fence-line. Pressing my cheek to the grille and looking to the right, I can see a street a way over – more old warehouses, but a few regular houses as well. A delivery truck is heading down that street. There's even a person, a distant rugged-up figure, walking their dog in the dawn light.

This isn't some secluded, never-to-be-found location. This is the suburbs. I could do something, I don't know what, but *something*. I could bang on the window frame, attract someone's attention . . .

Which would also attract the attention of my kidnappers – yeah, that'd go down like a lead balloon. They may not hurt me, given I'm their link to the information they need, but the scene with Paul last night wasn't particularly reassuring.

It's still better, knowing I'm *somewhere*. I have options. I don't know what they are, exactly, but I have some hope.

I hobble back to the bed. I pull the blanket around myself and start tidying up. With the front hem of my flannie, I soak up a little water from the bottle and scrub the blood out of my hairline.

I take stock of what I don't have. My vest, which would come in handy right now. My satchel. The idea of losing all my papers makes my stomach roil, but I'm not going to worry about passports and air tickets at this juncture.

Patting myself down, I feel a hard little square in the key pocket of my jeans. I fish out the square and my mouth opens. It's my matchbox, my London Town matches from the Sherlock museum. *Will Flame In Wind Or Rain* . . . How about flaming in a wooden warehouse?

I don't want to set my jail cell on fire right now, though, because I have to think. I could do something with these. It's a miracle I've still got them. I tuck the box into my left sock, against my ankle, in case they decide to search me at some later point.

Just as I'm pulling my jeans leg back down, the bulb in the room comes on.

I get the drill now. Light comes on, bad guy comes in. The light splashes inside the room, making me squint. Now the run-down quality of the wooden floors and walls is more obvious. I think I liked it better in the half-dark.

The door opens. It's not the Colonel. This guy is in his mid-twenties. Short, black, well-built, like a rugby player or a wrestler. His leather motorbike jacket stretches across his shoulders. He's carrying a brown plastic tray. Something on top of it smells mouth-watering – a paper-wrapped roll.

'Breakfast.' The guy stands there holding the tray in my direction.

'You're gonna have to bring it closer than that.' I'm not getting up again unless it's for something useful, like an escape attempt.

The guy snorts. 'Paul was right. You are bossy.'

This guy is English, like Paul. I recognize the accent now, vowels broader than Mycroft's – something more like Cockney. How do two working-class English guys get mixed up with some Russian mafia dude?

I cock an eyebrow at him. 'And how is Paul this morning?'

The guy just glares at me. 'Got what was coming to him, didn' he?'

He squats – he has powerful legs – and puts the tray on the

floor. Slides it towards me, keeping his eyes on me the whole time: a fifty-kilo girl with a gammy leg and probable concussion. What on earth does he think I'm gonna do? Attack him with my nonexistent nails?

But I could fight, if I had to. I stare at the guy. He returns the stare, staying near the door as if I'm a vicious animal in a cage.

Give me a chance to show you how vicious.

Right now, though, I'm a hungry vicious animal. I keep my eyes on the Colonel's latest henchman as I lunge for the paper roll. It's a kebab – warm, grease-spotted, smelling fantastic.

The guy watches me clamber back awkwardly onto the mattress. 'Sorry, princess, no gourmet.'

He has a gap between his front teeth. The gap and his build remind me of Mike Tyson. Dad always liked watching Tyson box. I don't think he'd like this guy, though.

I'm already peeling back the paper, the foil underneath, demolishing the top edge of the kebab. The meat is salted and juicy. My stomach growls in appreciation – it's been a while since yesterday afternoon's limp cafe sandwich.

Tyson retrieves the tray, and I remember: I don't just have physical skills, I have a brain to process information, except I'm sorely lacking in information right now. This could be one of my only opportunities to find something out, but I'd better start with something innocuous.

'What day is it?' I talk around a mouthful like some sort of ravenous street urchin, chewing at the same time.

Tyson blinks at me. He glances out of the room at something, then his eyes come back. 'Wednesday. It's Wednesday.'

So, I've been here since yesterday afternoon – Tuesday afternoon. It already feels longer than that. Gardener was killed last

Friday. The Folio was stolen the previous Sunday. They've been looking for it for over a week now. They must be getting pretty desperate.

'So you guys really don't have any idea where the Folio is?' I peel some more foil and rip off another chunk of kebab with my teeth. 'How can you lose something so big and heavy?'

Tyson's face is stony. 'You tell me.'

I shrug, keep chewing. 'I dunno. I told you everything yesterday, so I'm all tapped out.'

'Then after we find your boyfriend, you're not much use to us, are you?' Tyson makes a tight smirk and pulls the door shut. The light goes off.

I swallow the lump of meat and lettuce in my mouth. If they find Mycroft, they'll put the thumbscrews on him to get what they want. And once they have it, he'll be nothing but deadwood. They've already killed Gardener – another body or two would hardly be a blip on their radar.

The kebab doesn't taste so great anymore. I take another half-hearted bite, then fold the foil over the rest. I swig water out of the soft-drink bottle, but the lump in my throat doesn't want to go down.

———

Being a kidnappee is frightening, painful and awkward. But above all, it's excruciatingly boring.

I'm stuck in my prison room with nothing to do for the rest of the morning. I chew my nails, eat a bit more cold kebab, go through of the rest of my pockets. There's a twenty-pence piece, the ticket stub from my Oxford bus trip, and a lot of lint. Nothing else as useful as the matches. I hanker for my satchel, which has the Conan Doyle book in it – at least that'd be something to keep my mind occupied.

At one point Tyson comes in, with an expression like he's rolling marbles in his mouth, and refills my water bottle, replaces my smelly bucket with an empty one. After that I get up and limp around, check the window again, try my weight against the bath. It won't budge. But my right knee makes it hard to put in any effort. I pull the blanket around myself and drop my jeans to have a look.

I have to peel the denim from the joint, the way I peeled the paper off the kebab. My knee is swollen, red with heat and starting to bloom an ominous fuchsia around a graze on one side.

It's not dislocated. Mike dislocated his shoulder once when he tripped over a ewe and hit the ground hard. A dislocation is incredibly painful – if I'd dislocated my knee I'd be writhing. The way it is now, I think it's either a bad bruise or – worst case scenario – I've cracked my kneecap.

I can't do anything about it, either way, so I carefully pull my jeans back up.

Sunlight shifts through the security grille on the window, making grainy lemon squares on the floor, blue pools of corner shade. Nobody comes in to check on me and there's nothing to do except sit and brood.

It's pretty obvious now, the sequence of events that led to the Folio's disappearance. Paul wormed his way into a job at the Bodleian. Gardener 'worked' on the Folio, then hid it somewhere in his office. He gave another book, disguised with the replica cover, to Collette Nichols. Unknowingly, she tucked the fake into the safe for the weekend. Then, at some point, Gardener walked out with the real Folio.

Gardener must have expected Nichols to trust him, with her genial personality, and their mutual appreciation of books. Showing her the replica cover, with the 'repairs' he'd done, must have been a bit heart-stopping, but Nichols wouldn't have expected Gardener to screw her over.

Then Paul, my old buddy, cracked the safe on Sunday night. He even bragged about it to me, that he was first on the scene when the safe was discovered open. He took out the fake Folio, ditched the book's worthless innards on a shelf, disposed of the replica cover before more security arrived on the scene in response to the alarm. Paul could just hold up his hands and say 'Yes officer, it was open when I got here'. And Gardener made sure he had an alibi for the night of the theft, by going to London that evening.

Except Gardener would have *had* to get the real Folio off the library premises before the safe was opened. He must have walked out with it on Friday. He wouldn't have wanted the real Folio discovered in his office when police searched the place . . .

But how do you just walk out with a book that big? What could you conceal it as?

I think of all the stuff in Gardener's office. Stuff that would look like a big rectangular package. A lever arch file. A file box or a . . .

He had his jacket half on, and a bundle of copy paper and a sandwich in one hand . . .

A ream of photocopy paper.

I suck in a breath. That's . . . That's it. That's what Nichols saw, and she didn't think anything of it, because she trusted Gardener and was familiar with his eccentric untidiness . . . I remember opening the photocopier drawer, seeing the full stack of paper

214

inside. Wondering why someone had opened a new ream of paper and put it on the table beside the copier.

Gardener used the glossy paper from around the ream to disguise the Folio when he walked out with it.

Bloody hell. What a ballsy thing to do.

He must have been scared. I imagine Gardener in his crumpled trousers, spectacles askew, his jacket half on and hugging an armful of stuff – his keys, his sandwich, a ream of copy paper – while he's sweating under his shirt. Saying goodbye to other colleagues on the stairs, fumbling his jacket the rest of the way on, all the while carrying one of the world's most valuable books out of the library . . .

I have to think further than that, though. What did Gardener do with the Folio after he took it? It wasn't in his car on the day he was killed, because both the murderers and the police searched there. It wasn't in Gardener's house, because Mycroft said the house had been turned over by someone else before SOCO arrived.

Which I realize, now I think about it, means that the Colonel or Paul or Tyson must have been the ones to do the searching. So Mycroft was right – Irina Addington was just a cover story. They set up the Folio theft with Gardener. And when Gardener didn't deliver the goods, when they thought he was about to squeal to the police, they murdered him.

And now they've got me.

This is bad. That useful fact emerges out of my mental filing cabinet to confront me, but I can't . . . I can't think about that. I have to concentrate on logic, on rational thoughts. Okay.

Okay, so the Folio wasn't in Gardener's car or his house, and it wasn't anywhere in Gardener's office – I didn't get the chance to do a thorough search yesterday, but I'm sure both the police and the Bodleian staff would have searched there.

He could have hidden it in the library somewhere. If not there, somewhere else. I think about places like Heathrow, where you can store your baggage in lockers, or post office boxes. Mycroft and the police could be investigating those places. They could be looking for *me*, right now, in Oxford . . . Except they'll be looking in the wrong place. I'm not in Oxford anymore.

Morning sun slowly warms the room. I turn the problem over in my mind until my mind gets tired. All this anxiety running around inside has left me drained.

I close my eyes, just for a second.

———

I wake up, disoriented.

My first look around brings my heart-rate back up. Maybe the Colonel and his mates are going to contact Mycroft, get the info, then shoot me in the head and dump me somewhere. Maybe, even simpler, they're just going to leave me here in this room. If they clear out, I'll be trapped.

I prop my back against the wall. My knee is throbbing steadily and my body aches, as though I'm running a fever. The room smells of mold, something slowly falling to rot, and my stomach rolls.

Bands of light score the walls beside the mattress. It must be near midday. That's four a.m., Melbourne time. Is Mum dreaming of me right now? Can she feel my fear across the miles, as she turns in bed at home?

Maybe she and Dad are hugged up together, worrying, in that soft body-heated tent under the quilt . . . When I was little, I used to love burrowing in tight between them, listening to the outside sounds of birds stirring, the dogs rattling on their chains, the early sun making the tin roof groan.

That world was such a smaller, more manageable place.

Coming to London . . . Flying halfway around the world to see a boy who doesn't want me any closer than skin, coming to another city where I can't see the stars, smell the fresh wind, soak up the sun unobstructed by buildings . . . What the bloody hell was I thinking?

Now I'm trapped. I'm *stuck* here.

My chest fills up with claustrophobic pressure. I hug my arms around myself. When the light comes on, I have to scrub at my face to make myself focus.

The door opens. The Colonel scowls. 'Come out now. We continue our discussion from yesterday.'

'I don't want to come out.' My voice quavers pathetically.

The Colonel's expression changes to something like pity. 'You are scared. I understand. These circumstances, they are unfortunate.'

I don't say anything. I sniff.

'There will be no more scenes like yesterday, I promise. We will only talk.'

'M-my knee hurts.'

'I give you more painkillers for your knee. Come out. You want to leave this room for a while, yes?'

I do want to get out of this room. But I don't want to go from the frying pan into the fire.

'Come.' The Colonel ushers with his hand, like a butler. He's wearing a navy T-shirt today, but the same tracksuit.

I lever myself up carefully. The blanket is my only armor, but it gets in my way so I dump it on the floor. The Colonel edges out the door and I follow slowly, a sheep being led by a bellwether.

Brassy light streams from clerestory windows high above us. Dust-motes float like wrigglers in a jar of water. An extra chair has been added to form a triangle of seats. I don't see anyone but the Colonel – god knows where Paul is, and Tyson isn't around either.

'Sit. Please.' The Colonel makes the royal wave again.

I ease myself down.

The Colonel takes the same seat as before. 'I have tea. Would you like tea?'

Two chipped mugs steam on the table beside the Colonel's chair. He moves to hand me one. I take it warily – it's hot under my cold fingers, smelling sweet. The first warm sip is like ambrosia. It makes me shudder all the way down.

'It is better, yes?' The Colonel smiles. 'Tea is very good. The great panacea.'

I nod, slurp more. If we're talking about tea then we're not talking about anything else. Anything hazardous to my health.

But the lull can't last.

'Now, Rachel, we share thoughts. Details.' The Colonel sips from his mug in a civilised way, leaning back in his chair with one thumb tapping on his tracksuited thigh. 'Any little thing. Something maybe you forget to share when last we talk.'

My hand shakes, so I rest my mug on my bad leg. The warmth of the mug tenderises the spot there, the swollen skin crying out for a hot compress.

'I didn't really see much of anything.' I let out a breath. 'I mean, I saw Gardener's car, but you already searched that.'

'How do you know this?' The Colonel frowns.

I raise my eyebrows at him. 'You . . . you lifted the spare tire to check underneath, and then forgot to screw it back in. There was no way it could've come loose in the crash. I know a bit about cars. Enough to know that.'

The Colonel swears under his breath in what I assume is his native language. His eyebrows meet in the middle – it reminds me of Principal Conroy.

He sets his mug on the table. 'What else? You saw the home?'

'No. Not the house. I wasn't allowed. I saw Gardener's body. The autopsy.'

'You have a strong stomach, eh?'

I shrug in a lopsided way. 'I guess. There was a little parcel of effects – just a few receipts, the photo of his sister and his niece . . .'

The photo that got me into this mess in the first place.

The Colonel seems appeased – he's nodding his head, rubbing his chin. 'Yes. Hokay. This is good.'

I don't know what's good about it. I haven't given him any information at all. I'm not sure why he's wheeled me out of my prison room to 'chat'. He already seems confident that I don't have a clue where the Folio is.

There's a clatter on the steps, from the floor below us.

The Colonel glances in that direction before turning back to me, all smiles. 'Yes. So we make good decision, yes, to contact your friend over internet. He will know more.'

I lean forward automatically. My knee pinches hard enough to make me gasp.

'You've contacted my boyfriend?' I lick my lips. 'Is he . . . Did he say he'll trade information? Will he—'

The noise rises up the stairwell, drowning me out. The Colonel isn't paying me attention in any case. He's swivelled in his chair to look towards the staircase, so I look too.

Clomping footsteps preface the arrival of three figures – they rise out of the stairwell gloom like three bodies floating to the top of a black lake. One of them is Tyson; he seems overheated in his leather jacket. On the other side is Paul. He looks ragged, bashed and bruised all over his face, as if he should be in a hospital.

But Paul's personal health has faded into the background for me, because he and Tyson are leading someone else, the middle figure, by the elbow. And that person, his head covered by a hessian bag, is a tall, lean figure, limping forward in black jeans and a red-striped hoodie . . .

'*NO.*' The word spills out of me like a sob. I drop my mug – the brown liquid sloshes onto the wooden floor.

'Ah.' The Colonel swivels back to face me. 'Now we can ask the questions to your friend in person, yes?'

Tyson yanks the hessian bag away.

Mycroft's brown curls are a bit squashed from the bag. He spits hessian dust out of his mouth, his eyes scanning fast.

'Watts.' His whole face relaxes when he sees me. He grins. 'Have you been having fun without me?'

CHAPTER SIXTEEN

I make this awful noise and stagger up from the chair, except I can't stand properly. I have to brace myself against the chair back.

Mycroft tries to shakes himself out of Paul's grip. Paul glares at him with bloodshot eyes until the Colonel says, 'Please. Let them come together.'

Then Mycroft is in front of me, and I let go of the chair and throw my arms around his neck.

'*No no no no no . . .*' I whisper, but I can hardly even get that out. I clutch Mycroft as though I'm drowning.

He's all corded muscle and tension. Beneath the smell of hessian is the scent of cigarettes and sweat and that guy smell, Mycroft's own smell. His breath is warm on my ear, on my neck.

The combination of relief and horror inside me is so strong I feel sick.

Mycroft glances over his shoulder at the Colonel. 'Do you mind?'

He's lifting his arms backwards and I see his wrists, fastened together with a cable tie. I sob again. The Colonel pulls a switch-blade out of the pocket of his track pants. He looks all too natural, flicking that switch, but at least now Mycroft can put his arms around me.

Mycroft grabs me in a crushing grip. I wail into his neck, I strangle the fabric of his jacket, hanging on to the hard planes of him underneath.

'Hey, hey . . .' Mycroft strokes my hair, lifts my chin with one hand as he keeps my body tucked protectively into his. 'It's all right. Come on.'

He wipes my cheek with his thumb and I realize I'm crying.

Of course as soon as I realize this, it makes me cry harder. 'Oh *god*, you weren't meant to *come*. You were supposed to give them the information *online*, you weren't supposed to—'

'Hey. Shh, it's okay.' He curls me against his body, whispers low in my ear. *'Nothing on earth could've kept me away.'*

I make this noise again, this gasping, lowing groan, because I wish, oh *god*, I wish that Mycroft wasn't here, in this place. But the way we're holding each other makes a mockery of my wishes.

The Colonel puts up with this outpouring for a few seconds longer, then claps his hands. 'Excellent. Very good. It is touching, this moment. Now you will both sit down, please, and we continue our discussion.'

Still holding me tight with one arm, as if he's never going to let me go, Mycroft turns slowly to the Colonel. 'Right. A discussion. Nice accent, by the way, very post-Cold-War. That's Serbian, is it?'

The Colonel just gives one of his neutral, enigmatic smiles. I'm starting to recognize that he does this when he's irritated.

I tug on Mycroft's sleeve. 'James—'

'Because there's this kid in Year Eleven, he speaks the same way,' Mycroft goes on, staring the Colonel straight in the eye. 'Exactly the same. And he's Bosnian-Serb. Except, yeah . . . with better dress sense. So am I on the money?'

The Colonel says nothing. He glances sideways at Paul.

Paul marches over and grabs Mycroft by the arm. He's torn away from me so suddenly I wobble and lose my balance, flomp back onto my chair. Tyson takes up station behind me.

Paul hauls Mycroft over and pushes him into chair number three. He stands behind Mycroft, with one hand pressing down on Mycroft's shoulder. Mycroft glances my way, then glares at Paul's hand as if he'd like to bite it off and spit it on the floor.

The Colonel seats himself. 'Thank you, yes, for agreeing to come. You are Rachel's boyfriend, James Mycroft.'

And I feel, for a moment, as though my lungs have been removed. I've just realized something vital, maybe fatal. When I provided the Colonel with Mycroft's name, I didn't think about his history. His theory about the carjackers now seems horribly right, and suddenly I feel stupid, and sick, and scared, all at the same time. Has the Colonel made the connection between Mycroft's name and the name of the family he most likely put to death seven years ago? If he has, he's not giving away the merest flicker.

'Yes,' the Colonel continues. 'Very funny guy. Very clever. This is good. We need clever people to work out this little problem we have.'

'The problem.' Mycroft nods slowly. His eyes are dark as midnight. 'Right. The problem being that you don't know where your dead librarian dumped a six million pound book. Unless you're referring to the other problem, the one where you've kidnapped an Australian national.'

The Colonel spreads one hand. 'Please. You are angry. This is unhelpful. Your girlfriend is here, you are worried for her, but she is well. We treat her very courteously. Rachel, we treat you courteously, no?'

My eyes skitter from the Colonel to Mycroft and back again. I bite my bottom lip, make a tiny nod.

'You see,' the Colonel says, 'she is fine. Her knee is bad from her arrival here – this was accident. We give her painkillers, food, water. She is not mistreated in any way. We only seek for . . . cooperation. Yes. We have mutual interest.'

'Mutual interest.' Mycroft mouths the words. His jaw is knotted tight as a bowline.

'Yes, of course. You have some information for us. You give us this information, then you both go free, yes? That is all.'

Mycroft stares at the Colonel: he's got that look, as though he's mulling something over. But I don't want him to mull, I want him to just give up the information. Then we can tell the Colonel where to go, and get the hell out of here.

'Okay,' Mycroft says finally. 'I give you the information, and we go free.'

'Yes.' The Colonel smiles, a genuine-looking smile this time. 'You understand.'

'I have two conditions,' Mycroft says.

My mouth falls open. The Colonel looks equally surprised, except he doesn't gape, just lets his eyebrows rise to his hairline.

'Forgive me, but you are not in very good bargaining position, no?'

'No.' Mycroft shakes his head, hessian drifting out of his hair. 'I'm actually in an excellent bargaining position. I have six million

224

pounds worth of info that you can't get anywhere else. So I have two conditions.'

He reaches into his jacket pocket. Paul reacts immediately, grabbing his elbow like the scruff of a cat's neck. Mycroft gives him a look.

The Colonel frowns, glances at Paul. Paul's grip loosens enough for Mycroft to pull a pack of cigarettes out of his pocket.

'See? Just the same pack of smokes you found when you searched me.' Mycroft waves the pack, cocks an eyebrow at the Colonel. 'Your guys here really need to dial it down.'

The Colonel says nothing.

Mycroft pulls out a cigarette and balances it on his lip. 'Got a light?'

The Colonel lifts his stare to Tyson. Tyson snorts, but walks over and pulls out a plastic lighter. He lights Mycroft's cigarette, then walks back to me.

'Right.' Mycroft flaps at the smoke. 'Here are my conditions. The first one is this. Whatever you get out of me, whatever happens, if you find the Folio or not . . . Rachel gets released. That is Condition Number One. Non-negotiable.'

'Mycroft—' I start.

'No.' He looks at me, back to the Colonel. His face is determined, dead serious. 'Agreed?'

'Agreed.' The Colonel nods slowly.

'Condition Number Two.' Mycroft takes a long drag, blows it out. 'You give *me* some information. About a job you worked seven years ago. A car on the A1, with three people inside, they smashed into a road pylon . . .'

My breath gets sucked into a vacuum. Because I didn't see this coming, but I should have. I *should have*. I'm sitting in a room between Mycroft and the man who destroyed his life. Suddenly I remember Mycroft's face when he said *I had my father's brain matter in my hair when they pulled me out* and oh Christ, I can't breathe—

'This . . .' the Colonel says, frowning, 'this is not useful. This information is not for you. My employer is not interested in sharing this information with other parties.'

Mycroft shakes his head, flicks ash onto the floor.

'That's terrible. That's a terrible shame.' He looks at the Colonel, his eyes blue as balefire. He takes another drag and blows it skyward. 'Your employer, yeah? Then I guess you better get on the blower and convince him otherwise. Because that's what I want. Condition Number One and Condition Number Two. Or I'm going to find it very hard to recall all the facts in this Gardener case. There's a lot of detail, and I might leave something out, or just forget about it by accident.'

The Colonel is staring. I'm staring. Mycroft looks very calm, in control. I'm used to him launching into theater for some useful purpose – I think of the Deputy Coroner, which was only yester-day, my god – but this is the performance of a lifetime. His eyes are dark-circled, he looks tired, but his hands aren't even shaking.

'I guess you could hammer me,' Mycroft goes on blithely. 'That might work for a bit, you might get something that way. But the human brain does funny things when it's under stress. My mind might suddenly become completely blank . . .'

Mycroft's voice is almost blasé, but there's a look in his eye I'm familiar with. The razor-edged look, the one that unnerves Princi-pal Conroy and makes me think of loose electrical wires sparking.

The Colonel, for all that he doesn't know Mycroft from Adam, seems to recognize that expression somehow. Maybe he's seen it before, in his 'work'. Maybe he sometimes wears it himself, I don't know. But now he examines Mycroft's face with a narrow-eyed wariness, which I think may be as close to respect as he ever gets.

'I am familiar with this job you speak of,' he says slowly. 'Your family name . . . *Mycroft*, yes?'

Mycroft seems to have forgotten his cigarette. Curls of smoke drift into his eyes.

'Yes.' The Colonel looks down at the floor, squeezes his knee. 'It comes back to me. A white car. This was . . . some time ago.'

'Seven years.' Mycroft's voice is clipped, hoarse. 'Not a long time. Seven years is just like yesterday, isn't it?'

The Colonel inclines his head. 'Not yesterday. But not so long. This was very simple job. Find this person, trace this car, make an accident. Very simple.'

Mycroft's eyes glitter. His face suddenly appears a lot more hollow. 'But it didn't turn out to be quite so simple, did it?'

The Colonel shrugs. 'The method was . . . a little clumsy. Not so effective. There was some attention from police, from media, so my employer was not completely happy.'

Mycroft drops his butt, grinds it out carefully with the heel of his Con. 'You've improved the process since then.'

'I am more efficient now.' The Colonel waves a hand. 'But the objective was achieved, all the same. Eliminate this man, eliminate his family . . . Nothing is traceable and nobody makes connections. My employer is satisfied, I am satisfied. Everybody wins, yes?'

Everybody wins.

So casual, the way he says it. My shoulders and legs start trembling. A mental image crashes into me: Mike's old Five Mile mate, Harris Derwent, with a wicked grin and a lit match, standing beside the garbage pile he's just poured petrol on, saying *This should make a nice little bang, eh?*

Mycroft's eyes are fixed on the Colonel and his cheekbones jut out. He sucks his bottom lip into his mouth. His hands grip his knees as though he's only barely holding it in, the urge to rise, to launch himself at the Colonel, lash out—

This should make a nice little bang.

I almost jump out of my chair, knee or no knee.

'I want to go back to my room now. Please. My leg is hurting, and I'm . . .' My breath hitches. I'm lopsided with the shakes. 'I feel sick. *Please*. I just want to go back to my room.'

The Colonel looks over as if he's forgotten I'm there. Mycroft startles, stares at me.

Tears start pooling behind my lashes. My head is pounding. '*Please*.'

'Of course.' The Colonel stands politely. 'Rachel, my apologies. You are unwell.'

He steps forward and extends a hand, as though he's going to help me walk. Suddenly Mycroft is there, blocking the Colonel.

'Don't you fucking *touch* her.' Mycroft puts his arm around my waist, his eyes lasered on the Colonel.

The Colonel straightens with a sneer. 'Of course. You are her protector now, yes? A great pity, certainly, that you were unable to protect her before, when she is taken because of your involvement in this investigation . . .'

Mycroft's lip curls into a snarl. 'Why don't you *get stuffed*, you fucking—'

I've got to get these two separated before they go for each other's throats.

'I want to lie down. I'm gonna be sick.' I stagger towards the room. Mycroft is forced to keep up. 'Just a little—'

I take a wrong step and come down hard on my knee. The pain is . . . *oh*. I hear this shriek and realize I'm the one making it. The air around me goes flashy and sticky, my lungs filling up, and nothing is . . . nothing is . . .

'*Watts*.' Mycroft's voice, his arm firmly around me, holding me up. 'Come on, Watts. I've got you. Nearly there.'

Then we must be there, because I hear the clunk of the door being locked, and the light is dimmer. Mycroft's arms surround me and we are alone.

'Are you going to throw up?' Mycroft leans in to find my eyes. 'Rachel—'

The pain is still there, making everything sepia-toned. But I'm telescoping back down. It's becoming more manageable. I shake my head, which isn't really the best idea, so I stop.

I concentrate on breathing. 'I don't . . . I'm—'

Mycroft's steadying me, and I shift in his arms. I throw myself into him. He squeezes me hard, so hard, gasps into my neck.

'Oh Jesus Christ, I thought you were dead.' His whole body is shaking. '*Fuck*, Rachel—'

I cry out, a desperate sound. Part of it is my knee, but even that's fading now with the feel of Mycroft's body, his warmth and his texture and his smell. The other part of it is this emotion filling me up. Because he is *here*, here with me, and I feel as if I'm being sawn in half.

'God, this isn't *happening*, you can't *be* here.' I alternate between whacking my hand on his chest and hugging him to me. 'Mycroft, these people will *kill you* once they get this information—'

He kisses me then, just like that. We're standing in the middle of this dingy room, our mouths coming together like this is our first kiss. It is passionate, and hungry, and so full of despair that my eyes well up.

When we break apart, I'm breathless. 'James—'

'It doesn't matter.' He pushes my sweaty hair back from my face, leans his forehead against mine. 'It doesn't matter. They're going to kill us anyway.'

'*What?*'

'They're going to kill us anyway.' Mycroft leans back and shoves a hand into his curls. His expression is helpless. 'That's why he's being so generous with his information, your Colonel. We've seen their faces now. We can identify them. That's why I had a go at trading with him, because I knew we didn't have anything to lose, and I thought there was a chance I could at least get *you* out, so—'

'Then—' I pull back, shock and anger gurgling up inside. 'Then why did you *come*? For fuck's *sake*, Mycroft, you didn't have to meet them! You could've just—'

'Could've *what*? Opted out?' Mycroft stares at me, his eyebrows clashing together. 'Did you think I was just going to *leave* you here? Their message said you were still alive. I wasn't just going to pass over the information and wait around for your body to surface in the bloody Thames!'

He breaks away, breathing hard, one hand on his waist.

'But James, don't you get it?' I stand there unsteadily, looking at him. My rib cage is so tight it's about to implode. 'I could handle it when it was just me. But now *you're* here, and for god's sake, I'm as scared for you as I am for me! Don't you—'

Mycroft pulls me back into him, cutting me off. I think I'm going to cry again, but I can't do anything except gasp into his

230

chest. I'm completely exhausted. Just clinging on to him takes all my strength.

'It's all right,' he whispers. 'We'll figure it out. I emailed Walsh before I met with them. He'll know about this by now, he'll tell the cops to start looking. We'll get out of here.'

'*Both* of us,' I say. My whole body quivers. 'Swear it.'

'I swear it,' he says.

When I look into his eyes, I almost believe it could happen.

Once my shuddering has subsided I clutch Mycroft's shoulders as he helps me hobble to the mattress.

He eases me down, kneels on the dirty floor. 'Come on, let's have a look at your leg. God, they really fucked you up, didn't they?'

'No.' I shake my head. 'The Colonel was right, it was an accident during the struggle when they first grabbed me. They haven't been breaking my kneecaps or anything.'

Mycroft touches the denim over my knee with the pads of his fingers. I try to be tough enough not to wince.

'We've got to get your leg out of these jeans. Shit, they wouldn't even let me bring a pocketknife . . .' He casts around at the floor. 'Can't see any loose nails. Hold on.'

He leans forward and suddenly his head is in my lap. His hot breath eases through the denim of my jeans – he's biting the fabric halfway up my thigh. *Will Flame In Wind Or Rain*, I think, and warmth rushes into my face, and bloody *hormones*, they have no sense of propriety at all.

I give a hoarse laugh. 'I can't believe you're doing this.'

'What?' He looks up, all innocence, but there's a blush on his cheeks. 'I can't think of any other way to do it.'

'Well, hurry up and do it, before we get distracted.'

He lowers his head again, grinning. 'This is distracting you?'

231

'Yes. You're ripping my jeans off with your teeth. I'm getting kind of turned on.'

He snorts and busies himself with his task. Sooner than I'd like he's made a hole big enough for him to slide a finger into, and from that point he can just rip down and across.

I hiss. A dreadful mix of pain and relief hammers into me as my knee is freed from the denim.

'Jesus.' Mycroft eases back the fabric carefully, grimaces at the offending part. God, it looks hideous now – an eggplant-colored swollen lump, with pieces of blue thread stuck in the graze.

'Right, I'm just going to . . .' He touches my knee with fingertips that are barely a whisper. 'Is that okay?'

I nod, bite my lip.

'Right, can you bend it at all? Can you lift your leg?'

I can, barely. The effort makes me break out in a shivering sweat.

I let him prod gently for a few more seconds then blurt out my own diagnosis. 'It's broken, isn't it? I mean, it's not bad enough to be shattered. But I think I've cracked it, at least.'

He lets out a breath. 'Yeah. I think you've cracked it here on the outside edge, but you'll need X-rays to confirm. We need to immobilise it. Hang on.'

He gets up and looks around, seeing the same as me – a grotty room with no chair to break, no useful item at all except bed, blanket, bucket, bath and soft-drink bottle.

'There's nothing for a splint,' he says, frustrated.

We end up using the ripped-off arms from my long-sleeved T-shirt as a half-arsed compression bandage. It's awful, squeezing my knee back into a constricted space. But it's all we can do, and my knee feels better now it's straight.

'How are we going to get out?' I whisper, as we finish tying off the fabric.

'I don't know.' Mycroft shakes his head, his soft curls tumbling. 'Shit . . . Let me think.'

He looks as exhausted as I feel. He climbs onto the mattress, props his back against the wall and pulls me close. I cuddle against him. The warmth of his chest is better than a thousand Panadols.

'Oh god, I nearly went out of my mind.' He hugs me to him, breathing into my hair. 'I didn't get back from Scotland Yard until eight last night, I thought you'd be so hacked off . . . But then you weren't at the hostel. And your phone kept saying your number was unavailable, so I tried Alicia, and she was still in Camden, had no idea where you were either. Professor Walsh said maybe you'd gone to a show, but you'd said earlier that you were going to meet me, and I just . . . I knew there was something wrong.'

'I didn't go to a show,' I sigh.

'Yeah, well. Alicia didn't think so either. We searched every-where we could think of – she was almost as frantic as me. Then finally, at about eleven, I nicked the Professor's car and Alicia drove us to Oxford, hoping to find you somewhere. The whole bloody place was like a tomb, and you were just . . . gone.'

'They must have brought me here early in the evening. I don't know for sure. I got kind of knocked out.'

'Christ.' Mycroft lifts my chin so he can look at my eyes. 'Yeah, your pupils are a little too big. Probably a touch of concussion.'

'That would explain the monster headaches.'

Mycroft's jaw is tight as a drum. 'I'm gonna murder that military prick.'

Lightning zigzags across his face and I know he's thinking about all of it – his parents, us, this. It's all rolled up inside him like a ball of snakes, and without something to focus on it's going to writhe around and bite at his gut.

'Mycroft, look at me.' I tug on his jacket collar, force his attention. 'Seriously, come on. No revenge scenarios, okay? I know you're angry, but we have to think. We have to concentrate on getting the hell out of here.'

He closes his eyes and turns his head, but he nods. My face tucks back into his chest.

'Y'know, the stupidest thing is . . . it's my fault.' I breathe into his T-shirt. 'I went to the Bodleian and introduced myself as Natalie Sutcliffe.'

'You *what*?'

I look up, blushing. 'Well, there was no way they were going to tell me anything about Gardener if I was just some random person. So I said I was Natalie, Gardener's niece. Except the guy you met earlier – the blond guy with the bruised face – was posing as a security guard. I guess he thought if he brought me in I could give them something useful about Gardener and the Folio.'

Mycroft lifts my chin again. He has this frustrated grin. 'You are bloody certifiable, d'you know that? My god . . . Were you the one who messed up that guy's face?'

'Partly.' I shrug, then shiver. 'It was the Colonel who did the most damage, when he realized he had the wrong girl.'

'Yeah, he's running the show, it'd be his responsibility. Bloody hell . . .' Mycroft grabs my hand, lacing our fingers together. 'When I finally got back to London and checked my email, and there was a Comments alert from the blog with a message about you . . .'

He's starting to tremble. I look at up him, raise my hand to his cheek—

The light comes on and the door bangs open.

It's Paul, walking in like he owns the place. 'Yeah, this is real sweet and all, but your bloke's got bills to pay.'

He strides up to the mattress and grabs Mycroft by the arm. We barely have time to disentangle.

I half-fall off the bed, overbalancing, my stupid leg stuck out straight. 'Don't you bloody hurt him!'

Paul gives me a leer. It looks ghastly, distorted with all his bruises.

'We're not gonna hurt him,' he says. 'We're just gonna tickle him a bit, yeah?'

Mycroft staggers, his arm twisted behind his back. We only have time to make eye contact once – this gasping white-eyed glance – before he's bundled out of the room.

CHAPTER SEVENTEEN

I do go all secret agent then – as much as it's possible to go secret agent with a broken kneecap. Crawling off the bed and pressing my ear to the door, I try to make out what's going on in the next room.

But then I wish I hadn't. I hear the low rise and fall of murmured talk, then the thud of something hard hitting something soft. Mycroft coughs, and there's another thud . . .

There's more talking than hitting, but the hitting still happens, like a flat, monotonous punctuation. Every time I hear it, I flinch. I sit there listening and flinching as the light outside the window shifts into late afternoon.

Towards the end, I can't stand it. I start banging on the door. 'God, don't *do* this. Please, he'll give you what you want, *please*—'

Suddenly the light goes on and the door rattles – I hobble upright and hold the wall. Tyson pushes the door open and shoves Mycroft back into the room.

The Colonel stands in the doorway now. He stares from me to Mycroft, sprawled facedown on the wooden floor. 'We will check this information you give. Please, this is not personal. I am sure you understand.'

'Sure.' Mycroft prises himself out of the dust with shaking arms, spitting stringy red blood onto the floor. His voice is hoarse. 'It's not personal. Just business. I get it.'

'Very good.' The Colonel gives a malign smile as he pulls the door closed. The light snaps off.

'*James*.' I hop over and sink down beside him.

Mycroft rolls over and props himself up on one arm. He carefully touches the purple lump over one high cheekbone. Sweat and dirt are smeared on his face. His bottom lip is cut, starting to swell, and the line of his jaw is bruised.

He tongues the space between his teeth and his cheek with his eyes closed. 'Yeah, that wasn't actually as entertaining as I'd originally thought it was going to be . . .'

He winces when I cradle his hot cheek with my cold hand.

I blink hard to get myself together. 'Can you walk? Let's get you off the floor.'

'Ah, *shit*.' His face contorts as he levers up, his hand sticking to his ribs. 'Okay, that hurts . . .'

'Come on.' We hobble and stagger to the mattress.

Now I can push his hoodie out of the way and lift his T-shirt to see the damage. His rib cage is like chewed steak on one side – I'm almost scared to touch it. When I check the bones for give, he hisses.

'Ah . . . Yeah, they really liked gut shots for some reason.' His eyes screw up as my fingers move gently. He looks incredibly tired. 'That guy with the jacket has really big fists. Although your mate

237

with the blond hair seems quite pissed off, too. He was enacting a bit of personal retribution on me, I think.'

'Why did they do this?' I shake my head. 'You agreed to come. You're giving them what they want. There's no point.'

'I think they just like hitting people.' He watches me as I grimace at the sore spots on his ribs. 'Actually, there was a bit of a point. I was trying to hold out for a while, to give us some more time if the police are searching . . .'

'Mycroft . . .'

He looks at me and sighs. 'We keep getting beat up.'

'I know,' I say miserably. 'It's not fair.'

'Lion pens, warehouses . . . As my events manager, you are officially sacked.'

He grins, the blood on his lip runs onto his chin, and the grin turns into a cough. He coughs with this wretched hacking sound, his face distorted.

I'm going to cry again if I don't do something. I drag the soft-drink bottle closer, unscrew the lid.

'Here, drink a little. It's water, it's okay . . .' I'm whispering, but my voice keeps catching.

Mycroft sips the water, gets his breath back. I sip too, pull off my flannie shirt to drip some water onto it and wipe his face.

We sit together on the mattress, both of us battle-scarred, and watch the pebbled light behind the security grille turn stormy gray. Rain starts drizzling down from a London sky.

'You're shivering,' Mycroft says.

'It's cold.' I hug my bare arms around myself. 'I feel like I've been cold ever since I arrived in this bloody country.'

Mycroft scoots me over, then eases off his hoodie and balls it up, puts my bundled flannie next to it for a meager pillow. He lies down on the mattress beside me. I open out the blanket and tuck it around us.

We lie snuggled up together, careful of my leg, trying to conserve our body heat. It's like lying in my parents' bed as a child, that soft, enclosed body-heated tent. We're face to face, holding our tangled fingers in front.

My voice is a bare breath. 'What did you tell them?'

'What I knew,' he says softly. 'Irina Addington finally broke down under questioning, admitted she was just a stooge for Gardener's murder. I think Irina's confession was only ever a delaying tactic. The Colonel said himself that she owed them – I got that much while they were laying into me. So the police've figured out that the Folio theft was an inside job, that Gardener actually was involved. I just told the Colonel about what the police have already examined: Gardener's effects from the car crash, the receipts, the bookie's slip, the photo. Plus the stuff from his house. And there were keys – one for a post office box. He also had a bank deposit box.'

'So the Folio might be in one of those places.'

'Honestly, it could be anywhere. He also had a regular corral at the British Library, so there's a chance he may have hidden the Folio somewhere there. They're searching those places now. The only thing they're really not sure of is how Gardener got the Folio out of the Bodleian in the first place.'

'I think I know. When I was there yesterday, I saw his office. He had pictures of the Folio, and a whole lot of equipment – leather, cord, varnish. I think he made a copy of the Folio's cover. He was an expert. He would have known exactly how to go about making a replica cover. Then he put it around another book of a similar size and weight, returned it to its box and handed it back to the

Head of Rare Books. When she signed it back in, she was signing in a fake.'

'So when they saw the safe had been ransacked and raised the alarm, everyone just assumed that the Folio had been taken from the safe.'

'Only it wasn't the real Folio at all. Paul, the beat-up guy who was working as a security guard – he would've just broken into the safe and removed the fake to make it look like the real Folio had been taken. He probably slipped the fake cover off the book and then disposed of it somewhere – down a garbage chute, or through a shredder, or even back in Gardener's office.'

'And Gardener had an alibi for the night of the theft.'

'Yeah. But Gardener's boss said she saw him take a bundle of copy paper home with him on Friday night, and I thought . . . Well, I think he might have just walked out with the real Folio, disguised as a ream of copy paper.'

'Jesus. What a gutsy thing to do, to walk right out with it under everyone's noses . . .'

'That's what *I* thought. But then Gardener started to have second thoughts, for some reason. When the Colonel came to collect it, he begged for more time, and eventually contacted the police. Somehow the Colonel got wind of it – a phone tap, maybe – and when they saw him leaving the next day with a parcel in the boot . . . It wasn't until after the carjacking that they realized their mistake. Gardener fooled all of them, in the end. Not that it did him any good.'

Mycroft is wearing an amazed expression. 'Bloody hell. That's really clever.'

'Gardener's sleight of hand, or me figuring it out?'

'Both.' He steeples our fingers together. 'It's good for me, you know.'

'What is?'

'You, being clever. Takes a load off.'

I raise an eyebrow. 'Gee, thanks.'

'No, it's not like . . .' Mycroft looks at our joined hands. His blue eyes leap out from the bruises. 'I mean, I can never take you for granted.'

'That's right.' I grin, but it's a wonky old grin. 'And you better not.'

'You were right about Gardener, from the start.' Mycroft slides our fingers together, curls them over each other like the tails of sleeping possums. 'And you were right about me. The Colonel confirmed what I thought about my parents, about the accident . . . It still doesn't make me feel more whole.'

'At least you know what happened.' My voice is very soft.

'I knew that already. I was there.' Mycroft swallows hard. 'I still don't know why my mum and dad were killed. But I don't think it matters. Knowing won't make it better, won't bring them back. I just . . . I have to make my own history. Rebuild myself, from the ground up.' He looks at me as I watch him. 'You knew that.'

'Yes.' The thickness in my throat is unbearable.

Mycroft stares. 'How did you know that? How do you know me better than I know myself? We only met six months ago.'

'I just . . .' I squeeze his hand in mine. Our palms join perfectly, key in lock. 'Maybe it's easier, from the outside. I've got the same facts as you, but you're all . . . boiling around inside with all these feelings, whereas I can be more objective.'

'Detached.'

'No. Not detached. Because I care. But I can be more logical, because I'm not right in the center of it.'

Mycroft's lips part, his eyes slip gently over my face. It takes him a second before he can form the words he's after.

'You're in the center, Watts. Right here.' He touches his chest, over his heart, with his other hand. 'You're always in the center.'

I blink at him. He's come here, gotten himself torn to pieces, and now . . .

I have to press my lips together before speaking. 'God, you should rest. You look exhausted. How much sleep have you had since Saturday morning?'

His eyes open and close, like clamshells. 'Can't remember.'

I touch his cheek with my fingertips. 'Does your face hurt?'

'Yeah.' He grimaces. 'My ribs are worse, though.'

'You need to sleep. Come on, spoon up with me.'

We take off our shoes and wriggle into a new position so I'm lying on my good side, with Mycroft fitted snugly against my back. I pull the blanket over us, curl his arm around my waist. We lie together for a while, just breathing.

Drizzle tap-dances on the roof and the air is cottonwool soft. Mycroft's arm over me is a warm, reassuring weight. If we weren't here, in this warehouse, I'd almost feel at peace.

Every time Mycroft inhales I feel it against my back. His shoulders settle with the movement, his chest presses against me. I have never felt so soothed, or – bizarrely – so protected.

Mycroft's breathing levels out: I think he's dozing. I pray he's getting some rest, something to recharge him for the who-knows-what ahead. After a while, I drift off into that pleasant faraway space between sleep and waking.

I don't know when it starts to change. The room has darkened – it could be the rain, but I think it's the start of evening. We've been lying here for a long time, in this private, languorous place.

Now the air starts to thicken. Every spot where Mycroft is pressed against me ripples into awareness.

The length of his body heats me up under the blanket. His hand is on my waist and his legs are gently jumbled with mine, supporting my damaged knee. My hair is coiled beneath my head, so Mycroft's face is tucked against the back of my neck. When he exhales, all the hairs on my nape shiver.

I don't know how long we have left, how much time they'll give us. The next time we're hauled into the other room, it could be to cop a bullet in the head. And no matter how tired I might be, I don't want to sleep through this. This is us. This is our spark, and I want to live through every last moment of it.

My head sinks into the makeshift pillow. Mycroft shifts by a fraction. His hot breath ignites the skin of my shoulder.

But it's his hand on my waist that has me humming inside – it's making these soft, rhythmic squeezes that are so light, so delicate and seductive. The skin of my stomach shimmers every time his fingers move.

I slide my hand up to his.

'Rachel—' he whispers, and his fingers still.

I push his hand higher until his palm cups my breast. His soft gasp resonates against my neck.

My voice is a whisper too. *'Don't stop.'*

With my hand over his larger one, I feel the tremble in his fingers when he makes the first tentative touch. His thumb smooths lightly across the swell of my breast. Only the thin cotton of my T-shirt and the lace of my bra separates us, and it feels *right*.

Everything inside me relaxes and tightens at the same time, and the circumstances don't matter. This is the way it should be. This is pure – just me and Mycroft and this slowly building inevitability.

I spin out of myself as his palm rubs, as his thumb does this careful little dance. My whole body pulses, my breathing shallow and short. Mycroft presses soft kisses to the skin of my neck and shoulder. Tension is thrumming through him.

Suddenly I can't stand not seeing him. I roll onto my back and he's there, propped on one elbow, gazing down at me. His eyes are huge, red-rimmed from exhaustion, black with pupil. His crazy curls tumble around his face, a deep brown cloud, and his pallor makes his darkened cheekbone stand out. In spite of the bruises and abuse, his face is beautiful.

He's breathing heavily, blinking at me with that same awed expression he had when I kissed him in the morgue.

He looks between his hand on my breast to my face, as if he's in shock. 'I couldn't sleep. You smell good. I'm sorry—'

'I can't smell good.' I smile. 'That's crazy.'

'No, you do. You smell like—' Suddenly he dips his head, tucks his face into my neck.

I gasp. His curls tickle my jaw and my chin lifts, granting him access. His lips meet the delicate skin at the base of my throat and he inhales deeply.

Something about the gesture completely floors me. I press my head into his jacket behind me, stretching my neck. My back has risen off the bed. Mycroft's hand on my breast makes slow circles, and I can't stop panting.

He kisses and sucks gently all the way up my neck. He's shaking so much I have to touch him. As my hands slide under his T-shirt, over the warm, soft skin of his waist, he makes a shuddering jerk.

I stop. 'Are your ribs . . . Are my hands cold?'

244

'No, god, your hands . . .' He swallows. 'That's just really . . . It's . . .'

'Sensitive?'

'Yes,' he whispers.

A thrill of power sings through me as I watch him with his eyes squeezed shut. It's one high, crystalline note that obliterates every thought.

I trace my fingers lower, to the silken line of his hip. 'And here?'

'Yes—' His voice cracks on the word.

'Here?' I'm fishing for a reaction now. My hand trails across his stomach, feeling the swell and dip of muscle. I scratch my fingernails through the short, soft hairs between his navel and the button of his jeans.

'*Rachel*—'

'Here is good?'

'Yes. Yes. Christ.' He shivers – it seems to echo down into the core of his being. He opens his eyes to look at me. 'We can't.'

'Why not?'

'Because we're being held captive in a grungy warehouse. Because you have a broken knee. Because I have cracked ribs. Because—'

'I want you,' I whisper, and it feels raw and right, but I don't think it's going to be enough. 'I want you, and I don't care.'

'*I* care. I don't want our first time together to be this kind of scared, desperate—'

I can't stand it, that he's speaking the truth, and I can't stand that this might be all the time we have. I reach up with one hand and pull Mycroft's face down to mine. I kiss him softly, slowly, careful of the split in his lip. My tongue sweeps into his mouth – he tastes like molasses and blood.

My other hand skims over his chest, under his T-shirt, gentle with his ribs, tracing the curves. He makes the noise I love, a low whimpering groan. His hand squeezes my breast unconsciously and I *ache* inside. A deep throbbing fills my bones, and my heartbeat is loud and powerful.

When I let him up for air, his face is amazing – so open, lips wet and swollen from kissing, cheeks fevered. His eyes are half-lidded, glassy and bottomless, the blue between his lashes an elemental darkness. The way he's looking at me now is different, as though he's about to cross some line he can't pull back from.

He stares right into me as he moves his hand from my breast. I want to cry out, but he's just sliding it down, slipping it under my T-shirt hem, dragging his fingers in long, deliberate movements across the skin of my stomach. I shiver, I can't help it.

'Tell me to stop,' he whispers thickly.

I swallow and my voice hardly works. 'I don't want you to.'

He slides his fingers up to my breast again, touching me through the lace. My back rises again, and my knee is hurting but I don't care, I don't care—

'Rachel, tell me to stop.' He's feathering kisses over my cheek, my jaw. His hand trails lower again, back over my stomach, lower still. His fingers dip under the waistband of my jeans, and I can't breathe—

'I *can't*.' I'm gasping. My voice is a shaking whisper I don't recognize. 'James—'

Suddenly there's a rattling bump from the other room. We both freeze, like rabbits startled by a fox. There's another bump, quieter, and the sound of deep voices.

It's as if I've had a bucket of icy water dumped over my head. I'm lying here, with James hovering above me. His hand is inside my jeans. We're both flushed and sweating.

But there are people out there, just *there*, who are ready to hurt us, right down to the marrow. We're just bones to them. And this intimacy is not what I want – not while we're helpless, hurt, beaten and stripped raw.

I want James, but not like this.

'Stop.' I'm stammering, whispering. My hands move his away. 'Stop, *stop*. I can't . . . You're right, this isn't . . .'

'It's okay.' He reaches up to touch my hair, my cheek.

I sniffle, and wipe my eyes and nose on the edge of the blanket, but it doesn't make me feel better. 'W-we can't cop a break, can we? It's like, every time we—'

Mycroft nods until he starts smiling. 'Between your parents and a bunch of criminals, we'll never get it together.'

My eyes are scratchy-hot, but I smile back. 'God, we have shit priorities. We could have been spending this time organizing an escape plan – instead we're snogging on the mattress.'

'I think my priorities are right where they ought to be, actually.' He grins, kisses the tip of my nose.

'Prioritise this.' I whip the blanket off. Like a bold-faced slap, the cold air is brutal but effective. 'Shit. Okay. Right. How are we going to do this?'

Mycroft tugs me as I start heaving myself up. '*You're* not going to do anything. You have a broken kneecap.'

'I can walk.'

'Save it. We'll probably need to do some moving around to get out of here. You should keep off that leg as much as you can before then.' He puts on his shoes, pushes himself off the bed. He covers his ribs with one hand as he stands. 'Ow, bloody hell . . . Okay, I'm going to poke about. Quietly.'

I sit on the mattress, bundled in blanket, working my boots back on. 'What am I gonna do?'

'You're acting in an advisory capacity. And you can give me a whistle if the light comes on, considering that seems to be the signal they're about to burst in and ruin the atmosphere.' He limps over to check out the window, sighs. 'Jesus. Second floor. Why can't it ever be ground level?'

Mycroft winces as he looks around the gloomy room. I don't know if it's because of his ribs or because he's seeing the same limited resources that I see.

'There's nothing,' I say.

'No, there's something.' He licks the cut on his lip as his eyes scan. 'What have we got?'

'A bucket. A blanket. A plastic bottle of water, a bath, a mattress.' I think harder. 'A window. Your pack of smokes . . . Oh, *wait*. Check this out.'

I pull the London Town matchbox out of my sock.

Mycroft's eyebrows rocket up. 'How the hell did you manage to hang on to that?'

'They did a pretty average job of searching me, I guess.'

Mycroft snorts. 'If nothing else, I guess we could start a fire.'

A thought butts against me, out of nowhere. 'Mycroft, if these guys are such pros, why didn't Gardener give them the Folio straight off? What made him think he could double-cross them?'

'I can't imagine. Maybe he was just dumb enough to think he could get away with it.' Mycroft walks the perimeter, frowning. He nods at the bare bulb in the ceiling. 'Okay, we have access to electricity.'

'I don't think Gardener was dumb. I think . . . he realized what stealing the Folio would really mean. I think he just cared about the Folio too much, when push came to shove.' I chew my thumbnail. 'But what about the Colonel's boss? What does he want with an un-fenceable book of Shakespeare's plays anyway?'

'Maybe he has a buyer – that's how high-end art deals usually go. Or maybe the boss is a collector himself. Or maybe he just enjoyed the idea of jerking Gardener around, and getting a six million pound book was the gravy.' Mycroft limps over to the bath and studies the door in the wall beside it. Filaments of light and shadow from the streetlamp outside snarl through his hair. 'What's on the other side of this?'

'Don't know. I couldn't move the bath to get in there.'

'Let's have a look.' He braces his back against the wall and puts both feet on the edge of the bath. He grimaces, grunts. The bath moves, scraping quietly but enough to make me nervous, until it's about a meter away from the door.

He rattles the locked doorknob, touches the floor under the bottom of the door. 'Cold air.'

I shrug. 'All the air in this city is cold.'

'Gimme a sec.'

Mycroft hunkers down into the space between the door and the bath. He digs his fingers around in the back pocket of his jeans, finally coming up with two paperclips.

I stare. 'You're going to pick the lock?'

'I'm going to tickle it.' His lips twitch mirthlessly. 'Actually I haven't done this in a while, so I hope it works.'

He straightens out the paperclips and slides them into the lock one after the other.

'Something flat,' he mutters. 'I need something like a card, or—'

I push off the mattress and limp over, holding out my Oxford bus ticket. 'Will this do?'

'Perfect.' Mycroft slips the card into the edge of the door. It takes barely a second before he cracks the door open with a flourish. 'Voila.'

'Impressive.'

'No applause, just throw money.' He grins, pushes the door wider.

The room is a small, thin rectangle with a stack of moldering boxes in one corner. It's darker in here than in our room, with a single tiny, high window. There's a sink attached to one wall, a pipe for a nonexistent loo. A shower rose is suspended on the wall at the end, which must have been where the bath once belonged.

Mycroft clears a few cobwebs and checks the boxes. 'Toaster. DVD player. Microwave oven. Toaster. If only we had a loaf of bread.'

'Or a socket to plug the toaster into.' There's nothing along the walls that I can see.

'Yeah. Hold on . . .' He rattles the contents of an open box, angles it toward the light. 'Toilet cleaner. Two cans of air freshener. Insect spray. Toilet paper. And a bunch of bathroom cupboard knobs, with accompanying screws.'

'The reno that never was.'

Mycroft weighs the box in his hands. 'We can . . . We can do something with this. Toilet cleaner. If I had some foil—'

'There's foil.' I say sharply. 'I've got foil. That kebab wrapper, in the corner.'

'Okay, we've got hydrochloric acid and we've got foil. It's a start.'

'Of what?'

He gives me a significant look. 'Of a chemical reaction that goes *poof*.'

Mycroft settles the box near the door of the narrow room and waves us both back into our jail. He closes the door, carefully jamming the lock with the remains of my bus ticket, then conducts a more intense survey of our facilities. He picks up the water bottle and shakes it, studies the bath shell.

I totter back to the bed. 'So you've done something like this before?'

'Broken out of a dilapidated warehouse while being imprisoned by a Serbian mercenary with a penchant for eighties fashion sportswear?' He glances over from his examination of the window sash. 'No, of course not.'

'Dork. I meant the toilet cleaner and foil.'

'Once.' He pauses. 'Okay, a couple of times. Last year, when Principal Conroy had this ban on practical jokes after orientation week, I let off a couple of minor charges on the library roof. Not enough to cause serious damage.'

'Right.'

'It was just a couple of tiles. Anyway, hydrochloric acid doesn't leave any residue. It's just a bit of noise and smoke, mostly. Doesn't everyone know how to make flash bombs out of toilet cleaner?'

'No,' I point out, 'not everybody knows that.'

He tests the security grille on the window, frowning. 'They do. It's known. It's just one of those facts everybody mysteriously knows, like that bats turn left coming out of a cave, or that you can't piss on the rail tracks in France.'

'You got that from a Tally-ho packet.'

'What?'

'That bats turn left coming out of a cave.' I narrow my eyes at him as he comes closer.

'I glean useful information from everywhere.' He eases back down on the bed, kisses my nose again. 'We're going to get out of here.'

I lean against him. 'Jesus, shut up. You'll put the moz on it.'

'No, there's no moz. It's going to happen. Because I want to see you do that panting thing again when we're somewhere we won't be interrupted.'

'So . . . sex is your incentive.'

Mycroft grins. For someone with broken ribs, being held captive by murderers, he looks very cheerful. 'It's an awesome incentive. Awesome. And it's keeping me going right now, so don't knock it.'

Of course, as soon as he says that, the light comes on.

CHAPTER EIGHTEEN

We're back in the other room.

I put up some resistance. But Paul looked like he was going to clobber Mycroft again, so I bit my tongue and hobbled where they wanted me to hobble.

Now it's all five of us, a happy little party. Mycroft and I sit opposite one another. I've got the Colonel's chair, near the table. They've got Mycroft pressed down in my old chair.

Evening darkness peels back all around us – the overhanging lamps are glaring. Something about the arrangement of the chairs, the way Paul and Tyson stand close, is very disquieting.

The Colonel walks back and forth between us, casting long, moving shadows. Maybe this is it. Maybe they've decided to kill us now. I don't know, and the not-knowing makes my heart flutter like a sparrow in my chest.

'Hokay.' The Colonel looks a little gray, tired around the eyes. 'Hokay. Here we are. Now I give you opportunity to tell me anything left over. Any small thing, yes?'

Mycroft and I look at each other across this bridge of air. I can tell he's wondering the same thing as me. What are they doing, questioning us further? It's meaningless and stupid, like the way you pretend to wring the last drops out of a bottle by squeezing the neck. Are they just going to squeeze us and squeeze us until the end?

Mycroft reaches for his cigarette pack. 'Look, if you're going to kill us, just do it. Just get it over and done with, because I can't stand the suspense.'

My gasp is very loud. I clap a hand over my mouth.

The Colonel's face goes stony. 'You are very gutsy boy, eh? You know this is not what I want. I am only wanting the Folio. And we have already done exchange of information, but maybe there is some other small thing you want to tell me, yes?'

'No.' Mycroft lips the cigarette. 'I gave you everything I had.'

'Everything. You are quite sure?' The Colonel's eyes glitter.

'Yes.'

'You are sure you give me everything.' The Colonel smiles good-naturedly. 'You see, I have some contacts with the police. Enough to tell me certain things. When a certain man will drive from his house to the police station, for instance. Or the details of a certain boy. You are English boy living in Melbourne, Australia.' The vowels sound very strange in the Colonel's mouth. 'You work with Australian forensic expert brought here for this case. You are unusual – a special boy, with special talents, and certain . . . insights, yes? You see, we know many things about you.'

Mycroft's eyes are glued to the Colonel's. He takes his cigarette out of his mouth and slides it back into the pack.

'Yes, many things.' The Colonel smirks, as though he's amused to have the jump on Mycroft. 'And also we know your girlfriend. She is very loyal, very pretty, yes?'

This question seems to demand a response. Mycroft locks eyes with me.

'Yes.' The word grinds out through his teeth.

'So . . .' The Colonel rocks on his feet. 'You understand, I am thinking, it is not in best interest of anyone for you to withhold information.'

'I understand.' Mycroft enunciates very carefully, glares at the Colonel.

'Because you are clever boy. You do not hold back one small thing, one bargaining chip?'

'No.'

'Maybe some theory that police have interest in. So maybe you give me all the information, but not this . . . *thread*, yes, that takes us from all these small things to this Folio—'

Mycroft puffs out a breath, finally losing control.

'Look, I told you. There *is* no thread.' He throws a hand out. 'If I knew something, I'd tell you. You think I like having my ribs used as a punching bag? I don't, okay? And I *don't know* where the Folio is.'

The Colonel frowns at Mycroft and sighs. He turns and takes two steps away, pulling out a phone from his jacket pocket. Paul and Tyson just stand there, looking menacing, while the Colonel makes a call.

'Yello. Yes, it is me.'

The Colonel's on my left, looking towards the roof of the warehouse, talking up the way you sometimes do when you're on the phone – such a normal, everyday mannerism.

'Yes,' he says. 'No, I don't think that is so useful. No. Well, it is possible. But the boy is . . .'

He glances at me in the pause. I don't like that glance. He looks back to the roof.

'Yes. Yes, I understand, Mr Wild. No, this is no problem. In the usual way, yes, of course. Thank you. I will. Goodbye.'

The Colonel disconnects the call and gives another heavy sigh.

'Hokay.' His shoulders straighten and he turns around to us. 'Hokay. This is unfortunate for you, but this is instruction from my employer. He is not convinced you share everything, so—'

Mycroft's face contorts. '*No!* What are you – I bloody *told* you everything!'

Paul and Tyson have taken up position on either side of him, and all at once a bitter taste whirlpools in my throat. My rib cage feels two sizes too small.

The Colonel leans to get in Mycroft's face. 'Yes, I am not convinced of this, what my employer says. But he is my boss, yes? He says jump, I jump. He says do, I do. So this is not my choice, yes?'

Mycroft grits his teeth. 'So you're just going to lay into me some more, is that it?'

'Well, this is problem, you see? Because you are very strong. You have maybe a touch of Irish in there, yes, with the eyes and the hair? Irish people are hard people. And you are hard also, like a little nut.' The Colonel looks up at Tyson. 'Please.'

Tyson walks to some place behind me, into the darker recesses of the room. I get a dreadful chill. The feeling gets worse when Tyson comes back with a short length of metal. It's a tire iron.

I groan, deep in my chest and stomach. 'No. Please, no. Please don't—'

'Right,' Mycroft says, even though he's gone pale. 'Tire iron, is it? Okay, that's—'

'No.' The Colonel frowns at him. 'This is not how we crack a nut, because we use something like this and we smash the soft meat in the center, yes? Which is not useful.'

He swivels suddenly and walks towards me. I back up in my chair, but he's offering me something from his jacket pocket. It's a pencil.

'Write your name,' he says.

'W-what?'

'Write your name. Here on this table.'

'You want me to—'

'Write. Just write.'

I'm flabbergasted, but I do as he says. I take the pencil and write 'Rachel Watts' with my right hand, straight onto the wood of the table. My hand is shaking hard, and the loops and strokes run together.

'Thank you.' The Colonel takes the pencil back. He looks at Tyson again. 'This time on the left, please.'

Tyson comes around and hands the Colonel the tire iron. Then he moves the table. Its feet grate against the wooden floor until it's over on my left-hand side.

And now I'm scared, I don't know why. I'm so scared my whole body starts to shake. My teeth chatter and my shoulders twitch. I am my own earthquake.

The Colonel turns back to Mycroft, who is watching this performance with such a look of horror that I can't stand it.

'Hokay. Now, I ask you only one more time, yes? I think you understand.'

'*I* don't understand,' I wail. 'What *is* it, god—'

Mycroft seems to get it, whatever it is. He starts babbling. 'Christ, I don't have anything. Please, you don't have to do this, please—'

'Ah, yes.' The Colonel walks back over to me. He stands near the table on my left, and he is giving Mycroft this look that is almost sorrowful. 'Now we see what the meat is like inside, yes?'

'*Yes*,' Mycroft says, he is almost sobbing, and I don't know why but it makes my eyes well up in response. 'God, fuck, *yes*, and I can only tell you the same thing I told you before, and *I don't know any more!*'

'Let us find out for sure,' the Colonel says.

Suddenly Paul is behind me, holding me around the shoulders. I twist, but he holds on tight. He is grinning and grinning. The Colonel grabs for my left wrist, puts my left hand up on the table, spreads my fingers. Mycroft makes a howl of anguish and Tyson has to hold him down with both arms.

And that's when they do it. That's when they break my fingers.

———

They break one finger each time they ask the question and Mycroft can't answer. By the time they reach the third finger they figure out that Mycroft honestly doesn't have any more information to give. But by then, of course, I have three shattered fingers.

You'd think they might have worked it out sooner. After the first finger, perhaps. Mycroft almost dislocates his arms struggling with Tyson, and he screams a lot. Probably not as much as me. He's being so uncooperative they punch him a few times, but I don't know what they do to him after that because sometime during the third smash with the tire iron, I pass out.

When I come to, I realize we're lying on the mattress again.

I seem to be holding a live coal in my left hand. Except shaking my hand to get rid of it doesn't help, it just makes the pain stretch out to an unbelievable level. But I can't cry out, because my throat is raw from screaming. My tongue feels huge in my mouth, as if I'm trying to swallow a wet sock. I can make a kind of *uh-uh* noise, that's about it.

But it's enough to make Mycroft realize I'm awake. He starts stroking my hair, and just the fact that he's there, curled around me, is enough to make me cry. I'm not really sobbing, though, because I'm so absent. Tears dribble down my face while my mouth makes this strange quivering *oh*.

Mycroft cups my head, lifts the water bottle to my lips, with soft gentle noises. 'Just a little sip now, come on . . . Shh . . .'

The water spills into my mouth, down my chin. I swallow reflexively.

'That's it . . . Come on . . . That's it . . .'

My mouth and throat are less dry now. Mycroft's arms pass over me, and he snuggles down beside me. He is bare-chested. His shirt is wrapped around my hand. His face looks like a plane crash. His eye is actually busted up now, swollen like a boxer's, a mess of purple, red and blue. Blood is streaked from his nose. He has tracks down his cheeks where tears have run through the dirt.

I see this, I take it in, but I'm not really here, not in my body. All my observations are just a bare recognition. My head is full of white noise, as if there's been some sort of overload. I can't absorb anything else. I can't remember who I am. My hand throbs to the beat of my heart and blots out the world.

Mycroft is talking, and I don't even know if I'm listening.

'. . . just saw these long brown legs and your boots, the flannie shirt, and your hair, god, your gorgeous hair. Do you remember?

And then Mai introduced you, and you looked so spun out. I didn't even realize it was your first day in an actual high school . . . wanted to get to know you. I just thought, fucking hell, I've got this super-smart bombshell living two doors away, maybe the gods have finally given me a break . . .'

He keeps stroking my hair with one trembling hand, before passing the same hand over his mouth. He's blathering, his voice running like a slow-moving creek. I'm only hearing about one sentence in three, snatches of talk as I fade in and out.

'. . . all that time, with you in my room, and I wanted to touch you, my god, so badly . . . and I just couldn't believe you'd stuck around, I never met anyone else who saw me like that. And I . . . just didn't want to fuck that up, d'you know what I mean? So I thought if I sorted myself out, then I'd be a whole person, because you deserve a whole person. But it doesn't quite work like . . . not like a jigsaw puzzle. You don't get the pieces together and there's this magical sense of completion, it's . . . but if you knew the details then maybe you'd get scared off, or you'd think "Shit, this guy is a lot of hard work" and . . . bloody terrifying, this feeling, like this is it, like you're the one, but I just . . .'

I'm suddenly overcome by this sense that I'm missing something. Something important is happening and I'm missing it. I fight my way through the haze.

Mycroft's forehead is almost touching mine. His husky whispers are right there, his lips trembling.

'. . . so fucking horrible that they did this. It should be me. I'm already broken, so it should be me with the broken leg and the broken fingers.' He touches my cheek and his eyes are wet. 'Rachel. Rachel, please be okay. Please come back. I am so sorry. Rachel, please—'

And suddenly I'm focusing. I have blinked back into this plane of existence. I can really swallow and I can really cry. Mycroft smooths his hand down the side of my face, down my arm. He makes this choking noise.

I lick my lips. The words that come from my throat are just air. 'Don't stop.'

Mycroft sniffs and swipes his cheek against the hoodie pillow.

'Okay.' His eyes dart around my face. 'Okay.'

We lie there, breathing together, holding each other's gaze. Then he swallows hard, and his face shows every emotion as he begins whispering.

'I don't remember the actual crash. I . . . I must have zoned out or something. The first thing I remember was this dripping sound. I couldn't breathe properly, couldn't catch my breath. But when I cracked my eyes open, Mum was right in front of me. I think the force of the crash kind of pushed her back and me forward . . .'

His words flow on and on – a torrent, a flash flood. I lie there, slowly being revived to life, as I listen to him tell a story about death. It's a story he hasn't told anyone, not a single soul, in more than seven years.

———

The coldness of the bed, Mycroft's absence, wakes me. He stands motionless near the window, arms hugged around himself. A thin shaft of light from the streetlamp outside slides across his profile and over his shoulder. The naked skin of his back is goosebumped in the night air.

I groan, sit up.

Mycroft speaks without turning. 'The jet lag is still putting me off. But I think it's just before dawn.'

I scrub at my face with my good hand. 'Have you got the water?'

'Yeah, sorry. It's here.'

'It's okay. I think I need to move around.' I get up slowly. I'm right to be cautious – my whole body is stiff. I don't remember a time when I've ever been so sore. Even after the lion pen and the scaffolding incident, I wasn't this sore. Playdough must feel like this, after all the squeezing and twisting and reshaping is over.

Mycroft steps closer with his hand extended to help. 'You okay to walk?'

'Good practice for running away.'

I fight off the dizziness and nausea, limp over to the window. Walking makes the pain in my fingers and knee flare to life, but I don't want to stiffen up even more. Mycroft opens the cap then hands me the water bottle. I grit my teeth, holding the bottle awkwardly, taking small sips.

Mycroft watches me carefully. 'That's good. You should drink more, you look dehydrated.'

He takes the bottle back and I return to the bed as quickly as I can. Everything hurts and my uncovered arms are glacial. At least the blanket is warm.

Mycroft goes back to staring out the window. 'I've been trying to think of a way to get out.'

'Well, standing there freezing your arse off isn't going to help.' I pat the side of the mattress next to me with my good hand. I want him near me. 'Come back to bed.'

It's such a strange thing for me to say that it makes him look over. I smile, because a phrase like that, in this room, on this bed, is anything but a come-on.

Mycroft limps over and eases himself down beside me, holding on to his ribs. The livid patches from yesterday have blossomed into ugly purple bruises.

He pulls on his hoodie carefully, zips it up to the neck. 'We have to talk about something. We're going to have to do something radical to get out of here.'

My sigh is very soft. 'Yeah, I figured.'

'Because I think today might be our last day.'

I swallow, because I know what that means. 'I guess they can't keep us in a holding pattern forever.'

'Yeah.' His shoulders straighten, even though the pain makes him wince. 'So if we're going to get out, we might have to . . .'

'. . . do something radical,' I say, nodding.

'Kill somebody,' he says.

'What?'

He looks at the thumbnail he's picking. 'It's just . . . I've thought of an idea. For how to get out. But it's risky. Chances are there'll be some collateral damage. Hopefully on their side.'

'Okay,' I say, but it doesn't sound very okay.

He glances at me, looks back at his hands. 'Rachel, I know you've seen death. But seeing it and causing it are two different things. And you've never seen someone actually die, like I have. It's messy and awful. Not like in the movies. So if you've got any qualms about it, now's the time to tell me.'

I look at him, sitting there, picking his nail. His whole body is tense with controlled nerves, with anger. His face is worse: he looks as though he wants to salt and burn the earth.

It's the same expression he wore when the Colonel said I was pretty. Just before . . . I get a flash of the tire iron descending, push it away fast.

And I remember something important. The Colonel is the man who killed Mycroft's parents. Mycroft has a vested interest in seeing this guy lose a limb or two.

I never considered these things. I never considered that we might have to kill somebody to save our own lives. Bizarrely, I wonder what Dad would think.

I know what he would think.

'Let's Mortein this joint,' I say.

CHAPTER NINETEEN

We have to do everything quickly, but quietly, so quietly. If one of the bad guys figures out we're moving around with purpose and decides to stick his head in, everything will be rooted.

Mycroft ends up doing most of the work. My leg drags, and because of my left hand, I can't hold any parts together. But my tasks are simple.

I ball up small pieces of foil from my kebab wrapper. I fold up a large piece of cardboard from the lid of the microwave box, slide it carefully under the bottom of the door. Now the door is chocked and it'll only be able to open so wide.

Mycroft helps me splint my fingers with cardboard. The bandage on my knee has lost much of its usefulness, and soon I'll need a greater range of movement, so we take it off. It all hurts a lot, but I can't cry out – I just have to suck it up.

Mycroft pulls the cords out from the two toasters, strips the wires with his teeth. He twists them together, then stands on the upended bucket to connect the wires to the light-bulb socket. He connects the other end to the plug of the microwave.

As he's loading the two air freshener aerosols and the fly spray and the cabinet screws into the microwave, I get an attack of nerves.

'Are you sure about this?' I whisper. 'What if it just steams up, or something?'

'It'll do more than steam up.'

'But what if it just blows up the microwave and nothing else?'

'It'll do more than that. Actually, I'm worried that it's going to fry *us* as well as the Colonel.' He closes his eyes, opens them. 'Look, I don't know. I don't know. This is total Anarchist Cookbook stuff. I've done stuff like this before, but never on this scale.'

I squeeze his arm. 'It's okay.'

'No, it's not.' He pinches the bridge of his nose, careful of his swollen eye. 'It's the kind of experiment you'd do in a large field, while you hid behind a bunker. I'm going to get both of us killed.'

'Breathe,' I order. 'We'll be okay. We're doing something. We're not just waiting for them to shoot us. It'll work out.'

He looks away, exhales shakily. 'Right, we need to move the mattress.'

This is harder. At one point I drop the end I'm hauling and it bumps on my knee. I have to stuff my fist in my mouth while Mycroft grips my shoulder.

It seems to take forever to get everything prepared. Occasional low noises from the next room make us freeze . . . and keep going. Light is coming in through the window, bathing us both in a sallow gold. Mycroft moves with greater speed, positioning the microwave on its box near the door, testing the wires a final time, turning on the oven timer.

He makes me get into the bath, then hauls the blanket and

the mattress up so they're not quite covering me. I've pulled my flannie back on, but the bath enamel is freezing.

Mycroft's already put the bucket on the floor in the corner where our mattress used to lie. He sits on the bath edge and takes a long pull out of the water bottle, gives it to me. I shake my head – I was desperately thirsty a short while ago, but now the urge to drink has faded – but he makes me finish what's left.

He looks at me intently. 'Are you ready? Because once we start, that's it.'

'I'm ready. Are you okay?'

'I'm worried.' His throat moves convulsively. 'I'm worried we won't be protected enough. This explosion is going to be multi-directional, and with the shrapnel . . .'

I look deep into his eyes. 'Mycroft, if we don't do it, they're going to kill us anyway. I trust you.'

'Give me the bottle and the matches,' he says.

He positions a small bundle of matches on the edge of the box and slides the lid closed to keep them there. He strikes one match he's saved and lights the bundle before sticking the whole box inside the microwave.

He shakes the water droplets out of the bottom of the bottle, packs in all the little foil balls I've made, pours in enough toilet cleaner to cover the foil balls. His hands are shaking something awful, and some of it spills down the side. He caps the bottle, swirls the contents around, walks over and tosses it into the bucket in the corner.

In the time it takes him to get back to the bath, I hear a faint sound coming from the bucket. It sounds like corn popping in a saucepan, the little yellow kernels spinning in the thin layer of oil . . .

Mycroft hauls himself into the bath with me. I've made a space, but it's still a squash. I grit my teeth as he accidentally jostles my hand.

'God, sorry,' he whispers.

But he doesn't need to whisper, because about two seconds later there's this ear-splitting *BANG* from the toilet cleaner explosion that makes us jump.

This is it.

Response time is about five seconds. I hear a sizzle, and the microwave comes alive. They've turned on the light, but they can't get inside the room because of the cardboard chock.

'Open the door, you little shits!' That's Paul.

'Get it open.' The Colonel's voice, then it's raised. 'Rachel, you must open door now, please—'

Well, actually, I don't have to open the door, you mercenary bastard, so suck on that. I haven't felt so powerful in days. It's heady.

'*Shove it up your arse!*' I yell.

Mycroft yanks me back down into the bath. He's pulling up the blanket and the mattress so they completely cover us. His eyes are huge, bloodshot and scared. He's sweating.

'Rachel—' the Colonel says loudly, followed by a short string of what must be Serbian curse words.

The microwave is still humming its little microwave tune, which is drowned out by the voices at the door. They can't get the door open and it's really shitting them.

'*Underneath the door,* you idiot!' Tyson's voice, and then, 'Oh bollocks, give it to me—'

They've got it, they must be loosening the chock. I look at Mycroft desperately. Our faces are only millimeters apart, and we're both shivering. It's deeply shadowed inside the bath with the mattress over us. Mycroft counts as if he's learning to read, mouthing the words without letting the sounds come.

'Hundred and ten, hundred and eleven . . .' he breathes, and then, louder, 'Rachel, block your ears!'

We lift our hands in unison, our bodies pressed together tight. I have time to hear Paul say 'Oh, *shit*—', I press my palms over my ears, and—

The world erupts.

There is an explosion of movement and sound. I was expecting a bang, like the bottle rocket. This is not a bang, it is a **WHOOMPA**, and it fills all my senses, pummels its way into my very bones.

The window above us shatters, showering glass. I'd scream, but the air's been punched out of my lungs. Everything lurches, as though the floor has dropped away. I fall into Mycroft, so hard and fast I don't have time to register that it hurts my leg, my hand.

There's a rumble, as if the entire building is rocking on its foundations. My teeth have clacked together – blood seasons my mouth – and my eyes have shut. I force them open. I can't hear. Mycroft mouths something at me, his eyes urgent. I can't hear it.

Then everything rushes back in an instant, and I hear crackling sounds and someone groaning.

Mycroft is suddenly audible. '. . . *move*, we have to *move*. Come *on!*'

'*Is it safe?*' I yell. My ears still aren't functioning enough for me to judge volume. But then I see Mycroft is pushing the mattress off us, and it's on fire. 'Holy *shit*—'

He sits up enough to pitch the mattress further away. Other stuff is on fire, too – the wall, the blanket, part of the floor. Red-orange feathers lick up the side of the door. Panic blooms inside me, the age-old fear of fire that all rurals have, and Mycroft doesn't need to tell me to move, I'm moving, I'm slinging my legs over the bath.

I stumble when my feet hit the remains of the microwave on the floor. It's busted open, like a—

'It's a net,' I say stupidly, 'like models of platonic solids, in Maths at school—'

Mycroft grabs my arm and pulls me away. The bath has listed – countless shiny bits of metal are buried in the arc of its fiberglass bottom. I shudder, and then Mycroft is pulling me further.

The door is open, part of the frame is on fire.

'*No*—' My voice cracks at the sight.

Mycroft puts his arm around my head. My hair, shit, my hair is gonna catch fire, but then we're out. The three chairs in this next room are pushed over from the force of the explosion.

Someone's lying on the floor, near the door, and he's lying in a pool of dark water. But it isn't water, and I can't see his face because of all the red, and something is crisped black – his hair, maybe – and parts of him are smoking. I recognize the leather jacket and the pale palms, when the rest of the skin on his hands is so brown.

Tyson's hands spasm in space. There's a piece of metal sunk deep into his forehead – the hinge from the door. Mycroft tugs on me but I have to see, I *have* to.

Tyson's body shakes, a delicate all-over trembling, before it twitches and subsides – it sinks, his whole body sinks, and it's like he's getting heavier somehow as his soul departs, and this is what they mean by a *dead weight*, I realize, and I make this awful garbled moan which is half a laugh. Then Tyson's body is still, in

270

that way Gardener's body was still in the morgue, and I know, I know it, he's gone.

He's gone.

Air puffs out of me. Pain spasms in my stomach, and Mycroft holds my elbow. He's pulling me on. I almost surrender to it when I see something glinting, some bright shiny thing, tucked into Tyson's dead armpit. I yank against Mycroft's hand.

'Rachel, we—'

I lean, using Mycroft's hand as a counterweight, and fumble for the shiny thing. The grip is sticky. It's incredibly heavy when I pull it out. I keep it pointed at the floor.

'Have you used a handgun before?' Mycroft's voice is too loud, he must be having trouble with volume as well. The sound of crackling from the fire resonates in the bigger room.

I jostle back into Mycroft. 'Come on.'

We find Paul over near the top of the steps. He's the one groaning, and he's crawling on his stomach. Blood slicks across one side of his head.

I start forward to help him, until Mycroft jerks me closer. '*Don't.* We're getting out of here.'

But the fire, I nearly say. I can't imagine anything worse than dying in a fire. It's ingrained in me, this fear.

Then something distracts me. Movement, in the corner of my eye. A glimpse of navy blue and a flash of something metallic—

I grab Mycroft by the head and shoulders, shove us both to the floor.

There's a ferocious report, and my knee is screaming, and the Colonel has emerged fully from the darkness at the end of the room. He is coming on, firing, one of his arms extended straight out in front of his body, and he has dust in his hair but no blood. Mycroft is gasping on top of me and I can't think, I can't think, and then I think.

I lift Tyson's gun with my right hand and push up, push Mycroft off me. He half-falls down the top step. I lift the gun onto the rail of the banister, because my hand is shaking, and I squint at the Colonel and I pull the trigger.

Nothing happens.

The Colonel makes this full-bodied yell, striding closer. Another report. A large piece of wood chips off the banister to the left of my head.

I press the safety switch on the side of the gun with my other finger, one of the broken ones, and I cry out and pull the trigger again. The solid weight of the gun thumps into my palm and the impact goes up my arm to the elbow. The noise is a boom, delayed. I'm only used to Dad's twenty-two rifle; this must be a heavier caliber than I realized.

The Colonel drops, but I don't think I've hit him. That would be the most insane luck imaginable, and we've already used up a lot of luck. I hear this crescendoing scream, I'm making it, and I don't aim, I just pull the trigger two more times. My palm goes numb.

'Watts, come on, that's enough.' Mycroft's voice, and he's tugging on my sleeve. 'Watts—'

I take a breath. It feels hot, as though the fire is sucking all the oxygen from the room and then blowing it back out. Mycroft pulls on me and I stagger upright, down the stairs. I don't know these stairs, I don't know where we are. God, my knee is dying. Mycroft knows the way somehow and he puts his arm around my waist as we tumble.

The rest of the building is a complete mystery to me, so I'm surprised by what I see when we get to the bottom of the second flight of steps. A van is parked inside the building. It's a white service van, at the top of a ramp leading towards a large pair of wooden doors.

Mycroft looks at me and we must be thinking in unison, because I'm not shocked when he lets me go abruptly and runs for the wooden doors. I hobble to the van, look through the driver's-side window and realize the keys are in the ignition.

'Thank god, thank god,' I whisper. I don't know why I'm whispering.

The seat of the van is vinyl and sticky, and I'm fogging the windscreen with my heavy breathing. My fingers are slippery on the keys, on the steering wheel. I rev the engine – powerful, nervous revs – and ignore my knee and wait for Mycroft to finish pulling open the doors.

Something thumps hard upstairs on the second floor and I flinch. A secondary explosion. Splinters of wood shower onto the windscreen.

I lower the driver's window and shout at Mycroft. 'Forget the doors! *Come on!*'

He runs for the van and he's about to launch himself into the passenger seat when there's a crack. The window of Mycroft's open door explodes. He yells, throws himself down.

The Colonel is standing on the landing of the stairwell. He looks like a maniac – nothing is left of the urbane tracksuited image of such high efficiency that he was projecting last night, yesterday, the day before. His hair is standing up and he is screaming those curse words I don't understand.

I take the handgun off the dashboard where I'd left it. I fire at the Colonel – one, two, three times, the kick knocking my elbow into the doorframe. I drop the gun on the third kick and I scream, '*Mycroft, get in the fucking car!*', and he does.

I gun the engine, like I'm doing donuts in the paddock bomb at home, and Mycroft has barely shut his side when I launch the van at the wooden doors. We jolt down the ramp, I don't even feel the whack on my knee, I just keep my foot planted.

The van's nose hits the edge of the door as we jink out into the street, fishtailing wildly from the impact. I hold on to the wheel for dear life. We both hunker down, in case the Colonel emerges and starts shooting at us.

I yank the wheel to straighten up and burn rubber to the end of the street. There's a corner, then another corner and I level out the vehicle.

Suddenly I can see the outside world again. The sky is a leaden color and it's very big, even with all the buildings. Muted sunlight spills into the front seat and there's a tree or two. My god, the world is enormous.

I hear this soft, keening sound. It's not until Mycroft leans over and puts his hands on both of mine, gripping the steering wheel, that I realize I'm the one making the sound.

'It's okay, Rachel, it's okay. You can stop. We're out, we're safe, you can pull over.'

I shake my head, hair flying into my eyes. I'm breathless. 'I don't want to. I want to keep driving, if that's okay.'

'That's fine.'

I squint at the world. 'Where . . . where are we?'

'We're in . . . Brentford, I think.' Mycroft's chest heaves. He moves his hands, puts one on my shoulder and one braced on the bench seat. 'Okay, yeah. There's a sign.'

'Which way should I go?'

'Is your knee hurting?'

'Just tell me which way.'

Mycroft clears his throat. 'We have to . . . Go left. We go left and cross the rail line.'

'Okay.'

I drive, and there are other cars nearby now. Sunlight folds around us, the air is crisp and clear through the windows, one shattered and one open.

Mycroft squeezes my shoulder. 'Rachel, you have to brake here. Brake here. *Brake*, Rachel, it's a traffic light.'

So I do.

CHAPTER TWENTY

We drive through the early-morning traffic in silence. At one point I start shivering – I can't seem to stop – so Mycroft makes me pull over.

I don't want to get out of the van, though, so I just open the driver's door and am noisily sick out onto the road. It's only water and bile I'm throwing up and my stomach hurts afterwards, but it makes me feel better. There's half a roll of toilet paper in the glove compartment and Mycroft gives me some so I can wipe my mouth.

'You shouldn't be driving.'

'No,' I gasp. 'I want to . . . I like to drive.'

'This can't be doing your knee any good.'

'I don't care.'

Mycroft brushes back some of the hair around my face with warm fingers, and I look at him properly for the first time in a while. He has a graze on the lump over his cheekbone now, in addition to the black eye and bruises on his jaw and split lip.

Blood oozes down the side of his neck – it's coming from inside his ear.

'Oh, your ear . . .'

'It's all right. Actually, I don't know if it's all right. It doesn't matter.'

We don't talk about how relieved we are, or how scared we were, or anything like that. Somehow I know it's a place we can't press on, or the dull film on the surface will crack and we'll both break down here, in the van.

So we maintain our surface tension. We look at road signs, work out directions.

I drive us all the way to Westminster in the crappy little van. As we get closer I start to worry about running out of fuel. It keeps me from worrying about my knee, which is now a constant subsonic chord that resonates throughout my body, keeping me alert. I feel incredibly awake. I notice everything: every car, every pedestrian, every building. My eyes are wide, all-absorbing.

Then we're in Victoria Street, slowing for traffic. Mycroft directs me on where to turn, where to brake. I bring the van to a tired, jerking halt right out front of this enormous glass building with a revolving sign that says *New Scotland Yard*. As soon as I pull up, a white-shirted guy with a helmet and a black flak vest strides purposefully towards us.

Mycroft has already gotten out his side and is limping around to open my door, help me out. I detach my hands from the steering wheel by force of will. Stepping onto the bitumen seems hard, wrong, heavy. I want to be in motion again, smoothly driving along. I want to be racing. I cling to Mycroft's jacket as I hobble to the pavement.

'Good morning, sorry, but you can't park here,' the officer says. 'There's a visitor's car park—'

Mycroft speaks in a calm monotone. 'We need medical attention, and I need to speak to DCI—'

'Son, I can see there's a problem, but you will need to move that—'

'Look, my name is James Mycroft. I need to speak to Inspector Simon—'

'I don't care what your name is and you're not speaking to anyone until you move that van. This is not—'

Which is all the officer gets out before Mycroft pulls back and clocks him right on the nose. And then we get a lot of attention straight away.

'*Shit!*' The officer puts a hand up to his nose. There's a beat, while he stares at the blood on his fingers, then he says, 'You are under arrest for assaulting a police officer,' and grabs Mycroft by one arm. I lurch back onto the van hood as two more police officers come pelting out of the station entrance.

One of them tackles Mycroft to the pavement. He goes down with an *oof* and I scream, '*Don't*, for god's sake, he's got broken ribs!', and the first officer says, 'This little prick just gave me a dint, Rob.'

The other officer grabs me by the wrist, and says, 'Come on now, sister, let's get you in.' But when he pulls me away from the stability of the van hood, I stagger. My knee is suddenly blooming hot as a rose, a sunburst, a mushroom-cloud explosion. I shriek and half-fall, landing on my left hand. Then everything goes white.

A while after that I realize I'm being carried. I can see the pattern on the ceiling as my head lolls back over someone's arm.

The ceiling has white stipples on its surface, like a pallid rash. I'm being put down in a chair, and I can smell Mycroft because he smells like something burnt. A glass of water is pushed at my lips.

'Here, just drink a little. That's it . . .'

And then someone else, who smells like leather car seats, which may be a kind of cologne, is kneeling in front of me. Mycroft's hands keep me upright in the chair and I lean my head into his hip.

'Can you identify yourself for me, love?'

'My name is Rachel Maree Watts.' I speak with my eyes closed. God, my voice is slurring all over the place. 'And I live at twenty-eight . . . twenty-eight Summoner Street, North Coburg, Melbourne . . .'

'Okay, Rachel. That's fine.'

I have a sudden urge to sit up straighter, but acting on it is almost impossible. 'It was . . . it was the Colonel. The man who . . . We were in Brentford. It was . . . the man who killed Daniel Gardener . . .'

'Can we get the EMT in here, please? Right now?' the leather car seats man calls urgently to somewhere over his shoulder, and then he turns back to me. He has brown skin and eyes, very black hair and a dark-green gabardine coat. His face is young and kind, in complete opposition to his cologne. 'That's fab, Rachel, well done. Now just give us a sec,' and he stands up.

I hear him talking to Mycroft, saying '. . . get her to check out the shots for identification, but that can wait. Are you seriously telling me you *blew up* a microwave? The LFB's been hosing down that warehouse for half an hour', and Mycroft says, '. . . couldn't have known. Let me look at the shots', and the other guy says, '. . . be an excellent idea, but first I want you to let the EMT have a look at you. And we've contacted Doctor Walsh, so he should be in shortly.'

'It's Professor,' Mycroft says. He sounds exhausted. 'Professor Walsh. Emmett.'

'Of course,' the other guy says. 'One minute.'

He leaves the room. I'm trying to stay with it, but I keep fading in and out, as though I've got bad reception. Mycroft gently rubs my shoulders, smooths my hair back from my forehead. My head is still leaning on his hip and I can't quite get my eyes to focus. Then there's another voice, female this time, soothing.

'Hi there, how're you going? I'm Patricia, and I'm just going to have a little look and see how you are, okay? Goodness, let's see what's going on with this . . .'

Patricia smells faintly medicinal and she has short hair. She takes my left hand in her soft one and carefully turns the palm. Then she puts my hand down on my left knee and folds back the split denim over my other knee.

'My, yes, you've certainly given yourself a bit of a bump. Okay . . .' She takes a penlight and shines it in both my eyes. 'How are you feeling now?'

'Shithouse,' I say. I hear Mycroft snort.

'Right.' Patricia gives a little laugh. 'Well, I'm glad we're clear on that, and yes, you look as if you could do with a bit of a rest. I'd like to give you a shot, now, if that's all right—'

'*No.*' My eyes gasp around as I flounder closer to the surface of the world. 'No, I have to talk to the police. I've gotta tell them . . .'

'It's okay, Rachel, you've just spoken to Inspector Gupta,' Mycroft says, and Patricia calls out to someone, 'Can we get the gurney in here? Thanks, Maz, that's great,' and Mycroft bends down and whispers, 'It's okay now, just hold onto me.'

His right arm goes under my legs, his left around my back. I cleave to him as he lifts me up. I think he was the one who carried me before.

'You shouldn't be doing that, sweetheart,' Patricia says. 'I haven't had a look at you yet.'

'I want to,' Mycroft says softly.

He settles me on a spongy bed with crinkling sheets. When my head sinks onto the pillow, I nearly cry with relief.

'Van for this one,' Patricia says to someone. She puts a rail up on the left-hand side of the bed. 'For both of them, I think. Maz, can you get a line in here? She's looking pretty dry. Now, sir, if you want to keep up the knight-in-shining-armor routine you'll have to let me check you out first, okay? Just sit down here.'

I lie there, feeling quite comfortable except for the vibrations moving through my body, while an older man with a bit of light gray stubble says, 'Hallo there, lass, this won't take but a second.' He adjusts the bed I'm lying on so my upper body is slightly raised. Then he swabs down my right wrist and I feel a pain as the needle goes in.

But I'm more focused on the conversation between Mycroft's voice and other voices, and Patricia tut-tutting, 'Oh, sweetheart, yes, that's broken, I'd say. We'll get some films. Let's have a look at your eyes . . .'

I lean over the rail on the bed. The stubbled man makes a quick grab for my wrist, which he's trying to tape.

My hair falls in my face again. 'Is he all right? James, are you all right?'

'He's fine, lass,' the man says, his hand on my shoulder, pushing me back gently. 'Patty's taking care of him, he'll be right as rain.'

'I'm okay.' Mycroft shifts position, so he's sitting in a chair facing me, and Patricia has to move around in the space to stay connected with him.

'Hey there,' Mycroft says.

And suddenly I can see him, sitting long and lanky and drained in the chair. He's got ash in his hair, and so many welts and cuts on his face . . . They look out of place in this clean, fluoro-lit room.

Patricia fusses with the side of his head, his ear. His eyes are Prussian blue, his thick eyebrows furrowed, making a hollowed cave. There's a shadow-trace of stubble on his upper lip, on his cheeks and chin. His hoodie is unzipped – I see the pale skin of his chest.

Mycroft's eyes search mine. 'God, do I look that bad?'

'Yes.' I hiccup, and my throat is gluey as I smile. 'No. You look great. Do I look bad?'

'Terrible.' He smiles. It changes the whole set of his face. 'No. You look like a million bucks.'

I sniff and I can't swallow because of my throat. 'Six million pounds. I look like six million pounds.'

'That's right,' he says gently.

Tears are dripping off my jaw. Mycroft shakes Patricia away so he can reach over the rail to cup my cheek and wipe with his thumb.

'You hit that police officer,' I say.

'Yeah, I did.'

'Will they charge you?'

'I don't think so.'

I want to hold his hand, but my fingers still have cardboard on them. 'Oh god, we got out. How did we do that?'

'I have no idea,' he says, and he sighs, deep into his chest.

Patricia says, 'Maz, help me out with this,' in a frustrated way. There's a brief delay before I feel something strangely cold enter through the door in my wrist. It seems to curl languidly throughout my entire body like white smoke and my eyelids feel sore now, so I close them.

I hear Mycroft saying, 'Rachel. *Rachel*—' and then Patricia saying, 'Let her rest now, sweetheart . . .' And then she fades, and everything fades. All I'm left with is the image of the Colonel, screeching and writhing on the back of my eyelids.

———

I wake up to discover that someone has dimmed the lights. Alicia Azzopardi is sitting on the side of my bed, a hairbrush in one hand.

'God, I had a weird dream.' My eyes are gummy. I'm floating, but heavy. 'I was in the paddock. Me and Dad moved the stock closer to the house because of the fire, and the sky was pink . . . pinky-orange . . . I closed the gate and the bar caught on my . . .'

Alicia reaches out with the hairbrush, runs it down through the loose, silky strands near my shoulder.

'Yeah, I have strange dreams sometimes, too.' She looks red-eyed, tired. She smooths my hair with a soft hand, curves it back behind my ear.

There's a weight on my left hand and another on my knee. The ceiling is unfamiliar; there's a television in a bracket high in one corner, green curtains covering a window on the right.

'I'm in hospital,' I say.

'Yes,' Alicia says. 'Chelsea and Westminster Hospital.'

'There really was a fire.'

'Yes, there was.'

'And Tyson died. His body was smoking, and he had bits of metal—'

I burst into tears.

Alicia shushes me and holds me. 'It's all right.'

'They . . . they *broke my fingers* . . .'

'I know.' I feel Alicia shudder. 'It's okay now. You're in a safe place now. That's it, come on.'

She wipes my face as I settle down, offers me some tissues and a drink from a cup. I have to suck on the straw for a few seconds before I get enough spit together to actually draw on it. My mouth tastes like dry chaff.

The water swirls around behind my teeth before I swallow. 'I'm . . . I'm still in London. What time is it?'

'About lunchtime. You can eat, if you feel like it, but the nurse said you might be nauseated from the anaesthetic.'

'Anaesthetic?'

I finally lift my left hand off the bed and it's a complete horror show – a metal splint with bandages, and the bits of visible skin are jaundice-yellow. I wasn't nauseated before, but I am now.

'Mum and Dad are gonna have a fit.'

'We can talk about that later,' Alicia says. 'You should get some rest.'

Then I remember something very important. '*Mycroft*. He was—'

'He's fine. He was sleeping for a while.' Alicia nods across me. I turn my head and see another hospital bed with rumpled sheets. 'But then he said he needed to ask the police something.'

'I'm supposed to talk to them.'

'I'm sure we'll get around to that.' She smiles wearily.

'God, Alicia, you must have been so stressed . . .'

'I was frantic. Mike would never have forgiven me if I'd lost you.' She laughs, small and tight. I'm not sure if it's a laugh. 'Bad enough that I'm sending you back in such a state.'

'It wasn't your fault.'

'Bloody hell. I'm glad you're back. So glad.'

She sniffs and I give her one of my tissues. We pass tissues back and forth, grinning shyly. It's the most normal thing I've done in days.

There's a knock on the door. The man standing in the doorway is about mid-thirties, baby-faced. I recognize the dark hair and eyes from the police station – and from before that, at the crash site in High Wycombe. There's another man at his shoulder, a tall, ascetic guy who would probably appear skinny if not for the elegant tailoring of his black suit. The two men come in together, but only the first man, the police officer, seems friendly.

'Hi there, nice to see you're awake. I'm Detective Constable Inspector Simon Gupta, from New Scotland Yard—'

'I remember,' I say.

'Yes. Sorry to barge in.' Inspector Gupta walks closer, preceded by his cologne. He smiles and nods to Alicia. The black-suited man doesn't smile, doesn't nod. He stands on the other side of the bed so I'm looking awkwardly from him to Gupta.

Gupta waves a hand to his colleague. 'This is Mr Worth, a representative of the British government.'

Mr Worth has sharp features and a dark comb-over. He meets my eyes squarely.

'You're a very lucky young woman.' He says it like he finds the idea distasteful. 'I'd like to offer the apologies of the British government, for the treatment you received when you first

285

arrived at New Scotland Yard. Naturally the police are wary of any suspicious activity in the vicinity of police headquarters, given the current climate of anxiety about terrorism and so forth—'

'It's fine,' I say. I wish he'd stop speaking. Or at least sound less bored about it all.

Gupta looks between me and Worth, a gentle flush on his cheeks. 'Yes, well, I'd like to apologize as well. On behalf of the unit. And we're very glad you and Mycroft made it out. I've also got some photos here, I was wondering if you'd be okay to—'

'She's just woken up,' Alicia protests.

'It's all right. I can look.' I push myself into a sitting position with my elbow.

Inspector Gupta seems relieved.

'Great. Mycroft has already given us quite a lot of information, but we need your corroboration.' Gupta shifts on the balls of his feet as he takes something out of the inside pocket of his gabardine coat. 'Now these are just preliminary ID photos. Have a good look, see if you recognize anyone.'

He lays the photos on the bed, in my lap.

I don't really want to bring them closer. I just point. 'That's Paul, the guy who posed as a security guard.'

Gupta nods. 'His real name is Nathan Collinson. We got the Paul Knox alias from the van registration. We're not sure how he managed to get past security ID checks at the Bodleian, but he'd been there for a month. Was he the one who grabbed you?'

'Yeah.' I blink at the other photo. 'That's Tyson.'

'Ronald Eames. Ronny, to his friends.'

I shudder. 'I wasn't his friend.'

'No, of course not.'

Jagged nausea suddenly makes my stomach roll. 'W-we didn't mean to kill him. In the explosion. It was—'

An accident, I nearly say, but it wasn't an accident. I remember the hinge in Tyson's forehead, and then I remember Mycroft's term: *collateral damage*. That seems worse somehow.

'Rachel, it's okay,' Gupta says softly. He licks his bottom lip. 'So these *are* the two men that held you?'

I nod. 'There was another man, the Colonel. He was the man in charge, he—'

Mr Worth takes one measured step forward. 'I'm afraid only these two have been identified so far, from prints and dental records. There were only two bodies in the warehouse.'

'Then Paul died too. And the Colonel escaped . . .' I feel dizzy.

Worth gives Gupta a significant look, and Gupta raises a hand. 'It's all right, Rachel, you're perfectly safe here. We've got officers on protection detail in the corridor, and we're—'

'I want to go home,' I say. I feel wrung out. I want warmth and light and the tang of Australian air . . . I miss these things. I miss my family like a sudden bereavement.

'I'm sure you do,' Worth says gravely. 'We'll arrange that for whenever your doctor says you're medically capable. But we also need to get your statement about what happened.'

'Do you think you're up for that, Rachel?' Gupta says.

I swallow. My throat is dry again. 'I have to talk about it?'

'Not at all,' Gupta says. 'I can give you some paper, and you can write it down. Are you right-handed?'

'Yeah.' A grease-dark memory of the pencil, my shaky loops and strokes, makes me catch my breath. 'The Colonel checked . . . He checked to see if I used my right or my left hand before he broke my fingers.'

Gupta frowns. 'That's an odd thing to do.'

'I think he was saving the right hand for later,' I whisper.

Alicia grips my arm tight. Her mouth is a narrow white line.

Gupta's eyes skate over my face, the sheets, the bandages. 'I'll . . . get you some writing materials from the nurses' station.'

He collects his photos and heads for the door, and Mr Worth gives me a smile as thin as himself.

'Thank you for your cooperation in this matter, Miss Watts.'

When they're both gone, I have another drink and fold back the sheets. A black brace is strapped to my right leg. The pale-violet moon of my knee peeks out through the Velcro and nylon. The whole thing looks like something out of a medical textbook and explains the weight I was feeling. My other leg is skinny and blotched in comparison.

My hospital gown is a colorless drab, bunched up around my thighs. I haven't washed in days, my hair is dirty, my face feels grimy – I must look awful.

I blink at Alicia helplessly.

'This report,' she says. 'You don't have to do it now.'

'Yeah, I do.' I sigh. 'Before I start forgetting the details.'

She tucks my hair behind my ear. 'I'm sorry to tell you this, Rachel, but you probably won't ever forget the details.'

This stills me for a moment, until I see another person standing at the door.

CHAPTER TWENTY-ONE

Mycroft's wearing a pale T-shirt and white flannel drawstring pants under a blue hospital bathrobe. The dark-chocolate riot of his hair stands out against the white, and the blue robe makes his eyes vivid.

'I was wondering when you were going to wake up.' He pads over in his socks. His smile is wonky from the stitch in his bottom lip. 'Love the knee brace. Très sexy.'

'I'm going to get you some more water.' Alicia eases off the bed. 'And maybe some rice pudding.'

'Oh god,' Mycroft says, 'not the rice pudding. See if you can get her something edible.'

Alicia grins as she leaves.

Mycroft perches on the side of the bed. 'You feeling okay?'

'I think so. Still wobbly from the anaesthetic.'

He shifts my bandaged hand gently onto his knee. 'Anaesthetic. Half your luck. I only got a bunch of shots.'

The swelling around his eye has settled, leaving behind a spectacular slate-gray bruise. I peer at his pupils, pinned and over-bright. 'Mycroft, are you hopped up on medication?'

'Broken ribs are why God invented pethidine.' He trails a finger down my arm to the bandages starting at my left wrist.

I'm not sure whether to grin or frown. 'Ribs. Plural. How many ribs have you broken?'

'Just two. Two seems to be enough. Having a bit of trouble breathing and coughing and so on.' His eyes wander down. 'Are you wearing one of those hospital gowns that opens at the back?'

'You should go back to bed, get some rest.' I tuck the fingers of my uninjured hand into his palm and it feels good. His long fingers, with the oval nails still dark with dirt from the warehouse, twist to grab mine.

'I can't.' He shivers, like a dog shaking off water. 'Can't keep still. Pethidine seems to do this to me. And I'm kind of amazed. We got out.'

'We did.'

'And I didn't blow us up. We're still, y'know—'

'Alive. I know.'

'Don't you think that's amazing? That explosion, my god. And the Colonel shot at us, and you! You were, like, all guns blazing . . .'

'I still can't believe I did that.'

'And then you drove all the way to Westminster with a dodgy knee. That was amazing. A-*mazing*.'

I grin. 'Mycroft, I think you're completely high.'

'I am. I am high. I still can't believe it.'

'I'm about to write a statement for Gupta.'

'I did mine already. Verbal statement.' He lays his hand on

the bed, on the other side of my waist. 'I left out a couple of bits though. The panting thing. I'm keeping that for myself.'

He leans over me, smiling. It's the full-voltage smile I'm familiar with. His ribs seem to be the last thing on his mind.

I bask in his energy, his warm smell. 'Can you kiss me with that stitch in your lip?'

'Let's find out.'

He has to suck in a breath as he bends. His lips are soft, except for the stitch, and I'm greedy for them.

When we come up for air, he's grinning again. 'Everything appears to be in working order. I think that's enough to be going on with, while you write your report.'

'I might leave out some things too,' I say. 'Like the bit when you told me about the accident.'

He swallows, and he looks incredibly vulnerable right in that moment. 'That would be good.'

Nerves run like ink through my stomach. 'Are you okay about it?'

'I wasn't sure how much you'd remember.' He twirls a piece of my hair in his fingers. 'Broken bones, and then my shitty memories . . . I think you got the rough end of the stick.'

'No,' I say. 'I needed it. It was important. For . . . bringing me back. But are you okay about telling me?'

His expression reassures me immediately.

'I'm okay. I'm great.' He snorts, looking slightly astonished. 'I feel light. It's kind of weird, feeling so light. Do you know what I mean? Like I could just . . .'

His face does this incredible shimmer, his eyes darting up and around. Lips parted in surprise, breath puffing out from between them, taking off, taking flight.

'Like you could float away?' I grin. 'You sure that's not the pethidine?'

'I'm sure. For certain. I mean, people talk about feeling a weight lifting, and I always thought it sounded like complete bollocks, but it's . . .' He looks back down at me wonderingly. 'Did you know it was going to be like this?'

Oh my god, I love this boy – it hits me like a lightning bolt. My eyes start to get wet but I blink the tears away, because I don't want anything blurry about this moment. My throat catches as I squeeze his arm.

'That's why I came,' I say as I smile.

―――

'. . . and then I got very ticked off when he nicked my car . . .'

Professor Walsh sits in a chair between my hospital bed and Mycroft's, balancing a bowl of saag paneer and rice in one hand while he waves his fork around with the other.

'. . . of course, I had no idea it was so serious until I got the email, but that was Wednesday morning.'

'I did try to impress the seriousness upon you.' Mycroft sits on the end of my mattress, swinging his legs. He dips a pappadum into his bowl. 'Alicia, this curry is bloody fantastic.'

'There's a takeaway place down the road.' Alicia's cross-legged on Mycroft's bed. 'I just couldn't come at the idea of hospital dinner.'

'Bravo,' Walsh says.

I try to steady the curry-filled bowl on my lap with my splinted fingers. 'I don't have enough working hands for this.'

Mycroft puts his food down and moves to swing the trolley tray over, putting my bowl right in front of me. 'There you go.'

'Much better, cheers.' I dig in with my fork, glance at Professor Walsh. 'So you told the police about it?'

'Yes, I bloody did.' Walsh snags a greasy green spot off his tie with a paper napkin, and that's the first time I've ever heard him swear. 'Mycroft had been told to meet them at such-and-such a place—'

'Outside the Natural History Museum,' Mycroft interjects with his mouth full.

'Yes, and not to tell the police. But nobody said *I* couldn't tell the police. Also, I thought the chances were high you'd both end up, well . . .'

'Dead,' I supply for him.

Walsh winces. 'Please don't say that. Anyway, I informed Simon Gupta. I have to say, I think you've both defied rather staggering odds, which I'm incredibly relieved about.'

'I'll be incredibly relieved when they catch the Colonel.' I jab at a piece of red chicken dotted with white rice.

Mycroft looks over sharply. 'They have. Didn't they tell you that? Rachel, they arrested him at a Channel crossing when he tried to leave the country.'

'What?' I put down my fork. 'When?'

'About two hours ago . . . Shit, I can't believe they didn't tell you. They've got him at New Scotland Yard right now.'

A vise-like pressure in my chest, that I'd barely acknowledged was there, suddenly releases. The room spins a little in its absence.

'Rachel.' Mycroft has put his food aside to squeeze my arm. 'Do you want the nurse, or—'

'I'm okay.' I rub my neck with my good hand. 'Totally fine. Better than fine. So he's in custody? They're questioning him?'

'Absolutely.' Mycroft's face is softly jubilant, and I remember that this is a personal victory for him as well. 'They've identified him. He's not cooperating, I understand, but they have his prints from the far end of the warehouse.'

'So who was he?'

'Well, he actually is a colonel. Or was. Colonel Stefan Moranovic. And I was right about Serbia. His prints and military history were on record. Inspector Gupta said he was already on a watch list for possible identity theft, so he's been flying under the radar for some time as an independent criminal contractor.'

My shoulders straighten. 'That's something I remembered, writing my report. The Colonel spoke to his employer on the phone . . .'

'Yeah. "Mr Wild".'

'So who's Mr Wild?'

Mycroft shrugs, holds my eyes. Lots of questions there we can't really ask each other while Alicia and the Professor are in the room. Who is Wild? How long had the Colonel been working for him – more than seven years? And if the Colonel was just following orders when he killed Mycroft's parents, was it Wild who gave the order? And why?

And I realize something else, something that makes goosebumps break out on my arms.

'Mycroft, that means *Diogenes* is—'

'The police have put Irina Addington into protective custody,' Mycroft says, shaking his head just a fraction. I close my mouth, look at my food. More talk for later. 'And they've still got nothing on Gardener. You'd never have thought a librarian would be a master of subterfuge, but the guy managed to hide this enormous book that nobody's been able to find.'

'They haven't turned up the Folio yet?' I'm amazed.

Walsh gestures with his fork. 'If they do, you'll hear about it in the papers.'

'The police have chased up all the leads,' Mycroft says, wiping his mouth on his sleeve.

'What about the safety deposit box?'

'Turned out to be too small. There wasn't even a clue inside it.'

'So it's like the Folio has just . . . disappeared into thin air.'

Alicia tears her paratha in half. 'Such a lot of bother over a book.'

'A book like no other.' Walsh raises his fork as he declaims, *'I have had a most rare vision. I have had a dream, past the wit of man to say what dream it was.'*

'Quoting *Midsummer Night's Dream*? You're a bloody Renaissance man, you are.' Mycroft grins at him, turns the grin on me. 'Personally, I prefer *Though she be but little, she is fierce.'*

'I've got one for you. *To sleep, perchance to dream.'* The nurse in the doorway has thin cornrows, strong arms and dependable hands. 'Slumber party's over, folks. Time for these two to rest.'

Alicia and Professor Walsh both assume slightly guilty expressions as they bundle the remains of dinner together.

Alicia gives me a hug. 'Try to get some sleep. I'm at the Professor's hotel now, courtesy of the police, so I've packed up all your stuff and brought it over with me.' She smiles, then sobers. 'I've been in touch with Mike, as well.'

'Oh god, my parents . . .'

'You'll see them soon. The doctor said you can fly out tomorrow, if you feel up to it. Mycroft's on the same flight.'

I nod, a bit dazed. Tomorrow I'm going home. Tomorrow I return to Melbourne sun, Melbourne skies, and Mum and Dad and Mike.

Alicia looks over at Mycroft, who's fussing with his blankets. 'Don't sit up all night talking. I don't know if putting you both in the same room was the wisest idea, but the Inspector said it was easier for the security detail.'

Mycroft abandons the blankets and steps closer, grinning. 'So we have an official sanction.'

Alicia fixes him with the evil eye. 'Make sure she gets some rest.'

'I will. Scout's honor.' Mycroft holds up three fingers, the wrong ones.

Alicia squeezes my good hand. 'G'night, Rachel.'

I watch her head for the door, catch Professor Walsh's wave with a smile. Mycroft takes off for a smoke outside, leaving me to endure the nurse, Caroline. She helps with a slow trip to the loo, then gets me to brush my teeth while she reclines the bed, checks my medication and sorts my pillows.

When Mycroft returns, she gives me the pointy finger. 'No shenanigans. That knee of yours is still swollen, and the bags under your eyes are bigger than the ones they give you in Tesco. So no musical beds – are we understood?'

'Understood.'

But of course, as soon as she's gone, Mycroft closes the door and sneaks straight to my bed. I wriggle over to make a space and he stretches himself out beside me, careful not to bump my strapped-up leg. Our faces share the pillow – Mycroft takes my good hand in his as he leans in to kiss me. When we stop to breathe, we're both blushing.

Mycroft grins. 'You taste like toothpaste.'

'Better than curry.'

I grab a handful of his T-shirt and pull him towards me again, until the heat comes off us in waves. The shower I had before dinner was awkward magic. Now I feel languid and sleepy, which is probably the drugs.

'That stitch on your lip is kind of scratchy.'

'And annoying. It keeps pulling on me when I smile.'

'Pest. I like it when you smile.'

Mycroft's face goes soft. 'And I like it when you—'

I kiss him again. When we make a space between us, he's wincing.

'Oh, your ribs . . .' I touch him gently, feeling the rough bandages under his T-shirt. 'You'll be sore. I should let you rest.'

'I am resting. This is very restful. Except for the heavy breathing and heart-rate-increasing part, of course.' He slides his fingers through my hair. 'And tomorrow we go back, so this is the last time alone we're going to have for a while.'

'I did consider that.'

'So . . . wanna fool around?'

I laugh, but Mycroft's face turns serious as he runs his fingers down the side of my cheek, the side of my neck. Down and down, tracing through my thin hospital gown.

I turn my head on the pillow as Mycroft leans in. The softness of his lips on my ear competes with the tickle of the stitch, and I shiver as my eyes close. His hand is heavy on my hip, and I listen for what he's about to say . . .

Nothing emerges but slow, even breathing. I turn back – Mycroft's eyes are closed, his mouth slack, his face pale as winter light. Whether it was the medication, or sheer exhaustion, or both, he's totally conked out.

I snort and give him a nudge. He burrows his face closer. I roll my eyes, settle myself against him, pulling his arm over my waist and tugging up the blanket.

This isn't really what I had in mind when I first imagined us sleeping together, but it'll do.

CHAPTER TWENTY-TWO

Traveling on a plane for twenty-three hours is a drag. Traveling on a plane with a broken knee and fingers is more than a drag, it's agonizing.

My knee starts to swell at thirty-four thousand feet, so I release the straps on my brace. A few hours later Mycroft loosens the bandages on my fingers as well.

I lean my shoulder against his. 'How are your ribs?'

'Average.' Mycroft's teeth are gritted, as though he's holding his fillings in. He examines my face. 'You need pills, Watts.'

I shake my head. I'm vibrating a little with the pain. 'There's hours to go. I'm gonna try to hold out as long as I can.'

They've put us in the front of the row, nearest the toilets. There's space in front to keep my leg extended. Between the two of us, we look like a commercial for an Emergency department. What the flight attendants think of us, I have no idea.

I'd feel better if Alicia were here, crashed out in a seat on the other side of the aisle. But Alicia's on her way to France. After she did all the running around, getting my satchel back from the police and organizing our trip back, I made her sit down and tell me *when* she was planning to catch the train to Paris.

'I . . . I can't go to Paris now.' Her fingers wrung themselves together. 'I should help get you home, or—'

'Not a chance.' I held her hand with my good one. 'Alicia, you've been planning this trip for *months* and—'

'But you're in a *wheelchair*—'

'—and I'll be fine once I get on the plane. Mycroft will be with me. If you don't go now you won't get back until Christmas, and then Mike will give me stick. I'll be all right.'

So she went. She called home for me, then she hugged us both goodbye at Heathrow, while our police security detail looked on.

It feels odd – unbalanced – without Alicia, and I miss her. But if I survived being kidnapped by a Serbian mobster, I can survive a plane trip back to Australia. All I have to deal with is the impossibility of maneuvering in the toilet cubicle. And the swelling-at-altitude problem.

'One pill,' Mycroft says. 'You can have another one later.'

'No. I had three before we boarded, and the doctor said to wait.'

'Even *I* feel like taking one pill.'

'Don't.' I grab for his hand. He's on my right side, in the window seat. 'Talk to me. Distract me.'

'All right.' He kisses the back of my hand. 'You have the most perfect breasts. If we ever get time alone together again, I'm going to—'

'*Mycroft!*' I duck my head. 'Not *that* distracting.'

'Oh, all right. I haven't got a completely one-track mind.' He grins. 'Well, okay, I do. But that's because I'm, y'know, a guy. But we can talk about something else. I can be steered onto other less interesting subjects.'

'Talk to me about what we couldn't talk about last night. When we were having dinner with Alicia and Professor Walsh.'

'Oh, that. Well, I didn't tell you everything I found out.' His expression sobers. 'I didn't want to freak you out.'

'Freak me out? About what?'

Mycroft kisses my hand again, examines it minutely. 'The Colonel is in custody, but his boss is still out there. And, in case you've forgotten, he knows our names.'

I shiver. 'I haven't forgotten. But Australia is a long way from the UK, Mycroft.'

'Mm.' He doesn't look convinced. 'What I'm really interested in now is finding out who Wild is.'

'Do you think the Colonel was working for him when your parents were killed?'

'I don't know. '

'Because if the Colonel was working for Wild then, it would mean . . .'

'Yes. That Wild was the one who ordered the hit on Mum and Dad.'

I watch him as he says it. He looks pensive, eyes flaring in the light of the cabin, the sun out the window making strong contours across his cheek and jaw. But the expression on his face is calm. There's none of the flinching, none of the choking in his voice he always gets when talking about his family.

Something in Mycroft has changed. He's the most peaceful I've ever seen him. Maybe that one time, when he had a chance to talk about the accident, was enough to release something.

'There's another thing, though,' Mycroft goes on. '*Why* did Wild order the carjacking? What were my parents involved in that made us a target?'

'Maybe they weren't involved in anything.'

He shakes his head. 'Something brought them to Wild's attention. Remember what the Colonel said – *Eliminate this man, eliminate his family* . . . It was something to do with my dad. I just have no bloody idea what.'

'Give it time. You'll work it out eventually.'

'Yeah. I guess.' Mycroft bites his bottom lip, winces as he snags his stitch. 'But what will I find out?'

I don't have an answer. The only reply I can give him is a kiss.

When I've kissed him enough to get a warm feeling inside, I lean my forehead against his. 'I don't know why you were worried. I've heard most of your story and I haven't run away screaming yet. None of this is freaking me out.'

Mycroft eases away. 'Ah. That's because I haven't got to the important bit yet. The bit about *Diogenes*.'

A fish-hook of anxiety snags inside my chest.

'The Colonel contacted you about me via the *Diogenes* blog,' I say slowly.

'Yes.'

'So what happens? You close the blog down, or let the police monitor—'

'No.' Mycroft shakes his head. 'I'm not willing to do that.'

I gape at him. 'Mycroft, that's—'

'Dodgy. Yeah, I know. I didn't actually tell Gupta that the Colonel made contact through the blog. I said the Colonel's men left me a note at the hostel, and told me to destroy it. And you didn't tell the police how they found me in your report.' He starts fast talking as I open my mouth to speak. 'Rachel, I don't want to close the blog. It's the only link I've got to Wild, and I need to find out who he is. I know *Diogenes* is compromised, but it's an untraceable site – and I promise I'll be extra careful.'

I stare at him, gobsmacked. 'Mycroft, you *can't*! God, it's too dangerous . . . This guy, Wild, he *kills* people!'

'It's too late.' Mycroft's face is like marble. 'Wild's already made contact.'

It feels as if the plane we're in just dropped a thousand feet. '*What?*'

'I'll show you.' Mycroft sucks in a groan as he leans over to fetch his backpack from under his seat.

He pulls out his laptop. The file he opens is a screenshot of the *Diogenes* site. Mycroft's last blog post is prominently displayed. It's not even a forensics article – it's a short odd-spot on how to gold-plate your iPod.

Down at the bottom I see the comments, with a variety of approving emoticons.

I peer at the screen. 'Where am I looking?'

'Check the last comment. It was made yesterday.'

I scroll down apprehensively, then my shoulders sag with relief. 'A list of chemicals. So what?'

'Read them out.'

'Iodine. Nitric oxide. Uranium.' I frown. 'What about it? It doesn't even seem to be related to the content of the post, so—'

'In the Periodic Table of Elements, each element has an identifying letter, or combination of letters—'

'Mycroft, I *know* that. What's that got to do with—'

'Read them out again. Use the letters this time.'

I blow out my lips. 'Okay. Fine. Let's see . . . Iodine is I. Nitric oxide is . . . Is that N_2O or NO?'

'The second one.'

'Okay. And Uranium is U, obviously.' I push my hair away, clumsy with my bandaged fingers. 'So that's it. Eye, en-oh, ewe.'

Mycroft gives me a little eyebrow raise. Suddenly I get it.

'Eye, no, ewe.' I look at him. '*I know you.*'

'Check the profile name,' Mycroft says quietly.

I do. Suddenly my lungs are not working, and I need them to be working. '*Moriarty.* Mycroft, the profile name is Moriarty.'

'Yeah.'

'That's the . . . That's the guy, the evil mastermind guy, that Sherlock Holmes always used to—'

'I know.' He runs a thumb across the name on the screen. 'I think this is Wild. It's too clever for the Colonel – he was too much of a blunt instrument. But this guy is smart. Or he thinks he's smart. I bet if I check the logged IP address it'd take me back to some random junk server.'

'But that means—'

'Wild can contact me anytime he likes. He knows me. He knows what we did to his people. And he knows you, he knows how tough you are. He knows we're a couple.'

The back of my neck prickles, as though a million tiny black teeth are biting me there.

Mycroft stares at the name – *Moriarty* – in bold red type. He rubs his bottom lip compulsively.

'If Wild really wanted to find us, he could do it without *Diogenes.* He knows our names, he has contacts. This message—' He flicks a hand at the screen. 'He's just trying to keep us scared. At least with the blog link we might have some warning. What I expect we'll find out next is how well-connected Wild is back in Australia, whether he's recovered from his last defeat. If he contacts me again, if he makes a move first . . . then we have to think about strategy. It's a bit like a game of chess—'

'Mycroft, it's not a bloody *game!*' My voice is too loud, too explosive in the quiet cabin.

Mycroft grabs my hand in one of his, uses the other to fold down the laptop. 'Rachel, it's okay. Shh, it's all right—'

'It's not bloody *all right*, either!' But I've lowered my voice to an angry hiss. 'Are you *trying* to get yourself killed? Because this is—'

'Rachel.' He dumps his laptop and cups my cheek. 'Rachel, I'm *not* trying to get myself killed. I'm not. And I'm not trying to endanger you either. But I've got to *know*.'

'Mycroft—'

'It's like . . . this big secret I've never known a thing about, and I *have* to find out. I already feel so much more—' He looks around for the word, finally catching it out of the air, '—*free*, just knowing some of it, sharing it with you. If the police do all the work they'll never let me in on it, and it could take years. This is my chance. My parents deserve to get justice.'

I stare into his face. 'But don't you remember what you said in the warehouse? Knowing won't bring your parents back. They wouldn't want you to risk your *life* for this – I don't want you to risk your life for this! Wild is too big, he's too dangerous—'

'Rachel, I need to know,' Mycroft says softly.

It's simple, and it's everything to him – I can see it in his face. But the Colonel's words keep running back to me, over and over: '*Eliminate this man, eliminate his family . . . Everybody wins.*' Wild is probably already pissed off at Mycroft for blowing up his henchmen. Seven years ago he wanted Mycroft's entire family gone, for reasons unknown. Does this mean that now he's aware Mycroft's looking into his parents' deaths, he'll want Mycroft gone too?

I don't know, I don't know. I hold my head in my cold hands and the splint on my fingers catches in my hair.

Everybody wins. That's how dumb the Colonel was, that he thought there could be winners in this situation. There are no winners. Mycroft won't win anything, even if he finds out all this stuff. And I won't win anything either, and it's making my chest ache, and my heart, my heart . . .

'Hey.' Mycroft hugs me gently, brings my hands down, smooths my hair.

I shake him off. 'I'm tired. I can't do this. I want the pills now.'

'I thought you said you wanted to wait?'

'I can't.' I wobble my head. 'My leg hurts. I know you said I was tough, but I'm not. I'm not.'

'Rachel—'

'Just give me the pills, James.'

He fishes them out of my carry-on, and I take them. But they don't make me feel any better. They just make me more tired. God, I'm so tired. My leg is still swollen and my brain feels swollen. And my heart is too full. It's straining at the seams, red and pulsing, ready to burst.

CHAPTER TWENTY-THREE

Painkillers get me through the rest of the flight. The meds alleviate the constant, ponderous throb in my leg, fingers and head, but they only scratch the surface. I'm desperate to stop feeling. I spend a lot of time half-dozing, knowing I'll regret it, but suffering from jet lag back in Melbourne is the last thing I'm worried about.

I'd been so relieved to say goodbye to panic and fear. When the plane took off from Heathrow, I could finally breathe again. It was such a release. But it turns out those feelings have followed me all this way.

If Wild has contacted Mycroft, if Mycroft is a target, then we aren't safe anywhere. It's as if the whole world has turned into that chill, comfortless room back in the warehouse . . .

When we finally land, I want to be first out the door – god, I want to kiss the tarmac. Of course, because of my 'disabled' status, we have to wait until last, so the airport staff can bring me a wheelchair.

Finally we're out of that tin can plane and through the maze of Customs. An attendant pushes the luggage trolley and Mycroft wheels me through Arrivals into the terminal.

The sun of my own country feels like a Paul Kelly song. I taste the crisp Melbourne air, see the tall, wide-shouldered figure patiently waiting in his Redbacks and jeans . . .

'*Mike!*'

I can't get out of the chair and run to him. I just lift my arms, like I'm a baby who wants a carry. Then my brother is there, on his knees, folding himself around me, crushing me to him.

'*Rache.*' He hugs me in the wheelchair, angling around my elevated leg. 'Rachel. Christ.'

God, he feels so good, so home-smelling and warm. His arms are squashing me and the zipper of his jacket scratches my cheek. He's sniffing a bit, too, I'm sure of it.

'I said Friday, yeah?' I smile like crazy, hold back tears.

'Yeah, and it's Sunday, you goose.' Mike blinks and grins. 'Not quite good to your word, but I guess we'll let it slide just this once. Ah, geez, Rache. Look at you.' My brother checks me over and shakes his head. 'Mate, you just love it, don't you? Getting yourself knocked around? Can't help yourself.'

I blush. 'There – there was an accident—'

'It's all right, Rache. You don't have to give me the bullshit story. I know most of it from Leesh.' Mike looks grave, then cocks an eyebrow. 'At least you brought back my jumper, that's nice. Top marks for that.' He gives me a pat on the head, wobbles my chin with his fingers. 'God, you look a right duffer with your leg sticking out.'

Then he smiles at Mycroft, who's standing awkwardly holding my crutches.

'Mycroft, mate, good to see you.' Mike clasps Mycroft's arm. 'So you're the man who rode to the rescue, yeah?'

Mycroft's cheeks pink up. 'We kind of rescued each other.'

'Right. Right.' Mike isn't going to let it go, though. 'Well . . . thank you. For bringing her home.'

Mycroft shrugs one shoulder.

'Anyway.' Mike lets go of Mycroft's arm. 'Angela wanted to come get you, but she's only just knocked off work. She looked buggered, so I volunteered to be the monkey who'd drive out here. Probably for the best, the way you two look.' He peers at Mycroft's black eye. 'Face is a bit worse for wear, eh?'

'I've had better days with my face,' Mycroft agrees.

'Well, you're home now. We can go back to the ranch and put a big steak on it or something.'

And then I realize what's missing from this picture. I glance at Mike, glance around the terminal, but I'm not seeing anybody else, I'm not seeing—

'Mum and Dad didn't come?'

Mike pauses in the act of hefting Mycroft's backpack onto his shoulder.

He looks at Mycroft, looks at me, lets the backpack slide off. 'Well, Rache, Dad's on shift, but he said to say welcome home.'

'Okay,' I say slowly. 'But . . . what about Mum?'

Mike sighs and hunkers down to my level. 'Mum's a bit trickier.'

'How's that?'

'Rache . . .' He scratches his head. 'Mum did her nana. She was really pissed off when you left. She went completely ballistic.'

'But . . . that's normal Mum, right? We knew she'd go off. And me and Mum fight all the time, but then we just—'

'No, Rache. This is different. She's . . . I've never seen her this angry. She's only just started looking at *me* again. And she said . . .' Mike clears his throat. 'She said she can't talk to you right now. She said—'

'Mum doesn't want to talk to me?'

'Basically, yeah.' He sighs at my expression. 'Just give her some time.'

'So Mum's going to ignore me.'

'Look, don't get yourself all worked up, Rache – it won't help. See how things pan out. It's a small house, yeah? She can't pretend you don't exist forever.'

'Okay,' I say, but my voice is tiny, and I'm staring down at my lap.

'Ah, Rache.' Mike hugs me again. 'We'll sort it out. Come on, let's get you out of here.'

I flounder for control, nod and blink and wipe my nose on my sleeve.

'Okay.' Mike squints at the luggage trolley, at Mycroft with the crutches, at my stuck-out leg. 'Right. Not sure how we're all going to fit into the car, but—'

'Maybe I can help with that,' a gravelly voice says.

Detective Pickup has strolled up on my other side. He's got a long overcoat covering his usual hulking self, and his knobbly nose is red from the cold. He nods his carrot hair at everyone in turn.

'Yes, good morning, afternoon, whatever it is.' He surveys the luggage landscape, looks at me and Mycroft. 'Nice to see you back. I'd say "all in one piece", but that doesn't seem to apply. The Poms phoned me, filled me in on your arrival time and so forth. So here I am, official police presence. Believe you've got something of mine.'

'Yeah. Hello, Detective.' Mycroft scrounges through his jacket pocket and comes out with a letter in a slightly crumpled envelope, which he passes to Pickup. 'Here you go. Professor Walsh sends his regards.'

'Right.' Pickup takes the envelope, tucks it away and turns to Mike. 'Hello again, Mr Watts. So as I was saying, I've got the car. Plenty of room. I'll take these two, have a chat on the way, if you don't mind.'

'Er, right.' Mike seems a bit overwhelmed by the official police presence. He leans towards me. 'Rachel, are you sure you don't wanna—'

'It's okay, Mike. It's fine.' It sounds as if Pickup wants to do a quick debrief, and he's offering a ride, so we may as well take it.

'Well . . . if you're sure.'

I'm not sure. I'm not ready for a bawling-out by our friendly neighborhood detective, but Pickup's got that look on his face like he's going to get what he wants regardless.

'I'm sure,' I say. 'You take off with the bags, we'll bring up the rear.'

Mike frowns at Pickup. 'Take care of her, okay? She's had a rough shake. Her and Mycroft both.'

Pickup nods gravely, his red-ferret eyebrows coming together. 'I will certainly take priority A-one care of the two of them. Got my word on that.'

'Okay.' Mike seems mollified. 'Then I guess we're off.'

I've got a police detective pushing my wheelchair, and I've come home to what sounds like major family dramas. But it's somehow reassuring to emerge into a typical gray Melbourne day. The smog, the bone-chilling wind, the awful traffic – all these things used to depress me. Right now, they feel like not-England. They feel like home.

Pickup has parked his car in the emergency bay, so at least it's close by. He helps me maneuver into the front passenger seat. Mycroft puts my crutches in the back and folds himself in with them. Compared to Walsh's little brown accident-waiting-to-happen, this car is like a cruise liner.

Once we've passed the exit ramps to Bulla, Pickup decides to go for it.

'Yes, well. Not at all what I was expecting, to get a phone call in the middle of the night from our good Professor, informing me that you had somehow managed to get yourself *abducted*, Miss Watts. *Abducted*. And that *you*, Mr Mycroft, had elected to go haring off after your girlfriend on a rescue mission, unaided, without informing the police in London—'

'Yeah, well—' Mycroft says.

'And *then*,' Pickup says, squeezing the steering wheel, 'and *then* to hear you've both somehow managed to blow up a warehouse. *Blow up*. As in, explode into bits, set fire to, wreak destruction upon . . .'

'It seemed like a good idea at the time,' I say.

'You two.' Pickup's eyes goggle between the road, me, and Mycroft in the back seat. 'You two are . . . I don't know what to say. It's beyond my ability to say anything. Not to mention that it wouldn't make any impression anyway. I've *told* you on a *number* of other occasions, I've *advised* you what you should do—'

'Yeah.' I nod. 'Keep out of it. Stay home, do schoolwork, listen to pop music, do whatever normal teenagers do.'

'*Yes*. But you *don't listen*.' Pickup unclenches his hands on the wheel, sighs out deeply, stares at the road. 'It's doing my head in.'

I pull against my seatbelt. 'If it makes you feel better, Detective, we didn't exactly win prizes for investigative excellence. Daniel Gardener is still dead—'

'But we did find out who killed him.' Mycroft's leaning between the two front seats to get his twenty cents' worth in.

I give him a quick, glaring glance. 'And we don't know anything about the Colonel's boss, the guy who contracted him for Gardener's murder.'

'Something will turn up on him,' Mycroft says meaningfully.

'And the Folio is still missing,' I finish.

'Ah, yes. Bit tricky, that one.'

'Do you mind?' I turn to Mycroft, glowering.

'Yes.' Pickup nods. 'Not to mention the fact that you both ended up in the hospital. *Again*. Miss Watts, I was under the impression you'd gone to London to *help*. If I'd known you were just going to inflame the situation, then I'd never have given you the information you—'

'Watts did help.' Mycroft sounds indignant. 'More than that – she worked out the events of the theft. And it was worth it. Not the nearly-getting-killed bit, I could've lived without that, but—'

'No, he's right.' I look away from both of them. The unattractive pre-cast concrete structures of the Tullamarine Freeway flash past my window. Soon we'll be on Bell Street. I'm almost home. 'I was supposed to be there as support, not getting myself held hostage.'

'Exactly.' For once, Pickup approves of my logic.

'But after seeing Gardener's body, I just . . .' I stare outside. I wonder if Gardener missed home, before he died. If he missed the suburban pasteboard and dry gum plantings of Melbourne, after the green, heritage grandeur of London. 'I felt sorry for him, you know? I mean, he did something incredibly stupid, stealing the Folio. But I felt sorry for him anyway.'

'Gardener made a choice,' Mycroft says softly.

'I know that. But he died a long way from home. Everybody he cared about was right here. His sister, his niece . . . They were his only human legacy. And he—'

'What?' Mycroft says.

'I said, I'd like to figure out why—'

'No. Not that bit.' Mycroft is really leaning forward now, staring at me urgently. 'Say it again. What you just said.'

'Er . . .' I rack my foggy brain. 'I just said that Gardener's family was all here, they were his only legacy, and maybe—'

'*STOP THE CAR!*' Mycroft thumps his fist on Pickup's headrest.

In a flurry of cursing, Pickup pulls over into the emergency lane. We're nearly at the Bell Street exit – the car rocks as high-speed traffic pings past us towards the city.

Pickup turns and glares at Mycroft as if he's a rabid animal escaped from a carrier basket. '*Would you mind very much telling me what the BLOODY HELL you're playing at?*'

Mycroft is scrabbling in the pocket of his hoodie. 'It's right here, I've got it—'

'Mycroft—' I start.

'Here!' Mycroft yanks something out of his pocket – the notepad he's been carrying everywhere. He leafs rapidly through the pages. 'It's *here*. I wrote it down, I'm sure of it. I can't believe I didn't think – yes!'

He finds what he's after and tears the slip loose.

'What is it?'

Mycroft angles forward through both front seats. His hair seems to have electricity in it and his eyes are lit up, fixed on mine.

'You know, I've never told you this, and I really should. I should tell you all the time. Watts, you're a genius.'

He cups my head in his hands and kisses me, a sweet yearning kiss that ends with a smacking sound.

Pickup doesn't look happy. 'Mr Mycroft, if you don't explain yourself in about *one second*—'

'Drive, Detective.' Mycroft grins at Pickup, which only turns the detective's face a darker shade of purple. 'We're going to North-cote. If you take us there, I promise I'll give you a big present.'

'I don't *want* a big present,' Pickup splutters. The car bunny-hops as we pull out and gain momentum. 'I want you to get the bloody hell out of my car!'

'*Please*, Detective. Here's the address – Raleigh Street, it's not far.'

I'm still recovering from the kiss, but I'm trying to keep up. 'Mycroft, what's going on?'

'Trust me,' he says.

The look he's giving me means I have no choice but to comply.

———

The house in Raleigh Street has a lovely front garden, with a loquat tree that's dropping leathery leaves everywhere.

Getting through the garden gate is a bit of a squeeze with my crutches. Mycroft walks in front and clears the slippery leaves off the brick path, but it still feels precarious. My splinted fingers hurt after just a few meters. Clearly this crutches business is going to take more practice than I'd thought.

Pickup insists he be the one to knock on the door of the wooden house. Mycroft and I stand behind his shoulder like two bruised sentinels.

'Yes, can I help you?' A woman about my mum's age peers out from behind the flyscreen door.

'Mrs Margaret Sutcliffe? I'm Detective Senior Sergeant Vincent Pickup, from St Kilda Road station. I understand you recently received word of your brother's passing in the UK, is that right?'

'Why, yes.' Margaret Sutcliffe straightens. Her mouth trembles. 'Yes. They phoned me about Daniel, to say he'd . . .'

Her eyes are wary. I'm sure she's read the news, heard the rumors of suspicion.

'Right,' Pickup says. 'So you've been informed of—'

'I haven't been informed of anything at all.' Mrs Sutcliffe drops her arms from around herself. 'When he's coming home, what the police have discovered . . . I mean, they said his girl-friend caused the accident, but I knew that wasn't right. Dan never said a word to me about a girlfriend, and he always told me about that sort of thing. I know they've assigned an Australian pathologist, like I asked, but I haven't been given any report, any news – nothing. The police just seem to want to brush it under the carpet.'

She presses her lips together. I feel for her: she's Gardener's sister, and she's been left so out of the loop. Even I know more about her brother's death.

'He cared about you,' I blurt. Margaret Sutcliffe's head jerks in my direction. 'He had a picture of you and your daughter in his wallet—'

'Miss Watts,' Pickup says.

Margaret Sutcliffe stares at me. 'How do you know—'

She's interrupted when a girl walks up from behind and puts an arm around her waist. 'Are you okay, Mum?'

Natalie Sutcliffe is immediately recognizable, although she's grown up a bit since the photo was taken. She's maybe fifteen, braces on her teeth and leggy as a colt, with a long ponytail of caramel hair. She's wearing jeans and a tank top that's too summery for the weather, with a pink hoodie unzipped over the top.

'I'm fine, sweetheart,' her mother says, her eyes brimming as she smiles at her daughter. It always amazes me how parents do that – comfort and reassure you while they're in the middle of crying themselves.

'What's this about?' Natalie glares at each of us in turn.

'It's all right, love,' Margaret Sutcliffe says. 'It's just about Uncle Dan.'

'Mrs Sutcliffe.' Mycroft squeezes forward. 'Could we have a moment of your time? I was with the coronial team investigating your brother's death—'

'You were—' Margaret Sutcliffe peers at him. 'So can you tell me what happened?' She takes in Mycroft's bruises, his black eye, then runs a glance over my crutches. 'But why are you—'

'It was . . . an accident,' Mycroft says. 'Miss Watts and I were in an accident. But your brother, I understand he sent you something. A parcel?'

'Oh, yes.' Margaret Sutcliffe collects herself, waves a hand with a tissue she's fetched from her sleeve. 'It was addressed to Natalie. But I haven't been able to open it. I just couldn't stand the idea of—'

'What parcel?' Natalie rubs her mother's back. 'Mum, what is it?'

Margaret Sutcliffe looks away from her daughter, looks at me. 'All I could think was, this was the last thing we had from him before he died, before this "girlfriend" . . .'

'Mrs Sutcliffe,' I say softly, 'you were right. About the girlfriend, about everything. May we come in?'

'Yes. Oh, goodness.'

Mrs Sutcliffe opens the flywire and ushers us inside. I go first, ungainly on my crutches. Natalie watches me as I make my awkward way down the hall, past the bedroom doors to a little sitting room.

'Are you okay? There's a chair right here—'

'A chair would be great.'

Natalie steers me closer to a wooden coffee table with two chairs and a small pile of books and magazines. There's a bookshelf in one corner of the sitting room and an upright piano in the other. A small stained-glass window lets in filtered light. The air is musty, as though it's not used very often, and the room is cold.

Mycroft and I take the chairs while Pickup lurks behind us.

'Would you like a cup of tea?' Mrs Sutcliffe says. 'I could put the kettle on.'

'If it's all right, Mrs Sutcliffe, we'd very much like to see the parcel first.' Mycroft sits on his hands nervously.

'Certainly.' Mrs Sutcliffe gives him a curious look and exits for one of the bedrooms.

Natalie balances herself on a wooden stool near the piano. She tugs at the zipper on her hoodie.

'Did you . . . Did you really see my uncle? I mean—' She swallows. 'Did you see his body? Mum's been so stressed about it, she just wanted to know if he was in a lot of pain when he died.'

I don't know how to answer. I'm relieved when Mycroft speaks up in my place.

'Natalie, your uncle was killed when his car was forced off the road.' He holds Natalie's gaze firmly. 'He would have been in shock, and not aware of anything too much before his death.'

I know this is a lie. I blink at my knee, stretched out in front, until I think I've schooled my features to look up.

Mycroft has already gone on. 'I'm sorry I can't tell you more details, but—'

'No.' Natalie shakes her head. 'No, that's fine. I mean, that's good. It was the only thing Mum really wanted to know, if Uncle Dan had . . . Well, you know.'

'I know,' Mycroft says.

Mrs Sutcliffe is back again, holding an enormous brown, padded parcel covered in packing tape and stamps. She places it on the coffee table in front of us.

'I left it at the post office, you know.' Mrs Sutcliffe scrubs at her cheek with the heel of one hand. 'Then I put it on top of the cupboard. Just left it there, because I wasn't ready to open it. I mean, it seemed perfectly harmless, but I was . . .'

'That's completely understandable.' Mycroft touches the parcel reverently. 'Do you mind if I open it now, Mrs Sutcliffe?'

'Please.' Mrs Sutcliffe flaps a hand. 'You do it. I just . . . I'll just stand here with Nattie.'

Mycroft attacks the tape and the brown paper, peels everything back carefully, and inside the wrappings is a cardboard box, corrugated, protective. On top of the box lies a thin packet of handkerchiefs, the Liberty logo embossed in one corner. There's also a letter, written in a hurried scrawl – Mycroft passes that to Mrs Sutcliffe.

'*Darling Maggie and Nat*,' Mrs Sutcliffe reads. Her eyes scan further. 'Oh goodness . . .'

She puts a hand to her mouth. Mycroft keeps going with the cardboard box. Inside the box is a thick layer of bubble wrap, and inside the bubble wrap is—

Mrs Sutcliffe drops her hand and frowns. 'What on earth . . .?'

CHAPTER TWENTY-FOUR

Pickup has walked closer, is peering down. Mycroft carefully folds away the plastic to reveal a book.

Its front cover is made of brown leather, pitted, worn and much abused. There's an aged sheen on the leather, from all the years of being touched by readers' hands – this volume of plays so well-loved, so often read, so unique in every way.

My breath exits in a soft sigh.

Mycroft wipes his fingers on his T-shirt before touching the corner of the leather cover. He opens it and turns the first few leaves so we can see the title page.

There's the famous picture, the one I've seen so many times online or in other books – the engraving of the man with the domed bald head and the mustache, the high, elaborate collar. William Shakespeare's face, if this is what it really looked like, seems full of wry weariness.

'My oath,' Pickup whispers.

'*Mr William Shakespeare's Comedies, Histories & Tragedies. Published according as the True Original Copies. London. Printed by William Jaggard and Ed Blount. 1623.*' Mycroft's voice is shaking. 'There you are, Detective, I said I'd give you a present.'

'That's a six million pound present,' Pickup says.

I can't speak. It takes a moment for my brain to catch up.

'Are you telling me I left a book worth six million pounds sitting in the post office?' Mrs Sutcliffe says.

Laughter burbles up out of my stomach. It only stops when Mycroft squeezes my hand.

————

We don't get home for ages.

Pickup doesn't seem quite sure how to proceed when it comes to antique works of literature. He ends up calling for another car, and then for a secure police van. Margaret Sutcliffe's sitting room quickly becomes crowded with police officers.

In the kitchen, Mycroft talks to Mrs Sutcliffe about her brother's death. I call Mike, to let him know what's happened, then Natalie helps me over to the piano stool. She has the presence of mind to take some photos before the Folio and the letter are whisked away in the secure van.

'They're the last things Uncle Dan ever sent me,' she says to me, scrolling through the grainy shots on her iPhone. 'He used to send me all sorts of crazy stuff. Presents from Harrods and Liberty. Funny monogrammed tea-towels.'

'Your uncle planned to return the Folio,' I say. 'He said in his letter that he didn't want the person he stole the Folio for to have it. He knew the real value of it. Not the monetary value, I mean.

I guess he knew you and your mum would take care of the Folio until he made it back.'

'I guess.' She smiles, in a sad way.

Pickup is still scurrying around, organizing people, and he asks us to give statements. But there must be something in my face – maybe I just look as gray as I feel – and I end up talking to another officer on the front porch of the Sutcliffes' home.

Mycroft pokes his head around the lintel of the front door. 'It's nearly four-thirty. You probably need some medication.'

I'm shaking a little. The breeze is fresh, and the loquats are really glowing in the afternoon sun. I have to tear my eyes away from them to blink.

Mycroft sighs out his nose. He comes closer and helps me to rise, puts my arm around his neck. We hobble off the porch, down the steps, along the little brick path to the car. Mycroft lowers me into the passenger seat, then hunkers down inside the open car door. 'I'm going down to the station, but I think we'd better get you home.'

'I can't believe we found it,' I say. 'After all that, it was right here.'

'Bit of a wasted trip, then, yeah?'

My hair blows in my eyes as I shake my head. 'No. We found out what happened to Gardener. And what happened to you. Just . . . If you need to tell me something, next time don't wait until I get my fingers broken to do it, okay?'

Soon after that, a female police officer comes to drive me home.

———

Now we see what the meat is like inside, yes?

I jerk out of sleep, blink stupidly at the window. A disorienting second passes before I register that I'm in bed. Cool blue light stains the curtain from outside, so it must be . . . morning? I'm honestly not sure, because the last few days have been a sleep-addled blur of jet-lag exhaustion, hospital trips and unsettling dreams.

'Wakey wakey, Rache.' Mike barges in and flicks the curtain open.

I sit myself up, rake back my hair. 'God, what time is it?'

'Three-thirty.' Mike pushes the mug he's carrying – tea, lukewarm, too milky – into my non-bandaged hand. 'Wednesday. Remember Wednesday? Detective Pickup's outside in the car.'

'Right.'

Mike squints at me. 'You okay? Because if you're not up for St Kilda, I can just go out and tell him to stick it where the sun don't—'

'I'm fine, Mike. Really.' I slug back some tea, then plonk the mug on the chair beside my bed, the one that's being used as a rudimentary table for glasses of water, silver foils of pills, and books I'm not actually reading. 'And Pickup said this guy from the UK is too much of a bigwig to come here, so it's not like we have a choice.'

'Whatever you reckon.' Mike shrugs. 'Although I'm starting to agree with Dad. A couple of days in the hospital might be a really good—'

This snaps me fully awake. 'No *way*. I don't need—'

'Jeez, Rachel, don't bite my head off. Forget about it then.' Mike makes a fist, bumps it against his thigh. 'Anyway, you're fine, yeah?'

I scowl. 'Turn around while I get dressed.'

Getting dressed involves a lot of difficult maneuvering. Putting on a bra is impossible, so I opt for a crop top under my long-sleeved red T-shirt. My track pants are ugly, and have a slit up one side. I sigh. I feel like a chicken wire girl – stiff and scratchy and bent out of shape.

Mike talks to the wall. 'Want help with your socks?'

'Oh . . . All right, yes. Bloody hell.'

Mike kneels in front of me to manhandle my feet into socks and then boots.

I force my voice into casual pleasantness. 'So is Mycroft outside?'

'Yeah, yeah, he's waiting for you.'

'But . . . you didn't let him in.'

Mike blushes a little, eyes back on his task. 'Well, better not to rush things, y'know? Mum's pretty scary. She still hasn't talked to you?'

I look away. 'I've heard her, if that's what you mean. She and Dad were arguing right outside my door yesterday.'

I remember Mum's hissing whisper, . . . *taking off after that mad boy, disappearing without a bloody word, without a thought for anyone else's feelings, and then a* car accident, *for god's sake! Why can't she just—*and then Dad's voice, in a tone I'd never heard him use with Mum before, *Jenny. Come on, not in the hall.*

Dad had come in after arguing with Mum. He'd sat on the chair beside the bed, shifting the books and pill packets, and patted my shoulder awkwardly. *Y'know, falling in love isn't a bad thing, Rachel, but you've gotta have a bit of balance. I know it and your mum knows it, except she's so caught up in feeling anxious about you that she's turned it into anger. But she still loves you, okay? If you're a parent, that love . . . It just overwhelms you sometimes . . .*

He couldn't go on then. He'd got all blinky and had to clear his throat, which made me feel even more guilty.

I'm not doing this on purpose, I'd blurted out. *I'm not trying to piss you and Mum off or anything—*

I know, love, I know. Well, it could be worse, eh? You could be getting tattoos all over yourself, or piercings or whatever.

Mike finishes with my boots, and pushes himself up to sit beside me on the bed. 'Look, Rache, Mum still doesn't know about the kidnapping thing, and we'd like to keep that nice and quiet for the time being, if you don't mind.'

'I get it, sure.' I chew at my lip. 'I'm just a bit sick of copping flak about it.'

My eyes go hot, and before I understand why, I'm leaking tears.

'Ah, Rachel.' Mike sighs. 'I know it's hard, but you put Mum through hell. Flying off like that, and then coming home like *this* . . .'

Mike grimaces at me, as though he's looking at a sheep that's lost condition. I know what he's seeing. I saw it in the mirror yesterday. My face is pale, green-tinged with bruises, my hair lank. But I got through everything that happened in London. I can get through this, too.

'I . . . I just need a shower and a bit more rest.'

Mike raises his eyebrows, then stands up, reaches for my crutches.

I clutch at his elbow to rise, immersed in a sudden panic. 'Am I losing my words, Mike?'

My brother turns. 'What?'

'I just . . .' I fumble my crutches into place. Making him understand the tongue-tied helplessness I've had since I came back is hard. 'It's like . . . I used to be able to talk to Mum and Dad. Explain things. And they'd *get* it. They'd get *me*. But I don't know if that's true anymore . . .'

I wonder if I'm losing the easy vocabulary I had when I was a child that explained things to my parents. Maybe I've changed so much that I've got a whole new set of words my parents don't understand. Whatever those words are, Mike doesn't seem to get them either. His eyes are gentle, but wary.

'C'mon, Rache.' He opens the bedroom door for me. 'Let's just get you to St Kilda, okay?'

It's silvery-cold outside, the air damp and blustering. The grass in our front yard is long, as if Dad's been neglecting the garden. Across the street, someone is playing an old Rihanna piano ballad through crackly speakers. My fingers chill in the icy wind – I realize I'm going to need a jacket, then discover Mike's already got one for me. He puts it around my shoulders before heading back into the house.

I find Mycroft waiting for me on the front porch, sitting on the low concrete balustrade. The wind blows his curls away from his face, exposing the yellow-green edges of his shiner. We've only been apart a couple of days, but I've missed him so much it hurts.

'Hey.' He stands and curls an arm around me, pecks my cheek lightly. He looks nervous, although that could be his proximity to the house. Mycroft is currently *persona non grata* here. If Mum saw him waiting like this, she'd get out the shotgun – if she were actually home, and if we actually had a shotgun.

'Hey, yourself.' I look over to see Pickup's car idling at the curb. It's slick with rain – for some reason, this sight makes me shiver more than the freezing wind.

Mycroft's gaze takes me in. 'Are you sure you're okay to move around? I mean, this guy can just collect the Folio and go home. We don't have to go all the way to the station for an official thank you.'

'I'm okay.' I examine Mycroft carefully. 'Are *you* okay? Are your ribs healing up?'

'Slowly.' Mycroft lips turn up, but only on one side. 'I would have come in, but—'

'You don't have to explain.' I lean into him as I clunk my way towards Pickup's car. 'Mike'll let you in, once things settle down. I wanted to visit you, but it's a bit hard—'

'Shit, Rachel, don't apologize.' Mycroft's hand is steadying my lower back, and I feel it jerk as he snorts. 'It's *my* fault your parents are on the warpath.'

I pull us both up short as we reach the car. 'How is it *your* fault? I was the one who left without asking.'

'And I'm the one who left without warning.' Mycroft has turned to face me, his eyes intense. 'Rachel, if I hadn't pissed off in the middle of the night without a word, you might never have made your way to England. I've gotta take some responsibility.'

'But you had no idea I was going to *do* that.'

'Maybe not.' His laugh is hard, short. 'But I should have, because I bloody *know* you. You did exactly the same thing I would have done in your position.'

'Mycroft—'

'Rachel, I'll make it right, yeah?' He squeezes my arms. 'I'm working it out, I'm working really hard. I know you're still mad about the blog thing, but I've started investigating the Wild connection, trying to get one step ahead—'

'Let's just get to the station, okay?' I balance on my crutches to hold his hand. The buzzy look in his eye, and the mention of Wild, makes my stomach flip-flop anxiously.

Mycroft opens the rear passenger door, and gets me, my crutches and himself bundled in.

'All set, you two?' Detective Pickup leans back in the driver's seat to catch my eye.

'Yep, we're good.' The car's interior is toasty. Pickup's got the heater cranked, and some hideous classic-rock station tuned on the radio, mercifully low.

The vehicle moves through the streets more quickly than I expect. I'd like to stay in this nice warm cocoon, avoid the buffeting cold of the city. Trees toss their branches, traffic ebbs around us, and the Melbourne skyline is a steel horizon of industrial refrigerators.

'It looks like London out there,' I whisper.

Mycroft takes my hand on the seat. 'It's just a normal Melbourne winter.'

'*Winter*. My god, how did that happen?'

'Oh, the usual way. The earth turns on its axis, seasons change, days march on . . .' He checks my face. 'We've got exams next semester, you know.'

'God.' I close my eyes. 'I hadn't forgotten. I just—'

'You'd been hoping the world had stopped for a bit, while you were otherwise occupied?' Mycroft's eyebrows are raised, though not unkindly.

My throat is thick. 'Yeah. Something like that.'

'Hey, it's gonna be fine. Mai and Gus have said they'll help you cram whenever you like.' Mycroft touches my fingers, gently rubbing his thumb over the nail of each one. 'I know you're not right yet, Rachel, but you'll feel better soon. And Mai and Gus and your family and me . . . We'll get you squared away.'

I don't know what to say. I'm upset, but I'm not crying or anything. I just feel sort of blank, hollow.

Mycroft's eyes travel over my face. I don't like him looking at me in that worried way, so I lean my head on his shoulder. He strokes my cheek all the way to St Kilda Road.

Then we're getting out, checking in at the security station in the foyer, crowding together in the lift all the way up. My crutches hurt my armpits and my wrists, but I make it to Pickup's office.

A man is standing near Pickup's desk. Whoever this guy is, he must be important – it looks as though Pickup has had a bit of a tidy for his arrival.

He's about fifty-five, with styled gray hair and a square face. His suit looks expensive. A black coat is draped over his left arm and he holds dark-gray leather gloves loosely in the same hand.

I'm immediately reminded of Mr Worth, the government representative who visited me in the hospital in London. This man has that same sense of . . . *containment*. He seems more agreeable than Worth, at least. He'd look like someone's kindly grandfather, if not for the high-end outfit and the clever eyes.

The eyes give it away, I think. They're gray-green, very bright and hawkish. I get the feeling he's noting everything, every detail in this room, every detail about me – my crutches, my clothes, my face. Every detail about Mycroft, his face especially. The man's eyes linger on Mycroft's face for a long time.

'Thank you for coming,' the man says. 'My name is Mr Cole, and I'm a cultural attaché with Her Majesty's government.'

He shakes my hand and Mycroft's hand in turn.

'I understand you were both instrumental in returning the Bodleian Library's copy of Shakespeare's First Folio to the author-ities.' Cole looks at Mycroft again then quickly redirects his gaze at both of us. 'And I hear you suffered some unfortunate experiences while you were investigating its disappearance.'

His words are clipped, precise. His London accent sounds out of place here.

'Miss Watts, isn't it?' Cole nods at me.

I nod back, feeling slow in the head. 'Um, yeah.'

'I'm here to convey my government's gratitude, for your role in the return of the Folio.' Cole smiles. His smile has a diplomatic sincerity that only comes with practice. 'I'm sorry for your injuries and any inconvenience. You must be a very strong and extraordinary young woman.'

I don't know what to say to that, but Mycroft is already replying for me.

'She is,' he says simply. 'Does this mean you're taking the Folio back to the library?'

'Yes.' Cole nods. 'That's where it belongs. Mr Mycroft, I assume?'

'Yeah,' Mycroft says.

'Our thanks go to you as well. The Folio is a historical artifact of great significance, and we're very appreciative of its return. I'll be signing the paperwork today and flying back with it in a few days.'

'Once you've liaised with ASIO or something, I imagine.' Mycroft looks strangely flinty. He's staring at Cole, with his dark suit and leather gloves.

'That's right.' Cole has a faintly amused expression. He looks past us to Pickup. 'Detective, do you have the paperwork at your disposal? I can complete those forms now, if you wouldn't mind.'

Pickup moves smartly. It's not as if he jumps to attention or anything, but he gets that brisk policeman's look.

'Yes,' he says, nodding his head, 'they're all in order. I can fetch them from Lieutenant Cross now, if you'd like.'

Pickup bustles away to collect the papers. I never imagined I'd see him relegated to paper boy, but there you have it. Now it's just me and Mycroft and Cole, standing in front of Pickup's desk.

Cole gazes out the window, towards the lawn-covered hill of the Shrine of Remembrance, before looking back at Mycroft. 'Yes, I wouldn't have imagined anything different. You're Edward's boy. You resemble him a great deal.'

My mouth makes this breath-stopped *oh*. When I look over, Mycroft has gone so pale so fast I think he's going to pass out.

'Yes,' Cole goes on, 'with the hair, of course, and your height. You've got your mother's eyes, though. I'm very sorry for your loss. I know it was some time ago, but please accept my condolences. Edward was a good man. Good to work with, and exceedingly bright. You seem to have inherited some of that.'

Mycroft's mouth opens and nothing comes out for a second.

'Are you . . .' He wets his lips and tries again. 'Are you saying my father worked with British intelligence?'

Cole just gives him a faint, enigmatic smile. He glances over Mycroft's shoulder. 'Ah, Detective Pickup.'

'Papers are here, as I said. All in order.' Pickup flashes a blue folder in his hand. 'Would you like to do this at my desk, while I take the young people downstairs?'

'That would be very good, thank you, Detective,' Cole says.

He shakes my hand again, and then Mycroft's. Before he drops Mycroft's hand, he holds out a white business card.

'There you are. As I said, I'm leaving in a few days, so if there's anything you should need . . .'

Mycroft stares at the card. He seems to have lost the ability to speak, so I snatch the card from Cole's fingers and jam it in the pocket of my track pants.

I nod. 'Thank you, Mr Cole, you've been very kind.'

'Not at all,' Cole says.

He turns away. We've been dismissed, and I have to pull at Mycroft's sleeve to get him to move. Pickup escorts us down the hall to the lift.

'Right, here we go,' Pickup says as the lift light pings.

I lean on my crutches and put my hand on Pickup's arm, which is something I've never done before. Pickup stares at my hand like it's turned into a zucchini.

'We can take it from here, Detective,' I say. 'We'll just wait for you in the foyer, until you're done with your guest.'

'You will?' Pickup eyes me suspiciously.

'Yep. No worries.'

'All right, then. Fine.' He doesn't look completely happy, but he seems relieved once we're loaded into the lift.

Then it's just us, just me and Mycroft, in the lift of St Kilda Road Police Headquarters, going down twelve floors. Nobody else gets in, and neither of us gets out. We just stand there, resting against the back of the carriage.

Mycroft's face is like a still life. I probably don't look much better. I put my weight on my good leg, wipe my palm on my track pants and fish out the white card.

I read the short lines of print. 'Jonathan Cole. That's it. And a phone number.'

'Right.' Mycroft stares at the lights on the lift panel as they descend in order.

'Are you okay?'

'No,' he says.

So we stand there. I lean against Mycroft's shoulder, and he leans against mine. My knee aches, and Mycroft's expression is a vacuum, and we have no words at this time.

We drop down through the levels, each floor like another tug of gravity, a tug from the ground. We sink lower and lower, our eyes closed together, the warmth at each shoulder, and we wait for this ride to end.

ACKNOWLEDGMENTS

Lots of people have said it, but I'll say it again: a book is a group effort. These thank yous can't really express how grateful I am for the support I've received over the last year, but I'll give it a go. All my love, and lots of feels, are owed . . .

To Geoff, for always, and for being such a rock, and for London – that was amazing, sweetheart, so thank you! (We should definitely go again). Also to my brother, Jared, my sister-in-law, Deb, and my Dad, for making such a wonderful trip possible.

To my sons, Ben, Alex, Will and Ned. You guys are the bomb. You put up with me squirreling myself away in front of the computer for hours on end, my frequent absent-mindedness, and that vague expression I sometimes get when you're trying to talk to me ('Uh oh, Mum's thinking again'). You are my support crew, and give the best hugs ever! I love you all more than I can say.

To my amazing agent, Catherine Drayton, for being so tireless in your support of the series, and working ridiculously hard to make it possible for Mycroft and Watts to find new readers all over the world.

To my lifeline, my support network, my editors! Eva Mills, Sophie Splatt and Hilary Reynolds, you have worked your butts off on this book, and held my hand when I needed it. I'm grateful every day that your incredible powers of deduction and reason are on my side!

To the amazing Alien Onions. This book wouldn't be here without you (literally!). The amount of effort and care you invest in every book absolutely staggers me. Let's do cake! I'd also like to say a special thank you to Lara Wallace, publicist extraordinaire, for being such a support and helping me every step of the way, and mega-thanks to the entire team at Allen & Unwin (Sydney), for being a fantastic, super-powered book squad and getting behind the series so much. You are all made of awesome.

I'd also like to thank Sylvia, Alison, Tara and the amazing family at Tundra – I feel very privileged to have such a cool and supportive team of committed folk backing the series and bringing Rachel and James to wonderful new readers. You have all been *incredible*. Tim Tams are on me. :)

To Alisdair Daws: once again, this book wouldn't have made it to the finish line without my partner in crime. Thanks so much, Ali, and to you too, Tahlia, for brainstorming ideas, giving me enormous encouragement, and getting me through.

To Carmel Shute and the sisters. Carmel, a mere 'thank you' is not enough! You have done so much, and I'm so very grateful. Rock on, Sisters In Crime!

I'd also like to say particular thanks to those who've had input into the creation of this book. Gratitude forever to people I've pestered about research details, and who've given of their time to wise me up. Massive thanks:

To Meg Philips – derby doll

To my sister, Dr Lucy Marney, who proofed some of the medical details, and is always on hand to help me work out the difference between a haemothorax and hypovolaemic shock (any screw-ups after the fact are purely my own)

To Dr Zac Miles, orthopedic surgeon, for advice on broken bones of all stripes

To M, who wouldn't want his name included, but who gave me excellent advice on how to blow things up with household materials

To the staff at The Sherlock Holmes Museum, at 221B Baker Street in Marylebone, London

And to staff at The Prince of Wales hotel in Pimlico, London, for large pints, and delicious and sustaining roast dinners.

I'd especially like to thank the staff of the Westminster Public Mortuary, who showed such grace in allowing me to visit, and enormous kindness and patience while answering all my tricky questions. Particular thanks to Lisa Richardson, Senior APT, who contributed hours of her time, as well as extraordinary expertise.

Above all, I owe a considerable debt to the staff of the Bodleian Library in Oxford, especially the Head of Rare Books, Clive Hurst, and conservator, Nicole Gilroy. I was amazed by your generosity during my visit, the hours you spent helping me to explore and ask questions, and your dedication to the huge responsibility you bear. Any poetic license taken with the facts, or descriptive error, is entirely my own. A million thanks to Mr Hurst, especially – being allowed to view and handle a copy of Shakespeare's First Folio is something I will never forget!

I've had huge props on the home front too, so I'd like to take the opportunity to send a big shout-out to the folks of Castlemaine, Victoria, for all the support, and special thanks to everyone who's shown up for launches and events, including the staff of Stoneman's Bookroom and the Castlemaine Library, and students from Castlemaine Secondary College and Castlemaine Steiner School. Lisa Thomas, Celia Connor, Nadine and Grant Saltmarsh, Simon Clay and Julie-Anne Hewson all read early drafts of this manuscript and said encouraging things – thank you, guys, you're the best.

Another shout-out to the incredible supporters of the series – bloggers, Twitter and Facebook friends, fans (I would include all your names here, but the list would be very long! Thank you all so much!). Other writers have helped me keep my chin up during this process – particular thanks to Michael Adams, stablemate and world-building pal (drinks are on me!); Melissa Keil, for being cool and for allowing my homage to 'farm-girl porn'; and my mentor, PD Martin, for being herself. A special mention for Helen Garner (you don't know me, but hi!), for her extraordinary article 'At the Morgue' (*True Stories*: Text Publishing, 1996) which set the mood for my descriptions of the autopsy scene in this book.

Thank you, over and over again, to my parents, Dan and Brenda Marney, for getting behind the series all the way up in Townsville, Queensland. Love you guys so much.

I've saved critical mentions for last: huge thanks to all the amazing librarians and booksellers out there who've plugged the *Every* series and supported it. And to you, the readers, who are the lifeblood of this series – I couldn't have written this book without you. I am full of awe and gratitude, and James and Rachel send their love.

ABOUT THE AUTHOR

Ellie Marney was born in Brisbane, and has lived in Indonesia, Singapore and India. Now she writes, teaches, and gardens when she can, while living in a country idyll (actually a very messy wooden house on ten acres with a dog and lots of chickens) near Castlemaine, in north-central Victoria. Even though she often forgets things and lets the housework go, her partner and four sons still love her.

Ellie's short stories for adults have won awards and been published in various anthologies. *Every Word* is the follow-up to *Every Breath* in her trilogy for young adults.

Drop in at www.elliemarney.com, send her a line on Facebook or follow her on Twitter @elliemarney.

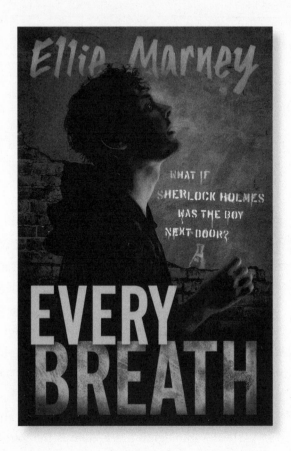

Rachel Watts has just moved to Melbourne from the country, but the city is the last place she wants to be. James Mycroft is her neighbor, an intriguingly troubled seventeen-year-old who's also a genius with a passion for forensics. Despite her misgivings, Rachel finds herself unable to resist Mycroft when he wants her help investigating a murder. He's even harder to resist when he's up close and personal – and on the hunt for a cold-blooded killer. When Rachel and Mycroft follow the murderer's trail, they find themselves in the lion's den – literally. A trip to the zoo will never have quite the same meaning again …